Wicked Surrender

Jade Lee

BERKLEY SENSATION, NEW YORK

THE BERKLEY PUBLISHING GROUP
Published by the Penguin Group
Penguin Group (USA) Inc.
375 Hudson Street, New York, New York 10014, USA
Penguin Group (Canada), 90 Eglinton Avenue East, Suite 700, Toronto, Ontario M4P 2Y3, Canada
(a division of Pearson Penguin Canada Inc.)
Penguin Books Ltd., 80 Strand, London WC2R 0RL, England
Penguin Group Ireland, 25 St. Stephen's Green, Dublin 2, Ireland (a division of Penguin Books Ltd.)
Penguin Group (Australia), 250 Camberwell Road, Camberwell, Victoria 3124, Australia
(a division of Pearson Australia Group Pty. Ltd.)
Penguin Books India Pvt. Ltd., 11 Community Centre, Panchsheel Park, New Delhi—110 017, India
Penguin Group (NZ), 67 Apollo Drive, Rosedale, North Shore 0632, New Zealand
(a division of Pearson New Zealand Ltd.)
Penguin Books (South Africa) (Pty.) Ltd., 24 Sturdee Avenue, Rosebank, Johannesburg 2196,
South Africa

Penguin Books Ltd., Registered Offices: 80 Strand, London WC2R 0RL, England

WICKED SURRENDER

A Berkley Sensation Book / published by arrangement with the author

PRINTING HISTORY
Berkley Sensation mass-market edition / September 2010

ISBN: 978-0-425-23636-9

BERKLEY® SENSATION
Berkley Sensation Books are published by The Berkley Publishing Group,
a division of Penguin Group (USA) Inc.,
375 Hudson Street, New York, New York 10014.
BERKLEY® SENSATION and the "B" design are trademarks of Penguin Group (USA) Inc.

PRINTED IN THE UNITED STATES OF AMERICA

10 9 8 7 6 5 4 3 2 1

*To Kate Seaver, who is the absolute best!
You've made this book ten times better.*

*To Pamela Harty, agent extraordinaire.
It goes without saying that this would
never have happened without you.*

*To Deb Miller, who made me keep going
when I had decided my only option
was to join a navel-gazing cult.*

*All three of you are incredible,
inspiring women. Thank you!*

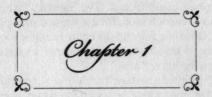

Chapter 1

"He's not here." Scheherazade Martin said the words aloud in an attempt to force her mind to stop looking for someone she didn't want to see. He wasn't in tonight's playhouse crowd, and she had no interest in being pursued by him anyway. She even prayed nightly that he would lose interest and leave her alone. But some desires went deeper than her mind's ability to block. And yet, it made no sense. Why did she want him so?

He was a lord pursuing a passing fancy. She was an actress and no lord would deign to marry her no matter what he whispered. Besides, her longing was only a symptom of a larger problem. Yes, she craved Lord Blackstone, but she also wanted . . . something else. Something elusive.

The word "love" whispered through her mind, and she ruthlessly shut the idea away. Love didn't come to the likes of her. Her goal was marriage and even that wouldn't happen with him. So it was best if she stopped looking for Lord Blackstone and concentrated on the task at hand. She turned toward the Green Room, moving so quickly that she nearly caught her skirts on fire.

"Move that lamp," she said to the newest stagehand, pointing to the offending lantern set casually on the floor where anyone could kick it. The Tavern Playhouse was small, barely enough room for a stage and fifty people, all standing. One little fire and the entire building would burn to the ground before she had the chance to scream. "Do you want to be burned alive?"

"Yeh," grunted the boy, barely ten years old, but he didn't move from where he was lying down, peering into a hole that led beneath the stage. Not until he was cuffed from behind by Seth.

"Ow!" he cried, leaping up, his fists raised. "Wot's that fer?"

Seth didn't answer, except to point at the lamp. He was a mute, but he still managed to handle an army of boys with seeming efficiency. Especially since he had the help of Joey, the oldest of Seth's helpers.

"That's Lady Scher, lackwit," Joey barked as he came around from behind the curtain. "We do wot she says as she says it. Or find yer bread elsewheres." He thrust his chin at the backstage door.

There was a tense moment when Scher thought the new boy would fight or bolt. Boys were the most unpredictable in their first week, but he looked at Seth's massive bulk and changed his mind. Slumping over to the lantern, he grabbed it with enough force to break the handle. Seth was beside him in a minute, pulling him to the door by his ear. The boy started bellowing, but Scher turned away. She didn't want to see Seth's brand of discipline. All she cared about was that it worked, and that it was a damn sight better than what waited outside the Tavern Playhouse doors. Besides, she was already late for the Green Room.

"Thank you for your help, Joey," she said.

"Yes, m'lady, yes! I'll finish up 'ere. I'll do it right an' tight, jes how you like!"

Scher managed a smile, and Joey's face lit up like a beacon. "You're a good boy," she said as she slipped past another curtain to the hallway that led to their tiny Green Room. It was a narrow path and dark, but she had been walking it her entire life, so she paid little heed to where she stepped.

She was just ordering her thoughts to the task ahead when it happened. She felt an arm on hers, a push from the side, and then she was spun around to face her attacker. She had only the vaguest impression of largeness—large hand, tall body, and a dull flap as his heavy cloak rippled around them. By the time she gasped, she was already pushed up against the wall. Her backside hit first, so she was able to prevent her head from banging painfully against a ladder, but that was all she could do as his body came hard and full against her, and his cloak hid her from sight.

Her hands fisted and her belly tensed. Slight as she was, she could still fight. And she was already drawing breath to scream. Seth and his boys would be at her side in a moment. No man dared accost Lady Scher, not in her own tavern.

"You're late," he said, his voice a dark shiver up her spine.

Him. The man who touched her too boldly every night— in person first, then later in her dreams. Tension coiled in her belly, as much from hunger now as from fear. Still, it took a moment for her to ease the breath from her lungs.

"Demanding crowd," she whispered. She lifted her head to see better, but he had braced his forearm and cloak on the wall above her head. All was darkness in the shadows he created, though she already knew every angle of his chiseled, masculine face. She concentrated instead on other impressions. His legs were spread just a little wider than her own, trapping her thighs between his. His belly was flat, but his groin was not, and she felt heat there like never before. But most of all, she smelled the mint of his breath. In a world of stale ale and men's sweat, mint was a beautiful, elegant scent.

But she had tasks to do and a reputation to maintain, so she pushed against his chest. "They are expecting me in the Green Room."

He eased back, but not because she pushed him. She could not have moved him if she put all her weight into it. But he was a gentleman, and so he moved off her. She would have sighed in regret, but he didn't go far enough for that. There was barely an inch of heated air between them.

"What's wrong?" he asked, startling her once again. "You seem sad."

She held her breath, stunned that he could read her so easily. Then she released it in a controlled laugh. "La, sir, but there is not—"

He caught her chin fast enough to make her gasp. "Do not lie to me, Lady Scher."

She didn't speak. She hadn't the breath, not with him so dark and so forceful before her.

"Tell me," he whispered as he bent his head to her neck. His lips began a slow tease to her skin, and she shivered in response. God help her, he was good at what he did. And when his tongue teased a circle just beneath her jawline, she was ready to do whatever he commanded.

She didn't. She couldn't. As the daughter of an actress, she'd learned early not to trust anyone, least of all a man. "I'm tired, is all. Delilah has the headache, which always makes her unpredictable, and Seth caught one of the boys pickpocketing. The child is turned out now, and you know how his life will go. It saddens me, 'tis all."

He didn't answer because he was ministering to her collarbone, right above the fichu of her modest, brown gown. But she knew he heard her. He was a man who used all his senses. He likely read the rapid pulse of her heart, the shallow whisper of her breath, and the feminine weakness in her knees. For her part, she knew his sharp features and his brown eyes, whether she could see him or not. She knew that taken piece by piece, his looks were average, his build unremarkable except for his height. But as a whole, he had *presence*. When he looked at her, she felt as if he were looking straight through her into her thoughts. And so he learned things that he should not. Like when she lied about her mood.

He pulled back far enough to hover over her lips. Below, his legs tightened ever so slightly against the outside of her thighs. "I don't like it when you lie."

"Of course you do," she countered. "You'd love it were I to lie *with* you, but that will never happen."

He brushed his lips across hers, and she felt her mouth swell from the caress. "Grammatical banter. I'm impressed," he whispered, and she could taste the mint on his breath.

"I went to school," she said stiffly.

"Then lay your troubles aside as you lie with me, and together—"

"We will lay all our lies to rest?"

He chuckled, the sound sending a low tremor through her belly. "Yes."

"No." She forced herself to push him away as reality intruded with the sound of raucous laughter from the Green Room. She was needed in there. Lady Scher's presence tended to dampen the worst of the high spirits.

"I must go," she said as she pressed her palms to his chest and pushed.

He didn't move. If anything, his legs pressed her harder against the wall. "Tell me what saddens you."

"I did."

"You didn't."

"Do not presume—" She got no more words out. His

mouth was upon hers. Not brutally, with lips and teeth mashed together. Not gently, as one might reserve for a virginal new wife. But assuredly, with nips of teeth against the edge of her lips and the tease of his tongue between the tiny seam she allowed.

She did not want to kiss him. She did not want the heat of his body to infiltrate her own. She did not like it that she opened her mouth to him, relishing every sweep of his tongue. She was no virgin, but neither was she a whore. Her role in the theater company was as a lady hostess, and so she needed the illusion of purity.

He stripped all that away. He did no more than kiss her, then invade her mouth and touch her until she was lightheaded from the joy of it. He didn't even press his hips against her so that she could feel his hunger. But she knew it nonetheless, and she knew her own. In barely more than a month, he'd become as vital to her as the cash in the cash box. This man was the newest and brightest light in her very gray and cluttered life.

He finished his kiss, and she damned herself for releasing a moue of regret. Even in the darkness, she saw his teeth flash white as he grinned. So she made her tone especially sharp as a way to salvage her pride.

"I must go. Tonight is not the night for Delilah to preside alone. She's likely to alienate someone."

"Tell me what has happened," he coaxed. "I might be able to help, you know."

She might have told him then. She might have spilled her entire malaise in a heated rush, but she couldn't explain what she didn't herself understand. So she shook her head. "It takes a lot more than grammar to gain my trust, Lord Blackstone."

"I can do more," he said, his every word a sensuous promise. "I will—"

"No," she said making sure her weariness showed in her voice. "I must go."

He stepped back and away, but before she could duck past, he grabbed her hand. His fingers were gloved, as they always were, and hers were blunt and chapped, as they always were. "I will come to you tonight," he whispered. "I will make it better."

"I am too tired."

His teeth flashed again with a boyish grin. "I will revive you."

How she wanted to say yes. The simmering of her blood clamored that she wanted him to bed her, to own her as a man owned a woman, but she would not walk that path again. When she was sixteen, she had believed a man's lies. Now she had that experience and the example of a dozen more actresses to know that the men who came to the Tavern Playhouse offered sweet kisses and pretty lies. That path led nowhere. The only escape for women like her was with a wedding ring, and that was not being offered by Lord Blackstone. "No, my lord."

He bowed in acknowledgment, though there was mockery in the movement. The kind of mockery all titled men had for their actress whores. "Yes, Lady Scher. Tonight."

She walked away, though she had to force her reluctant feet to move. She listened for the sound of his footsteps—either coming closer to her or withdrawing—but she heard nothing over the growing noise of the Green Room. Then she was pushing open the door with her customary quietness and slipping inside with the pretense of subtlety.

A few people saw her. Delilah was the first, her eyes flashing with a mixture of gratitude and irritation at Scher's late arrival. Their lead actress loved the flattery of her admirers, but sometimes their demands grew wearisome. Even from across the tiny room, Scher could see a pinched tightness to her smile, and most especially to her gestures. But at least she wasn't cursing anyone, and she looked like a queen seated at the only cushioned chair in the room.

Three other actresses acknowledged her with a flicker of

an eye or a slight nod. They held court in the other corners, but made sure in one way or another that their admirers knew Lady Scher was here. After all, so long as the "lady" was here, they could pretend they were "chaperoned" and cling to the illusion of being a higher sort of actress. It was a lie, of course, but one that brought in a better class of clientele. And that benefited them all.

Scher maneuvered into the tiny room as gracefully as possible. Not too many tonight—barely more than a dozen guests—which made it easier to breathe, but Scher feared for the company pocketbook. The Green Room offered special brandies and wines, all with higher prices. The more people crushed in here, the more who would drink while waiting for their turn with Delilah.

Scher scanned the crowd, memorizing the faces as she did every night. She saw men she genuinely liked, including Mr. Frazier, who stood in the corner playing with Annette's dog. He had a way with animals, and that made him a favorite. He glanced up when she passed and flashed her a warm smile, which she returned. But she couldn't tarry to chat, especially since a hand abruptly grasped hers in a sweaty clasp. She tried not to cringe. Even she, the "lady" of the tavern, had to suffer through being grabbed at every turn.

"Lady Scher! Lady Scher! Tell her she must give me a kiss!" It was Mr. Babbott, his thin features looking almost gaunt this evening.

"A ribbon!" called another young man, Mr. Phipps she believed. "I demand a ribbon that has penetrated her most precious hair!"

Ribald laughter followed that rather sad double entendre.

"Poor Mr. Phipps," Delilah trilled. "Have you been working on that all day?"

"All last night," he returned with a suggestive waggle of his eyebrows.

More laughter greeted his words. Scher smiled with a

vague kind of aloofness. As the "Lady" Scher, she was not meant to understand these things. So she gently extricated her hand from Mr. Babbott and gestured for tea. Mr. Babbott, she knew, did not like ale. And their brandy was too expensive for him.

"Oh, no," Mr. Babbott whispered as he shook his head at Nell the barmaid. "I am a little in arrears, these days, and cannot afford even tea."

How well she knew that, but he had other services to offer. "It shall be free, Mr. Babbott," she whispered into his ear. "If you can encourage your young friends to depart early. I believe Delilah has the headache."

His eyes grew misty for a moment as he looked at Scher's lead actress. "Of course," he said. "Of course I will, if you will but tell her of the service I do on her behalf."

Scher repressed an inward sigh. He had no hope with Delilah. Surely he knew that. But of course, he didn't, so with a rare show of generosity, she called for a bun as well. "A gift from me," she said when the food arrived. "So that you know you are valued."

Again, his eyes misted, but this time they were trained on her. "You are a true lady," he said as he quickly took the bun. He didn't even secret it away into a pocket but bit into it right there. It must have been quite a long time since he'd last eaten.

Scher patted his hand and moved away, her desperation growing. She was *not* a true lady, no matter what anyone here pretended. She was not a true chaperone nor an actress nor anything but a hanger-on in this gray life of the theater. She'd been born here. Twenty-five years ago, her mother had stood where Delilah now reigned. Over the years, Scheherazade had played the part of the baby Jesus, had toddled through the crowd pulling on wigs and pocketing coins, and then later tried her hand at acting. She had sung and danced and played the lute, searching for a place in the only home she had ever known.

But she didn't have the talent. She would never be a lead actress, could never become more than another singer/whore in the troupe. She had tried desperately to be the star, especially after her golden sister Cleopatra died. She had tried to fill the role, but she was not the beautiful nightingale that Delilah was. That Cleo had been. So Scher found a different way to be useful. She ran the tavern, she supervised the costumes, and most of all, she cared for the money. That gave her a role here, a function at the Tavern Playhouse, but it did not make her one of them any more than it made her a lady.

Meanwhile, Mr. Babbott finished his bun and tea, then began sniffing the air quite conspicuously. "Dear, dear," he drawled loudly. "I believe the air has gone stale." As he spoke, his eyes turned to Mr. George Hale who was cursed with frequent bouts of gas.

The man flushed red and began to protest his innocence, but it was too late. The damage had been done and he was forced to endure a great deal of mockery. That, in turn, gave Delilah just the opportunity she required to claim illness and escape. And with the lead attraction gone, others soon departed.

Scher continued to play the gracious hostess. She made polite, semiflirtatious banter with the clientele, and soon, she was rewarded with a quiet nod from Seth who had slipped in within moments of Delilah's disappearance. He would watch over the remaining girls. Most had already made their night's selection and would soon disappear upstairs or to the boarding house next door.

All was at it should be, and so Scher was free to tend to her more solitary duties. She turned to go but knew she would never make it. Kit was still here, chatting amicably with Annette, waiting until that moment when Scher was free. He truly was a sweet man, smart and charming with his sandy hair and freckled face. And now that the crowd had thinned, he crossed to her side.

"Mr. Frazier, how wonderful to see you tonight." It wasn't a full lie. She genuinely liked the man. He was a paying customer—one of their best in both pocketbook and lineage—and so she set aside her fatigue to chat with him. "Did you like the new act with the dog?"

"Kit," he said earnestly, completely ignoring her question. "I have asked you to call me Kit."

"Ah," she said, as she patted his arm, "but you know how very inappropriate it is."

He glanced around. "Please, Scheherazade, is there somewhere private we could go to talk?"

She thought of the hallway between the stage and the Green Room. She thought of the shadows and how in the entire theater, the most privacy could be had in those short minutes when Seth's boys were busy on the stage and the actresses were busy in the Green Room. But those minutes were gone. There was nowhere private anymore tonight.

"Mr. Frazier—"

"Aie, blimey!" interrupted Annette from the opposite side of the room. "I've forgotten me wig again. Come along, dears, and help me with the powder."

Scher looked up, feeling rather dazed as Annette shot a stern look at the other two remaining actresses. Within moments all of them had gathered their gentlemen and shuttled them out the door. One even picked up the dog. Seth held the door as all slipped out, then he turned back to her. With a slight nod of approval, he ducked away, pulling the door shut behind him. Faster than Scher thought possible, the Green Room was empty save for herself and Mr. Frazier.

"I don't understand," she murmured. And she didn't, she truly didn't. Mr. Frazier was the fourth son of a titled family. He was young, foolish even at times, but would eventually grow into a steady man. He was not one prone to taking mistresses, nor was he wealthy enough to have bribed the room to leave him alone with her. What could possibly be happening?

She turned back to her companion, only to gasp in shock at the sight of him on one knee before her.

"Oh, pray do not look so frightened!" he cried. "This is a joyous time, or rather I hope it will be." He grasped her hand in his own.

"Mr. Frazier," she whispered, her mind much too slow to follow.

"I wish to ask . . . That is, I want to beg, to plead with you. Please, sweet Scheherazade, will you do me the greatest honor of becoming my wife?"

Chapter 2

Scher's heart beat painfully in her throat, and she realized with some dismay that she was sweating. How could this be happening? How could she not have known it was coming? The gray haze that had covered her thoughts this last month abruptly thickened until she could barely hear Mr. Frazier's proposal of marriage. And in that near-suffocating silence, her mind brought forth impossible dreams.

She saw herself as a lady in a gown that did not have to be reinforced because of the many men who tugged on it. She saw her wedding in church with a congregation that didn't speak in cant, and the women wore gowns that fully covered their breasts. She saw her home in a village with green grass and birds that were not pigeons. She saw her whole life as it could be, if only she were respectable. And best of all, she saw her children—healthy children—who were attended by a doctor. She had lost her mother, her sister, and countless friends because the surgeon put them last on the list. The respectable patients always got treated first, got the best medicines, and always on time. She would never, ever have children until she could be assured that they would get the best care available. And that meant being respectable.

Meanwhile, Mr. Frazier tightened his grip on her hands. "Say something, Scher. Please."

She opened her mouth to speak, not even knowing what she would say. But finally words spilled out. "Your mother will never allow it."

Her eyes widened in shock. She never meant to say that! And as expected, his face flushed a ruddy red.

"I am a grown man!" he said with a note of defiance.

"Of course you are," she immediately soothed. "You have just taken me so off guard. I don't know what to say."

"Just say yes."

She closed her eyes. Her hand was still gripped in his, and she couldn't stop wondering why she was sweating at this most inauspicious time. "I cannot think," she whispered. It was a lie. She could think, but her thoughts would never come to pass. "It is beastly hot in here, don't you think?"

"Let me get you a chair," he said quickly enough. But he was down on one knee, so that necessitated him getting up. He jerked on her hand only a little as he popped up. In general he was very agile. Then quicker than she wanted, he was escorting her to an old wooden chair next to the wall. She followed him meekly enough, still trying to push through the heavy press of wishful dreams. But there wasn't enough time, and soon she was sitting down again and he was back down on one knee before her.

"Scheherazade, I know you are a woman prone to logic, so perhaps I should begin there."

"You are in love," she said softly. She did not sneer the word, but he must have noticed her lack of enthusiasm because he brought up his other hand to sandwich hers.

"Yes, I absolutely am, my dear. I love you, Scheherazade."

She shivered as he said her name. It sounded so odd. She was Lady Scher to everyone. Only Pappy called her by her full name, and he was gone these many years.

"I thought, I pray that you have some care for me."

"Of course I do," she responded automatically. "I have loved you since I first met you." He had been like the puppies that Annette raised, tumbling about and chewing on things. Not that he chewed on things, but that same earnest exploration of the world was common to him and the little creatures. She vividly recalled meeting Kit some years ago. He literally fell at her feet when his legs were taking him to the bar while his eyes had just caught sight of Delilah. His upper body spun toward the actress and his feet had no hope of recovering. So down he had tumbled to everyone's grand amusement, including his own. Indeed, he had thought it was so funny that he had called for ale for everyone such that he would not be the only one on the floor.

She remembered leaning down to him to chuck him under the chin, he was that adorable. Of course she loved him. *Everybody* loved him.

Meanwhile, Kit was continuing his ardent plea. "I can see that you require more than my love, don't you? Very well, then. Let me say that I have thought about this a great deal and our union makes logical sense."

She shook her head. "No, Kit, it doesn't. You are a nobleman, I am only an actress. And I am so much older than you."

He grinned. "You called me Kit. It means your heart knows the truth. Your heart wants you to say yes."

She didn't argue with him. She hadn't the breath. Damn the boy for offering her a dream that could never be. Didn't he understand how painful that was?

He must have taken her silence as encouragement

because he started to enumerate his thinking. "First off, you are not older, my dear. We are the same age exactly."

Were they? She hadn't thought so, but perhaps it was merely that he seemed so young to her.

"Secondly, I am the fourth son of a long and vastly ignored title. While you, my dear, have nobility on both sides of your family."

"My mother was an actress, my father . . ." She flushed and looked away. "Well, I am a bastard, and you know it."

"We'll say you are the bastard of a duke and you'll be all the rage. Much more interesting than—"

"One does not marry 'interesting,' Kit. That is not logical."

He abruptly perked up. "That is the second time you have called me Kit. I vow by the time you say it a third time, we will be engaged."

"Mr. Frazier—" she said tartly, but he shook his head.

"No, no, you have not heard the rest of my logic." Then he grimaced. "Forgive me, but my knee is killing me." He rolled to his side, then quickly got both feet under him as he grabbed a nearby bench and dragged it loudly forward. Within moments, he was seated before her, once again reaching for her hands. She did not fight him. She could tell he would insist, and she had no desire to play run and catch with her hand.

"Now where was I? Oh, yes, logic. I am not very good with it, you know, and there again is my next reason. Am I on four or five?"

"Three," she said softly.

"Ah, yes. See, you are much better at numbers than I."

She shook her head. "Really, there is no need—"

He grimaced, releasing the top of her hand to run a hand through his hair. It only made him look more dashing, of course. He really was an adorable boy. "I am botching this badly, but you see I am about to confess a great truth."

She winced. Nothing intelligent ever came out when someone called it a great truth.

"I was only indifferent at school. I have a moderate head for numbers and no interest at all in Latin."

"You are vastly intelligent, Mr. Frazier."

"Ah, we are back to Mr. Frazier again. That is because you are lying. I am *not* vastly intelligent. I am only somewhat intelligent. Which means I shall not add anything to the sciences, I will not return to school, and I certainly have no desire to wander around some hellhole being shot at by Spaniards or Frenchies or whomever. So the military is out."

She almost laughed. "So you want to wed an actress instead?"

His expression sobered, and his eyes grew serious. It was a sight indeed as he was rarely ever serious. "I am a fourth son with almost no means of support. No titled girl will want me."

"You don't know that—"

"And if they did, I don't want them. They are stupider than I am, Scheherazade. And if that's not a recipe for disaster, then I don't know what is."

She fell silent. She did not associate with the ladies of the *ton*, only the men. "You can still marry well, Mr. Frazier."

"See. You called me mister again, so it is yet another lie. I must marry a woman of intelligence, and you are the smartest woman I know. I must find a woman who can help me sort through the financials. With my respectability and your skills, we will become nabobs in no time!"

She laughed. How could she not? His prediction was ridiculous, and yet few men knew her skill. Money was the one thing she managed extremely well.

"Laughter!" he cried with obvious delight. "I am making progress."

"But that is hardly the basis for marriage, you know," she said softly. "I will help you without a wedding ring."

She would charge him a fee for her advice, of course, but that was only fair.

"Ah, yes, but you have forgotten all the other things. Recall that a ring will give you the respectability you have never had. I will own all the wealth you already possess—"

"Hardly an inducement in your favor," she lied.

"But you could live with me elsewhere. We could have children, you know. Charming boys and clever girls." He leaned forward, his eyes no longer earnest. In fact, they held a note of warning in them. "You would be honest as my wife, would you not?"

She straightened. "Of course."

He nodded. "I know of so many cuckolded before their first year. You would not do that to me. And I would be grateful every day for your financial savoir faire. You get a percentage of the take here, don't you?"

She looked away. It was true, but she didn't like admitting that. Her persona was as a lady, and ladies did not talk of money.

He drew her face back to his with a gentle touch. "Our marriage makes sense, Scheherazade. I need your stable intelligence. You need my respectability, and I think, my joy." His thumb tapped her lips. "You are too serious, and I make you laugh."

She felt her eyes widen in reaction, not to his words, but the sudden rush of wetness to her eyes. She was tearing? But why? He was wrong! She was *not* too serious. She was surrounded by actors, for goodness sake. If they did not deify levity, she did not know who did. And yet some emotion was gripping her belly tight. Something was feeding the malaise that she could not seem to shake. What was wrong with her that she could not simply be happy in the life she had built here as Lady Scher of the Tavern Troupe?

Her mind flashed to the dark shadows of the hallway,

to the kiss that had burned through her until she thought her blood would boil. "What of your . . ." She stopped her words. She almost said cousin, but none knew about her man of the shadows. "Your family and friends? They will sneer—rightly so—that you are marrying beneath you."

"Then they are not so good at logic, are they? I would be a good husband to you. I would never hurt you or our children. You would make sure our money is well spent, and there is one more thing."

She swallowed, her mind centered on the cramping in her belly, on the rush of sound to her ears. This would never happen. In the world's eyes, she was almost the lowest of the low. She wasn't even a famous stage actress, but someone who wandered about the backstage. At best, they assumed she was a madam, and they weren't far off. Kit would not be allowed to marry her. It was too far a step for him to take.

And yet, how she wanted it: true, honest, legitimate marriage. To the son of a peer! Her life would be respectable, her children safe from all the dangers that plagued illegitimate children. The longing for it was a deep ache that would not subside.

"I love you, Scheherazade," Kit continued. "And you have said you love me. When added to the other logic, can anything else be more perfect?"

She shook her head, her heart caught somewhere between her lungs and her mouth. "Your family will never allow it," she repeated. "Think of the reaction. Can you live outside of *ton*? Outside of all society? You love it here!"

"It won't come to that."

She sighed. "Yes, it will."

"But you forget something, my sweet." He lifted her clenched fist to his mouth and pressed a tender kiss to her knuckles. She winced at the sight of her dirty hands against his mouth, but he didn't notice.

"Do not say love again. That is a poor basis for anything."

He arched his brow in challenge, but then quickly conceded the point. "All right then, you have forgotten about the money. We shall be rich as Croesus, and that will solve the other. It is the way things are, as you have mentioned to me more than once."

"Money can only buy so much. Your family will still disown you. They would certainly never recognize our children." Her heart twisted painfully at that. How odd that she could feel pain for children that hadn't even been conceived yet, but she did. She most certainly did.

"We will not need them." He slid off his bench back onto one knee. He pulled her hand to his lips again and gazed at her with an earnestness that she found more endearing than she had before. "Please, Scheherazade, will you do me the greatest honor of becoming my wife?"

Could she do it? Could she spend her life away from the acting troupe and tavern? Could she exist in that gray place of the not quite respectable nor fully deplorable? Could she be a good wife to a man who was kind, if a bit young? Of course, she could. It was a far better life than what she had here.

But *he* could not. When it came right down to it, he *would* not. Well before they made it to the altar, the world would change his mind. And yet, she wanted it. She had wanted this forever.

"It will be hard, Kit. Harder than you ever imagined."

He smiled into her eyes, and she saw a strength there she hadn't expected. "Love will overcome all obstacles." And when she didn't answer, he sobered. "You will help me, Scheherazade. And I will help you. This I swear."

"Then yes, Kit. Yes, I will marry you."

It was many hours later before Scher sought her bed. Half the troupe had been listening at the door, so when she finally accepted Kit's proposal they had burst through with shouts of "huzzah!" Then there was champagne and brandy, the not-watered-down kind. And Scher managed to grab a bun before they were all gobbled down. In truth, she tried to keep the celebration modest. She didn't want the engagement talked about yet, and so she told everyone quite sternly to keep the news quiet. It wouldn't work, of course. No one enjoyed a good story like actors, and having one of their own marry the son of a peer was the best story of all. But some of them understood her worry. Some of them knew that Kit had yet to face the wrath of his family for his choice of bride.

In truth, she enjoyed every moment of the celebration. Whenever her mood started to sour, Kit was beside her with a word or gesture, something that made her smile. He really was a delightful . . . man. She could no longer call him a boy in her thoughts. He was a man grown, or so she hoped.

In any event, she was dropping with fatigue when she finally climbed the stairs to her bedchamber. She was the only one who lived on the top floor, and she cherished the privacy it afforded. The middle story was given over to props and costumes, plus four bedchambers, which were always occupied, though by different couples every night. And of course, the main floor was tavern and stage, plus the Green Room, which was really painted a soft brown so as to further highlight Delilah's pale beauty.

Scher hadn't even put her key to her door when she heard him step up behind her. She whirled around, her fist and lantern at the ready. But it was him, Viscount Blackstone, her fiancé's first cousin. He had warned her that he would come tonight, and though she'd told him no, she'd known he would come anyway.

He stood back in the shadows. His eyes were hidden in the darkness, but she could see the hard clench of his jaw beneath his morning beard. He was angry, and the sight pleased her. After all, he had made her angry often enough.

They stood there for a moment, her with the light in her hand, him just outside of the lantern's touch, silent and immobile. She struggled for something to say, but could come up with nothing appropriate. In the end, she sighed and turned back to her door. Let him stand in brooding silence all night if he liked. She wanted her bed. He spoke before she turned the key.

"You have accepted his suit."

She sighed again, her whole body filled with a sudden despair. She had held on to her joy among a score of people all shouting "huzzah," but now in the dark corridor before her door, she felt the fantasy slipping away. Why not get the pain over with quickly? The sooner she said the truth out loud, the sooner she could crawl into her bed and cry. And yet it was hard to say it aloud. So much harder than she might have guessed.

"Scher?"

"You need not fear," she forced out. "It will not hold. We are to dine tomorrow with his family to announce the engagement." She let her head drop to the side such that it rested on the door frame. One hand still held the lantern, the other had the key pushed into the lock. But the rest of her body sagged against the frame. "His mother will never let the marriage happen."

"So why accept the suit? Why tarnish his name with gossip? Why put yourself through the mockery?"

She shrugged. "He is a man grown and entitled to his choices."

"But if his mother—"

"Stop!" she hissed. She turned to look at him and was startled to find that her vision was excruciatingly clear. Despite the fact that he hid in the shadows, she still saw his every dark feature. "I want this wedding," she confessed. "I want the home and the children and the life he offers. I *want* it." She lifted her chin. "I do not know the future. I do not know that his family will break him. He is not the fool you think him."

His head canted to the side as he studied her. "I never said I thought him a fool." He reached out slowly to touch her, but she flinched away. She knew how it would feel before he connected. It would hold no tenderness, but it would burn across her skin like fire. And she had no business feeling fire with a man who was not her intended.

"He makes me laugh," she said clearly. Then she bit her lip, stunned that she had revealed so much.

He moved in close, too close for her to shy away, caught as she was against her door. He touched her only on her face, his rough male fingers exquisitely light on her cheek. And, yes, fire burned wherever he stroked. She closed her eyes, locking her knees against the weakness that would come.

Then his thumb slid to her lower lip, tugging the flesh out from beneath her teeth. "I can make you scream," he said.

She knocked his hand away, startling them both with the force of her refusal. Especially since her mouth was already swollen from his heat. "I do not like to scream," she said tartly.

"True," he said, and she detected a note of reluctance in his words. "You are the most quiet of women. It is why I like you so." Then he dropped the tenor of his voice to a low whisper. "Perhaps I shall make you sing, then."

"I stopped singing on my tenth birthday." Then she turned her back on him, wishing she could close him out of her thoughts as easily.

He had appeared in her life as most men did, as a visitor to the Green Room, a lord who wanted to dabble with the lower class for a time. He was clean, wickedly witty, and had a dark aura around him that she—and so many others—found intriguing. He never drank or became loutish, never pawed or groped anyone, and once he had saved Molly from someone who was both drunk and loutish.

That is what had softened her to him, a little more than a month ago. Before she or Seth had time to even notice the problem, Viscount Blackstone had caught the drunkard and sent him home. She had heard the story later from Molly, who was practically swooning from the romance of it all.

The very next night, Scher had thanked him with a glass of their very best wine. And in such a way, their conversations together began. Barely a week later, he had caught her between the stage and the Green Room. His touch had been dark and forbidding, just like the man. A touch of roughness, a dark need that sparked her passion as nothing else, and that wonderful whisper of minty elegance. She had allowed the kiss then. Five nights later, she had allowed a bit more.

He was a master at seduction, and she had gloried in it. But that had been weeks ago. Five times now, he had come to her doorway at night. Four times she had turned him away, though the things they had done in the hallway would hardly be considered proper. Still, she had kept him from her bed, but it had been a losing battle. They both knew her surrender was imminent.

If things had gone as usual this night, if Kit had not logicked her into agreement, then she probably would have opened the door tonight. She would have let him into her bed and her body. She would have relished every moment of her descent into the carnal, and in the morning . . . In the morning . . .

She did not know how she would feel in the morning, which is why she hadn't opened her bedroom door to him those first four times. And now the question was moot.

"I am an engaged woman," she said before he could renew his caress. "Please do not think I would betray Kit so easily."

He paused, his body still a good foot away from hers. And yet she smelled the mint, she felt his presence, and she knew her legs were weak despite the way she held herself tall and proud.

"You said the engagement will not hold," he said. "And you are still sad."

She huffed. "Because the engagement will not hold." She said the words, but in her heart, she thought something else. What if Kit held strong against his mother? What if the day went not well, but not so badly either? Then she would hold on to her dream with both hands and not let anyone end it.

"No," he said, his dark voice interrupting her thoughts. "There is something deeper. I knew it before Kit's impetuous proposal."

She stiffened at that, abruptly finding the strength to turn and shove him backward with one hand. "It was not an impetuous act!"

He arched an eyebrow at her, the dark slash an echo of the half-sneering twist of his lips. "That is your first show of spirit this whole night."

"Then it is a good thing it came when defending my fiancé." Her voice almost broke on the word "fiancé," but years of vocal training kept her emotions from affecting her words. "You underestimate your cousin."

He acknowledged her words with a shrug. "The boy does have excellent taste."

Scher shot him a grimace of disgust. "Flattery is not your strong suit."

"On the contrary, Lady Scher, flattery is simply not your weakness."

"Why can you not be my friend?" she asked, unable to look in his eyes as she spoke. "You know what life is like for a woman like me. I am accosted at night and sneered at by day. Even the poorest married woman is afforded respect, and her children have options as they grow." She forced herself to look into his eyes. "A friend would be happy for me, for this chance at a good life."

He didn't speak at first, but she read a desperate sadness in his eyes. "I want to be your lover, Scher. You cannot know how you haunt me."

"And I want to be respectable, Lord Blackstone."

"Kit is not your answer." He took a step forward. "But I could be. I could try."

She wanted to believe him. She wanted it the same way she wanted to feel his hands on her body, his male strength surrounding her—penetrating her—at night. But that path led nowhere. So she turned back to the key in her door, twisting it with a precise flick of her wrist. "I am too tired to match wits with you, my lord. I concede the victory. You are more brilliant, more witty, and more manly than any woman can withstand. I am fairly panting with desire. Too bad I am engaged to your cousin."

He was upon her in a moment, his assault too silent for her to hear, his strength too much for her to defeat. She hadn't even smelled the rush of mint until it was too late. He simply waited until her back was turned, then wrapped his arms around her, pinning her elbows to her side. She barely had the strength to keep the lantern from crashing to the ground and setting the entire theater on fire.

He quickly wrenched the lantern from her grip. And when she drew breath to scream, the sound came out as a squeak as he flipped her over his shoulder and carried her into her bedroom.

Chapter 3

Scher weighed next to nothing. That was Brandon's thought as he kicked the door closed behind him. For all her force of personality, for all the steel he felt beneath her surface, her weight was rather slight. Scher was flesh and bone, he realized, and that could be conquered.

He dropped her on her bed. He remembered at the last moment to protect her head such that it didn't bounce painfully on mattress or wall. He slid his hand to cradle her as she descended, but that brought him too close to landing on top of her. And if that happened, there would be no way to rescue the situation.

So he kept her head from bouncing, and then quickly stepped back. But he couldn't force himself to go far. He stood beside the bed, looming over her, as he contemplated her slim body. She was not lush like the portraits of her mother. Whoever her father was clearly had slimmer bones and more refined features. Brandon thought she was like a beautiful bird, slender enough for flight, long enough to be flexible, and with a crown of glossy reddish-brown hair that could mesmerize him. Did she know it changed colors depending on the light? Right now, it spilled about her head in dark waves, only occasionally glinting red from the lantern flame.

"Why aren't you screaming?" he asked casually. How odd that his organ was painfully hard for her, that he was thinking of doing the unthinkable, and yet could discuss his actions with the dispassion of the most hardened criminal. Perhaps that was what he was: a depraved, unrepentant criminal. "You are frightened," he noted.

Her eyes were wide, her breath shortened into tight whispered pants. She had braced herself on her elbows and coiled her legs together and back the moment her body hit the mattress. But beyond that—and a slow inching to the opposite side of the bed—she made no move to protect herself.

He looked to her bedroom door. It was shut, but not locked. Anyone could enter at any moment. Except that they were on the top floor, and he knew no one disturbed Lady Scher's rest. "One good scream from you and I shall have the whole troupe upon me."

She took a deep breath. He wasn't even looking at her, but he heard it nonetheless, and he reacted without thought. He was upon the bed, his forearm pressed to her throat. He didn't push, but the threat was enough. If she released her scream, he would cut it off before she could do more than whimper.

He waited that way until he felt her release her breath on a slow, steady sigh. He even closed his eyes to better feel the heated air whisper against his cheek and the gentle lowering of her chest as she exhaled.

"I suppose that is why," he said to himself. He felt his organ press against her thigh. Oh, she was so close. Damn his cousin for jumping the gun. Damn Kit for proposing today rather than tomorrow. He could have had Scher tonight if it were not for the stupid boy. He could have had her in a blissful sexual haze for nights on end. Enough to satiate his own hunger and dissuade the puppy from his ridiculous proposal. But Kit had not waited, Scheherazade had accepted, and now she would not submit to him without force.

It had seemed so easy a month ago. His brother, the earl and head of the family, had tasked him with distracting a scheming actress away from Kit. How hard could it be? Then he'd met Scher and found her infinitely more complicated than expected. And also infinitely more intriguing.

She'd been kissing him for more than a month now, teasing him with her hunger while simultaneously struggling to hold on to her respectability. He had felt the war inside her with every kiss. She did not want to desire him, but she did. And he had made sure that some of his friends knew of their liaison. Not the particulars, just enough to set the stage if Kit forced his hand.

And Kit *had* forced his hand, damn it all. If only the boy had waited one night. Kit didn't seem to care if the girl was virgin, only that she remain true to him now. So all Brandon needed to do was seduce her before the proposal, then brag about it in the right circles. But it hadn't happened that way, and now Brandon lay on top of her fighting his worst desires.

My, how he had fallen from his idealistic youth.

It would be so easy. All he need do is ease himself on top of her. One hand would pin her wrists. The other would pull aside her skirt. And if she screamed, it wouldn't matter. The deed would be done before anyone could stop him. Even if she cried rape afterward, there would be enough doubt. Kit would likely decry the engagement before tomorrow's family dinner.

His brother would do it. His brother would think it a service to Kit and to the family name. He could almost picture Michael standing over him, cursing with displeasure the longer Brandon avoided doing the deed.

She was back to her short panting breaths. In truth, he hadn't allowed her much more than that, so he eased off her throat so she could breathe deeper. He had no wish to suffocate her. But he couldn't force himself to move further—either on top or away. Her breasts were full beneath his chest. She had gotten that much from her mother. Ripe globes that he could feel distinctly even though she lay on her back.

He moved his free hand to her breast. His right arm still lay light across her throat, but his left shifted enough for him to caress her. He didn't tear off her clothes. She owned so few dresses. It would be cruel to destroy this one even though it was a dull, ugly brown. He could feel through her clothes. He shaped her and lifted her and rubbed his thumb across her nipple. She released a mew of distress, but he felt her pebble beneath his ministrations, and he wondered if her breath was short because of fear or desire.

"I do not want this," she whispered. It was always a whisper with her. Never had he heard her raise her voice or bark a command. An arch of her brow sufficed. Or a pointed finger. Once, he'd even seen her tighten a fist, but that was all. And when she was with him, her voice dropped even quieter, he thought because they shared such intimate confessions.

His hand had not stopped. His fingers continued to toy with her nipple, tugging it as much as he could, rubbing his nail across it when he could not. The fabric was a restriction after all, and he thought of ripping it away. He could always buy her a new gown.

"Stop," she said firmly.

"Cry off your engagement to Kit. Choose me instead."

"No." There was no compromise in her voice, not that he had expected any. He glanced at her face, wincing when he saw the whites of her eyes. For all that she lay still beneath him, he could feel her heart hammering in her chest and see the fear in her widened eyes.

He looked away.

"I have never raped a woman before," he said to her shoulder. "I have never considered it anything but the act of a depraved dog."

"Then why?" she whispered to him. "Why me? And why now? Am I not a person to you?"

He looked back to her face. Forced himself, actually. If he were to become a depraved dog, then he owed her the decency of looking into her face as he did it. So he looked into her eyes, and as he did it, he shifted his hips such that he lay directly on top of her. His organ pushed against her, and she shuddered. It was a small movement, one she obviously fought, but he felt it. There was desire there, if only just a tiny bit.

"You are a woman to me," he said.

"Then why?" she rasped. "You have a mistress. Go to her!"

He paused, pulling back with a frown. "I do not have a mistress." Her heart beat so fast beneath his hands. "You should not listen to gossip, Scher," he said. "The woman I brought back from India is not my mistress. She is but a child."

"What would that child think of this? Of what you are about to do?"

He shrugged. "She already wants me dead. This would be just another crime to lay at my door."

"Why me?" Was the burr in her voice because of him? Had he hurt her? Or was it desire? Either way, he eased his arm farther away from her throat. "*Why?*"

She slammed her fist down on his shoulder. It was the only thing she could reach and the blow caused a little pain. But it wasn't enough to overpower his lust, and his groin continued to push rhythmically against her.

"Because you have picked Kit over me," he answered.

She hit him again. "Vanity? You would rape me over wounded vanity? Are you so small a man?"

"Apparently," he answered. Then he caught her wrist and raised it high over her head.

"Are you drunk? Mad? Brandon, what is happening to you?"

She said his name. He closed his eyes for a moment to better appreciate the sound. But she had already spoken and so his name was gone. Still, he replayed it in his thoughts. *Brandon, what is happening?*

"I don't know," he answered. "I don't know."

Except he did know something. He knew he couldn't rape her. He couldn't do that to a woman, least of all her. And to do such a thing in service to his family name was beyond ridiculous. He shifted his weight, easing off her while he tried to frame an apology for his actions. He didn't get the chance.

She screamed. The sound was sharp and startling, and he recoiled backward.

How had he not felt it coming? How had he not known that she was drawing enough air to release so piercing a noise? And while he was jerking his ear away, she wormed a hand between them and shoved.

It was well placed and well timed. He was already flinching. She merely increased his movement, shoving with every ounce of her small frame. He fell off her and half landed, half crouched on the floor beside the bed.

She was on her feet in a moment, slamming her fist into his jaw with a power that stunned him. In truth, it pleased him. He had not thought she could defend herself so well. It was good for a woman in her position to know how to fight.

He blocked her next blow, slamming his arm against hers as he straightened up from his crouch. She countered, as he knew she would, but it was useless. She was trained in stage fighting, not real combat, and she was a small woman. He had her back down on the bed within a moment.

"They are coming," she gasped against the coverlet. "They will kill you."

She wasn't lying. If Seth had heard her scream, Brandon had no more than seconds to escape. The man was huge and could very possibly best him in a fight. And if Seth brought reinforcements, then Brandon had no hope.

He almost waited to see what would happen. But he wasn't suicidal, so he pushed up and off her. She whipped around to face him before he had fully gained his feet. Even in the dim light, he could see that hard accusation in her eyes. He dipped his chin in acknowledgment. He deserved her fury. He deserved that and very much more.

But a moment later he regained his equilibrium. He gave her a mocking bow and flashed his darkest smile. "This is not done between us, Scheherazade. In fact, it is barely begun."

He waited long enough to see his words hit her. He saw her blanche in fear, but also saw something else in her expression. Had she lifted an eyebrow in challenge? Had her lips curled slightly in interest? Or had his fevered mind only imagined it?

He didn't have time to find out. He heard footsteps on the stairs, and so he departed. Speed was one of his skills, and he used it to the utmost. He ran faster than he had ever run before, out the window and across the rooftops. He ran until his breath choked him from within and his feet stumbled beneath him. Then he dropped to the ground and tasted blood from the fall.

Pain. Pain in his side, in his hands, and even in his tongue from where he had bit it in his fall. Blessed, well-deserved pain.

It never lasted long enough.

Family dinners were tedious affairs. That's why Brandon tried hard to show up too late to be allowed in the door.

Unfortunately, Grandmama held the meal for him and so he was shown into the parlor to a bevy of cold, angry stares. He barely had time to flinch away from the sight of Kit and Scher standing at the fireplace before his grandmother's strident voice cut through the noise.

"Really, Brandon," she said by way of greeting. "India has had a terrible effect on your manners."

He crossed to her side immediately, struggling to *not* notice that Scher looked pretty in blue. It made her look like an English doll. She also looked more conservative than a nun since her gown had heavy fabric up to her chin. Then he saw no more as he bowed over Grandmama's hand. "One of the sad consequences of a hot and humid climate, I'm afraid. Makes one lazy and forgetful of the time."

"Well, you must sit down and tell us all about it," put in Aunt Adelia from the side.

He tilted his head in surprise as he looked over at Kit's mother. She was a pinched woman, in all respects. Her lips were perpetually pursed, her bun was wrapped tighter than a banker's vault, even her words came out clipped and hard. But she was family, so he quietly took his seat, though he didn't intend to talk about India. His whole family had heard about his disastrous trip when he returned sixteen months ago. Aunt Adelia asked after the women and the society there and if he were very rich. When his answer was "dull and not very," she had huffed in disgust and turned her attention to the latest English on dit. And now, looking into her eyes, he could see that she had no interest whatsoever in his answer. Which meant she had an ulterior motive.

He had only to look over at Kit standing before everyone to know his aunt's true purpose. The boy was going to announce their engagement, and everyone here knew it. After all, his cousin had been talking about a special woman for weeks now. His mother's sudden demands on

Brandon were merely a way of stalling. Unfortunately, Kit would not take the hint.

"Mother!" the boy exclaimed from where he stood before the fireplace. "I was in the middle of my announcement!"

"Yes, yes, dear," the woman returned. "But do you really need to do that now? Perhaps Brandon will finally tell us the details." She turned her gaze back to Brandon, her expression commanding. "Surely you can tell us now. What service did you do that gained you a viscountcy? We know there was a fire in an Indian factory. It was all the news for weeks! How many of those people did you save from that fire? Were they important? Is that why you were given the viscountcy?"

Brandon arched his brow, seeing the double ploy. Obviously, Kit had been trying—apparently for a while—to make his engagement announcement, while his mother had been carefully stalling, hoping to delay the inevitable. And what better way to distract everyone than by forcing him to reveal the truth behind his new title? But it wouldn't work on either account. Nothing on Earth would induce Brandon to tell the truth about his past, and he could see that Kit would not be deterred. The boy had even thrust out his chin and squared his shoulders like a pugilist. How quaint.

"No," Kit declared loudly. "I shall do this now with no more interruptions. From anyone." He glared at each and every member of the room in turn. As it was quite a number of attendees, that took a while. Unfortunately, he didn't have a while. Kit's mother was already heaving a dramatic sigh.

"Really, dear—"

"Miss Martin has graciously agreed to be my wife."

Silence greeted this announcement. Silence punctuated by a few very loud female sighs of disgust.

Kit raised the hand he'd entwined with Scheherazade's,

shaking it slightly in his vehemence. "We are engaged and will be married as soon as the bans can be posted."

"Is she pregnant?" Aunt Adelia demanded. "Is it yours?"

To the side, someone choked in shock at the bold question. Brandon looked around. It was Michael, his older brother and the current earl of Thornedale, gasping as he set aside his brandy.

"Really, Mother!" Kit cried, his hand fisting at his side. "Of course not!"

"Not yours or not—"

"Adelia," Grandmama snapped. "Do not be vulgar. I do not tolerate vulgarity in my home."

Meanwhile, Michael had at last recovered his breath. "Please, can we go into dinner now? I am starving."

"Oh, yes, let's do," inserted his lovely wife Lily.

"Oh, yes," drawled Brandon. "I'm sure this is just the conversation that makes a meal utterly delicious." Then he abruptly shut his mouth, stunned by his own stupidity. He had not meant to say a single word, and yet here he was, throwing in his own ridiculous form of dry wit. He should have stayed at his club for another hour.

"Harumph," Grandmama snorted as she pushed up to her feet. Brandon stood as well, helping her with her cane.

"I know," Aunt Adelia loudly declared. "We shall dine a la India in Brandon's honor. We shall go into dinner all willy-nilly. Kit, you take my hand."

Brandon stiffened, though he had to be careful of his grandmother's frail bones. "There is civilization in India," he said more coldly than he intended. "They observe—"

"Oh, do not be tedious!" she snapped as she tried to glare Brandon into cooperation. "And just for that, you shall stay at the back. You take Miss Martin's arm." She sneered every part of that last sentence, damning both Brandon and Scheherazade in one dark breath.

"No, no!" interrupted Grandmama with a fond smile. "Let Kit walk with me. I have not seen him in an age."

And there it was, Brandon's doom pronounced loudly enough for all to hear. While Aunt Adelia went on directing everyone's pairing, Brandon was finally forced to do the one thing he had been dreading more than this entire hideous meal. He had to look at Scheherazade.

He had been carefully avoiding such a thing, having no wish to face the condemnation in her eyes. But he was a man, a world traveler even, with more experience than most in his set. He could face one woman despite the hideousness of his actions. So, with steel in his spine, he forced himself to step to her side and offer his arm. And only then did he dare look her in the eye.

She appeared no different than usual. Her expression was as composed and aloof as every night when she oversaw the theater and its audience. Her eyes were clear but somewhat remote. Her skin was pale and her stance excruciatingly correct. And worst of all, there was no hatred in her eyes. More of a mute kind of acceptance of the slights to her person, the insults to her character, even his own abominable behavior. All was accepted with a tolerant pain.

And that made him angry. Furious even.

"Good God, where is your spirit, girl?"

She arched a brow at him, and her gaze sharpened. "This is Kit's show, and the audience has been quite restrained so far. But we are just past the first act. I am sure the entertainment will become quite exciting soon enough."

He felt his face heat in embarrassment. The last thing he'd wanted was to be cruel to this woman, and yet his anger would not abate.

"And so you duck off the stage before it has even begun?" he challenged. "You allow poor Kit to face the harridans alone? That does not sound like a marriage to me."

She tilted her head. "Does not chivalry demand that he protect me?"

Both their gazes shifted to where Kit patted his

grandmother's hand. He was chatting amiably with the woman, obviously working hard to please her as they began the procession into the dining room. Was Kit even capable of protecting Scher? Brandon doubted it, but then again, he was not a very good judge of character.

Meanwhile, he and Scher stood patiently for the end of the line, watching as relative after relative turned their backs on her. It was rudeness, covered by a veneer of politeness, and it set his teeth on edge.

"Willy-nilly is *not* how it is done in India," he growled under his breath, though that wasn't at all what he wanted to say.

She heard him, but she didn't comment. She simply arched a brow, inviting him to continue if he so wished. He did not. And yet, he most obviously did because words kept flowing from his lips.

"Everything in England is ordered," he said as they began the stately walk into the dining room. "We know where to sit, to stand, and exactly who everyone is within a moment of meeting them. Our lawns are precise, our livestock are put in their pens, and even our servants police each other to keep them in their subservience."

"I have never found England particularly orderly," she murmured in response. "But then we do not run in the same circles."

"We will soon enough. You are to be my cousin-in-law."

Her lips curved in a soft smile. He might have missed it as he was pulling out her chair for her. But having worked so hard to *not* look at her before, he found the opposite true now. He desperately needed to watch the hints of emotions that flashed so very briefly on her face. And in that soft, secret smile, he saw the truth. She wanted this marriage more than anything. Despite her cynicism and her reserve, he knew she wanted it with a hunger that defied everything else.

"Kit is not strong enough to withstand us," he said softly by way of warning.

Her fists tightened in her lap, but no other sign penetrated her quiet veneer. Instead, her gaze shifted to the head of the table, where Grandmama was positively beaming under Kit's attention. "He believes his grandmother will swing others to our cause," she said so softly that he knew no one else had heard it.

"How sad," he commented as he took his seat beside her. "Kit will soon learn that the one who loves him most cannot help him at all."

She shot him a fearful look. "As bad as that?"

He shrugged. "She dotes on him. And were he to gain her approval a decade ago, then there would be a contest indeed. But Grandmama is not the force she once was."

"How sad that your family power has devolved to another." Her eyes went to Aunt Adelia and her pinched lips.

He could tell she understood. Assuming Kit was correct—which was by no means certain—then Grandmama would do everything in her power to see Kit happy. But was she a stronger force that Aunt Adelia? Or more powerful still, Lily, the countess of Thornedale.

"Power among women is not something I have ever sought to understand," he said dryly. He watched closely for her reaction to the news, but beyond a quick glance at Lily, no expression formed on her face. In fact, the opposite happened. She opened her fists, smoothed her skirt, and waited in all patience for the first course to be served.

As he sat beside her, he was excruciatingly aware of the growing hostility in the room. Truly, Kit was a fool to have thrown down the gauntlet like that, announcing their engagement at the beginning of the meal. That was something best reserved for the end of an evening, just after a nightcap, when bride and groom could then disappear from the ensuing war.

"What do you think?" Scher murmured beside him. "Am I to be served up with the main course? Or shall it wait for dessert?"

He glanced at Aunt Adelia's furious stare. Kit's mother had the most venomous look, but hers was not the only angry expression. Even demure Lily, his brother's wife, was growing flushed at being seated near Scheherazade. "I believe you shall be like the center candelabra," he said, "held up for all to see and burned with every course."

"Naturally," she said with dry humor, but he heard the pain underneath and knew she was not as composed as she appeared. "Then by all means, light the torch and let the games begin."

As if on cue, Aunt Adelia began her first sally.

Chapter 4

Scher pretended to sip from her wine, but didn't actually swallow. She used it as a way to keep her hands busy. Otherwise, she would worry her dress to shreds and that would be yet one more strike against her. Meanwhile, Kit's mother began her attack. The woman started sweetly with a false smile and a tight expression, but there was no disguising the animosity that radiated off her. Which made it all the more odd that she addressed Brandon.

"Do tell us more about India, Brandon. It sounds quite wild and fascinating."

Brandon frowned, obviously thrown. Probably because he'd been back from India for a year and a half now, but he shrugged and complied. "They have a market called a bazaar. The noise was deafening and the smells . . . In that hot climate, the smells can become quite pungent."

"But you liked it, didn't you?" the woman pressed. "I distinctly recall you wrote that it was thrilling."

Brandon didn't comment. If anything, his face tightened

into a grimace, though Scher couldn't tell if it was because of his aunt's probing or because of the tepid fish soup being set before him. Scher took a few dutiful sips from her bowl, but Brandon did not even try.

"Curry," he abruptly said as he waved the soup away. "They have quite the fondness for curry. And such colors as I have not seen, all mishmashed together."

"But you made a vast amount of money there, right?" continued his aunt. She seemed to be able to drink soup and speak at the same time as she at last turned her attention to Scher. "Don't you think that would be amazing, Miss Martin? To wear exquisite clothes in India?"

Scher nodded politely. "I'm sure it is a fascinating country—"

"There is money practically littering the street. All you have to do is scoop it up! I think anyone with the means ought to go there as soon as possible! Before the opportunities are all gone."

Scher blinked. Did the woman think Scher would pack her bags right then and disappear to India? Just like that?

From the top of the table, Kit pushed away his own soup. "Would you like to live there, Miss Martin? After we're wed? I'm not sure I could stand seeing animals in the middle of the street, and it is beastly hot. But if there is money to be made, I should like to consider it."

"Don't be ridiculous," his mother snapped. "You would hate it there."

Scher felt her eyebrows raise despite her resolution to be completely demure. Surely her plan was not so crude as that? To get rid of Scher simply by saying there was money in India? "Of course, I should adore to live wherever you wish to go," she said smoothly to her fiancé.

Kit's grandmother smiled benignly down the table. "That was a lovely response, Miss Martin. A woman should always be directed by her husband."

Scher was just framing a response when the countess

released a delicate snort. "What an insipid answer. I would have thought you could come up with better, given your parentage."

Scher didn't laugh. She had expected to be picked at from all angles, but she was tired of playing the demure miss. It was time to start her own assault. She leaned forward with her first true smile. "Ah, but you did not ask my parents. My mother would respond that bizarre customs are the greatest inspiration to art. And she would say it with a florid arm gesture. What my father would say shall be left to your imagination." It was left to *everyone's* imagination as she had no idea who her father was.

Meanwhile, Brandon waved a lazy hand. "I feel compelled to add that there is *not* money lying about the streets of India. Orphans and cripples are more the norm."

"Still," murmured Kit, his forehead puckered in thought. "If there is money to be made, I shouldn't mind traveling a bit. England can be quite stifling at times."

"Indeed," spoke up the earl from the foot of the table. "I believe that is exactly what Brandon once said."

"And what an ignorant fool I was," Brandon murmured. Scher wasn't sure if everyone heard him, but she certainly did. Not that she could inquire as Kit's grandmother made her own florid gesture at the footman to remove the soup dishes.

"We have returned to the vulgar again," the elderly woman drawled. "Miss Martin, I should perhaps have to instruct you that polite conversation does not include the topic of money."

Scheherazade bit back her tart response. In point of fact, it had been Kit's mother who'd begun this discussion, but she knew better than to challenge the reigning matriarch. So she dipped her chin.

"Of course, my lady. I am most grateful for your education."

Brandon shot her a surprised look. Meanwhile, Kit

touched his grandmother's arm. "I say, Grandmama, that's hardly fair—"

"Tut-tut, Kit," interrupted his mother with what was probably meant to be a smile. "Do not belabor the point. She has apologized and learned something as well."

For a moment, Scheherazade thought that Kit would fight his grandmother on her behalf. He had made the initial attempt, but after a glare from his mother, he subsided into a mulish silence. Scheherazade suppressed her sigh. Kit was not handling this well. In that one exchange, he showed that he knew they were treating her badly but was unequal to the task of defending her to his mother. Well, she was hardly surprised by that, still she couldn't help feeling disappointed. Could she not have a man defend her honor just once? Could not someone else fight the battle for her?

Pushing aside her self-indulgent thoughts, she turned her attention to the battle, mentally tallying her allies and enemies. The mother and countess were against her, that much was expected. Kit's grandmother was an unknown, but as Scher had little experience in turning a proper lady into an ally, she decided to ignore the females and lead with her strengths. She would focus on the men, most especially the earl. He was the head of the family, his parents having both died of a fever some years before. Fortunately, he was seated to her right and so she smiled warmly at him.

Bad choice! His wife Lily sat directly across from her and stiffened most noticeably. Scheherazade immediately chilled her expression. She would need to appear friendly, but not too friendly. But how did one converse politely with an earl? If she were at the Tavern Playhouse, she would simply offer him a service or inquire as to how he liked the show. Given that they were in his grandmother's dining room, she had to find something else to discuss.

"I understand you are sponsoring a bill in the House of Lords against slavery. Have you always been an admirer of Mister Wilberforce?"

She thought it was a perfect topic. Lord Thornedale was known to be involved in politics, had supported the antislavery movement, though not as loudly as others, and what man didn't enjoy talking about his life's work? But when Scheherazade waited politely for him to start talking, the earl stared at her in shock. As did everyone else at the table.

Scher turned slowly around, scanning each face for a clue. Even Kit seemed completely blank.

"*I* have been the supporter of Mister Wilberforce," Brandon said softly. "My brother prefers a less reform-oriented policy."

"Truly?" she said. Had she confused the two brothers' politics? She hadn't thought so, but now she was committed to this line of conversation. "But what a wonderful thing that two brothers can disagree on politics and still be brothers! Do you debate with one another often? Or just choose not to talk about it?"

Brandon leaned forward, his eyes dancing with merriment. "Ah, well, that's the problem. I can never tell with Michael. Some days he wishes to talk cows, and the next day slavery."

"I find an unrelenting focus on one thing to be tedious," his brother responded flatly.

"When a country treats a cow better than a man, then perhaps there is a fundamental problem."

"I see," she inserted smoothly. She wanted them talking, not coming to blows. "Viscount Blackstone keeps a steady eye on the reforming prize," she said with a wink to Brandon. "While Lord Thornedale wields a more balanced hand. How wonderful it is that the body politic needs both of you!"

Success! Both men turned to her, their expressions varying degrees of surprise and relief that she had found a way to ease them away from an argument. If this were the Green Room, they would have smiled and deferred to her.

But she was not the reigning hostess here. That was their Grandmother, who snorted from the top of the table.

"Are you a close follower of politics, Miss Martin? I find that especially disreputable in a woman, you know. Too much familiarity with the common elements."

Scheherazade waited a respectful moment. She pretended to be thinking deeply about the lady's comment, but truly, she was waiting to see Kit's reaction. Would he want her to disavow any understanding of the issues of the day? Would he prefer she cede politics to the men? Or did he value her mind as he claimed?

Typically, he said nothing. She got the unfortunate feeling he was waiting to see how the others reacted to decide on his opinion. Which left it up to her again, and so she smiled brightly while phrasing a deferential answer in her mind. Unfortunately, she never got to use it as Brandon pushed forward.

"But don't you see, Grandmama, any government that doesn't understand its people is doomed."

"An understanding?" inserted Countess Thornedale from beside her husband. She spoke softly as befitted the wife of an earl, but everyone heard her clearly. "What is there to understand? They require bread, a home, and the chance to ply their trade."

"Do you find that true of your servants?" retorted Brandon with a hard edge to his voice. "Are there no petty rivalries, no squabbles, no tensions among your staff? Ever?"

"There is always silliness among the staff. I try not to involve myself in it, but it is necessary at times."

"Now imagine that type of bickering on a grander scale. That of a whole country. What if you as governor had no understanding of why those arguments existed? And if one of those servants was a thief or a murderer? What would you do then?"

Brandon's voice was tight with anger. It was not liquor

because Lord Blackstone did not drink. Clearly, there was some other wound here.

"Now see what you have done, Miss Martin?" Kit's mother inserted with a huff. "You have brought everyone to murder!"

"Don't be ridiculous, Aunt Adelia," snapped the earl. "Miss Martin has done nothing but encourage Brandon in his politics, and that is never a good thing."

Scheherazade didn't speak at first. She was too busy pressing a hand to Brandon's leg beneath the table. He was practically vibrating with fury, and she feared he would do something unseemly. It would be bad for him, of course, but completely ruinous for her, as whatever he did would be squarely blamed on her. So she gripped Brandon's hard thigh beneath the table, hoping to restrain him from below while she went on the offensive above. It was time to become more bold in her determination to wed Kit despite all the harridans that surrounded them.

"Yes, politics can be a heated subject," she said, "one probably best left to the men. Obviously, I could never be a political wife. My birth makes that an impossibility. But there is much that a woman of vast fortune can do. Either to support someone's political ambitions"—she glanced warmly at the earl—"or to embark upon grand adventures in other countries." She smiled up at Kit, not daring to look at Brandon who clearly thought India was something far darker than an adventure. "So shall we discuss this later, Kit? Exactly where and how we shall invest my fortune?"

"Of course, my dear," Kit responded immediately. "I'm pleased that you value my advice."

"Vast fortune?" drawled Kit's mother. "I assure you, Miss Martin, that a few hundred pounds in your coffers likely *feels* like a vast fortune. But in our set—"

"My lady," Scher responded tightly. "Do you not understand? I spend a few hundred pounds daily. I have simply chosen to spend it in support of my mother's playhouse. But lately, Kit has been expanding my thoughts to a new stage, so to speak."

"Can it be possible?" mused the grandmother as she turned to look at Kit. "Have you found yourself an heiress?"

"Impossible!" snapped Kit's mother.

"Oh, but she is," said Brandon. Beneath the table, he wrapped her hand in his and squeezed. Scher had no idea what his message was. His leg was still as tight as it was a few moments ago. There was no lessening in his fury for all that his voice had dropped to a silky drawl. "Did you really think Kit a total idiot?"

"Well, of course not," snapped Aunt Adelia. "He's just a little naïve, is all. Taken in by—"

"Do not say it, Aunt." Brandon's words vibrated with warning. Surprisingly, Kit's mother stopped speaking, her mouth hanging open in shock at his tone. Meanwhile, Brandon continued speaking while his gaze scorched everyone at the table. "She is kind, rich, has a sweet wit, and an unfortunate birth. But Kit is no prize. Accept her and she may deign to loan you some of her money some day."

To the right, the earl stiffened in outrage. "We have no need of money from the likes of her!"

"Really," drawled Brandon. "Not you perhaps, but what of her?" His gaze slid unerringly to Kit's mother, who flushed a bright red. Then he lowered his voice until he was almost gentle. Beneath the table, his body slowly released as well, and his fingers began to stroke the inside of her wrist with the gentlest of touches. "Aunt Adelia, look at your son. Can you not think to give him this happiness?"

There was a moment when Scher thought it would work. Kit's mother lifted her chin and took a long look at Kit. Then her eyes slid slowly around the table, presumably to look at Scher. But she stopped short, her gaze halting on Brandon. "It is for him that I do this," she said stiffly.

"Then you are a fool," he said. Below the table, he moved away from her wrist, choosing instead to entwine her fingers with his.

Meanwhile, Kit stiffened as all eyes turned toward him, clearly wondering if he too would defend Scher. But before he could speak, Grandmama set down her spoon with a loud click.

"Outrageous, Brandon! Wherever did you get such ideas?"

Below the table, Brandon's leg twitched as if he had been slapped, but his body above the table remained absolutely still. Meanwhile, Kit now took his moment. He threw down his napkin with dramatic flair, then stomped his way down the table to stand beside Scher.

"Come along, Miss Martin," he said stiffly. "I believe my cousin is in his cups."

Scher stared at her fiancé in shock. Surely he wasn't turning on his cousin, especially since Brandon did *not* drink? Below the table, Brandon clutched her other hand, refusing to release it. And between the two men, Scher felt well and truly caught, uncertain of the right thing to do or say.

Meanwhile, Kit's mother was not done with her own dramatics. With a clearly staged sob, she screeched down the table at the earl.

"Michael, you're the earl. Stop this now!"

Like everyone else, Scheherazade looked to the earl, but he had no answers. He glared at the three of them equally, but his eyes lingered longest on Scheherazade.

"This is not seemly," he said firmly.

Brandon snorted. "A lot of things happen in this world that are not seemly."

Scheherazade's patience was suddenly exhausted. This squabbling would get them nowhere. She pushed up from her chair. It was hard given that Brandon still possessed her hand beneath the table. "Brandon," she hissed, "let go!"

He released her, but his eyes still burned into hers. "You have other options, Scher. This will never work."

Other options? She almost laughed at the idea. She had only the options that had been available to her throughout her life: to become a whore or not. Kit was the only man offering her anything else. So Scher straightened, forcibly removing her hand from Brandon's grasp, though she wrenched her wrist to do it. Then she turned her gaze to the rest of the family, all gaping at her as if she was the one who had created this disaster. Looking at their faces, she made her decision. She had tried sweetness, she had tried to speak moderately, and even dressed in the closest things she owned to a nun's habit. It mattered not at all. And so she would say her piece to all of them.

"Kit and I have made our decision," she said firmly. "We had wanted to keep this polite, had hoped to win your support. But now I see we should just travel to Gretna Green."

"Scotland?" squeaked Kit's mother in alarm.

"Here, now," inserted Michael. "There's no need to elope."

Beside the earl, the countess dabbed her lips with a napkin before speaking in her own quiet tones. "This has been a difficult meal," she said. "But really, Kit does have a certain status to maintain. A mad flight to Scotland would start things off on a terrible foot."

"Would it?" she said turning toward Kit, her brow arched in question. "Or would it simply end all the ugliness early?"

Then from the top of the table, Kit's grandmother chose to speak with a power in her voice that surprised everyone. "My grandson will *not* elope! I wish to be at your wedding, Kit. Do not think to deny me that!"

There was a moment's silence as everyone turned to stare at the elderly woman. She was practically vibrating in her chair and her face was flushed a becoming shade of rose. Then Kit broke the silence.

"You shall be in the front pew, Grandmama," he said. Then he turned to Scher. "See, all will be well. A proper wedding stops wagging tongues."

"Does it?" she wondered aloud. But he knew polite society better than she, and so she bowed her head. "Very well."

Kit smiled as he tucked her hand against his arm and began to lead her out, sparing no more than a glance farewell to his grandmother. "I shall post the banns immediately."

Scher nodded. "I would be grateful." Three weeks. Could she endure three weeks of this before the wedding? Could he?

They were nearly out the door before Brandon spoke. Scher had been excruciatingly aware of him sitting there, watching them with dark eyes and plotting . . . something. He obviously hadn't given up his fight for her. She didn't dare look back at him; her entire being had to be focused on Kit.

But it came as no surprise that he had the last word. He was a man who chose his timing well. "I *am* your friend, Scher."

There were many things she could say to that. Some part of her agreed. He had tried to defend her, though it clearly hadn't helped. But were his motives truly so pure? Or did he simply think that she would turn to him if a family disaster made Kit cry off? Meanwhile, Kit stiffened and was about to turn and say something scathing, no doubt. But Scheherazade stopped him with a quiet squeeze to his arm. "Pay no attention, love," she said loud enough for all to hear. "Your family's squabbles mean nothing to us."

She said the words and knew from the silence behind her that they were effective. No one would speak until they were out of the house, assuming they moved quickly enough. But in her heart, she knew there was more to Brandon's story than a dissolute lord who was peeved about

losing a mistress. Something darker had taken hold of his
soul. Something that tortured him and intrigued her.

But he was not her future. She had no business being
interested in a man who was not her fiancé. So she turned
her attention to Kit as she rushed them both out of his
grandmother's home. Unfortunately, the moment the door
shut behind them, she knew she had erred. Kit's face told
her as much as he turned to her, his expression angry.
"Damn! I have not brought a carriage."

She blinked, startled by the vehemence in his tone for
something so small. "Um. Did you need a carriage?"

"Do you not recall?" he snapped, though not really at
her. He was snarling more at the street. "I rode my horse
here, and you met me a block away such that we could
arrive together."

Yes, of course she remembered. It had been her idea.
"It's no matter, Kit. I can find my way back—"

"You don't understand," he said as he ran his hand
through his hair. "I wish to talk to you, Scheherazade.
Privately. But I haven't got a carriage, and it wouldn't be
proper anyway."

She nodded, her heart sinking with his every clipped
word. As she feared, he had changed his mind. He could
not withstand his family's pressure, and now, judging from
his expression, he would blame the disaster on her. She
turned away, blinking back the tears even as she struggled
for some way to salvage the situation.

"There is no reason to fret about your family, Kit. We
both knew that they would resist. And I thought you quite
dashing in your final words."

"What?" He blinked, obviously turned from his thoughts
by her compliment. "Dashing? How?"

"About posting the banns."

"Oh." He shook his head, running a hand through his
hair. "Damn it, Scher, we need to speak. But it isn't proper
without a chaperone."

She didn't know whether to be touched that he thought about her respectability or saddened that he clearly planned to cry off their wedding. Either way, she could tell he would insist on speaking his mind.

"Shall we walk then?" she said softly. "So long as we keep our voices down, we can talk with complete respectability."

"Walk? It's a long way back to the playhouse."

"I don't mind," she said. "I like the exercise."

"Very well," he said with a sigh. Then he set off down the street, his steps too rapid for her to easily keep pace.

"Kit!" she gasped. "It will be easier to talk if I am not breathless!"

He immediately shortened his steps, mumbling an apology. But then, as they settled into a more sedate pace, he didn't speak at all but continued to stare angrily down at the cobblestones.

Well, at least she could be consoled by the fact that he was obviously distraught by the idea of crying off their marriage. Still, the pain of it cut deep. So deep, in fact, that she was becoming angry.

"Kit—"

"You called him Brandon," he blurted. "You shouldn't know my cousin at all, and yet you called him Brandon."

Her step hitched, though she tried to cover. She obviously failed because he turned to her, his expression more hurt now than anything else.

"I told you, Scher, that I would not be a cuckold."

Her eyebrows shot high. "Do you trust me so little? I swore I would not betray you."

"You called him Brandon," he repeated. "You are on familiar terms with him!"

"And from that you assume that he is in my bed?"

"Is he?"

"No!"

"But you know him. Well."

She sighed. There was no avoiding it. The information would come out eventually. She had just hoped that Kit would discover the truth later. "I know him. He has been trying to make me his mistress for nearly a month now."

"A month!"

"He has not succeeded," she said harshly. "Men have been trying to seduce me since I turned ten. You know that!"

"But I did not know it was my cousin!"

She slowed her steps even further, forcing him to either stop walking or move ahead of her. He stopped, but when he turned back to her, she could see such fury in him that she was stunned.

"My God, Kit," she whispered. "What is it? Why does Brandon—" She quickly corrected herself. "Why does Lord Blackstone infuriate you so?"

"He doesn't. He—"

"Kit!" she snapped. "Our marriage is much too important to be thrown aside because you will not speak honestly to me."

Her fiancé sighed, and again he ran his hand through his hair. She could tell he was struggling, his male pride unwilling to talk. So she tried to make it easier on him.

As they were gaining attention from other strollers, she grabbed his arm and resumed their slow stroll. "Let me explain something first, then. I have always longed to be respectable. From the moment I first realized how vulnerable an actress was, I wanted to be a married woman. I wanted to be able to protect my family. No men hanging on my dress, no need to fight off drunkards or reprobates. No fear for my next meal—"

"That's not entirely true—"

"And no daily display to the worst sort of men." She took a deep breath to steady her nerves. She was not used to confessing such a close-held secret. "I want to be married. I want a home and children who will not suffer as I have." She tugged him slightly so he would look her in the eye. "I can have that with you, and I would not jeopardize that for anything. Not for your cousin, not for a million jewels, not for anything, Kit."

He studied her face, his eyes searching for reassurance. He must have found it because eventually he nodded and turned back to the street. "Brandon is five years older than I, but our situations are similar. Younger sons of respectable pedigree."

She nodded, though he couldn't see her. His eyes were trained on another couple, smiling politely to them until they passed beyond hearing.

"He is so much more than I," Kit murmured.

"What?"

"Smarter. More handsome. Better horseman too. And now with a title and money, women flock to him."

"You fear that I shall dash right into his arms. Really, Kit, do you value yourself so little? Or do you think I am so inconstant?"

He shrugged. "Neither. Both. I don't know."

He did know. He was afraid, pure and simple, and that was something she understood very well. "Kit . . ." she began, but he interrupted her.

"There is something that I have done very well, Scheherazade. Something I have always done better than Brandon."

"Yes?"

"Love."

She frowned, not understanding. "But you said that women flock to him. And even I have heard of his exploits—"

"But that is not love, Scher." He put his hand atop of hers on his arm, and he gripped her tight for all that they were simply strolling side by side. "Something happened to him in India. I don't know what, but I know that he came home changed."

"That is to be expected—"

"No. Truly changed. Do you not feel it? The darkness in him?"

"Yes," she whispered. She felt it, and she wondered.

"I . . . I do not think there is any love left in him. I think whatever happened in India killed it."

She gasped, horrified despite her determination to remain unaffected by Brandon. "Surely it is not as bad as all that!"

Kit shrugged, more at ease now that they were speaking of his cousin's failings. "I am not sure, of course, and there is always hope. But I have seen him in a rage . . . It was frightening." Kit turned to her. "Don't be fooled by his charm. He is empty inside."

She smiled and touched his cheek. "Again you question my loyalty. Why are you so anxious about me?"

"Because you do not love me. Not yet, at least. And until you do, I shall never be easy."

Her breath caught and her steps faltered. She had not thought him so perceptive. "Kit . . ." she began, not knowing how she would finish.

"You will love me," he said firmly. "Of that I am sure. But you must give me time."

"Then marry me quickly," she returned. "After that, we shall have all the time in the world."

He flashed her a grin. "I shall post the banns immediately. Unless you were serious about Gretna Green."

"Very serious," she answered truthfully.

He thought about it, but in the end shook his head. "I want to marry you openly, respectably. Nothing hurry-scurry about it." Then he flashed her a grin. "Plus, I promised Grandmama."

She smiled, her heart tightening sweetly in her chest. Heaven help them if his grandmother turned against them as well. "I shall be the happiest of brides."

He grinned, tucking her arm tight to his side. "And I the most fortunate of grooms."

They walked farther, in quiet accord for many minutes. Scher was just beginning to relax, enjoying the simple pleasures of sun and air, until he tightened his grip.

"Just how wealthy are you, Scher?" he asked.

She sighed. Again, she had hoped to delay this discussion, but she was the one who'd thrown down that particular gauntlet. She could hardly blame him for bringing it up now.

"Wealthy enough if the playhouse does well. We shall never lack for food or clothing."

He didn't answer. She could tell he was thinking, but she wasn't sure about what. In the end, she took a stab.

"Did you perhaps want to see the documents? Would you like to know the particulars?"

"I think I should, don't you?"

No. No, she didn't want him to know. She didn't want anyone to know because once he knew the information, others would too. And then everything would change. Money always changed things. But he was to be her husband, he would be in charge of all her accounts. It was only right that he see it all beforehand.

"Of course, Kit," she forced herself to say. "But I must beg for your discretion."

"Naturally," he said with a lightness in his tone that she had not heard this day. "It shall be a great secret between us!"

She nodded, but her heart told her otherwise. Kit was not a man who could keep secrets.

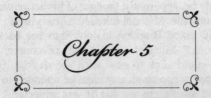

Chapter 5

"Is it true, Brandon?" Aunt Adelia's voice was strident enough to make him wince. "Does she truly have a fortune?"

Brandon waited long enough to think of the brandy decanter, but he was not going to allow Aunt Adelia to push him back to that particular devil. So he set his empty glass down. "Well, as to the exact amount, I haven't been able—"

"You said she had a fortune. You said she had more than you."

Brandon released a loud and heartfelt sigh. "Financial matters are hard to determine."

To his right, Michael leaned forward, his eyes accusing. "You also said you would handle this."

"Obviously," snapped Aunt Adelia, "his powers of seduction are vastly overrated."

"Mind your tongue, Adelia," Grandmama retorted, her blood obviously still running high. "You were disgraceful at dinner. And what's this about setting someone to seduce Kit's fiancée?"

Brandon turned, arching a brow at his elder brother. His task was supposed to be a quiet one between gentlemen. No one else was to know. But somehow Aunt Adelia and now the entire family knew of his disgraceful behavior. Sadly, only he, apparently, thought of his actions as deplorable. Meanwhile, Michael released a heavy sigh.

"I only asked Brandon to look into her background, Grandmama," Michael said. A lie, of course, but one Michael would stick to now until the day he died. "Kit told me weeks ago about a woman he intended to marry. I merely did my duty to see that he was protected."

Adelia responded with a huff and muttered, "Kit is *my* son. I should know what is happening. Especially if he intends to wed a whore."

Everyone ignored her, most especially Brandon, who pushed aside his congealed beef with a grimace. He knew better than anyone that defending Scheherazade's virtue would be useless to this set.

"What we need are details," Michael stated. "Exact details as to how much the chit is worth—"

"And how to best use her to your advantage?" Brandon drawled. "Perhaps we could mug her and grab all her coins. Or better yet, find a footman who would have her. A man whom we could control such that *he* takes all her money for us to spend."

"Yes, yes," Michael snapped as he drained his own glass of wine. "We are all well aware of your democratic attitudes. But the fact is, she is an *actress*."

"And therefore not fit for my son!" Aunt Adelia added with a sniff.

"Are you so very sure?" Brandon said, his voice low enough to be a hiss. "She is smart, demure, and rich. Kit could do much worse."

"And he could do much better!" his aunt retorted.

"Please, please," interrupted Lily. Her voice was soft, but like Brandon's, her words carried clearly to all. "This does not help us at all." She turned to Grandmama. "Is there any amount of wealth that would make her acceptable?"

"No!" snapped Adelia, but Grandmama frowned, clearly thinking.

"Money can be a great equalizer," the elderly woman mused, her gaze on Aunt Adelia. "I believe this is a question for the earl. Michael? Do our coffers require an infusion?"

Brandon's brother flushed a mottled red. "No," he said firmly.

"That settles it!" snapped Aunt Adelia.

"However," Michael continued. "Ready blunt never goes amiss. I could think of a dozen or more projects that would benefit greatly."

Brandon idly toyed with his knife. "Does anyone care that it is not our money? It is hers."

"It is her husband's," Grandmama said.

Brandon pinned her with a dark stare. "Then it would be Kit's money, not Michael's."

His grandmother lifted her nose with a sniff. "Kit has always been a good boy to me."

"And me!" Adelia said clearly. "Though if anyone's projects were to get the money, it would be Kit's oldest brother. The earldom doesn't need more, whereas the baronetcy could expand significantly."

"And yet," inserted Lily, as smooth as any countess could be, "you have said no amount of money would make her acceptable."

"And," put in Michael, easily backing up his wife, "if Kit were amenable to direction, we would not be in this situation at all. He would already be married to someone else of your selection."

"And if Brandon had done as he promised," snapped Aunt Adelia, "then this entire dreadful evening would never have occurred."

Brandon didn't respond. How could he? She was correct, damn her. He thought it a simple thing to seduce an actress.

It would do a service to his family, keep his cousin from a terrible mistake, and occupy his thoughts for a while. "Sometimes," he said softly, "the lady is not what one expects."

There was a host of feminine retorts, most in the form of snorts and huffs of disgust. Fortunately, Lily was of a more refined sort.

"I'm sure Brandon has done his very best," she said softly. "But perhaps we are going about this the wrong way. Perhaps we should find someone else for Kit."

Aunt Adelia slammed her hand down the table. "As if I haven't been trying! I have dragged Kit to every social event I could imagine. Every eligible girl has been thrust under his nose. He's always very polite, of course, but as soon as possible, he runs off to that whore!"

"Adelia!" Grandmother snapped.

"Well, it's true!" the woman returned mulishly.

"If it were true," Brandon said, a hard edge to every word, "then I would have already accomplished my task."

It was several moments before anyone spoke. They were staring at him—and the knife he held gripped in his fist—with varying levels of alarm. Finally, Lily chose to break the awkward silence.

"As I said before, Brandon is doing all he can. But perhaps I should have a quiet tea with a few ladies perfect for Kit."

"I already have—" Adelia began, but Lily rolled coldly right over the shrew.

"We do not run in the same circles, Adelia. Do not presume to think you know the same women I do."

Grandmama leaned forward, her eyes alight. "Excellent notion, Lily! I shall prepare a guest list of my friends' relations immediately!"

Lily nodded her head, but her eyes held a glittering anger that Brandon could only applaud. "Why, thank you. I shall be, of course, grateful to see any names you suggest. Perhaps for a ball later. As for my tea, I will make it small. And exclusive."

In other words, Grandmama could keep her interfering nose out of things. "Bravo, Lily," he said softly. She acknowledged she heard him with a very aristocratic arch to her brow, but before she could respond, Aunt Adelia chose to spread her venom. Again.

"Be so good as to hold your opinions to yourself, Brandon. We still hold you entirely at fault for this disaster."

He turned slowly, a darkness seeping through his body. Pain came with it, but in a cold way, freezing him outside of his own body. And in that moment, his family ceased to matter to him. It was an odd position to be in. He had been raised on the glory of brotherhood in Mother England, but all that had abruptly disappeared.

"You are quite right," he heard himself say. "I am useless to you. Next time you require the debauching of an innocent, pray do not call on me."

"She is not innocent!" retorted Aunt Adelia, but no one paid her the least mind.

"Everyone, stop being so dramatic!" Grandmama said with a sigh. Her face looked wan again, and he could see that her strength was leaving her. "No one asked for debauchery." Clearly, she didn't understand that Michael had indeed asked for exactly that. "But I would be grateful if you could discover the details of her money. How ridiculous would it look if after all this to-do, Kit discovered himself saddled with a *penniless* actress."

"And," continued Aunt Adelia when Grandmama had fallen silent, "if *that* requires your more manly skills, then you should stop acting so *democratic*"—she practically spat the word—"and get on with it!"

Beside him, Brandon heard his brother sigh. It was echoed as well by Lily. Neither of them appreciated Aunt Adelia's vulgar moments. But Brandon had a different reaction: He smiled. But in his distant place he felt none of the joy of his smirking expression. And no satisfaction either as he pushed to his feet. "No," he said loudly.

"No?" Aunt Adelia retorted. "No, what?"

"No, I am not up to the task. Nor will I ever be." And with that, he threw down his napkin and departed. His steps were long and fast. He covered the ground to the doorway with maximum speed. And yet, he was still not fast enough to prevent hearing his grandmother's parting words.

"Now you've done it. You insulted his pride."

He didn't catch his aunt's waspish retort, only the tone. And then he was mercifully out the door. Unfortunately, he couldn't escape his grandmother's words. Everything he'd said, everything he'd tried to express had been boiled down to hurt pride. Not a one of his family would ever think of Scheherazade as anything more than a rich purse or a scheming whore. And any words to the contrary from him would simply be put down to hurt pride.

Bloody hell, he hated England. Or perhaps it was merely the English he despised. Either way, he was done with them all. He intended to board the next boat to . . . to where? Back to India? Never! Besides, he would be shot on sight. Scotland? There were only more English there, except that they spoke funny. Australia, perhaps, to reside with the transported criminals? He was not that suicidal. Perhaps he could go to the colonies, though he very much feared it would be just like Scotland only with a different accent.

Which left him right back where he was. London and the English. Was there anyone in this entire benighted place who thought of people as people and not resources to be exploited? Yes, a few. William Wilberforce was one such reformer. And he had many admirers. So Brandon turned his feet toward his club, hoping that someone would be there. Someone who understood the difficulty of expressing democracy to people who refused to hear.

Besides, he thought with a sigh, it would be hours yet before he could sneak into the Tavern Playhouse to see Scheherazade.

* * *

Brandon became sharply alert the moment he heard someone's steps on the stairs. He had been lurking up here in the hallway beside Scheherazade's room since the beginning of the farce. It was the best way to be sure of seeing her, and truthfully, he had little interest in the show. He found the Tavern Playhouse fare rather crude. Funny, but crude. And after the first showing, there was little to be gained by repeat viewing.

So he had climbed the stairs to her bedroom and waited like a lost dog for her return. And now his patience was about to be rewarded. Except, the tread on the stairs sounded rather heavy. He had little time to do more than frown before the burly stagehand Seth appeared. Fortunately, the man was followed a moment later by Scheherazade, but that didn't stop the stagehand from tightening his hands into fists and bulking his shoulders until he looked like a furious bull.

"Hello, my lord," Scheherazade said sweetly. Her voice was slightly hoarse and she appeared tired, but that didn't stop him from thinking she was beautiful. He didn't even know why the thought filtered through his mind. He'd seen women more lovely in a purely physical sense, but that didn't change the lust that heated his thoughts. Somehow, Scher was different. She was better.

"Hello, Lady Scher," he said equally gravely. "I had hoped for a private word with you."

Scher smiled at him, her expression falsely sad. "I'm so sorry, but as I'm an engaged woman, it wouldn't be appropriate."

"I mean you no harm," he said softly, his eyes still on Seth's fists. He could probably best the man in a fight, but only if Scheherazade didn't help.

She raised her eyebrows and thankfully didn't comment. Of course, her very silence spoke volumes about what he had done to her last time. But still, he appreciated her restraint, and so he held out a jeweler's box.

"This is for you. An apology for my abominable behavior."

Seth stepped slightly aside so she could take it, but Scher didn't move. "Again, my lord, I'm an engaged woman. It wouldn't be appropriate—"

"What we did before wasn't appropriate either, but we did it. And in this very hallway." His words were tight and his face was heating as he stood there with the box in his hand. But she was adamant. He could see it in her face.

"My lord," she said softly. "Brandon. You must go now."

He shook his head. He even took a step forward, but Seth stood squarely between them. "We need to talk, Scher."

She didn't answer, but he knew better than to think she had agreed. She was a woman of few words. Instead of arguing needlessly with him, she pulled out her key and moved for her door. He stood in her way, but she merely stared hard at him. He stepped backward, shame heating his face.

A pressure built in his head and the tightness in his chest made it hard to breathe. She meant to cut off all contact with him. He could see it in her firm stance and her huge bodyguard. She would be completely removed from him. But that was unacceptable.

"I am not a patient man," he said softly as she pressed her key into the lock.

She arched a brow back at him, obviously startled by his odd statement. He was too. He did not usually talk about himself like this. But he always said the strangest things around her.

"I am not a patient man," he repeated, "but I have waited for you, dangled after you, and loitered in hallways like a dog."

"Then you should be happy to be rid of me."

He took her arm, but Seth raised his fist, and he released her. He had been gentle, the idea to get her attention, not to harm her. But obviously her stagehand was being overly zealous. "You won't take my gifts, you won't talk to me, how can I apologize for what I have done? How can we discuss . . . your future?"

She turned then. Her door was open, but she didn't step through. Instead she looked at him and shook her head. "You are not part of my future. Can you not find a woman on your own? Must you pester your cousin's fiancée?"

He winced even though he knew the jibe was coming. And in truth, what she said was absolutely correct. Kit had won her. Brandon ought to leave her alone. Hadn't he said as much to his family? And yet, he could not leave.

"You are still sad, and I am still your friend," he said softly. He didn't need to look to know that Seth had given Scheherazade a sharp look. Her grimace told him that much.

"It has been a very long day," she said dryly. "I am merely weary."

"No. I feel it too. A vague . . ." He gestured with his hand and was pleased to see that Seth did not tense at the movement. "Something is wrong."

She arched a brow. "Perhaps you should look to your own life then, and not mine. Good night, Lord Blackstone."

She stepped backward into her room and shut the door. He would have pursued her, but with Seth standing guard, he would accomplish nothing more than bloody knuckles. Or a bloody nose. Either way, he could not force the issue. So he did one of the most ridiculous actions of his life. He stood at the door and spoke through it.

"Please, Scher, I have come to help you."

Silence.

"I wish to take you driving."

Silence.

"In Hyde Park. At the height of the fashionable hour. It's all perfectly proper. I'll bring a high-perched phaeton, so there will be nothing untoward. You can ride with me and we can talk in perfect safety."

Still nothing. He was beginning to sweat beneath his shirt collar, and the feeling was excruciatingly uncomfortable.

"It will only aid your cause with my family. The more you are seen in public in a respectable manner, the more acceptable you will be."

He glanced sideways at Seth. The man had folded his arms, but his expression told it all. He glared at Brandon with total distrust, but he'd put away his fists, so to speak. Angry tolerance. He could work with that. Brandon turned and handed the jeweler's box to Seth. The man was no fool. He took it, though with no obvious promise to give it to Scher. Then Brandon pulled out a wad of pound notes and pushed those forward as well.

"I am giving Seth money," he said loudly. "It is so you can have a new dress made. Something fashionable. No more nun's habits. You aren't fooling anyone and it merely points out how unrespectable you are."

Seth snorted at that, but Brandon didn't stop.

"I like the color green on you," he said. "It brings out your eyes."

Again no response. She would be firm on this then. He sighed, making one last attempt to mollify her.

"I supported you against the family," he said to the door. "After you and Kit left, I defended you to them." He sighed. "I'm only trying to help, Scher. This marriage won't happen without help. A lot of good help."

He pressed his hand against the door.

"You need me," he said. "I shall come in two days, Scher. That's enough time to have a dress made." Then with a last sigh, he turned and left.

Chapter 6

"He has given me money for a dress, Kit. And he wants to take me driving in Hyde Park tomorrow."

Kit slouched in his chair and stretched his legs forward. He had obviously had a late night of it. His eyes were bloodshot and he could not stop yawning. But he had responded immediately to her urgent note, presenting himself in the Green Room well before noon. That was something at least, though she couldn't help being irritated by his lack of focus. She had stayed up at least as late as he and had risen just after dawn.

"Kit, I think I should go."

Her fiancé rubbed a hand over his face and frowned. "He says he wants to help us?"

Scheherazade worried at her brown skirt and wondered at Brandon's "nun's habit" remark. Did he think her gowns dowdy? "I want to believe he means well," she finally confessed.

Kit fully opened his eyes to look at her. His expression

was sour, but his words were calm enough. "There's not much that can happen in Hyde Park at that hour. The real danger is that you shall be bored to death."

Scheherazade ground her teeth. "No, Kit. The real danger is that he will ruin my chances in society. That he shall make me appear disreputable somehow."

Kit was silent a long time, obviously considering her words. Then he rubbed a hand over his face, speaking with the offhand way of a man trying to be gentle. "You already *are* disreputable, Scher. I don't see how he could damage you further."

She bit her lip, hurt by his casual way of dismissing her. "I have done my best to be an honorable woman, Kit."

"Well, of course you have. But that's the way of the world, isn't it? All actresses are damned by their very birth."

She looked at her skirt rather than allow him to see her tears. But a moment later, he was holding her hand and drawing it gently to his lips. "But that's the thing of it. You will never be respectable until we marry."

How did she tell him that she wished for the polite fiction? She wanted him to pretend she was as precious as any of the aristocratically born virgins paraded about Hyde Park every day. But that was illogical, and so she swallowed away her words.

"I shall have to get a new green dress as he suggested. I haven't anything else appropriate."

"Hmm? Oh, I quite agree. You look lovely in green."

Her head snapped up. "Kit! You know that's not what I was asking."

He was grinning at her, his expression mischievous. Clearly, he was teasing her, but she just didn't find this situation funny. Still, it was hard to be annoyed when he chucked her under the chin and planted a quick kiss on her lips.

"He has buckets of money. If he wants to spend it on a green dress for you, then I have no objection."

"But it's not respectable, Kit."

"And neither are you. Yet. Get the dress, Scher. Get two if you can manage it!" He pushed to his feet. "If it makes you feel better, I promise to show up as well. I'll be strolling or some such thing, and we'll meet as if by accident."

She stood as well, not because she wanted to but so she could touch his arm and try to impress upon him how worried she was. "So you won't feel odd that another man takes your fiancée out for a drive?"

"He's not another man, Scheherazade. He's my cousin." And with that, he shoved his hands in his pockets but he didn't leave. Instead, he cocked his head and looked at her. "He defended us to the family. After we left that disastrous meal, he said some nice things about you. I heard it from my mother, but of course she didn't put it like that."

She huffed. No, his mother would likely have damned both her and Brandon to hell. "That's a good thing, isn't it?" It was so hard to judge his mood this morning. Perhaps because she herself felt so unsettled.

He grinned. "It's an excellent thing! I believe my cousin got to know you and realized how wonderful you are. Just watch. It will be that way with the others as well. We just have to give it time." Then he turned around and strolled out the door. She heard his whistling all the way to the stage, and then it was lost as he undoubtedly walked out the back door.

A little more than a day later, Scher once again sat in the Green Room, but this time in a new green dress. And she was waiting for Brandon, not Kit. The other members of the troupe kept finding some sort of excuse to slip into the Green Room, but she shooed them out just as quickly. She was nervous enough about this afternoon's trip without their prying eyes and gossiping tongues. But it did little good. The moment one person left her alone to gather her thoughts, another stepped in from the opposite door. In the end, she just sighed and let them remain.

She was worrying at a crease in a particularly expensive part of the lace trim when he finally appeared. Nearly on time, she realized with surprise. It had felt like he was an hour or more late, but it was a mere seven minutes past the hour.

She straightened immediately upon his entrance, escorted by a dour-looking Seth. Brandon looked stunning, of course, in his coat of bottle green superfine. It was a darker shade than her dress but still matched her perfectly. She gritted her teeth against a sudden tightening in her chest. With matching outfits they would look like a couple.

He paused a few feet away from her. "You are frowning."

She immediately smoothed her expression. "Nonsense. I was just thinking something unsettling, that's all. Nothing of import. And now you are here to brighten the day." She gave him her most vapid smile.

"Humph," he said with his own frown. "If you are going to act the virginal twit today, it will be a very dull afternoon."

She moved slowly as she picked up her reticule. She should not be surprised that he was so direct with her, but it still disoriented her. "I thought it was to be a proper afternoon," she responded carefully. "I am being proper."

He rolled his eyes. "Then it will be a very dull afternoon indeed."

"Ah. So I was to be your entertainment? I thought you wanted to help me and Kit. Perhaps I should stay home, then."

He didn't answer for a moment. He kept his mouth shut and his expression blank. His gaze traveled the room slowly, starting with her, but touching on every member of the cast who had somehow managed to wander in. Eleven people in all watched and listened about the room without even the pretense of a reason beyond to gawk. But in the end, his gaze returned to hers and his voice was soft.

"This will be difficult for you today, Scher. You have not the flare to revel in being disreputable, nor are you callous enough to be cut and not feel it. It will be very hard."

She swallowed, knowing that everything he said was true. "You are trying to cry off, then. You don't want to take me."

"I am trying to prepare you. And to say that starting the trip at odds with me will only make things worse."

She looked away, uncomfortably aware that he was right. He could be a great aid to her and Kit, assuming he was dealing honestly. It would be unwise to battle him now.

"My apologies, my lord. I have no wish to fight with you."

"Nor I with you. But I do have a question for you."

She looked up, her belly tight with worry. "Yes?"

"Why is it so important to be respectable? You have much more freedom in your life now. Be very sure that you want to enter that jail of propriety before you marry. What you experience today will never ease no matter how long you are married or how rich you become. Be sure that it is what you want."

She shot him a grimace of distaste. "Only a wealthy aristocrat could ask me that. Of course it is worth—"

"Scher!" He held up two hands in surrender, but his expression was anything but repentant. "I merely ask that you think about it. That is all. Just . . . think about it."

She lifted her chin in disdain. "You act like I have never been snubbed before. As if I have never sat at a meal and been roundly criticized and humiliated by my fiancé's family."

She expected Brandon to flush slightly at that or maybe even acknowledge the truth of what she said. He didn't. His expression turned even gentler. "Today will likely be much worse, Scher. But I swear I will do whatever I can to make it easier."

She was touched despite her intentions. She didn't even fully trust him in this. She still feared that it was some twisted attempt to seduce her. And yet his expression and his words felt earnest. So much so that when he extended his arm to her, she went to him easily, touching her gloved fingers to the sleeve of his beautiful coat.

"You do look most handsome," she commented.

"Not nearly as divine as you," he returned. Then he maneuvered her easily around Seth and the others as they went to his phaeton.

The carriage was beautiful, tall and freshly painted. It bore no crest, but the boy who served as tiger moved smartly in his obviously new uniform of green and gold. He pulled the matched pair of chestnuts forward, bowed with excruciating correctness to her, then dimpled prettily when she smiled at him.

"Oy, miss," he began but was cut off by Brandon.

"Silence, Hank. Servants are silent."

The boy flushed and dipped his head, tugging on his forelock as he did. Brandon stared hard at the child a moment longer, then turned to hand Scheherazade up into the phaeton.

"I apologize," he murmured. "I have only just hired him. He is still young."

She glanced past his shoulder where Hank stood holding the horses' heads and simultaneously brushing some dust off his new uniform. "Where did you find him?" she asked.

"Hmm? Oh. Bad pickpocket."

She stilled to look closer at his face. "You hired a boy who was stealing from you?"

"Me? No, no, he was stealing from a drunken sot, but doing it so awkwardly that I could tell he wasn't a professional."

"You hired a street boy," she repeated quietly, startled by the casual kindness in him.

He laughed, the sound lighter than she expected. "Well, I needed a tiger, didn't I? Would hardly be proper for me to take you out to Hyde Park without a servant to play chaperone."

She didn't respond as he was helping her onto the high perch. His hands were large, his forearm pleasantly solid where she gripped him as she climbed. There was nothing at all sexual in his touch, and yet she felt him with sensitized awareness. Her back tingled in an expanding circle from his hand. And her bottom tightened just with the knowledge that—for a brief moment—her rear was eye-level with him. Then she was sitting down, quietly marveling at the new seat cushion.

Brandon leaped up beside her, grabbing the ribbons in a competent grip. Those too appeared new, and she turned to study the equipage more closely.

"How new is this phaeton?"

He flashed her a grin. "As new as my tiger. Couldn't bring you out in a shabby, old thing."

She tilted her head, completely flummoxed. "Are you trying to impress me?"

He sobered slightly. "I'm trying to show you that I value you. I respect you."

"By buying a new carriage?"

"And taking you to Hyde Park in it. Yes."

She didn't answer. Despite all logic, she was impressed. And pleased. She settled back into the cushions and tilted her head back so the sun could touch her face beneath her hat. The head piece was new as well, but unlike her dress, it was an annoyance. The ribbons fluttered about her left ear and her head felt hot, but propriety demanded that she keep it on.

"Did you paste your skin?" he asked in a low voice as his tiger jumped in behind them.

"Yes," she murmured. Her skin was an unfashionable light bronze color and even included a few freckles. No one noticed inside the darkness of the playhouse, but out in the afternoon sun? She had resorted to paste.

"At least it doesn't smell as horrible as my grandmother's," he commented dryly as he started the phaeton moving.

"Whores always know the best cosmetics. They have to be beautiful *and* not smell for their customers."

She was startled by his sharp bark of laughter at that. Her eyes shot open and she straightened in her seat, a blush heating her face.

"My God," she blurted out. "I am so sorry for saying such a thing. I cannot imagine—"

"No, no!" he chortled. "I was afraid that Kit had squelched all your spirit."

"Kit? Of course not! He is a delightful companion."

"But an indifferent lover?"

She stiffened in her seat. "You go too far," she accused even though she had been the one to take the conversation in a scandalous direction.

He bowed slightly in acknowledgment. "I see we are back to proper topics. Very well, shall we discuss the weather? I could regale you with all the details of my horses or this lovely carriage."

"All of it is quite fine," she returned stiffly, though secretly she wished she could pull off her gloves to feel the fine fabric of the cushion. "I had not expected the weather to be this sweet today."

"Last night's rain has made for a beautiful afternoon," he returned, though his attention was obviously not on their conversation. Neither was hers, for that matter, as they were just nearing the outskirts of Hyde Park and the crush of vehicles ahead.

"Whenever you wish to leave," he said under his breath, "just tell me and I will turn the horses."

"And what?" she murmured as she looked beyond at carriages, horsemen, and strollers all clogged together. "You couldn't move beyond a foot. Is it always like this?"

He turned to study her profile. She could see him out of her peripheral vision, but she didn't twist back to face him. The way he looked at her was so dark, so serious, it made her uneasy. What was he thinking?

"You have never been here before, even to look?"

"At the fashionable hour? Never," she lied.

"Why not? You are practically humming with excitement. You have wanted this for a very long time."

She looked back at him then, startled at his perception. "How could you know that?"

"It is no secret, Scher. You want to be among them." He gestured dismissively at the crowd of fashionable elite. "Surely you have stood at the edges and watched? When you were young, perhaps? I would wager when you were a child of no more than ten or eleven."

"Nine," she confessed before turning away. "I came the first time on my ninth birthday. Pappy brought me; he was an actor in the troupe. We dressed up in our finest clothes. He bought me an ice at Gunters, and then we strolled straight through the park pretending to be German royalty with terrible English." She giggled at the memory. "It was the best birthday I ever had."

"You did not come back again?"

"Every year until he died."

"Were you always German royalty or did that change?"

"Every year was different. Once we were scholars, another year religious reformers."

"And now you are here as yourself. You must tell me which you prefer."

She looked back at him. There had been no malice in his tone, but she knew the answer he expected. Slights directed at fake royalty were one thing. Insults to herself were quite another. But it didn't matter, they were here now. She was determined on her course. And as if on cue, Brandon pulled up alongside their first titled peer.

"Hello, Marcus," Brandon greeted with false cheer. "Fancy meeting you here."

The man smiled genially in response, his eyes vague enough that Scheherazade wondered how he kept a steady hand on his ribbons. Fortunately, the horses kept a plodding pace as the man laughed with good cheer.

"I am always here, Brandon. Wouldn't miss the exercise for the world."

"Lord Barstaff, may I present Miss Martin? She is my cousin Kit's fiancée."

"It is a pleasure to meet you, sir," Scheherazade said warmly. "Your son Jeremy has exactly the same smile. Quite handsome."

He arched a brow then lifted a quizzing glass to inspect her more closely. "You know Jeremy, then? I didn't realize he was making the polite rounds."

Scheherazade faltered. He was right, of course. She had not met Jeremy in anything resembling a polite setting. Fortunately, Brandon was able to smooth the way for her.

"Ah, but I believe Jeremy and Kit are good friends."

"Ah, yes, Kit Frazier. Fine boy, fine boy. Engaged you say? Well, felicitations, Miss Martin. I suppose there's no hope that you would want Jeremy instead, is there? The boy could use a pretty gel on his arm."

That he could. Jeremy was cursed with a rather unfortunate skin condition. "You flatter me, Lord Barstaff."

"Well that's what one does with pretty girls, eh wot?"

Scheherazade laughed happily, her shoulders and her breath relaxing with the sound. This was not so hard. Trading pleasantries with gentleman was something she'd learned to do when she was four.

"Viscount Blackstone! My goodness, it is you!" cried another voice from the opposite side. "I told Bea here that it could not possibly be you, but look, it is! And in a beautiful new carriage!"

"Miss Smithson and Lady Bea," Brandon said as he turned to the oncoming carriage. No one else would be able to tell that Brandon had tensed, but Scher caught an underlying coldness in his tone as he added another greeting. "Ashbury."

"Blackstone," returned the ladies' sullen companion. He was driving the carriage and looking rather disgruntled to be there. At least he was until he caught sight of Scheherazade. Then his eyes widened and he stiffened all the way from his belly to the top of his head.

He clearly wanted to voice some objection, but it was too late as Brandon made the introductions. "May I present to you Miss Martin. She is my cousin Kit's fiancée."

Scher smiled as warmly as possible to the trio of exquisitely dressed people. She knew of them, of course. Lady Bea and Ashbury were brother and sister, the only children of a highly political earl. And Miss Smithson was clearly a wealthy virgin on the hunt for a husband.

"Really!" gasped Miss Smithson. Apparently she only spoke in exclamation marks. "Mr. Frazier engaged? How delightful!"

Lady Bea smiled sweetly and leaned forward to extend her hand in greeting. "How lovely to meet you—"

"Sorry, must be leaving," interrupted her brother as he slapped his sister's arm down. Lady Bea gasped at her brother's rudeness, as did Scheherazade, but that was nothing compared to the venomous glare the man shot at Brandon. "New titles are always cheeky. I'll not forget that you introduced my sister to a madam!"

He clicked his tongue at his horses, but there wasn't a lot of distance for them to go. Their carriage moved forward only a few feet. Beside him, the ladies mouths had dropped open as they stared at her.

"I'm not a madam," Scheherazade said as firmly as possible, but it did nothing to cover her flush of humiliation. It was ridiculous, but she hadn't expected someone to accuse her so baldly and loud enough for other carriages to hear. She thought that respectable people didn't even say those words in polite society.

Meanwhile, Brandon released his own sniff. "And I am insulted that you would say such a thing about my cousin's fiancée!"

"Say what you want," Ashbury returned. "But I know you, Lady Scher." The way he said it made it sound like he bedded her every night.

She stared at him, wondering if he had ever come to the playhouse. Probably. Most young bucks about town did eventually, but he wasn't a frequent visitor.

"I'm sorry, Lord Ashbury, but I have no recollection of you at all. Do remind me, please, how we met before?"

As banter went, the sally was rather good. It implied that either Ashbury's sexual prowess was completely lacking— something that no young buck would admit—or that he was wrong about her identity. In the Green Room it would have drawn a bit of laughter. But out here in the fashionable throng, it only produced shocked stares.

Ashbury arched a brow at her, then reached into his pocket and flicked her a half crown which rolled onto the boards at her feet. "Perhaps that will jog your memory," he sneered, then he turned his back on her.

She stared down at the coin at her feet. It was covered by her skirt, but she knew it was there. She looked back up at the carriage, only to see the two other ladies gasp and turn their back on her. The cut direct.

"Mind your horses, Ashbury!" Brandon snapped loudly even though all the animals were well under control. "You should not drive when so deeply in your cups. Imagine confusing my cousin's fiancée with . . . well, with one of your set."

An excellent retort, Scheherazade thought miserably. Unfortunately, she could already see it would not work. Lord Ashbury was clearly *not* in his cups. And yet it was nice that Brandon had made the attempt to defend her. She had obviously not made good work of it.

It was a difficult minute or more beyond that as the carriages inched in opposite directions. Scheherazade didn't dare look behind them at the Ashbury carriage, but when she turned her attention to Lord Barstaff, it was to meet his confused frown before he too looked away.

Searching for somewhere else to look, she slowly scanned the nearby crowd. Everyone was staring at her, many of them whispering behind their hands. She could almost see the news of their confrontation moving through the park as one neighbor leaned over to discuss her with another.

Meanwhile, a pair of horsemen rode forward. They couldn't move quickly, of course, but they were clearly headed directly toward them. Scheherazade released a breath of relief. They were young men she knew well. Two gentlemen of modest means without titles. They were regulars at the playhouse and friends to Kit.

She smiled warmly at them. At least these two would be kind.

"What are you about?" Mr. Dempsey said to Brandon as soon as he was alongside.

"Pleasant afternoon, Mr. Dempsey, Mr. Tully," returned Brandon. "Please allow me to introduce my cousin Kit's fiancée, Miss Martin."

"I'm honored to meet you," she responded immediately, glad for the polite fiction that she had never met them. Unfortunately the young men flushed a dark red.

"Lady Scher," hissed Mr. Tully. "This really isn't the thing. You really—"

"This is *Miss Martin's* first visit to Hyde Park," interrupted Brandon. "She has confided in me that it is most exciting."

"Upsetting is more like," returned Mr. Dempsey, his brow furrowed in concern. "Engaged to Kit, you say?" He heaved a sigh and turned away. "Never thought you were grasping, Lady Scher. And unfortunate that you're helping her," he said to Brandon. "Come on, Tully, there's nothing to be done here but make things worse."

As they were on horses, the two men maneuvered easily down toward Rotten Row and away from the park. But they lingered long enough for Scheherazade to see Mr. Tully glance uneasily back at her. Twice.

"He called me grasping," she said under her breath.

"You knew that would be said. And much worse."

"But not by my friends." She looked up at Brandon. "I have known them since they first came to town. They are kind men."

"It's easy to be kind when the world is exactly as it ought to be," he returned. "But you are now upsetting that order."

She forced herself to smile at a nearby matron, who sniffed and obviously took great pleasure in giving her the cut direct. "I simply wish to get married, not overthrow any world order."

Brandon turned to her, his expression compassionate. "Sometimes the world is very cruel."

She had no answer to that, since they both knew it was true. And with that one shared look, she felt her world shift. Or perhaps not so much her world as her heart because she abruptly felt a kinship with Brandon deeper than anything she experienced with Kit. It seemed as if they were in this particular mess together. That he would stand by her side no matter what happened. For a woman who was perpetually on the outside looking in, this was so powerful it rocked her to her core.

He must have felt it too. She saw his eyes widen and his nostrils flare. Then he surprised her even more as a wash of gratitude filled his expression. She had no explanation for how she knew, but she did. He was grateful for her presence here beside him, when in fact, she was the one who needed his support.

"Scher," he said. One word, but it was filled with a longing that echoed through her soul. How could one whisper from him create such need in her?

Feelings overwhelmed her, swamping her thoughts. She ought to tear her gaze away. She needed to find her balance again or risk throwing everything away in a blind rush of emotion. But how he called to her! His eyes, his touch, his very presence beside her was a temptation stronger than anything she'd ever experienced. Without planning it, she leaned toward him.

He stopped her. He didn't want to, she could tell that immediately. But with a flick of his eyes, he indicated everything she had forgotten: where they were and who was watching. Good lord, they were in the middle of Hyde Park and she had been about to kiss him!

Scher spun away with a gasp of horror. She pressed a hand to her chest, willing her heart to steady. She scanned the crowd, not for any particular person, but as a way of reminding herself that every soul here watched her.

"Are you looking for Kit?" Brandon asked, his tone excruciatingly neutral. "He's over there."

She nodded but didn't dare look back at him. So she scanned the crowd again until she found her fiancé. He was strolling the grounds with two young women, one on either side of him. His gait appeared strained, but his laughter rang clearly nonetheless. Obviously one of his companions had said something clever.

"Oh, yes," she said, though the words were inane. "I see him now." Then she put on as brilliant a smile as she could manage and waited for her fiancé to look up to acknowledge her.

And waited.

And waited even longer.

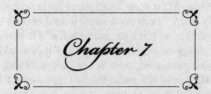

Chapter 7

She'd been about to kiss him. Brandon was sure of it. She'd been about to kiss him right here in Hyde Park and he'd stopped her. Idiot! If he'd just let her do it, let her fall into his arms right here, then everything would be over. No more engagement with Kit. No more possibility of a respectable marriage. And with that question gone, she would be his mistress within a week.

But he couldn't do it. He couldn't be the one to take away her dreams. And so he'd stopped her. And now she sat beside him, her body so stiff he wondered if she even breathed. As for the rest of the fashionable throng, Brandon lost count of the number of cut directs that Scheherazade suffered. They didn't all snub her, of course, but most could not afford to be seen speaking with her either.

"I'm sorry," he said, wondering exactly what he was apologizing for. Not ruining her with a kiss? Or sitting uselessly beside her as the English aristocracy expressed their hatred of her. "I suppose I overestimated my social power. I thought my presence would—"

"You warned me. I didn't listen." Her voice was flat in a way he'd never heard before. It gave him no clue to her thoughts. After their moment of total accord, this cut especially deep. "Perhaps a stroll would be just the thing. Stretch our legs as you meet up with Kit" He hated making the offer, despised making it easy for Kit to steal her away. But he had promised, and Scher had suffered so much already. He would not make the day any worse for her.

She twisted back to look at him, her eyes wide with alarm. "Do you think that is best?"

He recognized her look, one of a dazed and wounded animal. And she was turning to him for guidance. He almost laughed at that. He was the last person to whom she should look, but he didn't say that. Instead, he gestured to his tiger, who looked back at him with confusion.

Brandon sighed. "Walk the horses, Hank, until I return."

"Walk them? But—"

"Just keep them moving around the park. We will find you when we are done."

"Yup," the boy said, then jumped to the ground. He stumbled as he fell, having misjudged the height of the drop. His new uniform ripped and a dirt smear now covered the entire right side of his leg, but the boy never seemed to notice. He rolled easily to his feet and ran to hold the horses' heads. Brandon stifled a sigh, but beside him Scheherazade released a quick gurgle of laughter.

"As I said before," Brandon drawled, "he is very young."

"He'll notice it in a moment and be distraught, wondering how it could have happened when he had been so careful."

He turned. "You understand little boys."

"Seth does the work now, but there was a time when I was in charge of the stage boys."

"Lucky boys."

She arched a brow at him, so he was forced to explain.

"I merely meant they were fortunate to spend their days under your direction. You are a firm but fair-minded mistress. I'm sure most of them never met anyone like you in their lives."

Her lips curved in a near smile. "Have you resorted to flattery, my lord?" She glanced about them as yet another matron gave a loud sniff and turned her back. "Am I so pitiful a specimen now that I require—"

"It is not flattery if it is true. Now come and let us walk before Lady Rayburn gives herself a headache from all that sniffing and turning."

Scher's expression solidified into a real smile and he felt the tightness in his chest ease a bit at the sight. "Which one is Lady Rayburn?"

"Behind us to the right. She has been sniffing and gasping for the last ten minutes, desperate to gain your attention so she can cut you."

"Ah. Poor lady," Scher said with no sadness at all in her voice. "Unfortunately, I have no intention of looking her direction at all."

Brandon flashed a grin, pleased beyond measure that Scher was coming back to herself. No more dazed pain in her expression, but she wasn't exactly relaxed either. He leaped down to the street, then held out his hand to her. She moved gracefully to him, stabilizing her position with one hand while he grabbed her waist and lifted her free of the carriage.

How poised she was, he thought as she landed smoothly on her toes rather than her feet. There was no awkwardness of skirts or an anxious giggle at his touch. Though it appeared one smooth motion, he knew from experience that few ladies had the grace expected of the peerage. Lily had it, and she was a countess. Scher could easily have been another such woman but for the unfortunate fact of her birth.

"You are staring," she whispered harshly.

Brandon stepped back with a start. He had been noting the exquisite curve of her cheek and her stunning green eyes. Objectively speaking, her nose was too long for beauty, and her skin beneath the paint was not as creamy as the ideal, but something inside her screamed beautiful to him.

"My apologies," he murmured as he extended his arm to her.

"What were you thinking of so deeply?" She fell into step beside him. Propriety demanded a certain distance between them, but as a whole new group of aristocrats gasped and gave her the cut, she tightened her grip on his arm. He tucked it close to his chest and smiled.

"You would laugh if I told you."

"I could use something to laugh at right now," she murmured between strained lips. She held her head stiffly erect and he admired her strength. He would have cut his losses long ago.

"I was thinking how beautiful you are."

She laughed then, though the sound was a trifle forced. He nodded appreciatively at her. Obviously she was putting on a brave show.

"It is the truth," he said earnestly.

"And I was thinking that this is the very reason I never went on the stage."

He frowned. "I don't follow you."

"I hate being the center of attention. Goodness, you would think I had the plague."

He nodded. "You know," he drawled, "I believe I shall bring you every time I come to Hyde Park. This is the easiest I have ever moved through the grass."

"That is because everyone parts before me like the Red Sea."

"Well, Moses, I believe your destination is just ahead." There, rounding the path, was Kit, still with his ladies on his arms. Even from this distance, Brandon could see that his cousin was struggling. Though his expression held an easy smile and he occasionally laughed, there was a jerkiness to his gestures. In truth, Brandon had never seen his cousin so ill at ease, and that included that disastrous meal a couple days ago.

With a reassuring squeeze to Scheherazade's arm, Brandon lengthened his stride enough that they met up with Kit relatively quickly. "Ah, the happy couple reunites at last. Kit, your blushing bride has been delightful company. I envy you your future."

Kit looked up, his expression grateful, but none of the stiffness left his body. "Thank you, Brandon. And how are you faring, my dear? The sun is surprisingly hot, is it not?"

"Actually, I find the weather most refreshing."

"It is the company that she finds difficult, I fear," Brandon drawled, pretending he meant himself. Scheherazade flashed him an amused look. Obviously, she understood he really meant the aristocrats who continued to go to great lengths to walk far away from them.

Meanwhile, Kit gently disentangled himself from one of his companions to take Scher's arm. "Has my cousin been disagreeable again?"

"Far from it. He has been most generous." Then after a long pause, Scher turned to the ladies. "I am afraid I have not met your friends, Kit. Should I be jealous that you are spending time with such lovely ladies instead of me?"

Kit glanced warmly at Scher, his expression brightening measurably. "Are you jealous?"

Kit clearly missed Scher's clue to introduce her, and Brandon was on the verge of doing it himself, when the older of the two beauties dimpled prettily.

"I'm terribly sorry, but my grandmother has been gesturing most urgently toward me." She neatly caught her friend's hand. "Come on, Becky. You know how she is when her joints pain her. Lovely to see you again, Mr. Frazier,

Lord Blackstone." Then they both waved in perfect tandem before turning and rushing away.

"That was not well done," Brandon drawled, his eyes on their retreating backs.

"Yes, they have been trying to dissuade me from my disastrous course," Kit responded dryly.

"I meant you," Brandon snapped. "You should have at least introduced Scher."

"As you saw, they would not have permitted it. I had hoped to have some conversation first, so that they could see you were not some sort of monster," he said to Scher. "But you forced my hand, and . . . well, they are gone now."

Scher nodded. "And getting an earful from their grandmother, no doubt. I am sorry, Kit, I should have known you had a plan."

Brandon couldn't stop his snort. "Plan? Scher, they will not see you differently no matter how much conversation you share."

"That's not true!" Kit responded hotly. "Some will. The younger ones, and those who care for me."

"Like those two?" Brandon sneered. "And did it work?"

"You forced my hand!"

"Gentlemen, please," Scher interrupted in an urgent whisper. "Having you two argue publicly will only make things worse." Brandon opened his mouth to insert a dry comment, but she stopped him with a glare. "Yes, I know you do not think it can get worse, but the last thing I need is for my only supporters to be at odds."

Brandon dipped his head by way of apology, but inside his heart squeezed painfully. Did she truly think it could not get worse?

"Perhaps it is time we were done with the park," Kit said gently as he began to steer her along the path.

"Yes, thank you," she said softly, and Brandon was surprised by the jolt of disappointment inside him. Couldn't

Kit see what he was doing to Scher? If they went through with their ridiculous wedding, then Scher would suffer today's slights every moment of the rest of her life. Didn't he realize he was doing her no favor?

Kit glanced over his shoulder at Brandon. "Would you mind terribly, old man, if I escorted Scher home? I believe I can get her out faster than your phaeton." He tilted his chin toward where Brandon's vehicle was blocked in at the thickest part of the carriage crush.

"Of course not," Brandon replied smoothly, though he longed to plant his cousin a facer. Kit and Scher would remove themselves rather quickly on foot while Brandon would be forced to endure this for another half hour as he tried to maneuver out.

Scher looked around, her shoulders flinching only slightly as yet another group of ladies—young virgins this time—gasped in outrage and started whispering behind their gloves. "But how will we leave? Would it be proper?"

"We will walk, my dear," Kit said gently. "Grandmama's home is not that far from here. Then we can—"

"Not there, Kit, please. I couldn't bear it just now." It was the first admission from Scher that she was nearing her limits, and Brandon felt the darkness in him churn in response. He hated to see her in such pain.

"Walk toward there," he said with a gesture. "Go slowly. I shall extricate my carriage and meet you along the way."

"But—"

"Then Kit can borrow my phaeton and drive you home," he said though that was the last thing he wanted.

Kit visibly brightened. "You trust me with them? They are magnificent horses. I meant to say that earlier."

"And a new phaeton. Do not scratch it."

"I would never!"

Brandon didn't dare comment. His eyes on Scheherazade, he wondered if she could see how very young Kit was. Good God, the boy was exuberant over his horseflesh instead of worried about his fiancée. But when Scher's expression never wavered, Brandon began to wonder if it seemed to her that he was particularly old rather than Kit rather young.

Unfortunately, there was no way to ask, and so he bowed smoothly to them both. "I will see you as soon as possible." Then he turned and walked away. He couldn't move quickly for fear that people would think he was escaping, but neither did he wish to loiter and invite comments from the biddies and bastards that now pressed forward, all of them anxious to talk to him once he had left Scheherazade's side.

Best thing to do, he decided, was to shove his hands in his pockets and start whistling. A few people tried to stop him along the way, but he merely waved to them and kept walking. He could see by their expressions that they only wanted more fuel to gossip about Scheherazade.

This would not do. Neither Kit nor Scher knew what it was like to live outside of the only society they had ever known. If this marriage moved forward, Kit would lose his position, which was bad enough, but Scheherazade would enter a nowhere land too proper to associate with actors and yet still hated by the elite. She would lose everything to no benefit. She was a strong woman, but day after day of ostracism ate at a person. He had suffered it for months in India, and it had broken him. Two years ago, he had tried to live as a shining example of English and Indian cooperation, but he had failed in a most spectacular fashion. Scher would likely last longer than he had, but the end would be the same. She would end up broken and bitter, her soul battered to darkness. Except, of course, it would be worse for her because she could not escape as he had, coming back to London with a title and fortune.

He couldn't bear the thought of that, though he had no wish to delve into why he felt so deeply. He merely resolved to end Scher and Kit's ridiculous engagement as quickly as possible. By the time he made it to his phaeton, he'd formulated a plan. One that he could implement as early as tonight. In her bedchamber.

The first cut direct was hard on Kit. Scher felt his whole body go still with shock. To his credit, his step hitched only for a moment, but even though he obviously forced his feet to move, his eyes remained trained on the woman who had cut them.

Scher had no idea who she was, and she didn't dare ask. Kit was usually the one making her laugh, easing her tension. She didn't know what to do when he was the one in shock. So she simply kept walking while her cheeks began to ache from the forced smile.

The next cut direct merely elicited a sigh. It was a soft one, but she heard it. And if she didn't hear it, she could feel the slump to his shoulders.

"Kit . . ." she began, but he shook his head.

"Not now, Scher. Let me . . . Just not now."

"Of course." She buttoned her lip and lifted her face to the sun. If she closed her eyes, she could simply appreciate the beauty of the day. But the huffs of disgust and the more contrived gasps of outrage were loud enough to eat into her enjoyment. She already knew she was a pariah. Did they really need to make such a production out of snubbing her?

Tears prickled under her eyelids. She had dreamed of this moment for so long. Since she had first heard of Hyde Park's fashionable hour, she had longed to walk among the titled ones as one of them.

No, that wasn't exactly true. She walked among titled men every day. What she wanted was to exist alongside the women, to be included in a tight cluster of chattering girls, to wander beside a countess or exchange polite smiles with a duchess. She'd known it wouldn't happen today, but she had thought eventually it would. After her wedding, maybe.

But now she saw how very far she had to go for that to happen. Anyone who gave her the cut direct today would be especially resistant to changing his or her mind later. In short, it might never happen. Which meant her whole quest to become respectable through marriage might be a complete illusion.

She stumbled, her foot catching on some uneven root. Kit caught her, but the pain in her toe made her gasp. It wasn't really her toe, but she allowed herself the pretense. Between one breath and the next, her entire life's goal had come into question. All her life, she had been told that respectable women—married women—were treated fairly. Their children were doctored, their husbands had status, and with enough money, they could purchase whatever they needed. Her own mother had died because the doctor delayed coming to the tavern. Her sister had been shortchanged on the medicine she needed. Even Pappy's death came from a lifetime of cheap food and even cheaper ale. All that, she thought, would have changed if only they had been respectable. But now she saw how wrong that belief was. Or perhaps now she saw that no matter her marital status, respectability was far from her reach. And that thought brought tears to her eyes.

"There, there. It was just a rock," Kit said into her ear. She didn't know if he understood the real reason for her anguish or not, but either way, she could only nod and force herself into some semblance of composure.

"Come along, dear," murmured Kit as he continued to move them forward. She went willingly, grateful for his guiding hand. And eventually she wrestled her emotions back down. They were still perilously close to the surface, a roiling ocean of pain, but she kept them in check by force of will.

"Where the devil is Brandon?" Kit groused as they finally made it past the worst of the fashionable crowd.

"Has it been long enough?" she asked as she scanned the street.

"Probably not," Kit admitted, his shoulders more stooped than she'd ever seen before.

She almost said it right then. She almost offered to release him from their engagement, but she couldn't form the words past the lump in her throat. She still wanted to get married. She still wanted to believe it was possible. So she said nothing, merely gripped his hand and kept her eyes down. Fortunately, she didn't have to wait long. They shared only an awkward minute or two of silence before Brandon's phaeton rounded the corner. Within a moment, Brandon had hopped down before her, his expression anxious as he studied her face.

"How are you doing?" he asked softly. Could he tell that she was seconds away from sobbing her eyes out? Probably. Nothing ever escaped his notice.

"I am quite well," she responded smoothly.

He didn't look like he believed her but nodded anyway. Meanwhile Kit was moving toward the phaeton with clear awe.

"Thank you for the use of your phaeton. Nothing like a ride in a beautiful phaeton to brighten the day, eh?" he said as he turned to Scher. His eyes were shining and she could tell he was excited. How quickly he was able to brush off the experience in the park. She found she admired that about him.

Meanwhile she turned back to Brandon, who was the one who had made this all possible. "Thank you for your kindness today, Lord Blackstone."

"It was my honor," he said, his tones deep and serious. He didn't do anything beyond a slight bow, but when she looked in his eyes, she felt that same intensity as before. It shot deep into her heart and brought her right back to the moment when she had nearly kissed him.

Her face heated and she turned away, embarrassed and confused. "This has been a topsy-turvy afternoon," she said as much to herself as to the gentlemen with her.

"Then I shall get you home immediately so you can set everything to rights," said Kit as he grabbed her about the ribcage and lifted her up. A moment later, Kit leaped into the seat beside her and gathered the reins with boyish enthusiasm.

Scher shifted her attention to Brandon, who stood watching from the side of the street. His expression was smooth, but she had the sense that he was troubled. She wished she could speak freely to him. She wanted to thank him again. She especially wanted to tell him that she knew the half crown was gone from the floor, the one that Ashbury had so rudely tossed at her feet.

He had picked it up, she was sure. Not because he needed the money, but because he remembered it and didn't want her to be reminded. She smiled at him, wishing she could convey her tortured thoughts. His eyes widened in surprise, but there was no other shift in his expression. Then he was lost to her as Kit snapped the ribbons, jolting the horses forward.

Chapter 8

"I'd like to come up to talk to you, if I may," said Kit as they pulled up before the playhouse. "Privately. Um. In your room."

Scher smiled, her heart sinking. Did he mean to break their engagement? Should she? "It has been a difficult day, Kit. And we have tonight's performance as well."

"A few moments is all," he said kindly as he touched her hand.

Scher nodded. She waited a moment while the tiger jumped down to hold the horses' heads, using the time to think of a delay. She found it in the playhouse windows, where at least four faces peered out at her.

"They are going to want to hear all about it." She couldn't keep the despair from her voice. She didn't want to relay her humiliation to everyone else. She wanted to forget it had ever happened.

Kit straightened, frowning at the actors staring out at them. "This is beyond enough," he said firmly. "I will not have you subjected to that now." He hopped down and held out his hands to her. "I'll put an end to it. You'll see."

She swallowed, not daring to hope. "It is very difficult to silence actors, you know. Any type of scene only makes it more interesting."

Kit grimaced. "Gossips. Just like the fashionable biddies. Never mind. I have been watching Brandon, you know. He has a way of silencing everyone. I have been practicing it."

She was inching over to the edge of the bench when she stopped to ask. "Practicing?"

He straightened his shoulders back, tightened his features into a stiff glower, then abruptly raised one eyebrow. Or rather, she guessed it was supposed to be one eyebrow. He didn't have the knack of it, so both brows rose. Then he tilted his head to compensate. He ended up looking like a rather startled pug with gastric problems.

She burst out laughing. And when he blinked at her in true surprise, she immediately tried to cover. But laughter could not be credibly shifted to a cough, no matter how earnestly she tried. In the end she simply put her hands on both his cheeks and impulsively leaned forward to kiss him on the mouth.

In truth, it wasn't nearly as impulsive as she wanted to pretend. She didn't know what to do about their engagement. She wanted it to continue. She wanted their marriage. But could they make it work? Perhaps the kiss was a test. Could they be happy as a couple? And so she kissed him. Right there in the street, in front of the actors pressed to the window, the tiger holding the horses, and countless street boys no doubt watching them from every corner and rock in sight. She kissed him on the mouth and was grateful when his lips responded quickly to her advance.

She meant it to be a quick kiss. A swift drop on his lips to sample for joy and maybe the promise of love. But he was fast as he caught her shoulders, holding her mouth to his. The position was awkward. Her back quickly began to strain. But what held her attention more was the way his mouth moved over hers, all impulsive enthusiasm and sweet hunger. He desired her, that much was clear.

It was a long time before she heard the cheers from inside the playhouse. In fact, Kit must have noticed them first because he pulled back, blushing all the way through his ears.

"Um, er. Yes. Scher . . ."

She giggled. Lord, who would have thought she would giggle on today of all days? She smiled and reached out her hand, wincing only slightly as she had to straighten out her back. "Would you care to accompany me inside, Mr. Frazier?" she said sweetly.

"I would indeed, Miss Martin," he responded gravely through his grin.

He helped her down and escorted her inside, never once taking his eyes off her face. The playhouse doors opened as if by magic, and they strolled to the staircase without once acknowledging the dozen or more souls that watched them.

They made it up two flights of stairs before Kit grabbed her and pressed her against the wall. They were about twenty feet from her door, but he seemed too impatient to wait. She felt his groin first, hot and hard against her pelvis. Then his arms went to either side of her and his mouth descended.

She rose naturally into his kiss, feeling her heart beat in her throat. Her hat hit the back wall and tilted as he pressed her backward. The pins pulled at her hair and she gasped in pain. He took the opportunity to swoop inside her mouth, thrusting in with enough force to startle her.

His mouth was warm, the pressure on her lips uneven depending on his movements. Full dominance one second, more delicate stroking the next. She really had no idea what he was going to do at any given moment. Sloppy sometimes, delicate nips the next.

Then his hands abruptly dropped to her breasts, where he tugged and squeezed in awkward motions. She gasped in discomfort and tried to pull away. He also pulled back, though his hands continued to squeeze her.

"You have great breasts," he said. "I could do this for hours."

She didn't know what to say to that. Somehow "thank you" didn't sound quite right. And her breasts were beginning to feel slightly abused from the attention. She opened her mouth to say something—what she didn't really know—when he suddenly swooped down and kissed her again. His hands left her breasts to brace against the wall behind her and her head banged backward hard enough for her to wince. But that didn't stop his kisses. Nor did it stop her giggles when she repeatedly banged her head from his enthusiasm.

"Kit!" she laughed. "Ki—Kit!" She pushed back on his shoulders, gaining a small measure of separation between them.

"I cannot tell you how disheartening it is to have your fiancée giggle when you are kissing her." He didn't look nearly as forlorn as he pretended.

She pressed her fingers against his wet lips. "But that is the very reason I especially adore you. You bring such joy to everything."

"To you?" he pressed, his expression sobering a bit.

"Of course to me. What else would I mean?"

He shrugged with good-natured enthusiasm, pushing off her such that she could at last take a full breath. "Do you know I have been called adorable and delightful all my life? Every woman from my mother down to the scullery maid seems to see me in the same light as a favorite dog."

"That's not true," Scher said firmly, though privately she could see how it might be.

He looked at her then, his expression cooling by the

second. "I want to bed you now, Scheherazade. I want it bad enough that I could strip you naked right here."

She swallowed, her gaze quickly scanning both ends of the hallway. They were alone, as far as she could tell, but anyone might walk up here at any moment. It wasn't likely, especially given that the entire troupe knew that he was up here. But still, the idea of rutting twenty feet *outside* her doorway was mortifying, to say the least.

"Kit—"

"I want to, but I won't. We're to have an honorable wedding. I can wait until our wedding night."

She felt her face heat. "Kit," she began, but she didn't know what to say. Her heart was thundering in her ears, but she didn't know from what. "I don't know what to think."

He lifted her chin, stroking her cheek with his thumb. "I have sent the notice in. We can set the wedding date for three weeks from Sunday."

To her horror, her eyes abruptly teared. She blinked them back as rapidly as possible, but a few escaped.

"Silly puss," he murmured. "Did you think I meant to cry off?"

She swallowed, looking up to the ceiling in an attempt to forestall the waterworks. "I would understand," she whispered. "This is so much harder than I thought. And I'm not sure it will work. Today was just so . . ." She stopped speaking. She couldn't even express how terrible it had been.

"Horrible, wasn't it? But it will get better. Never you fear."

Would it? She desperately hoped it would. She straightened and wiped the tears from her lashes. He allowed her to do it, stepping backward before shoving his hands into his pockets.

"I'm going to leave now, Scher, before I dishonor you."

She released a short laugh at that. She was already

dishonorable, but she didn't argue. It was too kind a senti-
ment for her to disagree.

"I'd planned to see you tonight, but Grandmama has
insisted I accompany her to the Royal theater tonight. Says
I need to be exposed to good acting and won't hear the word
no. I think she was about to invite you, but Mama nixed it.
Insisted she would make a scene if you were to show up."

Scher sighed. "Wouldn't that reflect rather badly on
your mother?"

Kit grinned. "It would, but Grandmama is getting older.
She wants peace in her life. She will stand up for you, never
you fear. It will just take a little more time."

Scher nodded, praying to God that Kit was right. But
she very much feared that the power struggle between his
mother and his grandmother would end up with Scher on
the outs. Still, it was early. Maybe they would come around
and agree to the wedding. The worst thing Scher could do
now was try to step between Kit and his mother. That was
the surest way to appear the shrew and lose everything.

"Whatever you think best," she said as sweetly as she
could manage.

"I'll come by tomorrow afternoon. We can talk then
about the wedding itself."

"I'll be here," she promised.

"Excellent." He pressed a swift kiss to her lips. "Most
excellent."

Then he shoved his hands into his pockets, effectively
lifting his pants away from his groin, and strolled down
the hallway whistling with every step. She watched him
saunter to the stairs. She stood exactly where she was as
he descended from sight, and barely breathed for fear of
missing the sound of his whistle. When she no longer heard
anything but her own heartbeat, she let her head drop
against the wall.

She was going to be married, she thought. Despite
everything, she was going to marry the son of a peer. Her

sons could have a respectable profession and her daughters would not be whores. And when she called for a doctor, one would come.

Her knees crumpled beneath her. She slid to the ground not twenty feet from her door and began to sob. Long, loud wracking sobs of confusion. Nothing felt right. She was finally going to have everything she'd wanted her whole life, but she couldn't stop replaying that moment in the park with Brandon. No matter how she pushed it away, how much she focused on Kit, her mind kept bringing back that moment when she'd nearly kissed Brandon in the park.

Which meant what? Nothing had changed. Kit was the one who offered marriage, not Brandon. And so it was Kit who deserved all her allegiance. So why did it feel so very wrong?

The night's performance was awful. Not because the actors did badly. No, actually, they were especially energetic, which was always a crowd pleaser. No, what was terrible were the comments, the staring, the sly innuendoes, and the outright insults to Scher. She had a headache before Delilah's first song. By the time she was to enter the Green Room, Seth had appointed himself her bodyguard.

She hardly thought it was necessary. The crowd was heavy, but did Seth really think the gentlemen would actually damage her person?

Yes, they would. In fact, she barely made it in the door to the Green Room before the first brawl started. Someone loudly decried her as a whore and an upstart. Another shot to her defense. A man she didn't even know, but who was a self-proclaimed patron of the common man and woman. It took Seth and three of the largest of his boys to escort the brawlers outside. Scher took that excuse to disappear upstairs to her bedroom. She could only hope that no one chose to follow her.

She was wrong. One young man, the particularly earnest Mr. Tully from that afternoon, followed her up the stairs.

"Lady Scher! A word, please. Lady Scher!"

Scher winced as his voice got rather strident. Another bellow like that and everyone would be up here. So she turned around, pasting on a strained smile. "I'm terribly sorry, Mr. Tully, but my head aches so. Please, I must retire for the night."

"Just a moment please, Lady Scher." When she made to leave, he grabbed for her arm. She was no stranger to grasping men, so she twisted away. Unfortunately he was faster than she expected and managed to snag her sleeve, tugging it sharp enough that she heard a few stitches pop.

"Mr. Tully!"

"I know this is hard, Lady Scher, but you must hear me out."

They were near the top of the stairs, only three steps down. Another five steps and she would be at her door. So close, and her head did pound. With a sigh, she let her head rest against the wall, closed her eyes, and dreamed of a cool lavender compress across her eyes.

"I have a small cottage just north of London. It isn't much, but there are such trees there that privacy is assured. I had a bench put in the back near a small garden. In the fall, you can sit for hours and watch the leaves turn gold. I vow it is the most beautiful place on Earth."

His grip had shifted from her sleeve to her hand. He clutched it tightly, but she didn't open her eyes. In fact, she didn't react until she felt him lift her hand to his lips, where he pressed swift, dry kisses into her palm. Only then did she open her eyes.

"Mr. Tully? What are you about?"

"Your marriage to Kit will never work. Today was just the beginning. You are rapidly becoming a symbol of the common plight."

"What?"

He gripped her hand tighter as he pulled it to his heart. At least he wasn't kissing it anymore.

"Don't you see? You have become political."

"I am no such thing!"

"I know, I know! You had no wish for this. Truly, I understand. But it has happened nonetheless."

She straightened, a chill going through her body. "Please release my hand, Mr. Tully."

"Not yet, Lady Scher. Scheherazade. I wish to ask if you would, if I could . . ." He flushed a bright red that she might have thought was cute if her head weren't pounding. If he weren't still clutching her hand. "I wish to offer you my cottage. As my . . . um . . ."

"Mistress?"

"Yes!" The word was released on a gush of relief. "I have long admired you. Surely you know that. And I am a kind and considerate lover. You may ask Annette if you don't believe me. She said that very thing to me—"

"I am an engaged woman, Mr. Tully!"

He looked sadly into her eyes. She would have laughed at the sight except she could see that he really was distressed on her behalf. "Not for long. I am so sorry, but I know Kit. He was thrown out of his club today! Do you not understand what that means to a man like Kit?"

She arched a brow, reaching for every ounce of acting talent she possessed to appear as aristocratic as a queen. "You insult me," she practically hissed. "That would be bad enough, but to so malign Kit is beneath contempt. He is your friend!"

"Oh no!" gasped Mr. Tully. "I am *your* friend. Do you not understand? I am offering you a way out of this mess!"

"By offering me carte blanche?" She turned away from him, mounting the steps with precision. But he would not let go of her hand. Not until she looked back at him over her shoulder, giving him her most freezing look.

It took a while, but in the end he let go of her hand. Unfortunately, he wasn't done. As she topped the stairs, he followed right behind her.

"The offer stands, Lady Scher. You will find soon that you need to escape London. When Kit throws you over, when the political noise threatens to cripple the Tavern Playhouse, you can come to me. I will serve as your most devoted servant. I will—"

"Not follow me again." She had made it to her bedroom door, but it might as well have been on the moon. He was only a half step behind her, and she would not unlock her door as long as he was in the hallway with her. Where was Seth? What she wouldn't give for his burly presence right then. Or Brandon's. If anyone could freeze away an upstart, it was Viscount Blackstone.

Mr. Tully put a hand on her shoulder. "Do not forget what I offer," he said softly.

"Do you know," she said dryly, "that someone offers me carte blanche at least once a month, Mr. Tully?" It was a lie, but one she gleefully embraced. "If I had wanted to be a mistress, I have had plenty of opportunities."

"Not anymore," he said. "Not after this."

"On the contrary," she drawled, a chilling bit of insight burning through her. "If I am as political as you say, then I shall have dozens of offers soon. Anyone who wins me will be cause célèbre for a time."

He straightened, thankfully removing his hand from her shoulder. "But I am the only one who really cares for you."

She had no answer to that except an acid hole in her stomach. How could he imagine that carte blanche was a measure of respect or affection? And the arrogance of thinking he knew her at all! Just because he saw her every so often in the Green Room!

"Please, Mr. Tully, just go away. I cannot speak civilly with anyone right now."

She felt him hesitate. His breath hitched and he leaned toward her. She saw it in her peripheral vision. She tensed, readying to lift her elbow into his gut should he come any closer. But he didn't. Good sense must have prevailed because all he did was slide his card into her hand where she had flattened it against her door.

"I am a most considerate and gentle lover," he urged as he began to back away.

She wanted to crumple his card into a ball and throw it at his face. But to do so would bring him right back to plead his case. So she smiled at him and made a show of tucking it into her sleeve. The very sleeve he had nearly torn off her arm.

He grinned at her and left with a wave. Only after she heard his feet hit the landing below did she push the key into her lock. But when she turned it, she realized with some surprise that it hadn't been locked. It didn't matter. The sooner she got inside her room, the better.

So she pushed inside, crumpling Mr. Tully's card as she went. She closed the door, carefully locked it, then with a sudden fit of temper, she hurled the wad of paper as hard as possible at the corner where her chamber pot sat.

It never made it to the corner. A shadow reached up and caught it halfway there.

"Don't scream," said a man's voice. "It's just me."

Brandon. She turned away with disgust. "And what makes you think I won't scream when it's you?"

He stepped over to her bedside table and lit the candle there. The light bathed his face in a warm glow that did not help his features at all. He still looked harsh, mysterious, and not at all her friend.

She huffed as she dropped down into the nearest chair. "My head hurts too much to scream." She pulled out a long knife from beneath the book that rested within reach on the windowsill. "I'll just stab you instead."

He arched a brow at her, but then his eyes returned to

her crumpled card as he straightened it and angled it to the light. "Mr. Samuel Tully," he read. "Impertinent pup."

"You could have helped me out there, you know."

"I was at the door, ready if you required it." He turned, recrumpled the card, and neatly tossed it into the empty chamber pot. "But he was impertinent, not dangerous."

She closed her eyes and let her pounding head drop against the wall. It gave her a warm feeling to know that he had been ready to come to her aid. It was ridiculous, of course. She didn't want him to be her protector. She certainly didn't want him lurking in her bedroom. But it was reassuring nonetheless.

"Please go away, Viscount Blackstone. I have had all the offers of carte blanche I can manage today. But do feel free to shift your allegiance to Delilah or any of the other girls."

A hair pin slipped out from her bun. Then another. She started in surprise, shocked and appalled that he had crossed the room and was touching her hair while she was none the wiser. She raised the knife that she held, but he blocked it effortlessly. He didn't take the thing from her, but he kept her arm down and well away from him as his other hand deftly removed pin after pin. Her hair slipped out of its bun and the relief on her head was immeasurable.

"Pray do not gut me," he said softly. Then he released her arm to burrow both hands into her scalp. His fingers were strong, applying just the right pressure as he rubbed tiny circles all over her scalp. His hands started at her temples, but quickly flowed up to her crown, then spread downward toward her shoulders. She closed her eyes in relief. It felt wonderful.

She sighed in delight, all the fight going out of her. Her head relaxed fully into his large hands, and her eyes once again drifted shut. And then, wonder of wonders, his fingers slid lower on her scalp, flowing to the nape of her neck and lifting slightly such that her neck and shoulders began to stretch.

She hadn't even realized how tight her neck and jaw were until his touch allowed her to let it all give way. He didn't speak, thank heaven. She listened for his breath or his heartbeat or anything else of him but the press of his fingertips. She heard nothing but the muted noise from the Green Room and main playhouse floor. Clearly there was still a crowd down there. Her sudden political status might give her the headache, but it was doing wonders for the playhouse revenue.

She took her first full breath since this morning. And then she took another. Wonderful!

His lips touched hers first. Her mouth was slightly open in appreciation. Some part of her knew that he would not give her pleasure without asking for more. She'd known from the first moment he touched her head that he would be kissing her soon. A slow caress of lips, a mingling of breath, and a teasing nibble at the edge of her mouth.

She gave no response. He didn't need one. Like the caress of her scalp, this was done for her pleasure. She was relaxing in a sea of sensation for all that it was only on her mouth and the back of her head. Then, when he would have deepened the kiss, she lifted the knife.

She didn't even need to raise it high enough to get his ribs. It was just a tiny contraction of her wrist and he froze.

"I can take that from you, you know," he said softly.

"Are we back to force then?" she returned without even opening her eyes.

He sighed and gently eased her head back against the wall. She opened her eyes, mourning the loss of his caress. Her headache did feel much better.

He stood above her, a large shadow outlined from behind by the candlelight. But she needed no light to know the harsh angles of his face, the broad set to his shoulders, or the dark edge to his spirit.

"Tell me you don't desire me, Scher. I know you do."

She didn't have to see his eyes to know that they roved over her body. Did he see that her breasts were heavy and her nipples tight? Did he know that her thighs were relaxed, and her belly had gone liquid? Her every breath brought a slow tingle to that place between her legs.

She had never let him touch her there. They had shared countless kisses. He had fondled her breasts as well, rubbing her nipples through her gown until she was breathless with want. She remembered how large his hands were, how perfect in their seduction.

How had she managed to refuse him before? One night before Kit proposed, she and Brandon had done such things in the hallway. His kisses had been like black smoke, dark and drugging to her senses. He had loosened her gown and was pushing it down off her shoulders. Then Delilah came up the stairs, chatting with Seth the whole way. Something about how her costume was too tight.

So Scher had pushed Brandon away with an urgent whisper. She hadn't thought he would leave, but he finally gave in to her ardent shove. He had taken a moment though to lean in and whisper to her. "Tomorrow night, Scher, nothing will stop me."

That's what he had said. But then Kit had proposed the next night and everything changed.

"Damn Kit," he said now, though the words had no heat.

"Damn you for being so free with my bedchamber." He was standing over her like some demonic force, and yet, she had no fear. Just a warm heat down deep inside her belly. "Damn you for being so arrogant as to think I would fall into your arms just because you are a skilled lover."

He shifted and she opened her eyes. He now stood

enough in the candlelight so that she could see his confusion. Had she shocked him? She nearly laughed.

"You think I don't know?" she asked, incredulous. "Of course I know you could take my body to places I have only dreamed. One caress in the hallway, and my loins were on fire for hours. Oh, Brandon, the nights I have laid in that bed and thought of what we could be doing."

She gestured with her knife as a show of force. But inside, she knew that she was perilously close to throwing the blade away and allowing him to pleasure her in ways that she could only imagine. In her whole life, she had had only one lover—the cad who had taken her virginity. What would it harm her if she allowed one other, just for one night?

"You have tempted me beyond reason from the moment I first saw you," she confessed. "You make me question everything I ever wanted. Even marriage."

She saw her words hit him in the way his body swayed. His eyes seemed to burn as he stared at her, and when he spoke, his words were raspy and hoarse. "Scher, love, put down the knife!"

She raised it a little higher. "Has no one ever rejected you before, Lord Blackstone? No one felt desire for you and yet stayed virtuous?"

"Scores of women have turned their back on me, Scher. But none who claimed desire. None who knew . . ."

"What?" she pressed when his voice faded away. "That you are legendary in bed?"

"Yes."

"A careful and considerate lover?" she mocked, deliberately echoing Mr. Tully's claim.

His voice dropped to a tone that seemed to tremble through her skin and into her blood. "There are texts in India devoted to bed play. I studied them. I even spoke once with a master, trying to learn more."

She arched a brow, intrigued despite herself. "A master who instructs in bed sport?"

"A mistress, actually."

She allowed herself a small smile. "Of course."

He moved swiftly, dropping to his knees before her. His arms settled on the rests of her chair, and his face was level with hers. He was close enough that she could smell the mint. Close enough that the smallest movement of her knife and she would cut off his nose.

"Can't you see? You and Kit will never work. He is a boy, Scher. A good boy, to be sure, but you require a man." He dropped a hand to the floor then slid it under her skirt. "Think about what I can give you."

His grip tightened on her ankle. It wasn't painful. In truth it felt good the way he moved his fingers up her. leg, squeezing into her calf, then brushing soft strokes upward before doing it again.

"Did you learn that in India?" she asked.

"Yes. I also learned that there are points on a woman's legs that are especially sensitive." He shifted again, pulling his other hand down to untie the ribbons of her slippers. In the space between one breath and the next, her feet were bare and he was tugging at her toes.

She expected it to tickle. Her feet were extraordinarily sensitive, but his touch had just the right firmness as he kneaded her feet, slowly spreading the bones apart from the ball of her foot outward.

"There is a spot here," he said, as he pushed into her arch. She gasped. There was pain there, and yet the longer he held the point, the better it felt. Pain shivered into pleasure, especially as he began a slow circle caress. "There is a connection between foot and breast. I don't need to be stroking your nipples for them to become tight with desire."

Her mouth opened in surprise. She hadn't been thinking at all about her breasts, but at his words, her nipples contracted. And yes indeed, the moment he pressed a different part of her foot, she felt it as if he were at her breasts, stroking her there. She held her breath, her mind spinning with yearning. She didn't think she'd ever been more aroused in her life, and he was just touching her feet.

"There is more," he said as he moved his way to her ankles. One hand surrounded each ankle, and his fingers probed the soft flesh above her heel then farther up beneath her calves. "The Indians can make a woman scream in ecstasy without touching more than this. Just her feet and her ankles."

She would laugh at any other person who made such a claim. But right then, she felt his caress all the way to her core.

"Let me touch you, Scher. It won't mean anything. I won't tell anyone. It will simply be a restorative for you. There is such pleasure to be had, Scher, and of all people, of all days, you deserve this now."

She took a deep breath, allowing herself the fantasy. She had no doubt he could deliver on his promise. Her blood was simmering, her groin wet and tingling. Her thighs were already opening, and the desire was so strong! One more caress. One more moment of bliss. It would be so easy.

She swallowed. "Move one inch higher, my lord, and I will put this knife through your eye."

His head pulled back, but that was all that stilled. His hands still continued their magical caress on her calves.

"Release me, my lord," she said.

"Are you sure?"

She flicked her wrist. It was a quick movement, and she obviously caught him by surprise. Her knife sliced through his shirt sleeve. One glance at the tip showed that it gleamed red with his blood. Not a lot and barely the tip, but she had made her point.

He drew back with a curse, glaring down at the fine white linen. A red stain darkened the lower edge of the cut. She waited a moment, watching closely to see if she had gone too far. Would it bleed too much? Would he beat her in fury?

Taut moments passed as they both stared at his wound. But beyond the initial mark, the bloodstain did not spread. And when he turned back to look at her, she thought she read surprise and even respect in his face.

"I have never met a woman such as you," he said softly.

Was that a compliment? Or a curse? "Do not come to my bedchamber again, Lord Blackstone."

He grabbed her knife hand and pressed his thumb into her wrist. She didn't even see him move, but he was there, his hand incredibly large and horribly strong. His thumb dug into her such that her fingers went slack. She tried to kick him, but he blocked her legs with his knees, pinning her feet to the chair. And then the knife clattered to the floor.

"I am going to seduce you now, Scheherazade," he said. "I am going to spread your legs and put my mouth to your woman parts. And I am going to pleasure you until you scream my name."

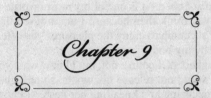

Chapter 9

Brandon shifted his hands, feeling the silky texture of her calves. Like all of her, it was soft on the outside, but one push and her strength was revealed. Scher was strong, both physically and mentally. And finally, he thought as he pushed up her skirt, finally he would get to touch her as he wanted.

"Did your Indian mistress teach you that?" she asked, her voice colder than he expected.

"I learned it in India, yes," he answered.

"She told you to force women? That they want to be overpowered?" She leaned forward and gripped his wrists beneath her skirt, holding him still.

He looked up, startled by the harsh tones in her voice. He expected many reactions from Scher. He had not thought she would be so . . . dismissive. Clearly he needed to go even slower with her.

He pulled back with a small frown. "I learned to listen in India. Not just to words, but to everything—body, clothing, even decor. All reveal something." He tried to shift his hands, but she held him tightly and he would not force the issue. Instead, he leaned forward and inhaled deeply. "I also learned to appreciate the smell of an aroused woman." He looked up at Scher. "It is one of my most favorite scents."

"And you think then because I am aroused that I must naturally succumb to enjoy the pleasures you offer? That I am ruled by my body?"

He laughed. "Of course not, but I know what you want." She still would not release his wrists, so he tightened his fingers, squeezing and kneading her flesh. "I know how to listen to a woman's body, Scheherazade. I know what she wants even before she does."

"I will scream. I will scream and fight."

He paused, her words too disconcerting for him to continue. "You want this, Scher. We both do."

"No, Brandon, I do not."

"Your body, your flesh. Your scent!" His hands tightened around her legs. He could shove them apart. He could take what they both obviously wanted. "And, yes, Scheherazade, some women want to be forced. It adds spice to the game."

She abruptly released his left wrist to grab his chin. Her fingers were sharp as they tugged his chin up. Never since he was a little boy had a woman thought to do that to him. He kept his desire in check as he looked where she intended. At her face. At her eyes. At the total implacability in her expression.

"No, Brandon, *no*! If you have any respect for me, any care at all, you will release me now."

He stared at her, his mind moving slowly. He saw no coyness in her, no game of saying no, but meaning yes. He knew she was aroused. Damn it, he *knew* it. *She had let him into her room!*

No, he recalled, he had picked the lock and surprised her.

But she had allowed him to touch her!

No, he realized, she had closed her eyes and he had surprised her. But she had certainly not stopped him.

Except, of course, she had. Her knees were firmly locked together and one of her hands still gripped his wrist.

"Let me show you what it can be like between us. We could be so much to each other."

She huffed in disgust. "Is this what you learned in India? Do the Indian women say something entirely different than what they mean?"

He swallowed. "I did not, um, enjoy Indian women. I kept to the bored British wives." His hands went slack along her calves. Suddenly his belly was sick with acid, but it was nothing compared to the turmoil in his mind.

"I am not bored," Scheherazade said. "We are not in India. Do you understand, Brandon? I do *not* want to go to bed with you."

But she was aroused. That one thought kept replaying in his mind. She was aroused. She wanted him. He could have focused on that knowledge. Even now he knew what to do, he knew the techniques to use, the shift of touch or tongue. He could make it good for her. He could make her enjoy it.

But her face. She no longer gripped his chin. She had released him the moment his hands had slid down her calves. He could easily turn away and not see her face, but that was a coward's act. No matter what her body said, no matter how it *smelled*, there was conviction in her face. She did not want to be seduced.

Despair consumed him. A crippling wave of burning pain that started in his chest and flowed outward. The first time he'd felt it—when fire had destroyed everything he'd thought to build—he'd felt sure his heart had given out. It grew worse when he realized the fire was only the beginning. There had been murders and theft, and no way for him to make the murderers pay. Then his chest had squeezed so tight that he thought he would never breathe again. Now he knew better. Now he knew he would still go on, still live only with the total loss. This feeling was devastation, an emptiness that left nothing behind.

He had felt it then. He felt it again now. She had kept it from him for a time. The game of seduction had pushed the agony away and given him something different to think about. Something wonderful to anticipate. Without her, he had nothing to stand between him and the despair.

"I have nothing else to offer you," he said more to himself than to her. "You already have money. You don't want tender emotions. You—"

"Respect, Brandon. I want to be—"

"I respect you!" he shouted back. He pushed up from the floor. He would not be on his knees before her. He would *not*! And yet, after two furious turns about the floor before her, he dropped back against the wall, his entire body slumping. He was not kneeling, but neither was he standing tall.

"I want you as my mistress, Scher," he said. He kept his voice soft and low, as was appropriate with a lady, while he prayed that the urgency within him somehow translated to her. His words came out in a rush, without thought or understanding. He would honor what he said, but he was too afraid of the despair to gauge his promises. "I will give you money, jewels, a home, and education for our children."

"Do you offer me marriage then?" she asked softly. Her expression was puzzled now.

"I . . . I . . ." He watched her expression harden and he damned himself for a fool. He would not lie to her. "I cannot," he forced himself to say. He couldn't even explain it to her. No one knew the extent of the problems he had brought back with him from India. A wife was simply not possible.

"Then you are right," she said. "You have nothing that

interests me." Oddly, she seemed disappointed by that. Her face had softened and her eyes held regret. Her perfume had dampened now that he was a few feet from her. All in all, she had given him his final comeuppance. Lady Scher, a failed actress had thrown him over.

She leaned forward, not to touch him, but to see him more clearly. She peered in his face and he read honest confusion. "You say you respect me, and yet you treat me like a trollop. You wait in my room, you try to seduce me with kisses and pretty words, and when I say no, you touch me anyway. Brandon, you are not this stupid! What are you thinking? What demons drive you to this madness?"

He looked at the floor as he spoke. He could not say these things to her face. "You were meant to be a distraction. A sweet way to pass the time between writing speeches and discussing English colonization policies. Michael suggested I seduce you—for Kit's sake—and I found you interesting enough to be worth the effort."

She fell back away from him, the disgust apparent in the huff of her breath. But he knew she still listened. And even if she did not, he could not stop his words.

"And then something happened."

"What?" she asked when he fell silent.

He shook his head. "I don't know, but it was the same in India." He lifted his head to look at her. There was only the glow of a single candle flame, but he didn't need it to see her face. Green eyes, glossy reddish-brown hair, and a serious expression. She managed an entire acting troupe, a playhouse, and unruly gentlemen with just a flick of her hand and arch of her brow. She had substance, and it inspired him. That was the word. "I grew inspired."

"You found a woman to seduce. That is hardly inspiring."

"No," he rasped as he stepped to her side and dropped to the floor before her. "I had already worked my way through the ladies. I had already learned about the secrets of bed play. In truth, I was bored." He sighed. "No, what inspired me in India was money, commerce, cooperation." He laughed, unable to hide the bitterness in his tone. "I was inspired to work, Scher. To fight for an ideal that would make both the English and the Indians a great deal of money."

She tilted her head as she looked at him. "But that was all to the good, was it not?"

"No, it was not. No good. No cooperation. Only . . ." Lies. Murder. Death.

"The fire in that factory," she whispered, finally understanding some of it at least. "When everything you had worked for was burned."

"Yes, the fire. It was deliberately set, you know. All those people murdered on purpose." He dropped his head into her lap. He had not meant to collapse there, but somehow he found that he had placed his head on her knees, and the feel of her fingers in his hair was the most exquisite of sensations. Neither sexual nor maternal, it was simply touch—human touch—and it made his eyes burn with tears.

"But what has that to do with me?" she asked. "How has that . . . that tragedy brought you here?"

Did she not understand? Of course not. How could she? He was struggling through the darkness himself. With great reluctance, he lifted his head. He caught her hand and brought it to his lips. She was passive in his grasp, but he knew he had not won her. Not yet.

"You inspire me," he said again. He felt her still, felt his words seep into her heart. Did she soften to him? He prayed so. "I cannot explain the reason or cause. I cannot explain any of this, Scher, except to say that I feel a fire within me whenever I see you. A fire that has not touched my cold, dark heart since . . ."

"Since India."

"Since before it all went bad."

She stroked his face, feathered her fingers across his cheek, and even touched his lips. He would have kissed her then, but she pulled back. He would have followed, but she held him off with a single look. "Disillusioned. I see it now. I see why you and I have this connection. Kit has never felt his world destroyed; certainly none of his set know what it is to give their heart and have it—"

"Burned."

"Betrayed."

He swallowed, nodding. Yes, he had been betrayed. Only a select few knew that the fire had been set by the English, not the Indians. She didn't know it was his superior at the East India Company who did the horrible deed, and that even the Prince Regent was complicit in the lies.

"And so," she continued, "we understand each other. We feel—"

"Connected."

She appeared to struggle with that word, and in the end she shook her head. "A resonance. A memory of pain. But Brandon, I cannot build a life on that."

He touched her arms, he looked into her face, he pleaded with everything that was in him. "Scher, look into my eyes, feel what I feel, know what I know."

"Brandon—"

"Just do it!"

She did. She looked into his eyes, and he saw something spark in hers. He saw her pupils dilate, her nostrils flare. He knew without looking that her body reacted to his, heating with a call that was more than just physical. She needed him, just as he needed her. He wasn't sure if it was truly in her eyes, but he wanted to believe it was there. He needed her to feel as he felt.

"Be with me, Scher."

"No."

"Live with me, have my children, inspire me for the rest of my life."

"Marry me," she said. "Anything you want, Brandon, but it comes with a wedding ring."

He tightened his hands painfully. "I can't!"

"Then neither can I."

He heard her words, pounding dully in his mind. He searched her face, looking for some crack, some spark of what he knew was there. He saw nothing. A shadowed face. A flat mouth.

"Scher . . ."

"I can't give up on that dream, Brandon. I have held it for so long, wanted it with all my heart. Don't you understand? You asked me why it is so important that I be respectable. Very well, I will tell you why. I had a sister once, did you know? Her name was Cleopatra and she was everything I am not. Beautiful, vibrant, with such a voice on stage that no one could fail to love her."

"You are beautiful, Scher—" he began, but she cut him off with a wave of her hand.

"Cleo was the light that everyone adored, including me. And one day she caught a fever. The surgeon came—a day *after* we had sent for him. We put all our money together to buy her medicine, but the man was a cheat. He sold us bad-tasting water and Cleo died."

He felt his gut clench and his hands tighten. He wanted to strangle the bastard with his bare hands.

"We were all devastated, but we were actors and whores. No one cared what the man had done, least of all the magistrate. A week later one of the actresses died in childbirth. We couldn't save her. She was a whore and we had no money to pay for proper caring, having spent it all on Cleo." Her eyes glittered as she looked down at him. "Shall I tell you how my mother died? Pappy? Or a score of others?"

He shook his head. He could lie to her. Tell her that her loved ones would still have died if they had been respectable, but the truth was that the lower classes received worse care. It was the way things worked in England, in India, in the world.

"Do you know why I work so hard?" she asked. "Why I watch the cash box and count the wine as if it were gold? So that there will be money to pay the surgeons when we need them. So the midwife will come for the gold. But it's not enough, Brandon. We still come second to anyone with a wedding ring. Any respectable family will be tended before us."

He could see it then, her aching desire for security. The need to assure by any means possible that the ones she loved would be well cared for. "You know, of course," he said softly, "that a wedding ring will not ensure safety. That people die in respectable families as well."

"I know," she said and he watched her eyes close in weariness. "I know, but I cannot escape the fear any other way. A doctor thinks twice before cheating a respectable family. And magistrates listen to a good wife as they do not hear an actress."

He couldn't argue with her. It was true. And even if it weren't, she had built so much of her life around the lie that she would not surrender it. Besides, who was he to tell her that she couldn't strive to be married like a normal woman? She was beautiful and smart. Any man would be lucky to marry her, including himself. But since India, that path was blocked for him, and nothing he did could change it.

"I cannot give you that," he confessed. "I can only offer you myself." He pressed his lips to her leg, feeling the cloth of her gown rough beneath his mouth. And yet it was part of her, and so he cherished even this tiny thing. "I need you," he said.

She sighed, the sound coming from deep within her. He felt her hands in his hair and her caress against his cheek. "No, Brandon. I will be a wife."

There was no fighting the finality in her words. He heard

it as dark and brutal as the crack of a pistol or the snap of roof being consumed by fire. She was sure, and nothing he could do or say would sway her. Nothing, of course, except the one thing he couldn't give her.

He slowly straightened away from her, standing though he could barely feel his body.

"Kit is a good man," he said. "He will be good to you." He looked down at his hands. "But he will never withstand the pressures of London society." He looked toward her door, the burning heat in his body now cooled to a gaping darkness. "Move as far away as you can."

She straightened, pushing to her feet even as he slowly fled. "Leave London?" she asked. "But everything I have is here."

He shook his head. "You must go somewhere where there is no British society."

"But that is not . . . not respectable. That is being expelled. Spit out like bad meat!"

He shrugged. He was so cold even with his new coat pulled on. "It is all you can have."

He opened her door and stepped out into the hallway. One of Seth's boys lounged in the hall, his eyes narrowed with suspicion. Brandon absently tossed him a coin.

"Tell Seth that I only spoke with her. I didn't touch her. I didn't hurt her. I only . . ." Failed. He failed completely and utterly to win her.

"Lord Blackstone," Scher called from her doorway. "Brandon."

He turned. Should he feel gratified that she looked troubled? He didn't. He felt so damned cold.

"What do you intend now?"

He arched a brow. Did he intend anything? Ever? The sneer came easily to his lips. "Do you think Delilah is busy?"

The boy answered. "She gots her man in her bed already."

"Hmmm. Well, perhaps at the brothel down the street then." He sketched a shallow bow. "Good night, Lady Scher."

She waited a moment, obviously trying to think of something better to say. In the end, she merely nodded. "Good night, Lord Blackstone."

He left quickly then, his feet taking him in aimless patterns through areas of London best left unexplored. It was hours before the blows came. Two thieves, possibly three. They came at him with knives similar to the one Scher had held. But unlike her, they wielded theirs with skill.

He felt the first cut on his back.

The next came to his chest, sharp and cruel beneath his ribs.

His last thought was that his blood was the warmest part of him, and it was draining away.

Chapter 10

"Have you seen Brandon?" Kit asked Scher in the Green Room six nights later.

Scher was distracted. The societal and political fury over their engagement continued to rage. Attendance at the Tavern Playhouse was at record levels, but so were the brawls. Seth had to hire extra men just to keep the furniture from being destroyed. Fortunately, the extra "actresses" were also enjoying a brisk after-performance business.

All in all, Scher's engagement had been an excellent business decision but a terrible personal one. In fact, demand for her presence in the Green Room was so high, it rivaled her mother in her heyday. After all, no one could toast to her success or damn her status-seeking immorality if she wasn't there to be applauded or damned. The worst night they'd had all week was the night she tried to spend a quiet evening hidden in her bedroom. They'd lost a dozen chairs and a score of glasses to a boisterous group demanding she hear their support of the lower classes.

It was ridiculous, but given the damage to the furniture, she never again hid in her upstairs room. She also made sure to never appear without Seth's protection. And after the second night, she insisted that Kit stand at her side as well. He was quite adept at diffusing the tension that surrounded them, always handy with a clever quip or a good-natured laugh. It was hard to hate Kit, even if one believed him the harbinger of the end of British civilization. Unfortunately, the strain was beginning to show on him as well.

Which was why his question about Brandon took her by surprise. Fully three dozen people were compressed in the Green Room tonight. Despite her hopes that the excitement would die out, she and Kit remained as notorious as ever. But as Delilah had just appeared—and in a rather scanty gown—Kit and Scher enjoyed a momentary respite from the crowd's attention.

"The wine tastes strange tonight," Scher commented rather than answer Kit's question.

"That's because I had Seth order a better sort. If I'm to be here for hours every night, I want to drink something worth the effort."

She arched a brow. He had never complained about the drink before. But then, he hadn't had to practically live here before either.

"Don't worry," he added as he drained his own glass. "It's just a few bottles exclusively for you and me."

And whatever guests he wished to treat. Not to mention the members of the troupe who would sneak a glass here and there. Kit would find that his few bottles didn't last nearly as long as he thought.

"What a nice idea," she lied. It was a terrible idea, but ever since she'd allowed Kit to look at the books for the Tavern Playhouse, he had started to meddle in the running of it. A bottle of expensive wine here. A new sort of cushioned chair there, the fabric already smelling bad. A suggestion on the new act, and a bizarre idea about the dog food.

Meddling, all of it, and Scheherazade hated it. It had taken her years to get all aspects of the Tavern Playhouse running smoothly. His little suggestions were already threatening to unbalance her hard work.

On the other hand, once they were married, all her ownership in the troupe and the building that housed it would pass to him. Which meant, he would soon own most everything here. It would be his right to meddle as much as he wanted. And she, of course, could say nothing about it.

"Kit, I think it would be better if we kept our wine in my bedchamber. It should be separate from the rest of the accounts."

"No one's seen him for days, you know," he said, completely ignoring her words. Which was only fair, of course, as she had ignored his. "I went round his rooms, and he hasn't been there for nearly a week."

"What? Who?" she asked, though she knew perfectly well.

"Brandon!" he repeated rather loudly. "Have you seen him?"

"Why would I see him? Last I knew, he was headed for a brothel."

"Scher!" Kit said with mock outrage. "Surely you don't know that."

"Of course I know that!" she snapped, irritated with this entire conversation. "He said so most explicitly."

"Well, that's hardly the thing."

Scheherazade stopped herself from rolling her eyes. "Nothing about Lord Blackstone is 'the thing,' as you put it. Nothing ever has been."

Kit released a sigh loud enough to be heard over the din of the Green Room. "A lady doesn't criticize like that, Scher."

That was another thing Kit had been doing more of

lately. He had started using the phrase "a lady doesn't . . ." with increasing frequency. Enough that she had to resort to her wineglass rather than risk an unladylike response.

It was some moments later before she permitted herself to speak. "I haven't the foggiest idea where Lord Blackstone is, nor do I wish to."

"That's unfair!" Kit responded. "He is my cousin, and he took you driving in Hyde Park."

"I remember who he is," she returned dryly.

"Yes, but do you recall that he has excellent advice sometimes? Most knowledgeable on politics and the like, though rather cynical."

"Extremely cynical," she muttered.

"And he was the only one who stood up for our engagement," Kit pressed.

"He did no such thing!"

"He drove you around Hyde Park."

"So that he could show us both how regretfully terrible an idea it was!" It was only with those last heated words that she realized conversation had lulled around them. In truth, the Green Room had gone relatively quiet as everyone turned to watch her and Kit in their disagreement.

Kit looked around, giving everyone a strained smile. "Nervous brides can have tart tongues, don't you know?" Then he turned to wink at her. "But it will all be better after the wedding night, my love."

Raucous laughter followed his words while Scher fought a wave of disgust. It never failed in the Green Room. A single bawdy comment and all was laughed off. Unless, of course, it was Lady Scher who made the comment. Then she was back to being a low-class scheming whore.

"Smile!" Kit hissed at her under his breath. "You look like you just swallowed a toad."

"It's the wine," she shot back, as she pressed her half-filled glass into his hand. Then she waved vaguely at the crowd. "I feel a headache coming on. Wedding preparations and all can be so exhausting." In truth, she hadn't done anything more than give their costumer instructions and coins to make her a simple wedding dress. She doubted it would end up simple. Mary loved to embellish, but Scher had made the effort.

"Perhaps I should escort you to bed then," said Kit with another broad wink to the crowd.

Scher turned quickly to press the flat of her palm on Kit's chest. She held it there, stopping him from moving forward. Then she slowly, carefully, raised up on her toes and pressed her lips against his. Her kiss was nearly chaste. Their mouths touched and when he would have deepened it, she held him back. She merely allowed him to explore lip to lip rather than tongue to tongue.

In the background, the crowd swelled with cheers and bawdy comments. She would never do this in the normal course of events. At least half the group would take this as proof positive that she was a scheming social climber. And by tomorrow night, everyone would be saying that she had stripped naked for Kit in full view of the entire Green Room.

It didn't seem to matter to her. Her attention was centered completely on Kit. She used all her skill to tease him—and the crowd—with just her lips, allowing just so much and no more. Then she pushed back with a smile even though Kit clenched his hands tighter on her arms, trying to keep her in place.

"No, no, my love," she said. "I think you should stay down here until the wedding night. I am a proper lady, after all."

Laughter erupted around her, peppered by more bawdy comments at Kit's obvious discomfort and his perfect expression of chagrin. But that was typical fare for the Green Room. What made the joke truly funny was the suggestion that Scheherazade was a lady. Clearly, their guffaws said, she was anything but.

Her smile tightened, anger churning inside her. How dare they judge her? She knew for a fact how very *immoral* most of these men were, and what sanctimonious asses the others were. But that was beside the point. Her temper was badly frayed. She needed to leave immediately before she did something very wrong.

So she curtsied and ducked out. Seth touched her arm as she was leaving, silently asking if she needed an escort. She shook her head. She had no fear of unexpected visitors tonight. So long as no one followed her upstairs, she would be fine.

She made it up to her room with speed, pushing inside less than a minute after leaving the Green Room. She had meant to drop onto her bed and apply a wet compress. Indeed, that had been her firm intent when she had decided to come upstairs. But by the time she unlocked her door, she knew her decision was in vain. No matter what she intended, she would end up in the very place she had been for the last five nights.

She didn't want to go. She didn't want to lie to Kit, to sneak out of the playhouse, to act like the very scandalous whore everyone thought she was. But she couldn't stop herself.

She changed her clothes quickly, donning a poor man's pants, shirt, coat, and hat. She'd had it made a long time ago for times just like this when she needed to be out by herself at night. And truthfully, the very shabbiness of the outfit added to the disguise. Moments later, she slipped out of her door and the playhouse, melding silently into the dark London night.

Wake up, sahib. There is a fire.

"Brandon. Please wake up. Try to drink this."

Sahib. Fire.

Cool liquid slid into his mouth. It was there, then it was gone.

Fire, sahib. Fire!

Brandon came alert with a gasp that made him choke. Ashes burned through his lungs, and his vision would not clear. Tears burned his eyes, pain wracked his body. The fire! Oh my God, the fire!

"Brandon! Stop! Brandon!"

Sahib!

"Drink this. Drink!"

Again the cool liquid on his lips. He had to get up. He had to go help. Oh my God. Fire! But he couldn't get the word out, and his head was spinning. The water was good in his mouth. How could it be good when . . .

"Fire," he croaked.

"There is no fire, Brandon. Just a fever. Drink more."

But there was a fire. And he was too late to stop it. Oh God, too late.

The water felt good. He swallowed by instinct, but he didn't deserve it. It was all his fault.

"My fault. My fault."

"Shhhh, Brandon. Try to rest."

"My fault."

A cool cloth pressed to his forehead. His muscles gave out. He was so dizzy.

"It was all my fault."

A fingertip touched his lips. A simple press, but it felt like a searing brand.

"Then you are forgiven, Brandon. Be at peace now. You are forgiven."

The words seemed to slip into his body from that touch on his lips. As if he inhaled what was said and from there it touched every part of him. He breathed deeper, pain splitting him from belly to chin.

Finally the pain went deep enough. Finally he felt the agony he deserved. And with that anguish came the release. Could it be possible? Had he finally suffered enough for his sins? No.

"Not enough."

"Sleep, Brandon. Be at peace."

"The fire," he mumbled, though his tongue felt so thick it could barely move.

"The fire is out. It is all over. You can rest now."

He felt the darkness grow, the numbness of sleep weighed his thoughts down. But he still had to know.

"Am I really forgiven?"

"Of course. You have suffered enough."

Truly?

"Sleep."

He slept.

Brandon opened his eyes. It wasn't a conscious decision. One moment he was drifting. The very next moment he had vision. Labels lined up in his mind. Names of things listed without judgment: torn blanket, urine smell, tallow candle nearly burned out. He blinked, sorting form from shadow. Woman asleep in chair. She wore men's clothing.

Scheherazade.

Scheherazade.

Scheherazade.

His mind stopped on her name, repeating it over and over. He didn't know if he could move his thoughts elsewhere. He didn't try. He simply stayed where he was, looking at her while her name repeated in his thoughts.

Scheherazade.

Scheherazade.

She wasn't here. Scheherazade wasn't here. He knew that without turning his head. If she were here, he would smell her. He knew she used lavender perfume. If his nose were against her skin, he would smell lavender and something else. Something that was uniquely her. But more often, he would smell every scent—heavy perfumes from dozens of people, heavy paints from the actors, and then the more acrid scents of sweat and dung that lingered throughout that area of London. Scheherazade carried all those scents with her, but they were not strong in this room now. Which meant she was not here.

And since he also didn't smell the overwhelming scent of onions, the other woman wasn't here either. That, at least, was a kindness. He really didn't care for the shrew. Or for the boy, Hank, his servant. They were like biting flies that bothered him when all he wanted to do was slip away.

With a sigh that was half regret, half relief, he closed his eyes. With luck, he wouldn't ever wake again.

Chapter 11

"'E asks after ye. Says yer name right and tight. An' when yer not here, he goes right back to sleep."

"So he can speak?"

"Jes yer name and none too clear."

Brandon stirred, hearing sounds from the other room, but they had no meaning to him. He tried to drop back into the oblivion of sleep, but the sounds became voices: Scher's voice and the other woman's. And with Scher's presence came interest, awareness, and eventually, meaning.

"But he can talk," Scher pressed. "And he lets you help him?"

"Usually just points. Lets me at him with the necessaries. Don't like my soup much, but 'e eats it. Then 'e sleeps."

Brandon's other senses roused. He could smell Scher now. Soon he would feel her presence like a tingle along his skin. He didn't know if it was true or just his fevered imagination, but he savored in it nonetheless.

"He didn't ask questions? Demand . . . something? He just—"

"The fight's gone out of 'im. Seen it afore. All 'e cares about is if yer 'ere."

He opened his eyes. He didn't see anything beyond shadows cast on the ceiling. He would try to sit up, but he knew from experience that it would be better if he did not. Besides, she would come to him eventually. He merely needed to be patient.

"You're awake!"

Scher stepped into his field of vision, bringing the candle with her. She wore a man's hat, which flopped ridiculously about her ears. It was a perfect match for the cheap men's clothing that hung on her slender frame. No one with any brains would mistake her for a man. She was too beautiful, her features too refined for anything but an angel.

She set down the candle, then took something from the other woman. Martha was her name, and she handed Scher a cup. With brackish water in it, no doubt. Scher leaned down, slipping her arm beneath his shoulders. He hissed as he tried to help her. How ridiculous that the mere act of lifting his torso produced such agony.

His head was swimming by the time Scher lifted him up enough that he could drink. He dutifully drained the cup, then clenched his teeth as she set him back down. Martha had put another pillow behind him, so at least he was higher up than before. He could watch Scher without straining his neck.

"How do you feel this evening?" Scher asked. Her voice held the gentle notes he remembered, but something else as well. An ease, he thought. So it wasn't really that there was something new in her voice, more that something was absent. The wariness was gone, replaced by a quiet ease.

He wasn't sure how he felt about that. He preferred it when she was on edge around him. He liked instilling excitement in her. But now, stretched out on this dirty bed, he was useless.

"Not feeling talkative, Brandon?" she said lightly as she pulled a roll out of her pocket. His stomach clenched at the sight. He was hungry, but so far his stomach had rebelled at anything more than greasy broth. Besides, he had no wish to eat her food. He knew from experience that this was likely the first meal she'd had all day. His gaze slipped to the window to check the time. Dark. It was probably well after the show then, two or three in the morning. He looked back to her. She looked tired.

"You are staring, Brandon. Did you want a bit of bread?" She broke off a small piece and offered it to him. She even stood up beside the bed, bringing her breasts eye level to him, but she wore that ridiculous men's shirt and so he saw nothing but cheap fabric.

She held the piece before his lips, but he shook his head. He would not take her dinner. She pressed her lips together in a tight frown, then shrugged.

"Very well," she said as she sat back down. "I'm very pleased that you are awake. The surgeon will return tomorrow, by the way. He said that you are very lucky. Very lucky indeed."

Yes, he had heard the surgeon's opinion. The man talked nonstop as he'd poked and prodded into wounds that were better off left alone. Brandon had endured it in sweating silence. "Lucky" was not a word Brandon liked. Certainly not when it pertained to him, though people insisted on calling him that.

He looked away. He wanted to use the necessary, but he couldn't move. He couldn't do anything by himself but sit and brood. The very idea disgusted him. What a waste he had become.

"It occurs to me that you have been lying there quite a while now. Do you need the pot?"

He looked at her, his eyes wide with horror. Good God, it was bad enough that Martha and Hank helped him, but Scheherazade? The mortification—

"Do not look at me like that! Do you think I have never seen a naked man? I provided most of Pappy's care for his last year. I assure you, you have nothing that will disgust me."

He shook his head, and his gaze slid to the door. Would she understand that he wanted the other woman to help him, not her?

"Martha has gone to bed and Hank is exhausted. They have had the care of you all day. It is my turn now." So saying, she stood up and grabbed the bed pan. But when she stepped close, he shoved aside her arm in irritation. He would do this himself!

Except the very act of pushing her away sent bolts of fire through his body. He bit back his scream, but he couldn't fight the weakness that made short work of all his determination. He grabbed her arm to steady himself, and then he pulled her closer, burying his head into her chest as he fought the agony.

She held him tightly, supporting him with both hands while she pressed a kiss to the top of his head. It was that kiss that broke him. How he had wanted her to hold him, to kiss him, to do any number of things. But not this way! Not like a mother to her babe!

He was furious with her, with himself, with the entire world. He wanted no one and nothing! Instead, he clutched her even more tightly and began to sob. Great wracking sobs of despair, and the knowledge horrified him.

He felt as if his consciousness stood beside him, a silent observer from across the room. That mental awareness watched in confusion as an ocean of darkness flowed from his mouth. Where did this well of sorrow come from? It wasn't the physical pain. He had endured that and so much worse before. This was a mental anguish that both stunned and revolted him.

He was a man, by God! And yet there he was in his sick bed, clutching Scher and bawling into her breast like a toddler. Worse, each wracking breath sent fresh torment through his wound. He'd been stabbed through his ribs. Did he want to tear himself open? He could still bleed to death. The wound could still go putrid. Worse, he could catch an ague in this godforsaken hovel. Did he want to die?

Yes.

The words came clearly to his consciousness as it stood apart from the bed.

Yes, he desperately wanted to die.

The knowledge was shocking enough that it translated all the way through to his body. His sobs stopped.

He wanted to die.

Then why the hell didn't he take some poison and be done with it? Why make the effort of healing up, of having Scheherazade nurse him like a child? Why endure the humiliation of her seeing him like this? Why not slit his throat now?

"Shhhh. It's all right. I've got a hold of you." She was murmuring into his hair. Then as his breath began to ease, he lifted his head enough to press his cheek against hers. "I've got you," she repeated. "I've—"

He kissed her. Clinging and awkward at first as he turned into her mouth. He could barely breathe, but he could press his lips to hers. He could thrust his tongue into her mouth. He could . . . he could . . . he could lose all strength in his body as he fell backward like a limp rag.

But she came with him. She supported him back down onto the bed. He needed to breathe, so she shifted to rain kisses across his lips, his nose, his cheeks. He had enough power in his hand to bunch her shapeless shirt tight in his fist. He clutched so tightly that his fingers poked a hole in the worn fabric, but he did not care. He would not release her.

Her kisses continued. His cheeks, his brow, even his eyelids, before she returned to his mouth. Once there, Brandon did not allow her to escape again. It was done with little thought. Even his consciousness that had stood apart, faded away to nothingness as he possessed her mouth.

On and on it went. Not because he didn't want to touch her breasts or fill her body. If he wanted anything in his entire misbegotten life, it was to thrust himself into her. But he hadn't the strength. He certainly didn't have the technique. He had only the desperate need to touch her.

Her hands were braced on his shoulders, her forearms pressed to his sides. Between them, her breasts were flat against his bandaged chest. He could feel her heart pounding there against his. And when she shifted again, he tasted her tears. He shifted his kiss, pressed his lips to the side of her mouth and her cheek. He licked away the saltiness and pressed light kisses to her closed eyes.

"Why, Brandon?" she gasped. "Why were you in that place? Why didn't you fight?"

Her words flowed past him without meaning. He heard anguish, not a question. He felt confusion without understanding.

"Joey and Hank followed you that night. I sent Joey after you because . . . because I was afraid for you. He and Hank . . . You remember your tiger, don't you? They said you just collapsed. You didn't fight. Why? Why didn't you fight?"

"There were two of them," he said, his voice hoarse from disuse. "I was surprised."

You wanted to die, commented his consciousness from that other place that wasn't his body. *You went there looking for death.*

She pulled back, her eyes widening with hope. "You're talking! You've been silent for days."

He swallowed. "I am not mute," he forced out. He sounded awful.

Her gaze traveled over his face, searching for clues. Her fingers touched him as well, roving over his stubbled cheeks and into his hair. "Do you remember what happened? Do you know where you are?"

He nodded. The other woman had explained. "Martha said Hank found me. And that he got help to bring me here."

"He didn't *find* you. He followed you, all on his own. He kept the thieves from killing you. Then we got you here."

His eyes widened in horror. "You went there?" he gasped. The idea of her in that area of London froze him so deeply he thought he'd never warm.

She nodded. "Do you know where you were?"

"Yes," he rasped. "You should not have gone—"

"Seth helped too. He had to. We couldn't have moved you otherwise. We brought you here to Martha's."

He closed his eyes. Boys had fought for him when he had gone there specifically to die. Scheherazade had risked herself to retrieve him. And now she nursed him and cried over his worthless body. His shame deepened until he thought he would drown in it.

"Why, Brandon? Why did you do this?"

He didn't answer. A few had asked him that question before. Only his brother Michael knew the answer, and even he did not know the full depth of it. *Tell her*, his consciousness urged from the bedside. *Tell her how useless you are. Then she will let you die in peace. She might even help you do the deed.*

Scher pulled back a little farther, her expression shifting to resignation. "Gone mute again, Brandon? Very well, then, perhaps I shall tell you what I have suffered in the days since your folly."

He lifted his hand to stop her, but she was far stronger than he. She pushed his arm away with no more effort than she would need for a pesky fly.

"I screamed when I saw you. You were lying in mud. The stench was overpowering, and your blood was everywhere. I did not even recognize your face. If it were not for your clothes and Hank, who held you in his lap, I would not have known it was you. Not until I was in the dirt with you. Not until I was close enough to taste your blood in the air."

Brandon closed his eyes. No death was pretty. No one smelled good or even left the Earth in angelic serenity. And even if they did, that would certainly not be his end. He tried to turn away. He had no wish to hear what he had forced her to suffer, but she grabbed his face and turned it back to her. She would not let him look away.

"A numbness entered my body. It is a place I go when the pain is too great. I can give orders. It is what I do best. I directed the lifting and carrying of you. We didn't think you'd live for the trip to your home, but we couldn't leave you in the street. I knew of Martha and that she would be grateful for the money you will pay her for your care. I sent for the surgeon and Joey hauled water for cleaning you. We worked the night through without rest, and all the time I wondered if you'd survive."

She was crying as she spoke, the tears flowing freely down her face. And yet there were no sobs or interruption in her words. The tears flowed, but her voice remained clear.

"Hank tried to tell me again and again what happened. It was a nervous reaction, I think, to speak without stop. He didn't understand it any more than I do. And he was afraid, of course. Would you blame him for not protecting you faster? For not warning you of their attack?"

"Of course not," he rasped, horrified that the boy would fear such a thing.

"I told him that. I told him he would be richly rewarded for his efforts. He has slept outside your door ever since. He helps Martha when I am not here. In the morning, Brandon, you *will* praise him. Now that I know you can speak, you will thank him for what he has done for you."

"Yes, of course." He spoke the words automatically, his mind already tallying the ways he might reward the boy. To show such loyalty after less than a week employed. How sad for the child that he had chosen such a poor person as his employer. Then Brandon gripped Scher's elbow. It was the only part of her he could clasp. "But what of you, Scher? Have you been here every night?"

"Yes." She lowered her voice, though she was barely speaking above a whisper. "We have not told anyone your name. People know Martha is being paid to nurse a sick man. They think you are a butcher and Hank is your son. If anyone knew the truth—"

"It would put everyone at risk. I understand." Kidnappings were not so rare, certainly not in this part of town. And if they knew he was more wealthy than a butcher— that he was a titled aristocrat—who knew what would happen in the dark of night? There were those who hated the aristocracy with a passion bordering on insanity. "Martha will be well paid for her efforts."

Scher nodded. "Good."

"But you have not spoken of yourself."

"I cried, Brandon. Even as I issued orders and cleaned the filth from your body, I cried so much. I didn't know I had that many tears, but I did. And when it was done . . ." She took a deep breath. "When I had to return the next night to the playhouse, I cleaned my face, changed into a dress, and pretended as if it had never happened. I have been pretending like that for five days now."

He didn't know what to say. She had cried for him? Worked night and day for the care of him? That knowledge stunned him. Then before he could think of something to say, she was standing up and he grabbed her arm in alarm. He didn't want her leaving him. Not yet!

"Hank!" she called, though she kept her voice low enough not to wake Martha.

The boy popped his head in, his eyes wide and his sandy hair askew. He looked as haggard as a ten-year-old boy could, with pale dirty skin and red-rimmed eyes. Had he looked as such these past few days? How had Brandon not noticed before? Meanwhile, Scher's voice continued without mercy.

"Come on in, Hank. His lordship requires some help and I cannot manage it alone. And I'd be so grateful if you could—"

"Right away, Lady Scher. Wotever you need." Then he glanced anxiously at Brandon. "I'm gentle, yer lordship. I'll be careful."

"Of course you will, Hank," Scher soothed.

Was there to be no end to the humiliation? But he had gotten himself into this situation. The least he could do was not complain about it.

Meanwhile, his gaze slid to Hank, whose gaze hopped nervously between the two of them. "You did well, Hank. And I thank you."

The boys face brightened like the sun, and Brandon felt more shame wash through him. "I tried, my lord. I tried real hard—"

"I know you did," he interrupted. "Your bravery astounds me."

Hank flushed red to the very tips of his ears, and he ducked his head. But nothing could hide the grin. "Thank ye, my lord. Thank ye."

Twenty minutes later, Brandon sent the boy to his bed. The child was still grinning despite his yawns, and Brandon made a mental note to reward him extremely well. Meanwhile, he was alone again with Scher. What would he say to this woman who had saved his life? Who spoke to him with simple honesty such as he had never heard his whole life. "Thank you, Scher. Thank you for everything."

She nodded her head slowly. "You have people who depend on you, Brandon."

She made to move away then, and he grabbed her hand. She could have easily broken his grip, but she stilled. "And what of you, Scher? How can I thank you for all that you have done?"

"I want no thanks."

He tightened his grip. "Then what—"

"I want to know why, Brandon." She rounded on him, her eyes fierce. "Why did you do this? I refuse you, and you rush out into the stews? Why?"

He swallowed and looked away, his mind dark. "I don't know."

"Unacceptable, my lord."

"I don't know!"

"I don't care!" Then she reached out and pulled his chin to her. Her eyes were bright with unshed tears, but he felt no softness in her grip. "You wish to thank me? Then find the answer."

He could have refused her, but he had no will in this. She was right, and it was long past time that he ceased his destructive path. "I will . . . I will find your answer."

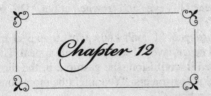

Chapter 12

Brandon was asleep. Scheherazade stepped silently into the bedroom, a quiet nod to Martha as the woman gratefully sought her own bed. The boy Hank was asleep as well, his curled form on a blanket and pillow set beside the fire. It was still cold enough at night that a burning ember was very welcome.

She glanced backward at the fire and noted the full coal bin. A sniff brought her the unusual scent of cooked meat. Chicken, she believed, and her stomach growled in hunger. Pulling out a hard roll, she tore off a piece as she entered Brandon's bedroom. The linens looked clean and fresh. And if she wasn't mistaken, the man had shaved.

She smiled as she sat down in the chair beside his bed. It was clear his temper had improved, but she was surprised that he remained at Martha's. Surely the mighty Lord Blackstone could have moved himself back to his apartments in the posh area of London. Why remain here if he could be infinitely more comfortable there?

She watched as he took a deep breath, then exhaled on a sigh. Mint. He had been chewing mint.

"You are here," he said without even opening his eyes.

"And so are you."

He opened his eyes and frowned at her. "Did you think I wouldn't?"

She shrugged. "I don't know what to expect from you, my lord. I never have." It was part of his appeal. Then when he frowned in confusion, she gestured in the direction of his bachelor apartments. "You might be more comfortable at your own home."

"Would you come visit me in the middle of the night there?"

She shook her head. "Of course not. It would be highly improper and someone would surely tell."

"Then I shall remain here, a butcher in Martha's care."

She tilted her head, pleased despite how inappropriate the feeling was. She should not be happy to sneak off and meet someone who was not her fiancé. "Do not expect that I will continue to do this. It has been a sore trial already, and I am dropping with weariness."

He raised his hand and brushed his thumb against her cheek. "Yes," he said softly. "I regret that."

She shivered at his caress. Everything was so confusing. "I do not know why I keep doing this," she said softly. "Someone is bound to discover it."

"So I can give you the answer I promised."

She lifted her chin. She had been nuzzling his hand like a stray kitten, but now her eyes leapt to his. "Answers, my lord? Truly? I am breathless with shock and curiosity."

"Do not take that tone with me," he said without heat. "I am a man of honor." Then he made a half-choking sound. "Or at least a man who tries to repay his debts. I promised you an answer as to my . . . er . . . motivations, and so you shall have it."

She stilled, her eyebrows raised. And when he still did

not speak, she leaned back away from his hand. She rested against the chair and folded her arms. She would not say anything until he did. But he shook his head.

"It is a hard thing to bare the soul, Scher. Give me a moment of your company first. Tell me what you have been doing. H—how are the wedding plans?"

She smiled at his slight stammer. He did not want to think of her wedding, but he was polite enough to ask about it.

"Do you know," she drawled, "that all of London is agog asking about my wedding plans? The playhouse has had record attendance since my engagement, a record number of brawls too. I cannot tell if we shall register a profit this month because of all the broken crockery."

He frowned, obviously startled. "They are brawling? Why?"

"Because I am either a champion of the people or a grasping shrew."

"And everyone wishes to voice their opinion on your life," he said with a grimace. "I am truly sorry, Scher. I had hoped that it would not become a matter of public discussion."

She tilted her head, looking at his expression. "Truly?" she asked. "You did not hope for exactly this . . ." Disaster? Trial? What word did she put on her nuptial plans? "This spectacle?"

He reached out and stroked the back of her hand. "I always hope I am wrong these days. And I would never wish you pain."

She believed him. "But you are never wrong," she said, knowing that he had predicted everything that had come to pass. There had even been political cartoons drawn lampooning her, and that was nothing compared to the scathing commentary on grasping women that was printed in today's newspaper.

"Do not encourage my pride," he commanded. "But,

yes, it appears that I am right when I expect the worst." He smiled at her and her heart stuttered in her chest. "It is one of the things that I most admire about you, Scher. You still hope, despite everything. You still think . . ." He cut off his words, but what he meant was obvious to her.

"I still hope that I will be happy with Kit."

"You could be," he said as he withdrew his hand from her. "But not in London, I fear. Not here."

He had said that to her before. He had told her to move far away, but she would not leave London. Primarily because she and Kit could not leave the source of their money. He had too little on his own. Besides, it could not possibly be as bad as what Brandon thought.

"Kit is not so inconstant," she said firmly. "He will marry me, and this . . . this notoriety will end."

He nodded, though she could tell he did not truly believe that. Instead, he shifted slightly in the bed so that he could look more fully at her. "Tell me what has happened. Perhaps there is a way to make you and Kit seem less interesting to the public."

She hesitated, trying to judge his earnestness, but in the end, she began to talk. She needed someone to listen, someone to hear how difficult this had been. Kit was in the thick of it with her, but whenever she tried to talk to him about the latest insult, he waved it aside. He had no wish to hear more. He lived it every day, as did she. So she never showed him the newest broadside that pictured her stepping up to the altar while a host of gentlemen bet on the paternity of her child. But she told Brandon about it, as well as all the other humiliations. To be able to talk with someone else about it was a godsend. Especially someone who understood British *ton* better than she.

So she talked, each word like a burden laid down at Brandon's feet. He listened without judgment and offered witty commentary when she faltered. All in all, he made her feel as if he understood. And when she finally finished, his advice was simple if completely impractical.

"Tell them all to go to the devil," he said.

She smiled ruefully. "I wish I could."

He grabbed her hand, trying to impress on her his point. "But don't you see? You can! Tell them that there will be no talk of weddings or class struggles or even babies in your presence." He leaned forward, then grimaced as he pulled on his wound. "You are Lady Scher. I have seen you lay a miscreant down with a single cold stare. I have watched as gentleman after gentleman made unseemly advances, and you simply waved a hand. They were escorted outside immediately."

She nodded. "Yes, of course I have, but that is entirely different."

"Only in terms of scale. Don't you see? You are *Lady Scher*. You have the power of a queen inside the playhouse walls. Of all places, you must make it your sanctuary."

She shook her head, her mind spinning with thoughts. Was it possible? Could she enforce such a rule? "But the ticket sales will drop."

"You have already said that the income is balanced out by the broken pottery and the brawls. How many more people have you hired to control the crowd?"

"Two."

"Then you must factor in their pay as well. Are you truly coming out ahead?"

No. A thousand times no. She looked at him, a new respect for him forming in her mind. "I will do it," she resolved. "I will create a place of peace in my world."

He smiled. "Your home must be your sanctuary, Scher. Wherever it is, you must make sure you have a place to be at peace."

There was an added note of seriousness in his words. Something that told her that he searched for that same thing. Had clearly searched and never found it. She realized her smile had slipped away, as had his. And in the silence, his gaze slid to the door. Was he thinking about a way to distract her? Perhaps he would call Hank and forestall the coming discussion. But she would not allow him to set her aside so easily.

"You have heard my story, Brandon. Perhaps it is time for you to pay your debt."

He swallowed, but to his credit, he did not run. "You said once that we have a connection because we were both betrayed."

She nodded. She well remembered every word of that night. And every caress. But she had been too simple in her thoughts that night. Their connection had more to do with listening to one another, not something that happened in their past. But she did not say that now because he was still struggling with his words.

"I was the betrayer, Scher, and because of me, good people died. It is something that I cannot undo. I cannot even find atonement for those who died. And so . . ." He looked to her, his eyes begging her not to judge him. "I want to die, Scheherazade. I want to end this farce I have become. That is why I left you. Why I wandered in the stews until someone beat me. I did not think that . . ." He gestured weakly to the room. "I just wanted it all to end."

She swallowed. She hadn't expected him to say such a thing so clearly, so firmly. So much of her life had been one endless struggle to survive. Her mother had never been good with money. It wasn't until she took over paying the bills—all the troupe's bills—that she was even able to breathe at night. She knew now that she had enough to pay for her next meal, for a good many next meals. But that had certainly not been the case when she was a child.

"You have so much," she whispered. "How can you wish to end it?"

His eyes were so clear. Even with the light of one candle flame, she saw deep into his dark pupils. An endless well of darkness. She gasped at the sight, stunned by the agony she saw there.

"You have so much," he said, his voice thick but still clear. "Does it give you what you want?"

She shrugged. "I have food. A home. People who care for me."

"And yet you strive for the one thing you can never have."

She swallowed and looked away. "I have spent every day since I was six working for the money to feel safe. I have that now, but there is a safety that can only be purchased with a wedding ring. With respectability."

He released his breath on a heavy sigh. "Marriage will not bring you safety. The world isn't a safe place."

"It will help," she said firmly, though in her heart, she questioned. It was so hard to accept that she would live with this fear all her life. That nothing could take it away. So much better to cling to false hope than succumb to despair.

He seemed to understand her terror as he nodded. "I will not take away your dream."

She shuddered because he had just brought her deepest fear to the surface. But then she remembered that they were speaking about him. So she pushed down the knot of anxiety in her stomach and turned back to him. "And will death bring you what you want?"

His smile was relaxed, so casual as they spoke of his death. "I cannot have what I want."

She arched her brow, silently asking what he *did* want. If he said he wanted her, that without her his life was meaningless, then she would stand up and leave. She would know that he was not speaking honestly and likely never would.

"Honor," he finally breathed. "Just as you can never achieve true respectability, I can never be . . . honorable." His voice hitched before his last word. It was as if he flinched before voicing the thought but forced the word out despite the pain.

She frowned, trying to sort through his words. "Honor for men is not something I have thought much about. For women, it is to maintain virginity outside of marriage. And that"—she shrugged—"that I lost a long time ago."

He gripped her hand, and she knew he wanted to ask, wanted to know her pain. But she shook her head. Her stupidity happened long ago. Or so she told herself.

"I lost my honor in India," he said softly. "I hadn't really thought about honor before then. But having lost it . . ." He sighed. "It is like an emptiness so deep inside me that I am nothing but empty."

"What happened, Brandon?"

He pressed his lips together, and he shuddered. But his eyes never left her face.

"You promised me answers, Brandon."

He arched a brow. "And does that require me to bare my soul?"

She nodded. "Yes, I think it does."

"People died because of me," he snapped. "Good, honest people who trusted me. And then they died. The men, their wives, and their children. Their daug—"

His voice collapsed on the last word, and his eyes teared as he turned away. He turned so hard that he gasped, his skin whitening in pain.

"Their daughters," she finished for him.

He swallowed. "Sons. Daughters. All dead." He turned back to her, his eyes shining with anger and tears. "They were Indian," he said, a challenge ringing in his voice.

She returned his stare with confusion. "They were Indian," she said softly. "Yes? How did they die? Didn't you get your title because of the factory fire? They say you went mad with grief," she recalled. It had been all the talk at the time. "Kit said you ran screaming into the fire, tearing through the flames to help, but you were too late."

"The fire was out by the time I got there. Nothing but ash."

But the grief was real. She could see that even now.

"And it wasn't just the factory," he said dully. "There were homes as well. Families. Children."

She bit her lip. Fires were a huge fear among her set. The great fire of London in 1666 was over a century past, but everyone remembered. "How is it your fault? If you weren't even there?"

He closed his eyes. She thought at first that he wasn't going to speak, but then he did, the words flowing from him as they might from a doll. If she didn't see his mouth move, she would have thought he slept.

"You know, Scher, that you are considered less than a full person by some. Because of your birth, because of your lack of virginity, some believe you are not fully a person."

She knew. She felt it daily. "Am I lacking or are they superior?" she wondered.

"Either way, the end is the same. You are considered less. They believe they are more."

"It is the way things are, Brandon."

"And why you so long to be respectable. So that you are no longer considered less."

She didn't argue. He was right, though the way he said it reinforced that she reached for an impossible dream. After all, some people would always think less of her. She pushed the uncomfortable thought aside.

"Imagine those people in a foreign country, Scher. You know how horrible they are to you here. Imagine how terrible they would be to people who are not English."

She sighed. "That is an ugly thought."

"It happened. It didn't matter that we were merely a handful of foreigners in their country. The English, as a rule, were arrogant, hateful, greedy pigs."

"Surely not all," she said. Then she squeezed his hand. "And certainly not you. Your pain says as much."

"My pain is because I was stupid," he snapped. "Greedy and stupid, willfully blind to . . . everything."

She sighed. "You are not the first person to be stupid in their youth, nor will you be the last. I am sorry that people you obviously loved died in a fire, but Brandon"—she squeezed his hand to soften her words—"this self-abuse is ridiculous."

He whipped his hand away from her, obviously unwilling to give up his agony. "You don't understand," he rasped.

"Of course not. You have not told me more than the sketchiest details."

He turned then to glare at her. His eyes were rimmed in red, though she had not seen any tears fall. "Do you challenge me?" he asked. "To see if I will tell you all?"

She arched a brow. "I do nothing but see to your wounds and sit with you for a time."

"You demanded answers," he snapped.

"And you have expressed nothing but self-indulgent pity. Brandon, either tell me what happened and why it eats at you or be done with this." She leaned forward. Perhaps it was exhaustion, perhaps it was the confusion in her own life, but she was impatient with the games he played with words. "You are in pain, that much is obvious. You believe yourself a fool who has caused people to die." She shrugged. "I cannot speak to that, except that whatever happened, it is over now. What do you build today on the ashes of yesterday?"

"Nothing." His gaze turned to the opposite wall. "Absolutely nothing."

She waited for a time, wondering if he would say anything more. But he remained stubbornly silent. It was his pride, she knew. For all that he was bitterly depressed, his pride stubbornly clung to his pain. But until he chose to release his personal agony, he was no good to anyone. She pushed to her feet.

"You are not worth my time, Lord Blackstone. Good

night." So saying, she left. She heard him gasp behind her. She doubted anyone had ever thought to walk out on him. But she was tired. Bone tired. She had nothing left to give a man who would not fight for his own life.

She walked home quickly. She could tell by the lights in the playhouse windows that someone was still up. Someone sat in the Green Room, though it was well past the hour when the troupe players were abed. She glanced in the window and released a moan of frustration. Kit sat at a table, her account books spread before him.

She must have made a noise. She must have done something because he looked up in surprise and their eyes met through the window. There was no help for it now. She would have to talk to him.

He was up on his feet in a moment, his eyes narrowed in worry. She gestured to the side door then picked her way through the broken glass and trash. He pulled open the door and stood there, hands on his hips as he glared at her.

"Scher! What are you doing out? And dressed like that? I thought you had a headache."

"I did. I do," she responded wearily, annoyed with his curt tone. "But Martha needed some help."

He stepped back as she slipped inside. Then he stuck his head back out the door, looking up and down the deserted alley, as if he expected to see the Prince Regent spying on her. When he pulled back, it was to watch her pull her ugly hat off her head with a pinched look to his face.

"Who is Martha?" he asked.

"She used to be part of the troupe. Had a wonderful hand with costumes. But then she got married and works in a shop."

"So why does she need your help?" His tone was getting surly, and she frowned at him in confusion.

"Her husband died, her eyes blur now, and her hands are none too steady." She folded her arms across her chest. "Why?"

He pursed his lips, his eyes visibly scanning her outfit. "You take quite a risk going out dressed like that. What if someone saw you?"

She blinked, her eyes feeling dry and gritty. "Who would see me? Everyone here knows me. I have been walking about at night like this since . . . well, since I could walk."

"But you cannot do that now that we are engaged."

He took her arm and escorted her back to the Green Room. She didn't want to go. She was tired and too likely to say something she regretted. But there was no help for it. Leaving now would cause a scene which would only keep her up longer. Still, she tried to find a way.

"I'm so tired, Kit. And I still have a headache. I understand that you're worried about my reputation." It was a lie. She didn't understand it at all. She was in her own neighborhood, for God's sake. But she didn't say that. Instead, she kept her tone conciliatory. "I'm so sorry. I'll try to do better—"

"It's not your reputation anymore, sweetheart. That's what I'm trying to tell you. Now that we're engaged, what you do reflects on me."

"I know that, Kit—"

"And my wife simply can't be running around at night dressed like that!"

She lowered her head and kept her voice soft. "I'm sorry, Kit." The words tasted bitter in her throat but she said them anyway. It was easier than sorting through whether she was feeling outrage because he was being high-handed or guilt because she had been seeing Brandon without telling him. Why she didn't just say she had saved his cousin from certain death, she wasn't sure. But she got the feeling that Brandon wasn't ready to let his family know what had happened. So until he chose to notify his relations, she would respect his wishes and stay quiet.

And while she was mulling over her conflicting feelings, Kit gestured her to his table. Even pulled up a chair so she could sit.

"There, there, Scher. No harm done. Let me get you some wine."

"That's not necessary—"

"But you're probably tired and thirsty. And as long as I have you in private, I have some questions to ask you about the accounts."

Scheherazade groaned. "Surely you don't mean now. It's almost four in the morning!"

"Is it?" He narrowed his eyes at her. "Awful late to go visiting."

He had her there. She shot Kit a glare. "Martha used to be with the troupe. She understands how late I work here. And as I was bringing her food, she could hardly complain about what time I brought it."

He cocked his head, his expression becoming a caricature of canny. He really wasn't very good at hiding his emotions, and what she saw now was suspicion. Pure, narrowed-eyed suspicion. "You took her food? Don't you think you have enough drain on the funds here?"

"What? Drain? Kit—"

"Just hear me out," he said, rapidly flipping through the pages of the book. "Look at this number for food and wine. That's for one week!"

"We sell that at twice the price."

"No," he interrupted. "You sell it at three times the price." He gestured at the board that listed the prices per glass. Then he pulled out a sheet of figures. "At that rate, we should be making money hand over fist, but we're not. Where is the extra money going? To people like Martha?"

She shook her head. "The money for Martha came from my own pocket." Her voice was tight, and her head began to pound. "But there are other costs. Spills, for one. Angry customers for another who are always soothed by a free glass of wine."

"That's ridiculous!"

"No, Kit, it's not!" She was fast losing control of her

temper and could not manage to keep her tongue civil. "Do you think I haven't thought about this? Do you think the playhouse turns a profit by accident? You have just now started to look at how we live. Do not assume you can understand us by a few days studying the books!"

"Now, now, sweetie," he soothed. "I didn't mean to suggest that you've done a bad job. By all accounts, you've done an incredible thing here. But now that I'm here, we can start to think larger. Bigger." His eyes started sparkling in delight. "Just look what I have drawn up."

He pulled out a sheet. It was a sketch, done in a rather fine hand. "That's lovely, Kit. Who drew it?"

"I did," he said with a slight flush. "Do you see it? Do you like it?"

"I do," she said honestly. "You have real talent."

He grinned. "Thank you. So you understand what I'm planning, what we could do here!"

Scher frowned, her gaze hopping from his exuberant expression to the sketch in front of her. It was a theater scene with boxes and a stage. She could tell that the stage was too small, as was the space for the floor audience. And the ornamentation on the boxed seats seemed too ostentation for her tastes, but it was a lovely picture nevertheless.

"I'm sorry, Kit. I don't understand."

"It's The Tavern Playhouse. *This* playhouse after a few renovations."

She blinked, her mind at last understanding what he meant. "That's much too grand for us!" she exclaimed. And the expense of renovating to what he wanted? It boggled her mind!

"But that is exactly the thing," he cried, jumping a little in his seat with his excitement. "It isn't too grand. It is exactly grand enough!"

"No, Kit," she said, pushing the paper back toward him. "It's not possible."

"But of course it is. It will take some time, of course.

And careful management, but think of the money we could make—"

"No, no!" she said, wishing she had the words to explain why it wasn't possible. "London already has two grand theaters—"

"We shall outshine them both!"

"But we can't! Not here. Not with our players." The objections lined up in her mind, too numerous to express all at once.

"Then we shall get better players. And you shall see. Once the money begins to roll, everyone will be happy!"

She sighed. "You, maybe. But not Delilah. Not Seth or Joey or anyone else in the troupe. Kit, don't you see? Your plans just aren't possible for us."

His face hardened, his hurt and anger palpable in the room. "You will see," he said firmly as he put away his sketch. "I mean to make these changes, Scher."

"No, Kit—"

"Yes. I didn't want to put it like this. I value your opinion, Scher, but I am in charge now. I will do what I think best."

A chill ran down her spine, the impact of his words hitting her like a club to the head. "You said that I was good with money, Kit. When you proposed, you said you would take my direction."

He straightened. "But I am the man, Scher. And I can see possibilities where you don't."

What he saw was a pipe dream, but he didn't understand that. "It will be a disaster," she said firmly. "And everyone here will suffer for your dreams." She pushed to a stand. "We aren't toys to be pushed around for your games. That is too grand a plan for us. If you do not see that, then . . ."

He stood as well, his expression almost sympathetic. "Then what, Scher? Do you say that you don't want to marry now? Will you give up on being respectable just because you are too prideful to let someone else manage the playhouse?"

"Pride!" she exclaimed. "You do not understand how a troupe of actors works!"

He took a step forward and touched her arms. His caress was gentle and there was pity in his eyes, but he did not soften his words. "You cannot manage the playhouse and raise our children at the same time. *Lady* Scher cannot be a respectable wife and mother." He pressed a kiss to her forehead. "I know this is hard, Scher, but if we are to marry, you must give up the work you do here."

"No," she whispered, stunned to feel the ache in her chest. How she had longed for what he offered. A home, children. "The Tavern Playhouse is my life," she murmured. "I was born in this very Green Room!"

"And now you will finally be able to leave it."

But she couldn't leave it in his hands. Not if he were to run the Tavern Playhouse into disaster! But of course, that was exactly whose hands would be at the reins. A husband automatically owned all a wife's assets. He brushed at her cheeks, and she realized belatedly that she was crying.

"It is late and you are overtired. Plus, we have Lily's tea party tomorrow."

She closed her eyes and her body swayed under the weight of it all. She had forgotten about the countess's party. Another afternoon of being picked at and judged.

He gathered her tight and let her rest on his chest. "You should rest. I want you in your best looks tomorrow. Have you got a new gown?"

"Yes," she murmured, startled to realize that Kit's clothing didn't smell so nice. She was used to the scent of men's sweat. There were times when she felt like she would never get away from the smell. He was cradling her body, holding her as if she could lay her burdens on him, and how she wanted to surrender to the illusion. But she couldn't, she realized with horror. She didn't trust Kit at all.

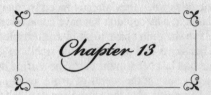

Chapter 13

Morning came late, thankfully, but when it arrived, it gave no mercy. Scheherazade was woken by Delilah, who brought tea and complaints. Her concerns were even written down in a rather ramshackle hand, but the words were clear enough. Kit had been meddling, and the troupe did not like it.

Scher dressed quickly, then went about soothing ruffled feathers. She told everyone she could that she would speak to Kit this very afternoon, that she would explain to him why he was wrong, that she would do everything in her power to keep things running smoothly. No one believed her.

The actors weren't stupid. They all knew that as soon as she married Kit, their lives would fall into his hands. And as happy as they were at her coming change in status, they did not want it to effect their lives. In short, it had taken Kit one week to turn everyone in the company against him and their wedding. By the time Scher was in a hackney on the

way to the countess's tea, her shoulders were bowed almost
to her knees. She had expected problems from Kit's family,
from his aristocratic friends, but never from the troupe or
the man himself. Never had she thought Kit would create
more difficulties when they already faced so many.

And damn it, why couldn't Kit have come by to pick her
up himself so she didn't have to sit in this terrible hackney,
crushing her skirts and picking up the smells of God only
knew what had last been in the cab? She sniffed delicately,
wrinkling her nose at the scents of urine, vomit, and stale
perfume. There was also the strong scent of cabbage. She
had on her own perfume, with extra in her tiny reticule
for after she disembarked, but it would not be enough. A
discerning nose—and she was sure that the countess had
a very discerning nose—would detect every vile scent that
clung to Scheherazade.

She thought fondly of Brandon's high-perch phaeton and
how she had felt when he handed her up. No noxious smells
then, just the sweet spring air and mint. It was ridiculous
to think that her affections could be purchased with a carriage ride, but she had felt especially grand sitting beside
Brandon in his phaeton. Or she had felt grand until they
made it to the park.

The countess's home was in the most reclusive part
of London. Pappy and she had once strolled through the
neighborhood on a particularly fine autumn afternoon. But
someone's butler had spotted their commonplace clothing
and chased them away. What would Pappy think now about
her attending a party at this exclusive address?

Probably that it was all well and good to pretend to
being royalty, but she should never try to walk among them
for good. He was happy to playact at being nobility for an
afternoon, but at the end of the day, he firmly believed
that every man—and woman—had a place in society. She
should not think to rise above it.

And that thought, she decided abruptly, was the last self-indulgent, pitying thought she would have for the rest of the day. Pappy was wrong. As were all the actors in the troupe. She was going to marry into the aristocracy and they could all take their complaints and their ideas of "place" and go hang! She would be respectable. In two weeks time, no less.

So with a sweep of her skirts, she stepped out of the hackney. She took a moment to pay the cabbie and sprinkle perfume across her skirts, then with a determined smile, she climbed the steps to the Countess of Thornedale's front door.

She didn't need to knock. The butler opened the door directly. He sneered at her, his disdain obvious, but she responded with a pertly raised eyebrow. And she held her stare long and hard until she was rewarded with a slight flush to his cheeks. She would pay for that flush, she feared. It was never a good idea to antagonize the butler of an establishment, but at that moment, she didn't care. So she swept into the foyer and allowed the man to take her bonnet and gloves.

She was greeted immediately by the earl. It almost felt as if he had been loitering, waiting here, but that was ridiculous. Why would he be waiting for her?

"Good afternoon, good afternoon, Miss Martin. I am so glad you were able to make it," he said as he brought her hand up for a quick kiss.

"Of course I would come," she said breathlessly as she half stumbled into her curtsey.

"The thing is," he said as she straightened, "I wondered if I might have a word with you about Brandon. Before you go into the tea and all."

"What?" she asked, her mind splintering in panic. "I-I mean," she stammered, "I'm not sure what I could know about Viscount Blackstone that you—"

"Well, he's gone missing, you see," he said as he tugged her down the hallway, presumably to someplace more private. "And I thought—"

What he thought was lost as the butler opened the door to three girls and their mamas. The girls were chattering away, as were the mothers, and the noise in the hallway abruptly became deafening. Then to complicate matters even further, the countess came down from the opposite end.

"Ah, there you are, Michael. And, Miss Martin! You look lovely, my dear. I can see Kit has helped you immeasurably in that regard."

Again, Scheherazade sunk into a demure curtsey, inwardly pleased with her choice of gown. It was a blue one, as Kit said he preferred, made to Brandon's instructions of *not* appearing as a nun's habit. And, yes, she did feel like she looked quite good in it. Meanwhile, the earl had released her hand so she was able to credibly greet his wife, but Scheherazade could not shake the feeling that he expressly wished to discuss more with her. What did the earl know? Did he suspect that Scher had his brother secreted away in a neighborhood his bootblack would disdain to enter?

"Come, come, enough of that," the countess trilled as Scheherazade stayed too long in her curtsey. "Come girls. As it is such a lovely day, I have opened the back terrace to the afternoon. We are having such a gay time of it outside." So saying, she led the way through to the back.

Scheherazade had no choice but to follow, though she felt the earl's eyes on her back. She didn't dare glance at him, but her imagination supplied a dark and rather disapproving stare on his austere face. And then there was no time to speculate as she stepped into a party of twelve, mostly women, all gathered outside.

She saw Kit immediately. He was surrounded by three ladies of various ages. He looked up upon her entrance but didn't spot her until she raised her hand in a wave. His expression lightened and he excused himself from his admirers to come to her side.

"You look lovely, Scher," he said warmly. "I knew that blue muslin was just the thing."

And how lovely it was that he announce to everyone that she had consulted him as to her dress. Especially since she had *not* consulted him. She gave him a pained smile and he chucked her under the chin.

"Chin up, old girl," he said sotto voice. "This will be a lovely afternoon."

Was he trying to be sweet? Or was he truly unaware that everyone was watching him reassure her? "Why, of course it will be," she said with false brightness as she turned to look at the entire group.

"Yes, yes!" laughed the countess. "Do not monopolize her, Kit, especially when I have worked so very hard so she could meet everyone else. Go talk somewhere else, Kit. Let me introduce her around."

And so Scher was neatly separated from her fiancé as the countess walked her about the terrace and even out to the grounds. There were mostly ladies about, all looking at her with a mixture of curiosity and loathing. Scheherazade tried not to be too sensitive at every stiffed greeting or slightly curled lip. Perhaps some of the women were suffering an illness. Perhaps their dresses were too tight. Or perhaps pudgy women dressed in too many flounces should not be so judgmental.

Then there were the men. Two, to be exact, plus the earl, who was sitting on the opposite side of the terrace and staring holes into her back. They seemed polite enough in this setting, but Scheherazade knew them all, as they were occasional visitors to the Tavern Playhouse. She dubbed them young, but tending to pompousness. They were not her allies, that was certain.

"Here is someone you must expressly wish to see, I am sure," said the countess as she walked her to a woman of middling height and soft features. She might have been pretty with her glossy brown hair and big eyes, but the coldness in her expression destroyed all pretense of beauty. "Miss Deidre Sampson," the countess continued. "An old schoolmate of yours from Mrs. Cabot's School for Young Ladies. I invited her expressly to make you feel more at home. Plus, it was thanks to her that I was able to invite another one of your dear friends, though he isn't here yet."

Alarms went off in Scher's mind, but she didn't have time to react as she finally remembered Deidre. She was younger than Scher, of excellent lineage, but possessed no money at all. Mrs. Cabot's school was the best she could afford. But even at five years below Scher in school, the girl had wasted no time in showing her absolute disdain of those with a more suspect lineage. Scher had been a particular target. The girl had been vicious and cunning, and now she sat next to Kit and smiled that horribly false smile. Was it possible the woman had changed from the girl? Scher doubted it but knew better than to express her true thoughts. Instead, she smiled sweetly. Perhaps she could turn Deidre's ways to her advantage.

"How wonderful to meet an old schoolmate. We shared such fun times as girls, didn't we?" And in this way, Scher linked her history with Deidre's. Perhaps the two of them together could turn the tide of aristocratic hostility.

"Mrs. Cabot had such democratic ideals," she said with a sigh. "It is, no doubt, why the school closed. Some concepts are really not meant to be."

Well, no ally there. And clearly Deidre hadn't changed a bit. Scher wasn't discomposed by that for she truly hadn't expected anything different. But she felt sadness that Mrs. Cabot's school had closed. The woman had been kind, and she was directly responsible for educating Scher in accounting and business practices. Without her, the Tavern Playhouse would surely have gone bankrupt years ago.

Meanwhile, Scher had no time to comment more as the countess spirited her around the terrace. And though the participants changed, the discussions took the exact same form. They always began with the weather, which was unseasonably cool, then progressed to one of three choices. First was dresses and that the color blue was overdone. Second choice was a lady's refined education at the overly democratic Mrs. Cabot's School for Young Ladies. And third was about upcoming balls or teas to which Scheherazade had never been invited. All innocuous taken one by one, all absolutely respectable topics, and every moment was designed to point out Scher's lacks.

And then something disastrous happened. Something Scheherazade had not expected at all, and she had been expecting the worst. But this was beyond worst. This was unforgivable.

Charles Barr joined the party. Apparently, he was the other "dear friend" the countess said was coming.

He had gained weight since she'd last seen him, but there was no mistaking his overdressed refinement or the mischievous sparkle in his eyes. She saw the truth now, of course. She knew that his wealth was only middling, his background as a second son of a viscount only average for this company. Of course, she'd known all that when she was sixteen too, but what she hadn't seen then was that his charm covered a calculating soul. That his intelligence was used half on the perfect form of flattery and the other half on how best to exploit his victims. In some dark ways, he reminded her of Kit—all sweet charm and boyish smiles. But at the core, Kit was kind. Charles was absolutely not.

"My apologies, my apologies for my tardiness, my lady," he said to the countess as he bowed over her hand. "My poor mother had one of her spells, you know, so I was delayed. But I am here now, and eternally grateful for this moment of joy you have brought into my life."

Scheherazade knew his mother, had indeed spent a great deal of time listening to tales of his mother's ailments. The lady thrived on her "spells," on creating all manner of illnesses such that all were forced to pity her.

And why, oh why, hadn't she seen that the son's character was not so far removed from the mother's? If she had seen that Charles played the suffering son as perfectly as the mother played invalid, then perhaps she would not have been so charmed.

"And how is your mother?" asked the countess, her face filled with concern.

"She struggles, you know, but I am able to help her as needed."

"And what a great son you are," the lady continued. "But come, this is a time for fun. Miss Martin, come see who I have invited just for you. Deirdre tells me you and Mr. Barr were the best of friends once."

"Why, yes," Charlie picked up, his expression boorishly enthusiastic. "I was her first admirer, you know, when she was sixteen. Not the only one, I am sure, but certainly the most intimate. One never forgets the first, and I am honored to have taken that particular place in her life."

Scheherazade felt her blood run cold. Raw fury could not stop the creeping chill that froze her where she stood. Right here, practically declared for all to see, was her first and only lover. She'd been sixteen and he'd promised her marriage. There had been mistletoe and a proposal. And then he had lifted her skirt and done as he pleased instead. When Christmastide was over, so were any plans for their wedding.

"You were never my friend, Mr. Barr," she said, forcing words out from stiff and cold lips.

"Come, come, my dear!" he chortled. "Of course we were. I still recall that sweet mole on your backside with such joy." He placed his hand on his heart in reverent memory.

She had no mole on her backside. She had nothing of the sort, not that anyone would believe her. She heard the gasps all around, most especially from the countess.

"Good God!" the countess cried with maximum

effect. "Mr. Barr, such topics are not for discussion in this place! You insult me, and I must demand that you leave immediately."

Charles was all apologies immediately. He stammered and bowed. He backed himself out of the terrace. But he never flushed, and he certainly didn't seem surprised at the lady's reaction. In fact, it was a rather poor performance, in Scheherazade's opinion. A badly rehearsed play by bad actors, but it was effective nonetheless.

The Countess of Thornedale had just created a juicy on dit. Scheherazade could hear the gossip already. At a tea to celebrate the engagement of her husband's cousin and Lady Scher, who should appear but the lady's first paramour! He created a scene and was tossed out, of course, but what can one expect when inviting *her* sort to a party? Likely half the gentlemen in London have already enjoyed her favors.

The agony of it was that it was all true. Not that she had shared her favors with half the men in London, but that the countess had indeed found her first and only lover. She turned her agonized eyes to Kit. She saw two things in stark relief. His white face was prominent. And then, of course, down almost out of view, was how Miss Deidre Sampson laid her hand on top of his arm in sympathy.

"Kit . . ." Scher whispered. It was a soft plea, but it did nothing to break him out of his tight-lipped shock. And then the countess was there, all false concern as she fussed over Scher.

"Oh my goodness, oh my. Please forgive the upset. I had no idea he was . . . That he . . . And you . . . Oh dear!"

Scheherazade's brain stopped functioning at that moment. She could see that the trap had been well and fully sprung. Any hope of a place in polite London society was over. Far from supporting them, the Countess of Thorndale clearly indicated her absolute hatred of this marriage. And without the lady's support, there was no hope that she and Kit would redeem the situation by themselves.

So Scher stopped the pretense. She walked over to Kit and firmly gathered his hand from Miss Sampson's. His skin was deadly pale and he moved as if a puppet. Worse and worse, she thought dully, but at least he disengaged from the party.

"Kit, would you mind escorting me home, please?"

He blinked. "Uh. Right. Uh. Not proper, you know. Need a chaperone."

She nodded. "Of course. Perhaps you could walk me down to Hyde Park. I can arrange for a carriage from there."

He swallowed, obviously coming out of his stupor enough to nod. "Yes. Yes, of course." Then he raised his eyes to Lily's. "How did you find him?" he asked.

"Ah, sweet boy," Lily said with what seemed like true regret. "It truly wasn't hard. Not hard at all."

Kit flinched and Scheherazade tightened her grip on his hand. She could not stand it if he deserted her.

He didn't. Then they moved together into the main house, heading toward the front door. He walked in silence, obviously thinking hard. They collected their respective hats and gloves, which necessitated letting go of each other. And in that moment, the earl came bumbling forward.

He moved awkwardly, his face flaming with embarrassment. "Miss Martin," he said. "Blimey this is difficult, but please. My brother, Brandon. Could you help me find him? Out of Christian charity? We are terribly frightened for him."

Scheherazade stared at the earl, stunned that he could ask for her help after his wife had just assassinated her character. Scher lifted her chin, startled to find that a frozen body could still move, could still talk. "My lord, you and your lady wife are no longer invited to our wedding."

And with that, she grabbed Kit's arm and quitted the earl's house. They walked in silence for a block or more. She prayed that he would say something. She wished that

Kit were a man to brush off such a public humiliation and comfort her instead. But no such paragon existed, and Kit was no exception. They were just nearing an idle hansom cab when he spoke, his voice low and rather dull.

"Is it true?"

"That I have had many lovers? No. There was only one, and I was too young to see how stupid it all was."

Kit nodded, then he raised his gaze to hers. "Was it him?"

She didn't want to answer. She wanted to lie and deny it all. "Yes," she said.

He touched the back of her hand, the caress exquisitely gentle. "Were you forced? Was it . . . rape?"

Tears flooded her eyes. How did she explain? How could she justify how dumb she had been? "He said he loved me. He said we would get married."

His hands fell away, first one, then the other until he stood before her with his arms hanging at his sides. "Charles Barr," he said dully. "My name shall forever be paired with that snake."

There was nothing to say to that. Nothing but to stand there and wonder futilely how she could redeem the situation. Now, twenty minutes after the fact, she thought of a dozen ways she might have put Charles in his place. She might have screamed that she had no mole on her backside, and he was a lying cad. She might have pulled any number of the ladies into the necessary room and proved to them that her bum was pristine white.

But she hadn't thought of that. And she doubted that would have helped anyway. Neither could she think of anything to say to Kit. So she remained silent, even as he opened the door to her and handed her inside.

"Oh, Kit," she said in the last moment. "Kit, I'm so sorry about this."

He flashed her a weak smile. He didn't say it wasn't her fault. He didn't even tell her he didn't mind, that he should have expected this when he proposed to her. He didn't do any of those things. He simply closed the door and gave directions to the cabbie.

She watched him as the hansom began to move. He stood at the side of the road watching her, his shoulders hunched and his expression morose. Her heart broke at the sight. He was supposed to be the exuberant one. Wasn't that what he said when he proposed? That she needed his lightness? How sad he looked then. How mortified.

She fell back against the squabs and looked down at her hand. Her engagement ring seemed to stare back at her, mocking her in its very dullness. The diamond was small, but she had polished the metal until it gleamed. What a foolish girl she was believing this was possible. Kit had not cried off, but his last expression haunted her. His face—that look—it was of a man suddenly tallying losses. It wouldn't be long now. The countess and his mother had won.

She swallowed, fighting the tears. She ought to be the one to cry off and save him the pain. They weren't right for each other on so many levels. She saw that now. And even if she didn't, the memory of his face said everything he hadn't. In just a short time, she had made him look morose. What would it be like in two months? Two years?

With sudden resolve, she pulled off the engagement ring. It slid off too easily, as if even the ring knew it would never be. And then, finally, the tears began to flow.

Chapter 14

Brandon was glad he'd bothered to shave when Scheherazade came in. She'd been crying, he saw that immediately. Then he saw her beautiful blue dress and remembered Lily's tea. Bloody hell. Last, he noticed that she didn't wear her engagement ring. Her left hand was conspicuously naked. He struggled to sit up, torn between anger at his brother's wife and elation that the engagement with Kit appeared to finally be over.

"You're awake," she said needlessly when she entered his room.

"You've been crying," he returned. Then he wondered exactly where his smooth tongue had gone. Wasn't he the one who could charm a woman into anything? He'd been told that in India a dozen or more times at least. Of course, a lot of things had been true in India that had since deserted him.

Scheherazade attempted a cheery smile. It failed miserably to meet her eyes. "A surly temper is a sure sign of improvement."

"So is an appetite. Tell that woman Martha to feed me something more edible than gruel."

Her smile warmed, though not enough to reassure him. "Food needs to be paid for, Brandon." She sat down in the chair beside his bed. "Is there a reason you have not removed yourself from 'that woman's' care?" Her eyes narrowed. "Why are you letting your family worry about you?"

He frowned. "Who is worried?"

A flash of fury twisted her features, but she smoothed them soon enough. "Kit has asked after you."

"And Michael no doubt." He reached out and touched her hand. "What happened? Was it Lily's tea?"

She nodded miserably and looked away, but not before he caught the sheen of tears in her eyes. She said nothing more, and he knew better than to press. She would tell him in her own time as long as he kept quiet. But it was a hard wait. Especially as he could do no more than touch the edge of her fingers with his own.

"I want to hold you," he said softly. The words were out before he realized how inappropriate they were. She would see him as a cad pushing for favors when she was at her weakest. "I-I'm sorry," he stammered. "I should not have said that."

She turned back to him, but her eyes were looking at something long distant. "When I was little, I used to curl up on Pappy's bed and read. I liked his tiny room and the smell of his sheets. I would wake in the morning curled into his side, my book laid neatly on the floor by my shoes."

"You slept nights with a man in the troupe?" he frowned. "What must your mother have thought?"

"I don't know that she ever found out. And even if she did . . ." She shook her head. "I spent all the time I could with Pappy. He was my father. Not my real one, of course, but in all other ways. Besides, Mama was more concerned with Cleo."

He frowned. "Your sister Cleopatra."

The corners of her mouth turned up in a vague smile. "My mother liked dramatic names." Then her expression faded. "Broke my mother's heart when she died. Cleo had the beauty and the talent to be a great actress."

"Whereas you have the intelligence to make the playhouse a profitable business. Is it heartless for me to say that I believe your mother undervalued you?"

She looked at him then, really focused on his face rather than staring vaguely in his direction. "That was terribly heartless," she said with a soft smile. "And Pappy used to say it too."

"And I am sorry for the loss of your sister. Between the two of you, the company could have done great things."

She shrugged, and her eyes brightened just the tiniest bit more. "She was born to play the great roles. But I don't know that our little playhouse would have satisfied her for long. She started talking about the Royal by the time she was eight."

"Isn't that what childhood is for? Grand plans? Great dreams?" And how quickly adulthood strikes them down.

She flushed and looked at her hands. "Kit has grand plans for the playhouse. He wants to remake it to rival the Royal."

What a disaster that would be! London already possessed two grand theaters. It would never support a third. He searched her face, pressing her to speak her mind. "And what do you think?"

Her lips quirked. "That he is young." She dropped her head into her chest. "I am so tired, Brandon. I don't know what to do."

He moved as quickly as he was able, grimacing against the pain. He slid to the side. The bed was large enough without his shift, but he wanted her to feel as comfortable as possible.

"Come lie down, Scher."

"I couldn't," she said, though he could already tell it was a token protest. She was hurting deep in her soul. She needed to return to that safe haven of childhood in Pappy's bed.

"I won't tell," he said. "And you are perfectly safe," he lied. He could never be sure of what would happen this close to her. Could he ever touch her and not want more? He tugged on her hand. "Come on."

She leaned forward, lifting a knee to climb onto the bed. Then she paused to grimace at her dress. "I will crush it."

"You could always take it off."

She flashed him an annoyed expression, and he immediately backtracked.

"It was crushed already, Scher. For once, don't think about propriety or other people or anything beyond this moment. Climb in. Close your eyes. Let yourself rest."

She did, though he could tell she thought she shouldn't. But the lure of lying down, of curling into herself on a man's bed was something she couldn't resist.

He was careful not to touch her. He had lifted himself up on the pillows and she settled low, facing him, such that not one curling lock of her hair met his raised arm. Two tiny inches separated her from his side, and he thought this was how she probably slept with Pappy. A little girl in a tight ball against his side or maybe even his back. How angelic she must have appeared, dark lashes against a child's pure downy skin. How beautiful she was now, though her lashes darkened the smudges beneath her eyes, and this close he could see the light freckles that dotted her cheeks.

"I won't let him do it," she said as she tucked her hands beneath her cheeks.

"Do what?" he asked. His fingers twitched with the desire to stroke her hair off her forehead.

"I'm going to cry off. I won't let Kit destroy the troupe or the playhouse," she returned without opening her eyes.

"Grand dreams are all well and good, but he is playing with our lives."

He noted that she said "our lives" not the actors' lives or even the company's life. As much as she longed for respectability, she still identified herself as one of the troupe.

"I believe you," he said softly. And if that was the excuse she gave for the end of her engagement with Kit, then he could allow her the deception. "Kit is a fool," he said with real feeling.

"Kit is young," she said softly. "And we have all been young before."

He couldn't stop himself. He arched his near hand down to stroke her hair off her cheek. Her lips curved in acceptance and she snuggled a little tighter to his side. Not yet touching, but not so far away either. An inch left between them, maybe less. And he was rock hard with the awareness of her.

"The countess invited Charles Barr to her tea."

Scheherazade spoke in a whisper, and he wondered if he had heard her correctly. What did that ass Charles Barr have to do with anything?

"He's grown fat and ugly. I don't know if that makes me feel better or worse, but he still dresses in the best style. And I think his smile is the same, though I didn't see what was underneath it before. I didn't see that his eyes are so cold."

His fingers stilled on her cheek. She had said "before." She hadn't seen that before.

"Why did Lily invite Charles to the tea?" he asked slowly.

"To humiliate me. To embarrass Kit. And it worked." She curled into a tighter ball. He could tell by the tension in her back that she held back her tears.

He spread his fingers, caressed her neck and shoulders. If he could, he would pull her right to his heart and cradle her there forever. "I'm so sorry, Scher. I'm so . . . sorry."

Why weren't there better words to use? A better way to say how deeply sad he was for her?

"He was the answer to my prayers," she continued. "I was sixteen. I should have known better. After all, I'd heard about men like him. And didn't some of the actresses try to warn me? Stupid. So damn stupid."

He was the one then, Brandon realized. The man who had taken her innocence. "No one is smart at sixteen." He reached his other hand around, trying to move protectively about her without seeming to. "He said he loved you and would take you away from your life," Brandon guessed. "He offered you everything you've ever wanted." He leaned down and pressed a kiss to her forehead. "It wasn't your fault."

She broke down then. Her sobs came hard, with a clenching of muscles as she tried to bury herself into the mattress. He could do nothing but hold her while her body shook. And as he lay uselessly beside her, he silently raged at Lily and that bastard Charles. He tarred them both with the same feather: the man for despoiling an innocent, and his sister-in-law for doing it again and so publicly. But in the meantime, Scher was still sobbing, her cries sounding like the release of a dam. Years of pain flowed out of her with every tear, and he wasn't in the least bit surprised to feel wetness on his own cheeks. He understood regrets. But whereas he had engineered his own downfall, she had been unwillingly duped.

He leaned forward and gathered her into his arms. It pulled at his wounds, but he barely even noticed. All his thoughts centered on her. And drawing her up enough that she released her pain into him and not the mattress.

"Come to me, Scheherazade," he said. "Let me hold you."

She resisted at first, as he knew she would. But in a moment, she reached out for him and wrapped her arms around his torso. He drew her up and back such that she lay on his chest, her arms a tight band that was both painful and so exquisitely wonderful that he could barely breathe.

She trusted him. She trusted him enough to climb into his bed and pour out her pain in his arms. That was a wonder to him, a miracle that he would do nothing to disturb.

It ended all too soon. Her sobs eased, her shudders slowed, and her body relaxed. She wasn't asleep. There was too much tension in her for sleep, but she was more at ease than she had ever been in his presence.

He didn't speak. He stroked her shoulder and even pressed a kiss onto the top of her head, but he didn't speak. He didn't know what to say. And then, unexpectedly, words flowed from his lips. Soft confessions spoken to the air above her head. And yet, every word, every thought was for her.

"I left for India when I was twenty-three. As a second son, I had no interest in war, but in commerce? In a foreign land? That intrigued me, and the money I could make there intrigued me even more. I went as an investor, but also as a worker. I would see to it that the money I put in would multiply a thousand fold."

She was listening. He could tell by the way she lifted her head the tiniest bit, cocking an ear to hear him better. Her mind had left her own misery to learn about his. And if confessing his sins distracted her for even a moment, then he would tell her all.

"We made our money in an Indian factory, weaving and dying cloth that was sold back here in England. Our only competition was a group of dyers. Artists really, and they knew how to make this color of blue that was exquisite."

He fingered the edge of her dress. How appropriate that she wore nearly the exact shade that had cost him so dearly.

"It was my task to hire the head dyer, the artist who had designed that most beautiful color. If he worked for us, then we would have the secret and the best fabric in the world."

"He didn't want to work for you, did he?" Her voice was rough from her tears, but he could hear her well enough. And her words proved that her mind was as sharp as ever.

"I offered him triple what the other dyers were paid. I became his friend, had meals in his home, played silly games with his children."

She shifted against his side, straightening enough to look up at his face. "The fire," she whispered, horror in her expression. "They say you got your title because of heroism trying to rescue Indians in a fire."

He rolled to his back, startled to realize how painful talking about this was, even now. It felt as if it had been yesterday. The wounds to his hands and face still burned as he remembered tearing through the debris, the agonizing shame. She started to raise up off him, but he held her close with his right arm. In truth, he was the one clutching her, not the other way around.

"Tapas would not come to work for us," he said. "How could he work for so much money when we paid his friends so little?"

"Did he work for someone else?" she asked.

"Worse. He put together a group of his fellow artists— dyers and cloth makers with incredible skills—and he started his own company."

She shuddered. "Did you burn them out?"

He looked down at her eyes, seeing the wide shock in them. He should nod and tell her the lie because it was so much easier than the truth. But he couldn't. "If we had, then they would have never given us the secret dying techniques. We needed that formula."

She frowned. "So what did you do?"

"They had skill but little money. We had money but no skill. I convinced them to work together with us. A joint venture. It took months of convincing. I had to prove to them that I was just like them, an honest hardworking man.

I dressed like they did, I attended their festivals and their market, brought expensive gifts to their children."

"They came to know you. They trusted you."

He touched her cheek, wiping away the streaks her tears had caused in her makeup. "We signed the papers. We had a grand celebration. Then Tapas showed me the formula. He was smart. He told me and only me. He didn't trust anyone else."

She sighed. "Who did you tell?"

"Charles Cornwallis, Marquess. My superior in the company." He made no excuses for his stupidity. The terrible thing was that Cornwallis seemed no different than any other Englishman overseas. He had a wife, a fondness for wine, and a genial disposition. Nothing in his manner that would indicate ruthlessness. Nothing except a slight dismissiveness of foreigners, a deeply rooted belief that the English were superior. That was bad enough, but Brandon realized now that the man didn't even consider the Indians real people. That was what created the monster.

He felt her hand on his cheek, a warm presence as she drew his attention back to her. "What happened?"

He shrugged, pretending to be casual when the very words sliced new pain into his mind. "I don't really remember. It was a . . . a celebration. I had been drinking. Cornwallis got me to explain the process. I have a good memory for facts and figures. I got the formula right, I know it."

"Of course you did. You'd been working for just that thing for months."

"Then he offered me another drink. What was one more? But there was opium in it. I was already drunk enough that I didn't notice the taste. I woke up two days later, long after the damage was done."

She frowned. "The fire. I thought you were burned in the fire as you tried to rescue . . ." Her voice trailed away.

"The Indians? Yes, I know that's what everyone believes,

but it's a lie. I woke up after the factory had burned to the ground. After Tapas had died when his home burned in an ancillary fire. They lived close to the factory."

She paled. "His wife? His children?"

"All dead save one. I went insane when I heard. One of the boys found me. A child of a different dyer discovered me in an opium den and told me everything. I didn't believe him at first, but then I went to the factory."

"You were mad with grief," she said. "That's what Kit said."

He snorted in disgust. "I tore through the rubble, screaming out my horror. I knew exactly what had happened. I had been played by the company. They let me befriend those people, they used me and them to discover the secret to their cloth. And when they had it, they killed them all and left me to rot in an opium den."

"My God," she gasped. "Could they really have done that? Couldn't it have been an accident?"

"A horrible, unfortunate accident?" he said, trying to not let mockery enter his tone. He knew that was the story, that was what everyone believed. "No," he said softly. "We did it. You have no idea the power they have there. What people will do just because they can."

"But it wasn't your fault, Brandon. You didn't know."

"Merely stupid rather than evil. Tapas and all the other artisans are still dead. I haven't touched a drop of alcohol since." He swallowed, and he allowed his focus to narrow to her breath against his side. The expansion of her ribcage, the gentle contraction back. Within seconds, he was breathing with her, timing his every inhale and exhale opposite to hers. As her breath expanded, his shrunk, and the reverse. So that he could pretend they shared the most basic of functions together. And in that sweet state, he was able to explain the rest.

"I was loud and very angry. I told them I would expose

what they had done, I would tell everyone in England, I would scream their evil to anyone who would listen."

"They hurt you to keep you silent." It wasn't a question, but he looked at her in surprise. "I cleaned your wounds, Brandon. I saw the scars."

Fists. Knives. Even threatened to shoot him. "They could burn a factory to the ground, murder Tapas and his friends, but they couldn't bring themselves to kill the son of an earl. Not when they had a more effective weapon."

He wondered if she could guess what they used to silence him. It didn't take her long. "They gave you a title, hailed you as a symbol of England's great charity to the Indians. Made it known here and abroad that you lost your mind in that fire."

"It is a small title, the lands mostly swamp. The line died out and no one cared. It was an easy thing to give me and a sensational story."

"And no one to believe the abuses that you saw. The horrors that were done to those poor people."

She understood. He could see it in her eyes, feel it in her body. He pulled her tight and pressed a kiss to her forehead. How wonderful it was to be with her like this. To tell her his sins and not be reviled.

"You must have refused at first. I know you," she said. "You would not have accepted anything from them."

He smiled. She was right. But days in jail showed him how useless his struggle was. He could do nothing from inside a cell. "Logic was on their side. The story was already out. Any objection I had would be seen as further proof of my madness. And with a title I would have a seat in the House of Lords, a place to create change."

"And your money too," she said. "They would hold back your money unless you accepted. You could be impoverished and insane or titled, wealthy, and—"

"And yet another shining example of British manhood."

Her eyes welled with tears. "Oh, Brandon, it is not like that. You are a good man!"

His emotions were not proof against her sympathy. He buried his face in her shoulder, the shame threatening to consume him alive.

"Brandon—"

"They died. They burned." He gripped her shoulder, would not let her move to look at him. "And I have a title and money. So much money."

"But you give it away. Do you think I have not heard? Do you think you could give away thousands of pounds in London and I not know it?"

It wasn't enough. It was never enough.

"The Marisa Orphanage," she said. "Such an odd name. Was that one of Tapas's children?"

"His wife. There are orphans in India too. She wanted to do more for them."

She eased him back, forced him to face her. "A good name. It is where you really found Hank."

Brandon grimaced. "I should have known you would figure it out."

She leaned close, pressed her cheek to his and her mouth to his ear. "I know, Brandon. I know that you are a good man. I know that despite all, you deserve your title and your wealth. And that you honor Tapas's memory by what you do and say."

"No one will listen to me. No one believes any Englishman could behave so vilely."

She pulled back just enough to look at him. "But you have a plan. You have been working on a possibility."

She was so beautiful, looking at him like that. With faith in her eyes. "There is a man," he said softly. "A great man, a great orator. William Wilberforce."

She nodded. "The champion of the black slave."

"He believes me. He understands."

She smiled. "See. You will make good. You will—"

"It's not enough. It's never enough."

She was silent a long moment, and he saw emotions flicker through her eyes too fast for him to follow. He saw pain, but he also saw a well of hope that had been so long absent in his life. It was what defined her, he realized. She hoped for a respectable life. She hoped that her past would not cripple her present. She hoped that he could live up to the man he wanted to be.

"I love you, Scheherazade. I have loved you since the first moment I saw you."

"You didn't even know me."

"I did," he said. He stroked her face, touched her cheek, brushed his thumb across her lips. "You are hope, Scheherazade. You give me and everyone else the heart to carry on."

She blinked, obviously stunned by his words.

"Let me touch you, Scher. Let me . . ." How he wanted to please her, to express his love for her in the only way he knew how. "I won't take you, Scher. I won't. But—"

She kissed him. Her mouth swooped down so fast, so urgent, that he could do no more than gasp in surprise. But that changed in a moment. In less than a second, he wound his arms around her. He tugged at her gown with his fingers and took control.

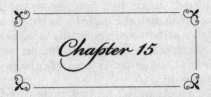

Chapter 15

He said he loved her. Scher knew it was a lie. Or more precisely, it was his truth at this particular moment. What else would a man in his sickbed say to the woman who oversaw his care? Of course he loved her. She was the reason he was still alive.

And yet, it didn't seem to matter. When he gazed at her like that, Scher felt like a goddess. She felt all powerful and wholly loved. Of course she would kiss the man who gave her that. And of course she would let him open her gown and touch her however he willed.

His kiss was so amazing that she didn't at first know what else was happening. She knew she initiated the kiss. She stretched up and pressed her lips to his. They had kissed before, so she knew to open her mouth to him, knew his swift possession with tongue and teeth.

Always before, he had taken his time. Toying with the seam of her lips, nipping at the edges until he slid almost slyly inside. This time he thrust into her almost before their flesh touched. His tongue delved inside, pushing against her powerfully, thrusting again and again while she arched her neck to open herself to him.

He was taking her in her mouth, she realized. He was pushing himself inside her, thrusting—owning—every part of her mouth until she tingled with the joy of it. She nearly laughed at the wonder, especially as she began playing back. She nipped at his tongue, pushed her own tongue against his teeth, and gasped in shock when he pinched her nipple in response.

She pulled back, arching her back as she gasped for air. The buttons on the back of her gown were undone. The arms of gown and chemise had been pushed down on one side, enough that the fabric was loose around her breast. Which gave him room to pinch and abrade her nipple with the fabric.

His hands were large as they shaped her, but she wanted to feel more. She wanted more, and so she shifted, easily slipping her arm out of its constraints so that half of her was bared to his touch. His eyes burned as he looked at her, and she held her breath. When had a man looked at her like that? With desperation and hunger?

She felt his touch on her skin, reverent even as he pinched and teased. He felt hot, or perhaps it was her own skin that was too heated to contain. Either way she trembled at the sensation, her breath coming in short gasps.

He rolled forward, pressing his mouth to her neck for kisses from just beneath her jaw down to her collarbone. His hands squeezed her, but it was the scrape of his nail against her nipple that kept her mind blank to all but the constant, building sensation. Each brush against her peak was like an expanding tingle that went deep into her chest. Soon every rub had her opening her front to him just to get more room to feel. She arched her head back; she helped him pull the rest of her clothing down. She wanted more and more of the blanking white sensations.

Lightning, she thought. His touch was like lightning flashing brighter, delving deeper, and soon she would burn like the sun.

He was drawing her higher on his body, silently urging her to rise up. She did as he wanted, knowing where he was heading. But her dress was too tight, her knees not well placed. With a curse of frustration, she undid the last of the buttons of her gown, pushing it down to her hips. But the chemise was too tight and she tugged at it in impatience to no avail.

It didn't matter. He pulled her forward so that his lips were finally at her breast, suckling in a rhythm that built the flashes of light in her mind. The firestorm of sensations continued at her breasts and deeper inside. Her entire body felt liquid with desire, and that liquid was quivering in a faster rhythm.

She felt his hands bunch at her back, the muscles of his arms tightening around her. Then she heard a steady rip as he tore her chemise apart and dragged it away. She felt the fabric pull at her belly, rubbing against her skin until it was gone and she felt so free!

She wanted him to touch her everywhere. Her belly, her thighs, her woman's core. She had felt desire before. She had known the moistening of female flesh. But never had she wanted as deeply as she did now. Never had she felt as adored as he returned to tonguing her nipples. And the quivers inside her deepened to ripples.

This was magical! she thought at the very same moment some sane part of her mind screamed that she ought to stop. "A little more," she said. "Just a . . . More."

Her gown was in the way. It restricted her knees and interfered with her balance. She was kneeling on the bed beside him, and he pushed her backward away from him.

"Lie back," he urged. "Let me get this off you."

"We shouldn't," she said as she did as he bid.

"Just feel," he said as he worked the gown over her hips,

pulling her legs up. She felt him gasp as he worked, and she belatedly thought of his wound. She tried to straighten up, to bring back some sanity, but there was nowhere to press her hand for support. His work on her dress had tipped her upside down so she was lying head down on his bed. The only place to support herself was on his hips. She had to stretch across him, to place her hand on his opposite side, which tightened the sheet across his groin and clearly outlined his rigid member.

She had never touched a man's member, not with her hand. And not when it was straining upward, even through the sheet. Unable to resist, she ran her hand along its length.

"It's so hot," she whispered. She had not expected such heat.

He groaned as he fell backward. She wasn't sure if it was because he finally tossed her gown completely aside or because of her caress. She looked at his face, saw that his skin was flushed, his mouth parted, and his eyes dark.

"I don't want to hurt you," she said.

"Lie on your side, Scher. Let me do this for you."

Her quivers were fading. Sanity was returning too fast. She lay naked reversed. Reversed!

"Do you know what I want to do, Scher? Do you understand—"

"Yes," she gasped out. She had talked to the actresses at length. She had a thorough education in the variety of positions before she was twelve. But knowing and experiencing were vastly different. And just the idea of what he wanted to do had her face heating to flame.

His hand was between her knees, trapped between her compressed legs. His fingers flexed, but his hand couldn't move.

"Have you ever experienced pleasure before? Do you know anything but pain in coupling?"

She swallowed. "Kissing is very nice."

"And the rest?" he pressed.

She looked away, slowly lowered her face to rest against his thigh. It was a surprisingly comfortable position given the awkwardness of what they discussed.

"Scher," he said gently. "If you don't want to talk about it—"

"It hurt," she pushed out. "It always just felt big. And . . . and wrong. We weren't married, so that was why—"

"It has nothing to do with whether or not you were married, Scher. He took no time with you." He leaned across and pressed his lips to the outside of her thigh. And then he did it again, opening his mouth farther to curl his tongue in a circle against her flesh.

She liked the way it felt. She liked what he did and closed her eyes to relish it more.

"I want to please you, Scher. I want you to feel what I can do for you."

She bit her lip. Oh, how she wanted it. She was wet and her legs were already relaxing. But it was wrong, wasn't it?

"Pull my leg toward you," he said against her thigh. "My wound. I can't move easily . . ."

She pulled back immediately. And then, at his direction, she tugged on his far hip, helping him roll onto his side. "Brandon—"

"Do you know what the scent of a woman does to a man?" he asked as he pressed his face back to her leg. He inhaled deeply, his eyes closed in reverence even as he lifted her top leg. She knew she shouldn't allow it. She knew she should be strong and moral and respectable.

But she wasn't respectable. Hadn't that been impressed upon her this very afternoon? Why not act the wanton everyone assumed she was. Why not allow what she so desperately wanted? Meanwhile, Brandon was kissing higher on her thigh.

"Put your hand on me, Scher. Feel how I react."

The sheet had pulled free as he moved, so she was able to tug the fabric away. And there he was, naked except for the bandages wrapped around his abdomen. She reached forward slowly, laying the palm of her hand across his organ. Heat seared through her, and his organ leaped into her caress. The skin was softer than she expected, smooth against her palm. But beneath the thin layer of skin, he was like a rock.

She knew the actresses engulfed their men with their mouths, but her angle was wrong even for gripping him with her hands. So she contented herself with stroking him, with exploring the length and texture of him. The mushroom head was wet and smooth. The girth was not perfectly round as she'd expected, but a little wider across the sides. And as she explored, she pretended to not notice that his mouth moved along her thigh, that he lifted one of her knees so that he could kiss the inside of her bottom leg. He was so close to her core that she ought to pull away, but she didn't.

He pushed her upper leg back, and she bent her knee so that she could open herself completely to him. His fingers were stroking her hair, rubbing first in a circle, then deeper. His hands were large, so it was easy for him to push her wider, and she felt her belly contract and her thighs tighten as she scooted closer to him on the bed.

Her breath caught on a gasp the first time he tongued her, not on her skin, but so deep into her curls. Compared to the other sensations, this was like a hard, wet push of light against her groin. A miracle of sensation, and she wanted him to do it again.

He took his time, using his fingers again to burrow, to open, to expose. And then he did it again. A flick this time. And then two more flicks in rapid succession.

She cried out. Her body was again that liquid pool of light, and the ripples were sudden waves with every touch of his tongue. The sensations were already so much that she could barely contain them. She pressed her face to his leg as a way to quiet herself, to contain what she felt.

Instead, it brought the scent of his organ to her mind, and the length of him right there. Right . . . there . . . She pressed her mouth to it. She needed some way to share with him, and this was it. She opened her lips and tongued him just as he had tongued her.

But then he was pushing her down, shifting more of his weight onto her top leg such that she had to roll back. His tongue continued to probe her, to stroke, and she widened her legs in response. Then he pulled back enough to press words into her thighs, muffled but audible enough.

"I cannot reach you, Scher. Touch your nipples for me."

She blinked, dazed by what he did with his fingers as he slowly pushed one inside. It did not feel wrong. It felt so wonderful, especially as he drew it out and then pushed in again.

"Can you touch yourself for me, Scher? Let me see it, please?"

He sounded so earnest that she did as he bid. She put her hands on her breasts, and lifted them to the ceiling.

"How does it feel?"

"Like light," she said. "Tingling light."

Then he pushed two fingers inside her, thick and hard. She groaned as she tweaked her nipples.

"God, you are beautiful."

She didn't see how that was possible, but she was too far gone to care. He made her feel beautiful. He made her feel exquisite!

He rolled his thumb up and across her flesh. Oh, she had never felt that! Not like that with a thick pad high and a hard thrust inside.

She arched, the ripples now becoming waves that pulsed inside her. She felt him move again and then there was his tongue. He used it in quick motions, pushing, stroking, exploring. It seemed random at first, but she didn't care. The waves were growing, expanding, and pulling her entire body in.

"Come on, Scher," he said against her skin. "Surrender. To me."

There was no thought except for *yes*. Her hands fell away from her body. She had nothing to hold on to as she undulated beneath his tongue. Then he began to suck. He kept his fingers inside her, moving as best he could. But it was his lips that absorbed her as he alternated between sucking and tonguing. The pull was incredible. Then a push, followed by a pull. Push. Pull. Not fast enough. Not fast enough!

She moved beneath him, her mind and body gone from her. She was the wave, powerful and complete.

Flick! Flickflickflick!

Bliss!

God, she was the most amazing woman! She had barely touched him, but he had exploded like a boy just from the sight of her pleasure. She had writhed against him and the look of shock and awe on her face had tipped him over the edge. He was a mess, but damn if he cared.

"Have I killed you?" he asked, half in jest. She lay so still, her eyes shut, her body languid and still open.

"Shouldn't I be asking you that?" she mumbled. Then she frowned and her eyes popped open. "Are you hurt?"

"Not in the least," he lied. "Though I would appreciate a cloth or something." In his own home, he would have used the sheets to clean himself, then ordered a fresh set. But he was not at home, and so he was forced to be neat.

She pushed herself upright, scanning his body and his mess. He felt his face heat, not to mention his neck and chest and God only knew what else. But the pain was lapping at the edge of his consciousness now. He was holding it back by sheer force of will, but his every breath brought it closer. He knew better than to try to stretch even to reach the far side of the bed, much less his washing cloth.

She smiled in understanding—and no small amount of embarrassment of her own—before rolling off the bed. It was not a graceful movement. She was still too boneless, though she regained her balance and a sense of purpose quickly enough. Still, it was a joy to watch her move, her breasts bobbing in front of her, her legs wobbly from what he had done.

"When I am better, I will teach you such things."

She looked at him a long time at that. He saw her expression slowly shift from languid to shuttered. It probably took only a second or two, but it felt like eternity. An eternity when he saw her slip away from him and yet he could do nothing to prevent it.

"It will be better next time," he said, trying to will her to look at him.

"It was wonderful," she said softly. There was a washbowl nearby and a cloth, which she wet then wrung out. Her eyes remained focused on her task, her body unnaturally stiff.

Fear trembled in his mind, but he refused to heed it. She was simply shy, he told himself. This was obviously so new to her. She returned to the bed, and when she would have cleaned him, he stopped her.

"I can manage," he said gently as he took the cloth from her. He did what was needed, and all the while he wondered what she was thinking. "I should be doing this for you. If I had done the proper thing, I would be drawing you a bath right now and feeding you sweetmeats."

She took the soiled cloth from him, then returned to the basin. Then with an apologetic smile, she grabbed her clothing and ducked behind the privacy screen. He heard her perform her own ablutions and then dress, and the sounds of fabric rustling brought his imagination to life. Damn these wounds! If he weren't an invalid, she wouldn't be dressed for days. Weeks!

"I know that this is new to you, Scher. I know you will take your time thinking about it. And I must soon return to my life. I have missed the last session of the House of Lords, but there are still people I need to talk to, if only to be scorned and ridiculed."

"Surely they are not so cruel," she said from behind the screen. Her voice was higher than usual, a little bit louder too.

"Oh, they are that and a great deal more," he said, his mind not on politics but her. What was she thinking? What was she feeling? "Nothing beats a British gentleman in that arena. Mockery is taught with our very first breath."

"Yes, I suppose that is true," she said in her polite voice. It was Lady Scher's voice from the Green Room, and the sound gave him chills. Were they back to polite banter? He huffed in disgust as he fought the panic. She could not draw away from him now!

"Scher . . ." he began, even though he had no idea what he wanted to say.

She stepped out from behind the screen, and he noted high flags of color in her cheeks. She was holding her dress on from the front, though it showed no signs of drooping.

"I'm afraid I need some help. Could you please . . ." She turned around and showed him her back and the four undone buttons. Truly, he was amazed that she could manage all the others.

"Of course," he said as he pushed himself farther upright. The pain made him grit his teeth, but he kept his hands as steady as possible as he caressed the pale flesh still exposed. How he wanted to be undoing her gown, not tidying her up.

He felt her shoulders tense at his stroke, and he was sure

he felt a tremble. "The buttons, if you please," she said, her voice slightly strangled.

His fingers froze, fears clamoring inside his head. But what could he say? Where were his pretty phrases now? He buttoned her dress, then fell backward, utterly exhausted.

"I am doing this badly, Scher. I want to woo you."

She turned and looked at him. Her eyes were dark and troubled, her expression frozen somewhere between terror and total civility. She didn't know what to say to him any more than he knew what to say to her. What was wrong with them?

He reached out and grabbed her hand. She allowed him to, though her skin was cool to the touch and her hand lay limply in his. She spoke before he did.

"You are looking very pale. You should rest."

"What do you want Scher? Name it and you shall have it! A home with a garden. Done. A carriage to take you wherever you wish. Certainly. Servants, jewels—"

"A ring, Brandon."

He swallowed, his bandage cutting painfully into his breath. "You have my heart."

"A wedding ring," she said as if he had not understood her the first time.

His gaze dropped to their intertwined fingers. How did he explain? "I can't, Scher." He felt her flinch, but he gripped her hand before she could flee. "It's not what you think. It has nothing to do with your birth or your background or any other such nonsense."

She tried to pull away, but he wouldn't release her. She had to understand!

"Listen to me!" he said, though she hadn't interrupted him. "It's not what you think!"

She stilled, but he still couldn't speak. He felt her breath shudder in and out of her, knew the tension in her hand was echoed throughout her entire body.

"I will give you anything you want, Scher. Anything, but I can't . . . It's not . . ."

"No," she said quietly. "No, no, no!" The word grew in force until it was an angry hiss. She whipped her hand out of his. "God, I am such a fool!"

"I'm married. Scher, I'm already married."

Chapter 16

Scher didn't go down to the Green Room that night. She didn't even speak to anyone, not that they didn't try. They were an hour away from opening the doors, and Kit had been meddling again. If the problem had been anything but Kit, she might have softened. She might have bowed to her responsibilities with ticket sales or costume repair. But it was Kit, and she had no interest in discussing men right then. Any man. So she waved them off as she grabbed her favorite bottle of wine and a glass. Then she climbed the stairs to her room and slammed the door.

She was halfway through her second glass when Seth came to her door. She recognized his heavy tread and his soft knock. As he couldn't speak to her, she condescended to open the door, though it was a near thing. But of all people, Seth didn't deserve her sharp tongue. So she kept silent as she hauled open her door.

He stood there holding a tray of cheese and bread. He peered at her, quickly taking in the glass of wine in her hand and the wadded blue dress in the corner. She wore her men's clothing merely because it was comfortable. And because she intended to get blind drunk just like any man.

His face tightened into a frown, but she simply lifted her chin in defiance. Then, to add to her pose, she drained the rest of her glass. A murderous darkness came into his eyes. She blinked, wondering if the wine had already started dulling her senses. But when she opened her eyes again, Seth was still standing there with fury on his face. She hadn't seen that look often, but she knew to step back when it appeared.

She did, and he stomped in, dropping the tray on the table. Then he hauled over a second chair and planted himself in it. She heard the wood creak under his weight, but it didn't break.

She blinked again, but there he sat, arms folded, expression mutinous. And when she didn't move, he arched a brow at her. Good God, he looked aristocratic when he did that. The man was huge, had a craggy face and calloused hands. He was everything that was hulking and brutally strong. But at that moment, he absolutely reminded her of Brandon with his arched eyebrows and his firm belief in his own power.

"Oh, Seth," she said more to herself than to him. "You deserve so much better than this life."

His second brow went up to match the height of the first. He sighed, and he slowly shook his head. She knew what he meant. Of all the people in the company, he was the absolute most grateful, most content with his lot. He may be mute, but he supervised an army of boys, was paid better than anyone else in the company, and at night, he graced Delilah's bed. They were married, though few knew it. She only pretended to act the whore, bringing a favored few into her bedchamber, where she entertained, but didn't whore. It was a bizarre situation, but one that seemed to work for her. The more she appeared to take favored lovers, the more the men dallied after her, hoping to become her next patron. It increased her attraction and the draw to the playhouse. But in the end, it was Seth who had her heart. God willing, one day they would be blessed with beautiful children.

Scher shut her door—without slamming it—then poured Seth his own glass of wine. He wouldn't drink it. As far as she knew, he never drank, but it was the polite thing for her to do. Then she sat down across from him and reached for a piece of cheese. She chewed it slowly, then grabbed the next one more quickly. She hadn't eaten anything beyond this morning's tea and found herself abruptly starving.

Down below she could hear the commotion of the troupe preparing for another show. The dressing chambers were on the floor right beneath her and excited chatter always filtered up through the floorboards. She wondered if they were discussing her, then nearly laughed. Of course they were discussing her. Everybody tonight would be discussing her and that disastrous tea. Was it only a few hours ago? It seemed like a lifetime.

She was chewing on the bread when Seth handed her his handkerchief. She wasn't even sure why at first. Then she realized she was crying. Tears leaked from her eyes and her nose was clogging up even as she chewed.

"What a mess I am," she said as she wiped her face. "What a mess *everything* is."

He didn't respond, but she knew he was listening. And bit by bit, everything came out. She began with the tea. Charles. Kit. The countess witch, and Miss Deidre Sampson, another witch. Seth frowned at that, probably at her language, but Scher poured herself another glass of wine, silently daring him to admonish her. He couldn't, of course, so he leaned back in his chair and continued to look at her.

Damn. He knew there was more. She looked away, but he didn't move. She had seen this technique before when he disciplined the boys. He locked them in a room with him and just sat there. All day, if necessary. She never understood it, but eventually the children couldn't stand the silence and confessed everything. And if they didn't, then they were tossed out unemployed.

He didn't have that threat with her, and yet the truth came pouring out anyway. He knew that she had been caring for Brandon anyway. Between Hank and Joey, he probably knew more than she did.

"He has a wife, Seth," she said to her wineglass. "Brandon has a wife."

He sat bolt upright at that, a grunt of fury filling the room. She didn't have to look at him to see that his hands were fisted or that her furniture was in danger. Seth didn't throw things often, but when he did, everyone ducked.

"He met her in India. The details don't matter. In truth, I didn't listen. I just left." She was starting to cry again, so she reached for the wine. Then decided against more drink, contemplated throwing the bottle. Then decided against that as well. She set it down beside her chair instead. It was too much work to throw the thing, especially since she'd be the one cleaning up the shards.

"He has offered me carte blanche." She glanced over at Seth and wasn't surprised when the man didn't react. For every woman in the troupe, mistress to a titled peer was the ultimate prize. Especially if that peer was rich and a good lover. And God help her, she was considering it.

"He listens to me, Seth. He talks to me." Conversation—real conversation—was the rarest thing in her world. Banter she had aplenty. Gossip and opinions, too. But no one listened to Lady Scher. She was there to listen to them. "No one listens like he does." She flashed a smile at Seth. "Except you, of course. But you're Delilah's, not mine."

She grabbed the last piece of cheese and offered it to him. He refused with a shake of his head, and so she began to nibble on it.

"I'd say yes if I thought it would continue. But you know what happens with a mistress. She's there to serve you. She takes your money and gives you attention in return. That's not what happens with a wife. You're bound to her no matter what. You have to pay her bills. If you have a home, she has a home. Her children are your children. I know there are marriages that become nightmares, but it wouldn't be like that with him."

She popped the last bite of cheese into her mouth and chewed with ferocity.

"Forget him. I got money. I got my own home. What need have I of more?"

Even as she said the words, she knew it was a lie. Her bed was lonely, and after today, she finally understood what was possible between lovers. And hadn't she been restless before this all began too? Before Kit's proposal? What of children and a home?

"I want a dog," she said firmly. "And green grass where he can run and piddle on my flowers."

Seth didn't even arch an eyebrow in response. And in the silence, she heard the opening fanfare as the playhouse doors opened. The musicians would continue playing as gentlemen filed in. The rumble of conversation wouldn't reach her all the way up on the third floor, but her mind filled in the noise anyway. She ought to go down. In her whole adult life, she had only missed a week or more of playhouse nights. But she couldn't stir herself to stand, much less clean up and face the gossip.

So she sat in her chair and stared sullenly at the bottle of wine. A moment later, she heard Seth stand. He picked up the empty tray in one hand and pulled the bottle out of her grip with the other. Then he stood there looking down at her, his expression filled with sympathy. She lifted the side of her mouth in a half smile, half grimace.

"You know, Seth, I'd have set my cap for you years ago if it weren't for Delilah." Or for the fact that he treated her as a sister. "You're a better man than all of them put together."

He grinned then nudged her head with his elbow. His hands were full or he'd have tugged on her hair. Then he pointed sternly at the wash basin before leaving.

She did as he bid and cleaned her face. It took her fifteen minutes to bestir herself, but in the end, she washed and brushed out her hair. The routine movements felt good, but she was exhausted by the time she'd taken out all the knots. She stared for a moment at the beautiful blue gown in the corner, but couldn't decide whether to shake it out or burn it. In the end, lassitude set her back to her chair where she stared out the window and brooded.

Hours passed without her even noticing. One of the boys came up to light the fire in her grate and bring clean water for her washbasin. He first chatted nervously about the light crowd tonight. Apparently, her declaration that Lady Scher would no longer tolerate discussions of politics or her wedding had taken effect. She wasn't even there to see it, but apparently Brandon had been right. Lady Scher had spoken and without the attraction of more brawls, the audience stayed away. She didn't know whether to celebrate or spit in disgust. She did nothing but stare morosely out her window.

And then, some time later as she sat drowsing in her chair, the door opened to another bottle of wine. It was held by a well-dressed arm, which extended the bottle into the room like an offering. The bottle waved back and forth in the air, and soon Kit's head popped in behind it.

"I come bearing gifts," he said. "May I enter my lady's chamber?"

She straightened and wiped the sleep from her eyes. She ran her hands over her hair, trying to smooth it, but there really was no point. She was a mess and there was no time to fix it.

Meanwhile, Kit stepped in, his expression sobering as he looked at her. "Ah, Scher, what have I done to you?"

She frowned, her mind still foggy. "Sir?"

He gasped as he pulled out the cork on the wine. "Are we back to that then? I was once Kit to you."

She pushed up again in her chair, wondering why she couldn't think. "Of course you are Kit. Oh, bloody hell, I've had too much to drink."

He laughed at that, the sound almost musical. But in her state, she didn't like the noise. He poured her a glass, but she waved it away. She was muddle-headed, thick-tongued, and out of sorts. And he was dropping down into Seth's chair and drinking the wine he had just brought for her.

"I like your hair down," he said. "It's pretty that way. Gives a man all sorts of ideas," he said with a waggle of his brows. "But I can't say that I care for the clothes."

She ran her hand over her hair again, then looked down at her clothing. It was her man's attire, cheap, gray, and shapeless. She allowed herself to slump in her seat. It didn't much matter if she sat like a lady in this clothing, so why bother? And she had a crick in her neck from how she'd been lying with her head dropped to the side.

"We had quite the afternoon, didn't we?" he continued as he refilled his glass. "Been thinking on it all day. And if I didn't want to think on it, there were all my *friends* . . ." He sneered the word. "Overflowing with ideas on how to help me."

She stood up. She had to get her mind working! Crossing to the water basin, she washed her face and hands. He watched her, of course. And then he must have seen the crumpled blue dress in the corner.

"You were pretty as could be in that dress, Scher. No man could expect a prettier . . . wife."

She winced at the sleight hesitation before that last word. Her mind was clearing enough that she finally understood why he was here. It was time to break their engagement. She'd known from the moment Charles Barr had stepped into the tea that her engagement was over. At least Kit was kind enough to tell her in person.

"I suppose . . ." Her voice was thick and coarse. She had to clear her throat and try again. "I suppose it was inevitable that you'd meet Charles. But I cannot forgive the countess for what she did."

"Lily's a witch, to be sure. Ice cold and shrewd. Miss Sampson called it bad *ton*, which is rather deplorable in a countess."

"Miss Sampson is the one who *told* Lily about Charles," Scher snapped. "Only the people who knew me back then would know his name. And she is the only one who could hope to run in the countess's circle."

Kit didn't answer except to grunt. She wasn't sure exactly what the sound meant, so she settled for her own heavy sigh. "I'm so sorry about all this, Kit. I should never have let things go this far, but I wanted—"

"I've been thinking a lot, Scher," he said, interrupting her words. "Had to take refuge in the lending library to do it. No one goes there but spinsters and nannies, so it was quiet. Paid them a guinea just so I could sit there like you were doing. Staring out the window and thinking. Your boy only found me when I went home."

"My boy?" she asked.

"Joey. Perhaps it was Seth who sent him. Anyway, the boy insisted I come here. Said it was urgent. Then when I got here, Seth pushed the bottle into my hand and pointed me upstairs. You know, for a mute, he expresses himself very well."

She had no argument against that. Only sadness that she couldn't find a way to make their marriage work. She didn't know if the fault lay with them or the world in which they lived. Either way, marrying Kit would only bring unhappiness. "Kit . . ." she began, but he waved her off.

"Been thinking I'm done with society for a while. What's to be done but gossip and tea parties? Had my fill of them! Don't like dancing. Don't like theater. Well, not the Royal stuff."

She held up her hand, trying to sort through his disjoined ramblings. As he was draining his glass, she had a moment to think. "I thought you wanted the playhouse to be just like the Royal."

He snorted as he poured himself more wine. "Well, that's what sent me to the lending library, don't you know. Been using my *friends*." Again he sneered the word. "Asked them to set us by way of a royal seal so that the playhouse could be more than a tavern act. Explained about my plans."

"Kit—" she began, but he waved her off.

"Got visited by a fellow. The God damned under secretary to the under secretary to somebody. Don't remember who. Doesn't matter. Told me in no uncertain terms that the Crown has determined that no other *house of entertainment . . .*" He sneered the words. "Like we were some damn bawdy house. House of entertainment. Bah!"

She swallowed. He had asked for a royal seal? Had he really expected it to succeed? "He said no."

"He said my tart had drunk too much gin and was leading me around by my balls. So, no, Scher, there will be no royal seal for the Tavern Playhouse."

She closed her eyes, the unfairness of it all hitting her hard. It was no more than she expected, but it hurt. It had been Kit's idea, but she was the one accused of stupidity. She was the gin sot who had Kit by the balls.

"I punched him, Scher. I punched him hard, but he was a quick little shit and dodged. Then I was obliged to leave my new club, which is when I saw the lending library. Quiet in there, but no drink." He lifted his refilled glass. "Have you got any cheese?"

She shook her head. It was hurting abominably now and she rested it back against the wall. She wanted her bed. She wanted Pappy. She wanted to sink into a gin-soaked haze for real. Except that she'd never really liked the taste of gin.

Kit grunted and drank more of the wine. "So I thought there in the library, I don't like society very much anymore. Maybe Scotland. Do you like Scotland, Scher? Or maybe the colonies. I hear that real aristocrats are quite the rage over there."

She hardly had to tell him that she wasn't a real aristocrat. Of course, neither was he when it came right down to it. As a younger son, he was nothing more than a regular gentleman. And a soon-to-be drunk one at that.

"I think you will feel better in a week, Kit," she said to the ceiling. "I think my head hurts and I want to go to bed. And I think you have drunk enough wine."

"Have I?" he said as he lifted the half-filled bottle. "I suppose on top of the brandy I had at home, this is rather much."

She lifted her head to look closer at him. His eyes were indeed owlish and bloodshot. His clothes were unusually rumpled as well as his hair. If she hadn't been so groggy, she might have noticed that earlier.

"Oh, Kit," she said. "We can't leave London. The money is here. And we can't live happily with everyone against us." She took a deep breath and forced herself to say the words. "We can't get married, Kit. It's just too hard."

This time he was the one who blinked, and his mouth went slack. Then he straightened in his chair, forcibly setting aside his glass. Thankfully it was both empty and strong, so it didn't break or slosh onto her table. "You're crying off? After everything we've been through, you're crying off now?"

"I'm so sorry, Kit. I should never have accepted."

"Of course you should have! Thought about it all demmed day. It was a good decision. One of my best."

She let his statement hang in the air. She repeated it in her thoughts and held it close to her heart, but it didn't change the truth. They were not meant for each other. "How can you still want to marry me?"

"Nobody else will have me now!" he said with a chortle. "'Cept that Miss Sampson and I've decided I don't like her now."

Scher leaned forward, bracing one hand on the table. "Kit, no."

"Yes!" he said with a drunken wave of his hand. "I'm in love with you, right? Said so when I proposed."

Was he? She could hardly believe it. "But why? I mean . . . how do you know?"

He smiled, his expression warming as he wet his lips. "'Cause you're pretty and smart. And I like the way you smell." He abruptly leaned forward and grabbed her arm, yanking her toward him. She had no balance to resist, and no feet beneath her for stability. She fell forward across the table. And as she was still gasping from surprise, he wrapped his hands around her ribcage and hauled her on top of him.

"Give me a kiss, Scher love." His thumb moved up and around, reaching for her nipple. It missed by a good two inches. "A kiss, my sweet. And then you can lead me around by my balls."

She smiled. Her head still hurt. Her mind was still thick and muddled. And she still had to end her engagement to Kit. But he did make her smile, and so she tried to hold him upright while she struggled to look him in the eye. Unfortunately, he wasn't in the least bit interested in just looking.

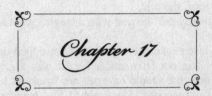

Chapter 17

Kit was quicker than Scher expected. He found her lips despite her attempts to avoid him. But at the first press of his mouth to hers, she realized two things. The first was that she didn't want to kiss him. Not after what she had done this afternoon with Brandon. If nothing else, that one thought told her she had made the right decision. She could not marry Kit.

The second thing she noticed was how very hot Kit was. The drink, obviously, but she was surprised his skin didn't crackle.

She pulled away with a gasp, but he was stronger than she expected. And more unsteady. Their foreheads bumped, jarring her headache, but she tried not to notice. She gripped his shoulders, trying to hold him back. He must have mistook that for a sign of need. He immediately dropped his hands to the bottom of her man's shirt, brunching it up so he could work his hands underneath. The shock of his hands on her skin was alarming.

Again his heat struck her as abnormal. Then she couldn't
think as his weight tumbled her fully off the table. He kept
her from dropping onto her face, which was very nice, and
he steadied her as she settled onto her knees before him.

"Kit, stop," she said.

"Don't struggle!" he said with a laugh. "Ain't so steady
right now."

Then, faster than she expected, he swooped down and
swept her feet out from under her. It was a grand gesture and one that should have set her firmly in his arms.
But she was surprised. She grabbed his shoulders as the
only things at hand. But it must have been too much for
him. He was filled with drink. They never had the right
balance.

Compared to their earlier tussle, their fall was graceful.
She noticed his blood-shot eyes bugging out with shock.
She felt her weight raise up as he lifted, then drop and
continue to drop as he could not support her. Her arms
were about his shoulders, but they did not halt her descent.
Instead, she pulled him down on top of her.

Down onto the table which splintered beneath her.
Down then onto the floor while she hunched her back in a
vain attempt to protect herself. Her head bounced painfully
on the ground and she felt a splinter dig into her shoulder.
Then there was a thud that was not the table breaking or
her own head hitting the hard floor. It was Kit as he cracked
some part of him somewhere. She lay flat on the ground,
her head throbbing like the very devil. Kit was sprawled
on top of her, and she was dimly aware of wet as the wine
likely spilled all over everything.

"Ung," she managed as she tried to move. Kit pinned
her too severely. "Kit." She pushed his arm off her nose.
She poked him in the side. "Kit!"

He didn't move. And then she became aware of an odd
smell in the room. It wasn't a wine smell at all. And the wet,

she realized, was not from the bottle. Blood. She smelled blood. And she was pretty sure it wasn't her own.

"*Kit!*"

"He's not dead is he?" Brandon couldn't credit the idea that vibrant, young, stupid, *young* Kit could be gone. But he had seen it enough to know that youth was no guarantee of immortality. "He just fell down?"

Scher nodded, her eyes wide and her face pale. She had come to his room just before dawn, looking as if she hadn't slept in a week. And he smelled a variety of wines on her. But what terrified him was the look of haunted panic in her eyes. And the way she wrung her hands in front and didn't step farther into the room than just inside the door.

"He knocked his head on my table," she said to the floorboards. "Or what's left of it. But he's not dead. No, not dead. Just . . . asleep." She shuddered. "And there was so much blood!"

"Head wounds bleed like the very devil, but that doesn't mean they are serious. What did the doctor say?"

"The same, and it was a surgeon. He stitched it up, said to keep him warm, and . . ." She shrugged, her eyes rising to his while embarrassment colored her cheeks. "And to feed him something other than cheap wine when he woke."

Ah, so there was the truth, Brandon realized. The boy had gotten himself drunk and fell down in Scher's chamber. He studied her face, unwilling to speculate why the boy was in her room and more unwilling to press her.

She was obviously shaken and on uncertain ground. So was he. There were so many unanswered questions. Not only about the nature of Kit's injury, but about Scher herself. Why, for example, was she here with him rather than at the playhouse nursing Kit? After the way they had parted before, he had thought she would never come to see him again. While he, on the other hand, had spent every moment of the last day dreaming of ways to get her back in his bed. If only she would let him explain, but she had refused to hear.

"Was he still asleep when you left?" he asked gently.

She nodded. "He has a fever, Brandon. I don't want to move him. It might reopen the wound and make things worse. But I can't keep him in my bed! His mother would have a fit." She released an anxious laugh. "How is it that I have come to hide away you both?"

"Bad luck?" he offered. He wished she would come closer. Wished she would let him touch her. Instead, she just sighed and closed her eyes, rubbing the back of her neck. "Scher, what is it? Why have you come to me?"

She raised her gaze and looked at him. There was no covering her feelings, no polite mask on her features. He looked at her and saw such weariness. It was as if the restlessness of before had been replaced with exhaustion and a creeping sadness. It wouldn't take much, he realized, for it to slide into despair.

"Let me help you, Scher. Let me—"

"I have come to ask you to return to your home. I cannot spend all my time nursing Kit. I have responsibilities at the playhouse that I have been neglecting. Martha is the one I go to for help with these sorts of things—"

"But not if she is here nursing me. Of course, Scher. I had not meant to burden her or you."

She shook her head, and her words continued in a nervous rush. "I do not mean to pry into your matters. It is none of my business why you chose to hide out from your family here. They were getting concerned, you recall. But if you wish to remain—"

"For you, Scher," he interrupted. "I stayed because you visited me here as you could never do at my home."

She paused, her breath suspended as she absorbed his words. Then she looked down at her hands, which she'd clasped again before her. "Perhaps it would be best all around if you went home and allowed your wife to nurse you."

"My *wife* cannot see me as it makes *her* condition worse." He looked up at the ceiling and wondered if ever there were a more damnable situation. He had tried to explain things to her. "If you but understood how this came about."

"It doesn't matter how it came about, Brandon!" she snapped. "You are married. And I am still engaged to Kit." She threw up her hands in disgust. "He doesn't know yet that it is over. I tried to tell him, but he was so drunk. He would not listen!"

He could see the frustration in her, and a bone-deep weariness. "How can I help you? Anything you need—"

She looked at him, her expression pleading. "Just go, Brandon, and let me sort things out."

"Let me help."

She pressed the heels of her hands into her eyes. "No," she said behind her arms. "It's too confusing, right now. I cannot think with you around."

He nodded. "I will wait in my apartments. You have only to send me a message—"

"No!" She bellowed the word with such force that he was taken aback. And when she dropped her arms, he saw such misery in her eyes. "I won't send a message. I won't contact you. I don't want to be a mistress!"

His jaw tightened. His hands were already fisted in the sheets, but it did not stop him from seeing the absolute truth. Her engagement to Kit was at an end, but that did not destroy her dream of becoming a wife and mother. She still longed for the respectability of a marriage. And only a cad would deny her such a dream.

He loved Scher. Of that he was certain. So certain, in

fact, that he could do nothing but accede to her wishes no matter that it tore his heart out. Though the very thought made him want to stab himself anew, he knew now that he could never have her.

"You may take Martha," he forced out. "Send Hank to me. I shall remove myself within the hour."

"You do not—"

"Within the hour, Scher! I will not discomfort you further." He pushed himself up until he was seated fully upright. But then he had to wait as the pain washed over him. He welcomed it. If he focused exclusively on that, then it washed away his other thoughts.

"I will send Hank to you," she said. She hesitated, hovering next to the door until he looked up, pain making his lips curl into a snarl.

"I must get dressed, Scher. Leave now or you shall see more of me than you want."

She blanched, then he saw a flash of anger on her tired features. Lifting her chin, she sketched a mocking curtsey. "As you wish, my lord." Then she departed, calling for Martha and Hank as she left.

Pain. Blessed pain. It never lasted long enough.

Chapter 18

Brandon groaned, clutched his handkerchief to his sweating face, and prayed that he didn't get sick in his own carriage. Smelling *that* for the entire trip would really put a cap on his misery. The carriage hit a rut and his left hand clutched the squabs reflexively. His hand was already cramping, but he hardly cared. If he focused exclusively on that single, steady note of muscle pain, then perhaps he would forget the rolling in his stomach. He should not have attempted the seventy-minute drive to Pottersfarm near Greenwich. Not without some sort of drink to knock him unconscious.

Another rut, this one deep enough to jostle his stomach wound. Pain exploded into his misery, and he cried out. Enough! He had to stop! Gathering his strength, he rapped on the carriage ceiling, then collapsed backward against the cushions.

It took long, sickening moments as the conveyance

slowed, dipping and swaying through the ruts. Then, eventually, Hank's face popped in.

"Yes, yer lord . . ." His voice trailed away as he stared at his employer. Then the boy scrambled inside, grabbing hold of Brandon. "I got ye."

They made it outside with barely enough time. Brandon was on his knees, casting up his accounts. The boy and the coachman held him up, doing their best to not jostle his wounds. They failed, of course, but perhaps it was for the best. If the pain became great enough, he would pass out.

He waited and hoped, but remained stubbornly conscious. Five minutes later, he collapsed to the side and lay in the grass. It was only because of Hank that he didn't slide straight into the ditch.

"It ain't much farther, my lord. Just about a half hour."

A half hour. A half century. It didn't matter. "Slit my throat, Hank. Finish me off. I'm begging you."

"You'll feel better once we get you home."

No, he wouldn't. Once there, he was likely to feel a good deal worse, but he hadn't the breath to tell the boy that.

"Here," said the boy as he pressed a torn piece of white bread into his hand. "Lady Scher gave this to me for you. She said if you get too sick, I was to give this to you to eat. Soaks up the bile, she said. Course she didn't think you'd be going all the way out here."

Brandon pressed his lips together, refusing the bread. The ache in his soul grew exponentially at the mention of Scheherazade. He wouldn't take anything from her. He couldn't. It wasn't honorable and she deserved better than the likes of him.

"Er, now," said the coachman gruffly from the other side. "Don't waste it."

"You eat it, Hank," he whispered.

"Can't," the boy responded cheerfully. "She said it were fer you. Don't make me into a liar, my lord. Not to Lady Scher."

Brandon didn't respond. A breeze was flowing over his body, drying the sweat on his face. He heard a bird call in loud notes from somewhere. Something else buzzed closer by. The ditch wasn't pleasant, but the breeze brought new scents to his nose, something floral and sweet.

"It's pretty 'ere," commented Hank. "I ain't never been out o' London afore." Then he sniffed loudly. "Smells nicer."

"Yup," responded the coachman. "There's a tavern up the way a bit. Good stew."

Scheherazade would like it here, Brandon thought. She would have her green grass and the sweet smell of flowers. Her children would have a place to run, and the neighbors were of a more tolerant sort. That's why he had settled Channa here, pleased that the locals seemed open to an Indian woman in their midst. If only Channa had made the effort.

He took another breath and was pleasantly surprised to discover he wasn't as nauseated as before. His pain had subsided to a dull misery. It would rise up again the moment he tried to move, but at the moment, he took another breath and felt grateful for the respite.

And when Hank pressed a mouthful of bread to his lips, he opened without thought. He chewed and swallowed before realizing that he had just eaten Scheherazade's bread. And damn if it didn't make his stomach settle just as she'd promised.

"Give 'im the water too," the coachman instructed.

A flask was pressed awkwardly to his lips. Brandon had no choice but to swallow or drown. He drank. Then he ate another morsel.

"'At's it, my lord," Hank said. "Lady Scher would be right pleased."

Brandon lifted his hand enough to grab Hank's wrist. "Hank," he rasped.

"My lord?"

"Mention Lady Scher again and you're sacked."

* * *

He slept for nearly a day, his thoughts miserable, his gut worse. But by morning of the second day, he was heartily sick of this tiny guest room on the sunny side of the house. Surprisingly enough, Hank was turning into an excellent young valet. With a little help from the housekeeper, he had hung up Brandon's small satchel of clothes, assisted whenever nature demanded that Brandon move, and best of all, kept everyone else away. And now that Brandon wished to bestir himself, the boy turned out to have a steady hand with a razor as well.

And he didn't once mention Scheherazade.

"There's bread and jam," Hank said cheerfully. "Mrs. Wiggins says there'll be berries and cream any day now. But for today . . . custard!"

It was a measure of Brandon's improvement that the words did not turn his stomach.

"She let me have a bit of honey too. Never had it afore in tea, but she says it's the best way to take tea."

"It is," Brandon agreed and nearly smiled when the boy pulled back enough to stare. Brandon arched a brow. "Is there a problem?"

"No, my lord! No! It's jes the nicest thing you've said in a week. Not a bit of a grunt or a moan in there at all."

Brandon frowned. That couldn't possibly be true. He wasn't completely surly, was he? "Finish my shave, boy," he said with a return of gruffness, but it was softened by his smile. "As I'm obviously not going to die, I intend to get up and dressed."

The boy's eyes widened. "Yes, my lord! Right away, my lord!" Then he returned with a great deal of enthusiasm to scraping at Brandon's face.

"Easy, Hank. After all this healing, I wouldn't want to die of a slit throat now." He would have taken the razor from the boy's hand, except Brandon's hands were much too unsteady. It wasn't that he trembled. The shakes only came when the pain became white hot. It was this damnable weakness. He felt quite fine for fifteen minutes, maybe twenty, but then he had to rest because he was utterly spent. Thankfully, he was much improved from yesterday and even the day before. At this rate, he should be healthy within a week. If only Scher were here to give him more incentive to remain conscious.

"Slow and steady," Hank said, referring to his work with the razor. The boy's eyes were nearly crossed with concentration, and he even stuck his tongue between his teeth as he worked. Eventually, the task was done without bloodshed, and Hank scrambled off the bed with obvious pride.

"I'll need help with my clothes," Brandon said, "and then I'd like to visit Mrs. Wiggins, please."

"Yes, my lord. Of course!"

Brandon caught himself just before he gave the child a fond smile. He ought to feel annoyed by such overwhelming enthusiasm, but he found he was not in an irritable mood. The sun was shining, his body was healing, and he felt true hunger for the first time since being stabbed. If he wasn't happy, at least he wasn't suicidal.

In short, it was time again to face his future and try for some sort of happiness. His mind immediately went to Scher, but he pushed the thought away. She had made her choice as had he. Dwelling on what could never be would turn him into . . . He flinched away from finishing that thought. It was time to move forward, he repeated to himself. And so he applied himself to donning clean clothes.

An hour later, he had finished his rather grim talk with Mrs. Wiggins and was now headed at an extraordinarily slow pace down the hallway to his wife's bedroom. In truth, it was the master bedroom, but he had given it over to her as she required the most care. Her maid was given the attached lady's bedroom, which relegated him on his infrequent visits to the small guest bedroom beside the nursery.

The maid, Nidra, opened the door quietly at his knock. She smiled prettily, then ducked her head in respect. Dark skin, dark eyes, and a pretty white frock. Nidra must be a teenager now, he realized, and enjoying England by the looks of her robust health. What a contrast to her mistress Channa.

His wife sat by the fire, staring down at the dancing flames. She was swathed in bright fabrics that wrapped her from head to toe, and yet she didn't appear to sweat in the blistering heat of the room. He saw little skin—only on her bare feet and face—but what he could see was sallow and dull.

"Not a good day, my lord," said Nidra in perfect English.

"My goodness," he responded warmly, "how wonderful you speak now."

She giggled at his compliment, then abruptly slapped her hand over her mouth with a frightened look at her mistress. Other times he had let the gesture pass. He knew Channa hated noise, any noise, but most especially joyful ones. His wife had sat before the fire mourning her family for nearly two years now. It was time for both of them to leave off this oppressive darkness of spirit.

So thinking, he reached out and pulled Nidra's hand from her mouth. "I like the sound of laughter," he said gently. "Never cover it up."

Her eyes widened at his unusual firmness. Then she nodded slowly at him, before her gaze once again hopped to Channa's. His wife hadn't moved. In truth, he wasn't entirely sure she still breathed.

"I hear that there is custard downstairs. You should go see if you can get some before my valet eats it all."

She flashed him a grin, nearly forgot to curtsey, then

dashed out the door. He smiled, watching her go. Indian or English, all children liked custard.

He stepped farther into the room, closing the door gently as he moved. "I remember running down for custard too, once upon a time," he said in his wife's native tongue, though there wasn't a Hindi word for custard. "And I understand that Cook's is excellent. I should have some brought up here for us to try before Nidra and Hank gobble it all down." He settled slowly into the chair beside the fire, though the heat was nearly unbearable. "Do you remember me telling you about custard, Channa? I promised you huge vats of it, I believe. And you laughed and asked me if it was something to wash laundry in."

She didn't answer, not that he had expected her to. She remained as she always did, according to Mrs. Wiggins. She sat day and night beside the fire, staring into the flames. Beside her was a basket of fabric and a pair of long, sharp scissors. According to the housekeeper, on Channa's better days, his wife cut pieces of cloth into fantastic shapes and designs. Then she one by one fed them to the fire.

He leaned back slowly, feeling the pull of his wound. He would not last long sitting up. The ache was already traveling up his back and down his legs. Soon he would not be able to breathe without panting in pain. But for now, he would sit and talk with his wife.

"I met a woman, Channa, a most amazing woman. The daughter of an actress."

He glanced over at his wife, trying to see some flash of life in her. She remained still, her eyes unfocused as she gazed into the fire.

"She is the most unrealistic creature on Earth," he said with a laugh. The sound was forced, but Channa gave no sign she noticed. Or even listened. "She believes that she can be respectable, Channa. She believes that marriage will give her everything she wants."

He sobered slightly as he looked at his wife. Her gaze had not moved. Neither had her body. So he reached forward, rooting through the fabric of her dress until he found one slender hand. She stiffened. He could tell that much, but he was determined. Slowly he pulled her hand out from beneath the cloth.

It was small and ashy in his palm. He recalled the way she had touched him so long ago. She had been shy, her hand tentative, and her fingers trembling with excitement. There had been such life in her, such wonder and giddy girl delight, and he had been seized by such lust at her fluttering caress. Now her fingers lay like dead things in his hand.

"She is ridiculous," he continued, "but the more time one spends with her, the more one believes. She has such strength that I cannot help but think she will succeed."

He entwined his fingers with hers. He tried to tug her closer, to somehow pull her gaze to his, but she did not budge. In the end, he was the one who moved. He shifted to his knees, putting himself before her such that she was forced to look in his eyes.

"If she can do it with her lower-caste upbringing, with her lack of anything respectable, then how much easier it will be for us, Channa." He reached up with his free hand, touching her cheek as tenderly as he knew how. "We were happy once. We can be so again. We merely need to try, Channa."

She didn't answer, but her gaze was fixed on his face. She was looking at him. Maybe he was getting through.

"Tell me what you need, Channa. Tell me and it shall be yours. I am a lord in this country, a wealthy man respected throughout." He tried not to wince at the lie, but it was true enough for her purposes. "As my wife, you can have anything. Fine clothing. Good food."

Of course, she already had all that this last year to no avail. So he swallowed and forced himself to offer what he never had before.

"We could travel, if you like. To the Continent. There may be a way to visit India. The northern parts, perhaps . . ."

There was a flicker in her eyes at that, but no response.

"Would you like that?"

No response.

"Or," he said softly, and then he again reached up and forced himself to caress slowly—sensuously—down her cheek. "Or if you would like to step into your life as a mother, we could try that as well. I am prepared to be a proper husband to you, if you want." He tried not to see another face as he touched her. Another smile, another skin, another woman. "We could have children."

He waited, his belly taut with pain, but his body still. He needed some sign from her, some hint that Channa was still with him. He didn't care if she wasn't the vibrant girl from two years ago. He wasn't even sure he could handle such a woman. He simply wanted a person rather than this empty shell. Anything could be accomplished if only there was still life in his wife.

"Channa? Will you try?"

She moved. Her eyes remained trained on him, but her free hand slid off her lap. He didn't dare look to see what she was doing, couldn't risk breaking the link of their gazes. But he was excruciatingly aware of her slow movement as her hand slid down her thigh to reach below the chair.

He didn't at first understand what she was doing. And when he did, he didn't believe. He still remembered her laughter, half hidden behind her hand. He saw the skipping, barefoot girl he had first met that day he walked to her father's home. His memory was filled with the happy echoes of her voice as she chided her sisters to stay away from the English master.

So when she grabbed her scissors and tried to stab him, he was both stunned and not surprised at all. She had no strength, and he was fast enough to stop her. Even as she strained with all her frail weight to impale him, he could not shake the echoes of her laughter the first time he had winked at her . . . and she had winked back.

He held her arm high and slowly twisted her wrist until the scissors clattered to the floor. He thought she was breathing heavily from the effort of trying to kill him. She was certainly panting from her exertions. But it wasn't until he'd pulled her empty hand back down to her lap that he realized she was speaking. One word, repeated over and over in a voice so unused to speaking that it sounded more like a grunt than a word.

"Mama," she said. "Mama! Mama! Mama! Mama!"

Her hand pressed to her belly and she began to rock.

"Mama! Mama! Mama! Mama!"

He pushed wearily to his feet, having seen this kind of fit before. When she began rocking like that, there would be no speaking to her for hours. She would continue like that, refusing food and water, soiling herself when her body demanded, completely unmanageable until exhaustion made her collapse. Any attempts to moderate the fit only made it worse.

He shuffled awkwardly to the door, hauling it open. He didn't need to call. Nidra sat outside the door, her eyes wide with horror as she peeked inside. For an insane moment, Brandon thought to block the girl's view. She shouldn't be exposed to such despair.

Then he realized he was being ridiculous. Everyone in this household was well used to Channa's fits. More so than he was. So he stepped back, pain biting into his chest as his belly wound pulled. He didn't leave though. This was his wife. He would stay and give what assistance he could.

So he stood there and watched as Nidra rushed to her mistress's side and began singing a Hindi lullaby. He didn't understand the words, nor could he really make out the tune. All he heard was Channa's word repeated over and over as she tried to kill him.

"Mama! Mama! Mama!"

He closed his eyes, leaning back against the wall when the pain from his belly began radiating through out his chest and back. Soon his own silent chant covered his wife's.

Scher. Scher. Scher.

Chapter 19

Brandon wiped Channa's spit off his face and wasn't surprised to find his handkerchief dotted with blood as well. She had used her nails this time to surprising effect. At least she hadn't gone for the scissors. Was that progress? Probably not, since he'd had the weapon removed after her first attempt to kill him.

A week had gone by in his country idyll. He daily tried to work with his wife, and as had happened all the other times, his efforts were steadily repulsed. There seemed to be no difference in her response whether he approached her with gentle respect or firm discipline or any combination of both. Touch didn't help. Neither did food, isolation, or firm commands. And the daily battle was wearing on them both. Channa appeared wilder every day, and he was retiring to his library earlier and earlier in the day.

It was almost noon when he heard the rider approach. He was in Channa's room reading to her from a book he had purchased in India. His understanding of her language was not the best, but it was a children's book and he could manage most of it. She was rocking herself, her eyes on the banked fire, but the chanting had stopped, so maybe she was listening. Either way, he heard the rider and set the book aside with a sigh of relief.

"Do you hear that, Channa? I believe that's the doctor. You remember him, don't you? Dr. Dandin has been studying in London. I'm going to go talk to him, and then bring him up here after lunch. Would you like that? Would you like to see Dr. Dandin again?"

Typically, she didn't respond, but Nidra perked up noticeably. The girl actually reminded him of how Channa used to be: bright, expressive, and so curious about the world outside her doors. And every time he looked at her, he wondered what Channa would be like if she had never married him, if he had never met her family, if he hadn't caused the death of everyone she knew and loved.

Pushing aside his morose thoughts, he stood with ease. His wound was almost completely healed, only twinging every now and then. And his stamina, thank God, was back to healthy levels. But he still moved warily, more to keep from startling Channa than hurting himself. He was halfway down the stairs when Mrs. Wiggins opened the front door.

"Good afternoon—" the woman began, but was summarily pushed aside.

"Is he here? Is Brandon here?"

Brandon frowned, recognizing his brother's deep voice. And if he didn't, the man was already in his front hallway, looking tired and dirty as never before. Good God, the man looked ten years older!

"Michael? What has happened?" His mind immediately jumped to Scheherazade, but then as quickly dismissed the thought. Michael would certainly not appear in such a state for Scher's benefit. Which probably meant . . . "Mother?"

Michael's eyes leaped up the stairs and relief flashed through his expression, only to be quickly replaced with annoyance. "Good God, Brandon, next time you decide to hurry off to the country, you should leave word with your man so we all don't go mad with worry over you."

"I have no man," Brandon responded as he made the bottom floor and clasped his brother. Could this distress be caused by worry? Surely not.

"All the more reason to get one," Michael snapped. Then he looked around the place, noting the housemaid, footman, and Mrs. Wiggins all standing within earshot. "Do you have a library in this place? Somewhere we could talk?"

"Of course," he said as he led the way down the hall. "I thought you were the doctor come to help Channa."

Michael paused, obviously searching his memory. "Your Indian mistress. Is she no better?"

"My Indian *wife*," Brandon stressed. "And no. No better."

Michael waved the niceties of religious law aside. He didn't believe that a Hindu wedding ceremony was recognized by British law, ergo his brother wasn't married to *that* woman. He preferred to refer to her as a mistress, which was almost laughable. Brandon wouldn't be in his current fix if Channa wasn't his moral, legal, and ethical responsibility.

But this was old territory between them, and obviously not relevant to today's matter, whatever that was. So both men crossed into the library without further discussion. Michael didn't appear to notice anything beyond the sideboard with a decanter of brandy. Brandon pulled his chair from his desk and arranged it facing the only other one in the room. He generally didn't like facing the fireplace, so he angled his furniture to the window to enjoy the view. Meanwhile, Michael poured himself a very large glass.

Brandon raised his eyes in surprise. Michael must truly be upset if he was drinking at noon without even asking if it were all right. But then, his brother was an earl and used to taking whatever he wanted without asking.

"What has put you in such a state?" pressed Brandon. "Surely not my absence."

Michael shook his head, then swallowed half his glass. It was a few breaths longer before he could speak. "I sent a missive here two weeks ago, but the housekeeper said you weren't here."

Brandon didn't respond. He was not going to explain his whereabouts to his brother.

"Then I put a footman inside your front door, waiting for news of you. Never would have known you were here if you hadn't sent that coachman for your papers."

Brandon's concern ratcheted up another notch. The coachman had only left this morning and wasn't due back until this evening. That meant that Michael rushed here within minutes of learning his whereabouts. "Michael, out with it! What has happened?"

His brother set down his glass, visibly pulling himself together as he spoke. "Kit's dead. Sorry to put it so baldly, but there's really no other way to say it. He's dead."

"Dead? From a drunken fall? That can't be."

"What? No! A sickness. Probably from that actress." He practically spat the last word.

"Is Scher ill?" It wasn't what he should have said. It wasn't even all he was thinking, though it was certainly at the top. But the words were out before he could think further.

Michael's brow creased with an ugly frown. "I have no idea, though she was in the peak of health last time I saw her. Didn't you hear me? *Kit* is dead! *Kit* was ill!"

"I heard you!" Brandon snapped back. But how was it possible? Scher said he was sleeping off a fall. Had she said something about a fever? He didn't remember. "What happened?"

Michael snorted, draining his glass. The man hadn't

even bothered to sit down. "I told you. Illness. In *her* bed."

Michael ran a distracted hand through his hair. "Aunt Adelia is beside herself with grief, and Grandmama hasn't left her room in days. The funeral is tomorrow. Small thing. Private. Just family." He shot his brother an irritated look. "Assuming the family can be *found*."

Brandon jerked on the bellpull before even realizing he'd crossed the room. Then, ignoring the pull, he hauled open the door and spied the footman. "Saddle my horse immediately."

"Good," grunted Michael from behind him. "But let's wait long enough for luncheon. I just arrived and need a rest. Besides, the funeral isn't until tomorrow."

Brandon barely spared him a glance. "Take as long as you like." Then he turned and left. He was on the road, riding toward Scheherazade, within three minutes.

She was in the Green Room when he found her. As pale and composed as ever, she was calmly wiping out glasses and setting them on the sideboard in preparation for the evening's show. So intent was she on her task that she didn't even look up when he entered, which gave him a moment to study her.

She wore a simple dress of light brown with a fichu covering her chest and stains on the skirt where men had tugged on her with greasy hands. She moved with precision and grace, as usual, but he could see the emptiness in every line of her body. She had always been composed, but now she was bleak. Where there had been energy in whatever she did, now there was a slowness as if every breath were an effort.

He saw all this in a moment. It took another for him to cross around to her side. And then she was in his arms, enfolded there and gripping him first lightly and then with increasing strength. Or perhaps it was his own desperation. He didn't know. He was too busy holding her slight body against his, smelling her scent, and pressing a long kiss into her hair.

They didn't speak. There was no need to. He understood her anguish, just as she must know how desperately he wished he could comfort her. He felt her body shudder against his and knew she was struggling against her tears. Reluctantly, he released her enough so that he could whisper into her ear.

"Come with me."

She shook her head. "I have responsibilities here." Her breath was a moist heat against his neck. He hadn't bothered with a neck cloth and in the heat of his pell-mell ride to London, he had allowed his shirt to open to the breeze.

"Do you really think you're good to anyone right now?"

She didn't answer, though he knew she wanted to. He didn't give her the chance as Seth pushed into the room, looking burly and protective. Brandon flashed the man a grim look.

"I am taking her with me tonight. And then tomorrow to the funeral."

Scher spoke to his chest. "They won't let me in—"

He squeezed her slightly to show that he heard her, but he continued to speak to Seth. "Can you have someone gather what she needs?"

Seth frowned a moment, his eyes darting back and forth between Brandon and Scheherazade. And in that second of indecision, Scher repeated her words. "They won't let me in the church. The earl made that quite clear."

"I don't give a good goddamned what Michael wants. You *will* be allowed in."

Apparently the ruthlessness in his voice was all that Seth needed to make his decision. He nodded smartly—to Brandon—then turned on his heel. Meanwhile, Scheherazade seemed to shrink against him.

"I won't cause a scene at Kit's fu—" Her voice broke on a choke, but when he would have pulled her into another embrace, she pushed him away. "I won't cause a scene. It's disrespectful. They've lost a son."

He touched her face, amazed that she could think of his family. "You've lost your fiancé." She released a snort of disbelief, and he was pleased to see that tiny show of spirit.

"It will be all right, Scheherazade. You deserve to be there, and I will see that you go."

She nodded, her eyes bright with tears. She tried to say something, but her words were choked off.

"I would walk through hell and back to help you, Scher. Surely you know that."

She stilled, her gaze meeting and holding on his. He couldn't read her expression, nor did he have the chance to ask as Annette and her little dog came rushing into the room. The animal was clearly excited, rushing around and yapping at everything in the way of nervous dogs. Annette was no less agitated, though she covered by speaking non-stop as she hauled in a large satchel.

"I put in clean underthings and your paste and rogue pot. The only black dress we got was the costume for last year's Lady Mountback. You remember the play? It won't fit you perfect, but there's pins in the skirt to tighten it up. Mind you don't put it on without pulling out the pins first, else you'll be bloody and black. Your shoes are already black, so there's no worry there, though you'd be better with slippers so as not to clunk down the aisle of St. James."

"Thank you," Brandon said, disentangling the heavy bag from Annette's grip. He began to steer Scheherazade from the room, but the woman trailed after, still talking and still followed by her yapping dog.

"We're all real sorry, Scher. And don't you worry none about us. Delilah and me can handle things. And Seth can handle the money. You know he can. So don't you worry 'bout us. We're all real sorry. He was such the nicest man. Polly always liked him. He never hurt her even when she peed on him."

They had made it through the hallway and into the main stage area. Brandon was occupied with maneuvering both Scheherazade and the large bag so he didn't at first realize who had lined up in the room. The entire troupe was there, even the stage boys. And as they moved through the room, the men doffed their hats and the woman curtsied, all of them murmuring their condolences for Scher.

It was an odd sight to see. Brandon was used to such displays from liveried servants as they greeted the earl and his countess. Never had he thought to see such a thing from a motley crew of actors and hands, and giving such reverence to Scher. It bore home exactly how treasured she was to these people.

He looked down, wondering if she realized the magnitude of the love they offered her as she passed. She did. Her eyes were wide, her face open in a stunned kind of gratitude. She didn't cry, but she acknowledged every man or woman's words like a lady born. Brandon was forced to release his hold on her as she accepted a handkerchief from one man, a black bow for her hair from a girl, even a copper from Joey. "For the poor b-box. In his honor," stammered the boy.

Scheherazade accepted it all, but Brandon could see the toll on her. Though she carried herself well, her shoulders were beginning to stoop and her movements had become jerky with emotion. He had to get her someplace private fast.

He tossed one of the younger boys a coin. "Find us a hansom cab." The boy nodded and was gone in a flash. Then Brandon turned to Seth. "Can you get my horse to my stable? I'm going to ride with her."

Seth nodded smartly and disappeared after the boy.

Then all Brandon could do was wait as Scheherazade stopped at the threshold, turning back to face everyone.

"Thank you," she said, her voice thick with unshed tears. "You all mean so much to me." She started to say something else, but clearly the words deserted her or her throat closed down. In the end, Brandon stepped up beside her, finishing with what he guessed she wanted to say.

"Whatever the future holds for Lady Scher, this is where she comes from. You are her family. She could not face tomorrow without your love today. Thank you." Then he bowed as deeply as he knew how.

The cab pulled to a stop in front of the playhouse. Brandon passed her bag up, then gave directions to the cabbie. Lastly, he assisted Scher into the carriage, followed her in, and shut the door.

She didn't turn to him until they felt the horses start. And only then, in the darkness of the carriage, did she bury her face in his coat and begin to sob.

Chapter 20

Scher was accustomed to death. Her sister had gone first.
Her mother went next. Then Pappy, plus a score of others—
young and old. Death was not common so much as an ever
present specter lurking in the back of her mind. She had
cried before at funerals. She had held her friends as someone precious was laid to rest.

But Scher had never known the racking despair that
she experienced now. It seemed as if her soul had crawled
inside the deathbed with Kit. Her body was the only part
that existed in the outside world. The rest of her remained
stubbornly with Kit.

She took a breath, belatedly realizing the carriage had
stopped. Her tears had dried, but her face was still pressed
tight to Brandon's chest. When had it stopped?

She straightened away from him and felt the heat of
his hand on her shoulder slide to her back. The rest of her
remained warm, still flushed from her tears and his body.
The handkerchief she clutched in her hand was already

a mess, so Brandon used his own as he wiped her face clean.

"Can you walk?" he finally asked.

She nodded. Of course she could walk. Except that her legs felt leaden, and the air seemed thick and resistant. Still, her pride made her move when he pushed open the carriage door. How long had she been lying against him with the cab just sitting in the yard?

With his help, she disembarked from the hansom only to frown at their location: the Barking Dog Inn on the edge of London. She had never stayed here, but she knew of the place. It was clean, catered to merchants and the like, and was *not* frequented by the aristocratic elite.

Though she didn't ask, Brandon answered her unspoken question. "I cannot take you to my bachelor apartments. I have no servants to tend you. But you can have good food here, a hot bath, and a warm bed. Whatever you need, and no one to bother you. I will get a room next door so you can call me, but you don't need to fear."

He was guiding her inside with a hand on her back. At his words, she tucked tighter to his side. It wasn't a conscious movement so much as an instinctive one. A part of her recognized that she was suddenly pressed along his hip. A part of her knew that she could not stand to be alone tonight. But the rest of her existed in a silent cocoon where she couldn't speak and could barely move.

Fortunately, Brandon didn't need words. He glanced sharply at her, searching her face, then his features tightened into a frown.

"I will be right next door, Scher. Only a cad would—" He broke off as the innkeeper bustled forward. Scher didn't listen as Brandon began issuing orders. She didn't even blink as she saw a golden guinea pass into the man's hand. She simply moved as Brandon directed, the push of his hand the only real thing in her life. His warmth, his presence, his direction as he helped her climb the stairs to a large and spacious chamber.

Brandon guided her to a seat by the window. He settled her in it, then whispered into her ear. "Just a few moments, Scher. Let me get everything settled."

She didn't respond. He had removed his hand from her back, so his warmth no longer heated her and his presence no longer motivated her. She sat and stared out the window.

What had happened to her? she wondered in that distant part of her thoughts. She had been working just a few moments ago, doing something at the playhouse. She had found the ability to work, to handle the accounts, to clean glasses. Why now was she abruptly too exhausted to move? Why was she lost now? It made no sense.

But as bizarre as it seemed to her, she could not break through her lethargy. Brandon had shown up and taken control. She had no will to resist him. And having now given over to Brandon, she found herself with no strength of her own. So she sat. She stared out the window as the leaves of a nearby maple fluttered in the late afternoon light. They were young still, as this was spring, but the green looked ever so pretty in the light.

"Have some bread, Scher. It's excellent fare."

She took the piece he handed her. It was dipped in a stew, so it was sticky on her fingers. She ate it as he directed. His face was nicer to look at than the trees, so she turned her attention to him. He smiled at her, though his expression was still serious with worry. She wanted to say she was fine. She wanted to tell him so many things, but the more she sat, the more lethargic she became.

"You should try this stew," he said, as he offered her the bowl. "It's simple, but hearty. I like it."

He pressed the bowl into her left hand and the spoon into her right. She lifted it and began to eat because he directed her to.

"Do you like it?" he asked.

"It's very nice," she said, though she couldn't taste it at all.

He gave her a warm smile that didn't reach his eyes. His eyes were dark brown, she noted. Almost black. And his breath still smelled of mint. She breathed in. She loved the smell of mint.

"Don't stop now," he said as he gestured to the bowl. "You should finish it before your bath."

She ate the entire bowl, not because she was hungry, but because he continued to chide her until it was gone. Then he pointed to the side.

"Your bath is ready now. This is Marie. She's going to help you while I take this bowl back downstairs."

He stood, pulling her up as he moved. She was a doll, she thought, moving when he directed, stopping when he disappeared. He hadn't disappeared, of course. He had merely stepped to the side, but the effect was still the same. She simply stood there.

Then the girl Marie came to her, taking her hand and tugging her forward. It was too much effort to resist, though her eyes sought out Brandon's.

"Marie will help you, Scher. I'll be back when you're done. Do you understand?"

"Of course I understand," she returned pleasantly. And she did. But after he nodded to her and left the room, she felt her little interest in the world desert her. In her mind, she was back in her room at the playhouse, looking down at Kit. Gray-as-cheap-wax Kit. What her body did now wasn't important.

Marie undressed her. Marie set her in the bath and washed her. Body. Hair. It mattered little. Except the warmth of the water, the food in her stomach, all combined to bring her slowly awake. Some of the cocoon of silence parted and she peered out—more aware than she had been in days.

By the time the bath was done, she was able to stand on

her own. She could assist in drying her own body. She was even able to wrap herself in a dressing gown as she returned to her seat by the window. The late afternoon sun was lowering, lengthening the shadows, and painting patterns on the cobblestones. She heard noise from the taproom—the rumble of voices, the occasional spark of laughter. It was a sound she'd grown up with. The playhouse sounded much the same from her bedroom. It was warm and familiar and as soothing as the food and bath.

She took a deep breath, smelling mint again. Turning, she saw Brandon standing in her door. He appeared to have bathed as well. His hair was wet, his clothing wrinkled but clean. He wore dark pants and a white shirt, open at the collar. And no shoes. He came in slowly, shutting the door behind him without once taking his gaze from her face.

"How are you feeling, Scher?"

She liked his voice. It was cultured. Smooth without the thick-mouthed accent of the lower classes.

"Much better, Brandon," she responded. "Thank you." His expression eased markedly, and she felt her lips curve up in a smile. "Surely you were not so worried as all that. Was I really so sad a case that simple conversation relieves your mind?"

He crossed the room, taking the seat opposite her. "Scher, I have never seen you so lackluster before. It was . . . disturbing."

"I think the food helped. I should have eaten earlier."

He was up again in a flash, bringing over a tray of bread and cheese that she hadn't even noticed. He set it on a nearby table. "There is more."

"So there is."

And because he so clearly wished it, she broke off a piece of cheese and ate it. She could taste it now, and she smiled because it was good. They sat a moment in silence. She chewed and found that she was still hungry. He relaxed back in his chair, watching her eat.

"Where did you go?" she asked. "I sent a message to your apartment, but no one was there. Not even Hank."

"I have a home in a village a couple hours from London. It is sunny and quiet there. A good place to recuperate."

She wondered if his wife was there. If she had tended his wounds, sat by his bed at night, and prayed that he would live to morning. She wondered, but she didn't have the strength to ask.

"You look better," she said instead. "Your wounds—"

"Healed. Though they still ache when I do too much."

"Did you ride to London on horseback?" It was only now, thinking back, that she remembered how he had looked in the Green Room. And had he said something to Seth about his horse?

He smiled. "The bath helped." He leaned forward, his expression sobering. "I am sorry I wasn't here before. Michael only came this morning. I didn't know."

He didn't explain *what* exactly he hadn't known, but Scher understood. No one had expected what had happened, least of all herself. Not to Kit. He had been so alive.

She felt Brandon's hand on her cheek, and she looked up at him. She hadn't even realized her gaze had dropped away, but now she saw the concern in his face. The apology for not being here when it happened. And the question, of course. The same question that haunted her: What had happened?

"It was so sudden," she said, speaking to his ear rather than his eyes. "He had a fever. The surgeon said to let him sleep off the drink. But then the cough began."

His hand dropped from her face to settle over her hands. She had them clenched together in her lap and his warmth easily surrounded them all the way into her wrists.

"Maybe if I had called for a doctor rather than a surgeon, but I was busy, and Martha said he'd heal. I knew he was ill, but I didn't think . . ." Her voice trailed away as guilt clogged her throat.

"Kit was young and strong. You could not have expected this."

Maybe. Maybe not. "He was in my bed. I sat with him and held his hand. But in the morning, he was gray. Even in that dark room, I could tell. Gray." Like Pappy. Like her mother and her sister near their end. "I sent Seth to find you."

"I'm so sorry, Scher."

She shook her head. She knew there had been no reason for him to stay in London. Certainly not for her. She had already sent him away.

"When you were not home, I had to contact the earl. His family deserved to see him. I could not keep him in secret, in my bed. They deserved—"

"Nothing, Scher. Kit chose you. I'm sure he wanted to be with you."

Scher bit her lip. It was true. Kit had said as much in one of his few moments of lucidity. Between coughs he'd said the last thing he wanted was to see his mother's pasty face every morning. Or worse yet, the countess's. After the tea party, his opinion of Lily had been colorful and heartfelt.

"But his mother deserved to know. To see him . . ." One last time. To say good-bye.

She couldn't say the words aloud, but Brandon understood. He reached over and gently gathered her in his arms. She went willingly. Burrowing against his shirt, she listened to his heartbeat, felt his heat, and smelled the mint of his breath. There was nowhere else in the world so wonderful.

"I suppose Michael began issuing orders the moment he saw the situation. It's what Michael does best: take over."

She nodded. "After one look at Kit, he'd told me to say my good-byes. He knew. We both did." He'd spoken simply, bluntly, and with the absolute force of an earl. "He said I would not be allowed near again. It would be too cruel to his mother."

"Bastard," Brandon snapped.

There was nothing more. The earl had taken Kit away, and then a few days later, she had received a cold note informing her of Kit's death. She never saw the obituary that appeared in the newspaper. Logic told her that it would have been the topic du jour in the Green Room that night, but that had no place in her mind. A sob tore through her, harsh on her throat. Then she felt Brandon's arms close about her as he lifted her up and set her on his lap. She curled into his embrace and let the feelings out. She cried as she never had before. She cried until she knew no more.

She woke hours later, still secure in his arms. Outside the window, the world was black. A storm was coming on, so the stars and moon were hidden behind clouds. Which left the eerie feeling that there was nothing beyond this room, nothing except her and Brandon in this chair together.

He'd been sleeping, just as she had. His head was set against the wall, cushioned by the edge of the chair. But somewhere between her awareness of the dark outside and the silence below stairs, he had come awake and was looking at her now.

She shifted her eyes to his and smiled. "You must be uncomfortable."

"Not at all."

It was a lie. It had to be, but she liked that he would hold her despite the discomfort. He must have read the thought off her face because he was shaking his head.

"I'm not lying, Scheherazade. Yes, my back may ache and my neck will not straighten just yet, but that has nothing to do with how I feel. To hold you like this is a comfort. I feel comfortable with you. It would take a great deal more than a crick in my neck for me to disturb that."

She touched his face. How could she not? He was holding her and expressing the exact peace she felt. "Thank you," she whispered.

"No, thank you," he responded. "Comfort is no small thing."

She smiled, but it didn't last. Her mind was waking, her body as well. And in this secluded moment out of time, odd thoughts surfaced. "Kit never held me. We didn't touch like this. He wasn't . . ." What was the word she wanted?

"Mature enough?" To his credit, it didn't sound like a criticism.

"I was going to say quiet. Always moving, always doing."

"He had energy. And he made you laugh."

"Not just me. He made everyone laugh. Even as he was turning their lives upside down." That had been the most consistent thought from the troupe. That he was a good fellow all around. Stupid about the playhouse, but a jolly, good fellow. High praise from the troupe players. "But he never touched me like you do. And he never looked at me like that."

Brandon's eyes shot up. "Like what?"

"Like your next breath depends upon mine."

Brandon shifted his gaze away. His eyes fell on the banked fire.

"Kit was . . ."

"A jolly good fellow."

She felt his laugh as a hitch in his breath, a slight jolt in his body, but otherwise all was serene in the cradle of his arms. "Yes," he said. "A jolly good fellow. The world needs more like him."

She closed her eyes, allowing her mind to drift into silence. She knew the lift and lower of his breath, the heat from his body, and the sweet smell of mint. Since the moment the earl had carried Kit away, Scheherazade had felt as though she were cocooned in cotton, insulated from the world and unable to communicate with it. She still felt cocooned, but the place was larger. Her space of peace was now this room, this moment, and Brandon was very much part of what kept her alive here.

Alive. She was alive, and she hadn't felt so in such a long time. She tilted her head such that her lips were near his neck, so her nose could be right against his skin.

"Touch me, Brandon," she said. "Please touch me."

His breath stopped. His hands froze. She knew he was holding back his reaction, keeping his thoughts apart from her.

"I think sometimes I died with Kit," she continued, not really thinking of her words but just letting them spill forth.

"You're not dead, Scher. You will feel again."

"I feel now. With you. Because of you."

"You will regret it tomorrow."

She pressed her lips to his neck. He was warm, his skin slightly rough. She brushed her mouth back and forth, feeling the texture against her skin, knowing his pulse hammered just beneath the surface.

"No, I won't. I will think back on it and remember what it was like to be alive."

Then she reached up and tugged his head down to her. He resisted, his muscles giving way in jerks. But she kept the pressure firm, never wavering in her intention. In the end, he gave in with a groan.

His mouth took hers, kissing her with the fierceness she remembered. He needed her, and when he kissed her like that, her every sense came alive. Within moments, she felt her own desires heat, her own needs surge.

He plundered her mouth while she clutched him tight, anchoring herself to him. The kiss went on forever, and when they finally broke apart, she pressed her face to his shoulder and gasped for air. And while she struggled to contain the pounding of her heart, he lifted her up. In a single abrupt movement, he tightened his grip on her and stood up from the chair.

"Brandon!" she gasped, surprised.

He looked down at her, his eyes in shadow but his expression clear. He stood there a moment, holding her suspended in the air. She understood what he was thinking, what he was asking.

"Don't stop, Brandon. Make me feel everything."

He didn't answer. He searched her face. And then in two long strides, he took her to bed.

Chapter 21

Brandon was not a small man. That was Scheherazade's first thought as he knelt alongside her on the bed. His body was tall and lean, his muscles sinewy. What softness she'd noticed before had been whittled away by his recent injuries. That left him a man of stark contrasts.

He was large beside her, his body hard, and yet when he touched her face, his hand shook with the effort to be tender. She looked into his eyes and saw a focused intensity, a fire that burned for her alone. But when he leaned in to kiss her, she found his caress almost leisurely. The brush of his lips, the touch of his tongue was slow, casual, and too light.

She lay on the bed in a dressing gown that had once been her mother's. It was plain cotton worn nearly gray with age. If it ever had lace, it was long gone now. Beneath it was an equally serviceable sleeping gown. Which meant she stretched out beside Brandon in attire that would be better suited for an elderly matron.

He didn't seem to care. Her hair was a wild tangle about her face. He leaned in, kissing her forehead and eyes, using his nose and his fingers to push away curling strands of her brown hair. She gripped his shoulders, wanting him to return to the kisses of before, the thrusting tongue and demanding possession, but he did not. He inhaled the scent of her hair and tasted the shell of her ear, but he did not *take* her as she'd asked.

"Brandon," she said as his breath heated the hollows of her ear. She arched her neck and pushed her body harder against him. He still wore all his own clothing, but at least she could feel the thick heat of him below. "Don't be delicate with me."

"Darling," he said as he pushed her back from him. She rolled until she lay flat. He followed but not as close as she wanted. He touched her hair with his one hand, stroking and playing with her curls, while he nuzzled the curve of her neck. "I have wanted this for so long, you do not expect me to rush now that it is here, do you?"

She did want him to rush. She wanted him to overpower her, to take her, to overwhelm her senses until she was swamped in what he did to her. But in this, he would not comply. She touched his chin, tilting his face so that she could look at him closely. He returned the look, his eyes serious, his expression open. Waiting. In the end, he arched a brow in query.

She had no words, no question. She knew the answer without even looking. He wanted her to choose, to touch, to enter into this as fully aware as he was. Her hand stroked across his cheek then fluttered past his mouth. His nostrils flared at her caress, but he didn't move, and in time, her fingers fell away from his face.

"Yes," she said. She wasn't even entirely aware of what she was saying yes to. Hadn't she already told him to take her? But perhaps this yes was to her fuller participation, to her meeting him as a partner in this act rather than an overwhelmed girl.

She smiled and stretched her lips to his. They met without deepening, their flesh touching, moving, caressing without tongues. And the restraint sent a shiver of awareness throughout her entire body. In that one moment, she felt every inch of his body as just outside of her touch, just beyond her reach, and yet so tantalizingly near that she ached.

She extended her tongue, touching his upper lip with just the tip. She felt his mouth curve in a smile as he opened enough to meet her just beyond his teeth. Their tongues touched, teased, dueled, but never penetrated either of their mouths.

She wended her fingers into his shirt, unfastening the buttons by touch alone. But she could not reach all the way down, and when she tugged, he lay too heavy on it for her to pull it free. In the end, she gave up, choosing to brush her fingers across his chest instead. The texture of his skin was soft beneath the coarse dusting of hair, and his nipples were tight knots that were so interesting to her. Especially when he shuddered at her stroke.

Their mouths were still touching ever so lightly, but now—at last—he leaned forward, rolling into dominant position as he deepened their kiss. He pushed his tongue into her mouth as she opened to him. Her hands were crushed against his chest, so she maneuvered them around his ribs to his back. But his shirt pulled tight, restricting her movements, and she whimpered her frustration.

He didn't seem to care. He was too intent on possessing her mouth, and she was happy to let him. For a time. Until the moment she surprised him by pretending to bite down. He drew back a bit and she stole the opportunity to thrust her tongue into him.

She liked this game, she thought. She could play this

with him forever. Or rather, for a little bit longer. Or not so
long because soon she was clutching his back, drawing him
closer to her while he used his higher position to take her
mouth in the domination she'd craved at the beginning.

She could feel the hammer of his heart against her chest.
Or perhaps it was her own as her breath was speeding up,
her body heating unbearably, her legs growing restless as
she clutched at him.

His shirt was an annoyance now, and she tried to tear it
open. She couldn't, but finally her need broke through the
haze of his kiss. He rolled back with a gasp and yanked off
his shirt while she lay panting. How pretty the light was as
it played across his skin, golden red from the fire embers
and shifting as his muscles clenched or relaxed.

He pushed her robe off her shoulders, but there was the
larger issue of the gown beneath. He abruptly levered himself upright and circled her calves with his hands. He made
a long caress of lifting her gown off her. She had to lift
her hips to help him as he pushed the hem over her knees,
up along her thighs, and over her bottom. Then he slid his
hands underneath her gown to press into her lower back
helping her to lever upright.

She did what he wanted, sitting up and raising her arms
overhead. His fingers stroked along her sides, his thumb
rolling over ribs and breasts as he maneuvered the gown
upward. He paused a moment while she sat there with her
arms ridiculously lifted, fabric bunched at her neck and
face. His thumbs rolled back down over her breasts to
tweak her nipples again. And again.

"Brandon," she gasped. "Brandon!" Then when he showed
no desire to finish his task, she hauled off her gown, tossing
it aside before shaking her hair out of her eyes. Then she
glanced at Brandon, only to see that he sat mesmerized by
the sight.

Was it of her? She smiled and shook out her hair again,

this time lifting her breasts enough that they bobbed with her movement.

"Tease," he accused, but he was smiling and his eyes had not left her chest.

She straightened, excruciatingly aware that she sat naked before him, this man who was not her husband and never would be. Despite her thought earlier that this was a moment out of time, she could not suppress the awareness that she was accepting a man into her bed outside of wedlock. Her dream of becoming respectable was disappearing by the second. Or perhaps it was long gone.

"I am beginning to think and I don't want to," she whispered to Brandon. "We are going too slow." Then she reached forward and tried to maneuver her hand beneath his waistband.

"Then you have the advantage of me," he rasped. "I find I cannot think at all." He lifted her hand away from his clothes, unbuttoning them with quick movements. He stepped off the bed long enough to shuck all of it away until he was as naked as she.

Her eyes went to his organ. It stood large and proud, outlined clearly by the glow of the fire. He meant to come to the bed, she knew, but at her focused stare he stilled.

"Are you afraid?" he asked.

She shook her head, her eyes still on his organ. Then she stretched out her hand and slowly traced the full dimensions of him. She knew the wiry texture of his hair, the velvety suede of his skin, and the ridges from veins. There was a distinct edge at the mushroom head, and she traced the near circle of it before sliding on top. The wetness there made her finger move in a circle, spreading the moisture around before she wandered back down. And as she went, she leaned forward so she could curl all her fingers until she held him fully.

His buttocks tightened, pushing him against her palm.

She hadn't kissed him before. Not there. Not like he had done to her, and so she stretched toward him with that intent.

He stopped her with a hand on her cheek. Then he cupped her chin and pulled her gaze up to his.

"I will never last," he said. "Is that what you want? For me to not . . ."

She shook her head. She wanted him inside her. She wanted her belly filled with him. She even wanted his child, but she shuddered away from that thought. The implications of that were too huge.

"I will try not to spill my seed in you. I will try to—"

"No. There are other ways." She had learned of such things from the actresses. She scrambled off the bed and crossed to her bag. Annette had packed it, and Annette was especially careful about these things. "Can you light a candle?" she asked.

He did, bringing it to the dresser where the mirror doubled the light. Searching through her bag, she found what she was looking for: a glass vial and a sponge. She should soak the sponge in the vinegar solution and insert it now as deeply as possible. It wasn't a perfect method, but it was enough.

She straightened, smiling at him in the mirror. She didn't have to speak. Their eyes met and held, and he understood. Then she watched as he came up behind her. She felt his heat on her back and the push of his organ against her bottom. Then he bent his head and began to kiss her neck, just beneath her ear. His hands circled around her, sliding over her belly and then up to cup her breasts.

She stretched upward into his arms, lifting her breasts into his hands, and thrusting her bum against his organ. Her head dropped back against his shoulder. His hands were doing such wonderful things to her breasts, holding them, tugging at her nipples, squeezing and twisting. Soon she was writhing beneath his touch.

"I should use the sponge—" she gasped.

He tightened his grip on her, keeping her exactly where she was. He wrapped one arm more fully about her torso while he began a rhythmic push against her bottom. She wanted to lift up higher, to let him seek between her legs, but he positioned his organ along her spine well away from what she wanted.

"I won't risk it," he said against her ear.

"It will only take a moment," she said, but she didn't push out of his arms. She wouldn't mind so terribly to have his child. Any child was a joy, but his child . . . The very thought filled her with a silent yearning.

"I won't risk it," he repeated. Then his right hand roamed down over her belly. Her legs were already weak. It was easy for him to push his fingers between. She was so wet that he could slide easily over her mound and between her folds. "Lean forward," he said, as he pressed his chest against her back.

She bent at the waist, bracing her hands on the dresser. In the mirror, she could see herself reflected clearly, her left breast held in his hand, her nipples hard and pointed. He was bent over her, the angles of his face chiseled and dark. His eyes met hers in the mirror, caught and held her gaze. And then the fingers between her legs began to stroke her.

She had little room, encircled as she was by his body. His arms trapped her torso, his body pressed against her back, and his legs slipped between hers, spreading her wider and wider. His organ pushed hot and hard against her bottom, upward between the fold of her cheeks. And his fingers pushed deep inside her only to pull up in a long, full stroke.

She gasped, shuddering at the exquisite feel. He pressed a kiss into her shoulder, a nip against her neck. She arched, feeling him push two fingers deep inside, only to pull out in another long stroke.

A flash fire of heat seared her skin. She arched again,

but there was no place to move. She felt his organ pulse in response. He was pushing hard against her. Or perhaps she was arching backward. Then her thoughts splintered as he pushed his fingers in again.

Deep push, then the long slide out. Punctuated by a pinch of her nipple.

Her breath stuttered. She was leaning forward, her arms barely able to support her weight. Mostly, he held her. He stroked her. In. Out.

She whimpered, her gaze still held by his in the mirror. Faster. He was moving faster and her breath was coming in rapid pants. Her entire body was moving forward and back in time to his strokes.

Faster.

Deeper.

Yes!

The ecstasy hit as an expanding wave of pleasure. It centered on his hand, but rushed inward, pulse after pulse of bliss. He held her throughout it all. She had closed her eyes in the end, arching with a cry.

The waves had just begun to slow when she felt him shift his grip on her body. He slid to her hips, holding her steady as he pushed against her bottom. Not inside. Vertically, along her spine, but with a ferocity that caught her attention.

His face was taut, his eyes blazing with hunger. She held his gaze, silently communicating her joy to him, and then his own pleasure gripped him. He thrust hard and she felt his spasm along her whole spine. His head was thrown back as he lost control. She watched his throat stretch and his chest ripple. Her own pleasure returned just from seeing his.

Another ripple of her own. A gasping moment of delight. Pleasure suspended out of time. So sweet.

So sweet.

And then it passed. Time started again. Their bodies

collapsed forward onto the dresser, their arms trembling, their breaths still short and quick. Another moment more and he slowly straightened.

It should have felt awkward with the way he cleaned her. There was a pitcher and bowl next to the dresser, cloths hanging from a rack on the side. He wet the cloth and washed her, taking care to be gentle on her sensitive skin. It should have felt awkward, but it didn't. The business of afterward was comfortable, the rhythms easy even though they had never done this before.

Then he helped her to bed, settling her down on the pillow before climbing in behind her. He intended to pull her backward against him, but she didn't want to face somewhere else. So she rolled over to set her head on his shoulder, her arm on his chest. He wrapped his other arm around her, pulling her close.

There were no words. They didn't need any. All was in silent accord as she closed her eyes. His free hand reached up to hold hers where it lay on his chest. And soon she felt his breath deepen into sleep.

She lay there a little longer, her mind replaying the events of this night. She remembered her own pleasure, but what she relived the most was the sight of him arched in release. He was a beautiful man, she thought, lean and powerful. More than that, he was a good man, careful of her in ways that no one else had ever been. What man denied himself so that she would not risk pregnancy? What man thought to bring her to a private inn, arrange for food and bath without expectation of more? And what man listened as she spoke, understood her in all her moods? Even when she had no understanding of her own?

No one in her life.

Again the question resurfaced, troubling despite the bliss that still saturated her body. What would she give up to be with this man forever? Kit was gone, but her dream of respectability still lingered.

This night of sex has been amazing. But was the temporary joy of their coupling worth the loss of her hope of becoming a wife and mother? How would she feel about him, about this in the morning?

She didn't know. Worse, she didn't want to know. If it had been up to her, he would have buried himself in her, releasing his seed into her womb and damn the consequences. Damn her reputation and forget the life that waited for every child born as a bastard. Another boy raised in the theater? Another girl who could aspire to no better than to become an actress/whore? What did she care when he held her so sweetly?

She hadn't cared at the time. She did now. And she absolutely would have cared in the morning if she found herself pregnant.

He had taken care that that didn't happen. He had seen that she didn't worry, and for that she adored him. But what of next time? What of the future? Would he always be so concerned? And would she always feel that another night like this, suspended away from the world, was worth the disdain that waited in the daylight?

Could she live with the consequences if she became his mistress? Would she give up becoming respectable, being a wife to an honorable man and a mother to legitimate children? Was this moment of bliss worth a lifetime without respectability?

No.

As wonderfully amazing as this night was, the answer was still no. There would be another man for her. Not Kit, obviously, but someone. She merely had to lower her standards and *not* look among the aristocracy. She should allow her financial status to become known. Fear had always kept her silent, but if everyone knew how much money she had, dozens of respectable men would vie for her hand. The only reason she hadn't taken the step before was because she had held out hope for something different, something special.

Brandon.

Everything she wanted was in Brandon. But he couldn't give her respectability. She sighed, burrowing tighter to his side. Could she? Could she really be happy wed to someone who wasn't Brandon?

Yes, she lied. A thousand times yes. She could be respectable and happy with someone else. And if she kept repeating that, then eventually she would come to believe it. And in the meantime, she would sleep here, curled tight to the man she . . .

She would not say "love." She absolutely would *not* believe that she loved Brandon. That would be a folly beyond any other folly she had ever committed. Thinking that she loved Brandon would be like opening her heart and soul to a raw dagger. If she thought she loved him, if she said the word in her mind or—God forbid—out loud, then she would be committed. Something in her soul would link with him and never be satisfied with less.

She would not do that to herself. She would not open herself to misery with no hope of redemption. She absolutely, positively did not love Brandon and never would.

Chapter 22

Brandon watched Scheherazade dress. Her movements were efficient, her manner calm. She appeared happy, smiling at him with warmth whenever their gazes connected. But there was a reserve in her, something that he could not assign to one action or another. A stillness that was from sadness or maybe even despair.

Perhaps he was being maudlin. Perhaps it was his own emotions he was sensing. But he could not shake the feeling that as wonderful as last night had been, he and Scheherazade were further apart than ever. He waited until they were in a hired carriage to press her. He hadn't meant to mention it at all, but the isolation of the vehicle invited confidences, and he could not stop himself from trying to bridge whatever gap had formed between them.

"Are you anxious about the service? You won't be turned away."

"Yes, I will," she said softly. Then she lifted her chin.

"But it doesn't matter. I will stand outside of St. James if I must. I will show Kit proper respect."

"You won't be turned away," he repeated firmly. He would see to it. It was the one thing he could do for both Scher and Kit. "He would want you there."

She didn't respond, and they both lapsed into silence. He sat across from her, feeling the space between them widen. He studied her profile, the curve of her face, the length of her neck. Objectively speaking, she possessed above-average beauty. Her face was well formed, her eyes expressive, but the stresses of her life showed. Dark hallows haunted her eyes, and even when she smiled, she rarely showed her teeth.

And yet, when he looked at her, he saw so much more than her skin or her eyes or her teeth. He knew the solid strength of her as she went about her days, managing the playhouse and the troupe, handling financial crises as well as medical ones. Her skills were beyond amazing. This morning, in the time it had taken him to tie his cravat, she had pinned and adjusted her gown to fit her slender frame.

She would make an excellent wife and mother. Competent in all manner of care, with a loving heart and a generous spirit. She wouldn't be one of those overly anxious or hysterical mothers. She would manage all with a firm but loving hand. But it would be a sad home, he thought as she turned to stare out the window. The children would bring life into it, she would bring quiet strength and love, but who would bring the laughter? The joy? Kit would have. He understood that now.

"I shouldn't have tried to stop you and Kit," he confessed. "I was wrong."

Her eyes barely flickered. "And now?" she whispered. "Now that he is gone and you no longer need to save him from me—"

"Now someone needs to save me because I do not think I can leave you be."

She arched a brow. "Even if I say no? If I declare no more, my lord? If I bar my door to you and ban you from the Tavern Playhouse?"

He shrugged, his hand dropping away as he admitted the truth to himself as well as her. "Even then I will pursue you."

"Because my wishes mean nothing to you?"

"Because there is no place in the world that would not be better with you in it. No part of my life feels whole without you. Even in my own mind, I cannot turn around without wishing I could share my thoughts with you."

Her eyes widened in shock at his words. He, too, felt shaken by the absolute truth of what he had just said. And in that stunned silence, the cab slowed to a stop. They had arrived at St. James.

He helped her disembark, his eyes scanning the crowd of carriages. He could already tell that the service would be well attended. Though only a lesser son, Kit had been universally liked. And no one in the haut *ton* missed an opportunity to attend the funeral of someone related to an earl.

He saw Michael immediately. The earl was obviously waiting at the front, scanning the crowd. Lily stood at the very door, greeting people as they entered. She looked just as a countess ought—appropriately severe in black even with the fashionable cut of her gown.

Michael's body slumped in relief when he spotted Brandon. But then his expression tightened into a dark frown when Scheherazade stepped into view. Not surprisingly, a number of the crowd noticed her as well. Brandon caught a number of pointed fans and outraged gasps.

"I'll take care of everything," he murmured to Scher as he extended his arm to her. Then he silently offered a prayer to God that he could keep his promise.

She squeezed his arm, reassuring him when he had tried to reassure her. Then together they glided forward.

Michael met them well before the door, his every movement radiating total disapproval.

"Good to see you alive, Brandon," he drawled. "We expected you last night."

Brandon shrugged. "I cannot help your expectations, brother. Next time, you should make your orders more clear."

"Yes," he drawled. "Apparently I have been too vague in the past. I shall attempt to remedy that." His cold stare shifted to Scheherazade. "You are not welcome. I do not know what wiles you have to so besot two otherwise perfectly normal members of my family, but I assure you, I am immune."

"Have a care, Michael," Brandon growled to no apparent effect.

Michael gestured to a waiting carriage and the two large footmen standing beside it. "You will climb into that carriage there. It will take you wherever you wish, then you will never again contact any of my family."

"Or what?" snapped Brandon before Scheherazade could speak. "You will destroy her reputation? You have already done so. Threaten her person?" He glared the two footmen back. "Already done. Do you plan next to burn down her playhouse? Shoot her in the head?"

Michael reared back, his expression shocked. They all three knew of the tragedy in India. They all knew what had been done there by Englishmen who pretended to be honest, moral Christians.

"Do not thrust your demons onto me, brother," Michael snarled.

"Kit would want her at his service."

A cold female voice cut in. It was Lily, speaking with the gentle tones appropriate to a countess. "But Kit is gone; his wishes no longer matter. Kit's mother, however, is alive, as are his brothers and his grandmother. Kit's *family* has no wish for a scene at Kit's funeral."

Brandon straightened. "Then step aside and there will be no scene."

There was a moment of taut silence. Michael and Lily stood together, a solid wall of aristocratic arrogance. Brandon faced them, his every breath radiating his absolute determination that Scher be allowed to grieve her fiancé in an appropriate manner. What Scher thought was a mystery.

Michael's hands tightened into fists. "Have you taken leave of your senses? She is an *actress*."

"I was his fiancée," Scher said, her voice so soft as to be nearly snatched away by the wind. "Our banns are no doubt still posted right over there." She pointed to the board where St. James hung marriage announcements.

"Allow her to grieve at the service as is *appropriate*." Brandon stressed the word even though he knew Scher had broken off the engagement. What might have happened was no longer relevant, and Brandon refused to give them the satisfaction of knowing the truth.

"I will sit at the back and be silent," Scher said, "but I *will* honor Kit's life and memory."

"Your very presence is a dishonor—" Lily hissed, but Brandon cut her off.

"I have the ring Kit gave her. Their engagement ring." He pulled it out of his pocket and held it up to the light. It was a lie. The cut and setting were the same as Scher's ring, but the diamond was a good deal more than anything Kit could have purchased. As expected, Lily's eyes narrowed on the brilliant gem.

"Brandon . . ." Scher began. She was likely going to protest that it was the wrong ring, but he turned to her, speaking over her words.

"It is yours, Scher," he stressed, praying that she would accept his lie. "Kit gave it to you in good faith, but would you trade it to be at the funeral? To sit inside St. James and honor Kit as you would like?"

She swallowed, and he saw the shimmer of tears in her eyes. "Yes," she whispered. Then they turned together to Michael and Lily.

"Very well," snapped Lily as she tried to snatch the ring from Brandon's fingers. "But you sit in the back."

Brandon was faster than her. Rather than lose the ring, he caught Lily's hand and held her still in a bruising grip. "No, Lily," he said softly. "Scher will sit where she chooses and stay as long as she likes."

"That will not help your political ambitions," inserted Michael. "Wilberforce is here, as are most of the political families. Appearing to support her so openly will only harm your agenda."

"On the contrary," returned Brandon, the truth of his words crystallizing as he said them. "It shows my absolute support of the idea that every man should be allowed to choose his own path, his own bride, without the meddling interference of British society."

Michael obviously bristled, likely more from the tone than the idea. And Lily remained poised in between them, trapped by her own greed since she would not release her hold on the ring. And into this frozen tableau, Scheherazade once again inserted her quiet words.

"I will sit in the back." Then she touched Brandon's arm. "I have lately begun to value compromise." She looked at Lily. "I will cause no more noise, no further scene. I will not even cry loudly, and I swear to leave directly after the service. And for that, you may have the ring." Then she turned her eyes back to Brandon. "Thank you, Lord Blackstone. Thank you for being my best champion."

He frowned at that. There was an extra measure of meaning in her words, a message he could not understand. He leaned toward her a moment, needing to ask, but this was not the place. So he pressed his lips together and nodded to her, pleased by her compliment despite the situation. He released his hold on Lily and the ring, curling his lip only slightly as his sister-in-law secreted the ring into her glove. Then she spun on her heel and stomped directly to the St. James board, presumably to rip down the list of banns. Michael followed his wife a moment later, leaving Brandon and Scher free to climb the steps.

The service proceeded as an aristocratic funeral usually went—with stares and loud sobs, ponderous tedium and a closed coffin. When it was her turn, Brandon escorted Scheherazade to the casket. She lay her gloved hand on the polished wood and whispered something no one could hear. But Brandon was close enough to see the movement of her lips and knew what she said.

"Thank you, Kit, for everything. I am so sorry that I was not the woman you deserved."

Then he escorted her out the doors. They walked past his sobbing grandmother and furious mother. They ignored the gossiping aristocrats and more gasps of outrage. Brandon took her straight back to the carriage he had hired this morning.

He helped her inside, then gave his instructions to the coachman. Moments later, his plan was set in motion. It would be some time before Scheherazade realized what he was doing. Hopefully at least a half hour before she thought to look out the window and see the scenery. But whether she realized it immediately or not, the end would be the same.

She was coming with him to Pottersfarm. He was abducting her.

They were just outside of London when Scheherazade finally took stock of her surroundings. Her mind had been so full of things—the funeral, Brandon giving over an expensive ring that was not her engagement ring, what they had done together last night. All of it was jumbled together in her thoughts, nothing really preeminent except that Brandon featured in all of it. But it was too early and too complicated to think about him, so she had allowed her mind to drift to Kit and the ring that she still had in her pocket. The ring that she had taken off the day of that terrible tea and had never put back on.

She pulled it out of her pocket now and held it before her. Kit was gone. His plans for the future buried with him. She had resolved last night to look for a future for herself, to no longer exist in the gray life she had lived. It was time to find her own happiness. She shouldn't have let Brandon give over a different ring while she held on to the real one.

"Here," she said as she held it out to him. "Perhaps you can switch it later and get back the other one."

"I don't want either one of them," he said, his voice a solid presence in the murky light of a closed carriage. "Kit gave that to you. You should keep it."

"Kit is gone as is the woman I was when he proposed." She tried again to offer it to him, but he steadfastly refused to move. "I do not need a ring to honor what he has taught me."

Brandon arched a brow at her. "And what is that? What have you learned from my feckless cousin?"

She smiled at that. There was no condemnation in his voice. If anything, Brandon's tone held a gentle respect for his "feckless" cousin. "To try again," she said. "To learn to laugh without him."

Brandon leaned forward, his eyes narrowed as he searched her face. "Kit was never beaten down as you were. He never suffered in the way you did."

Or you, she added silently. Brandon knew better than most the pain of betrayal and loss. "But that doesn't matter," she said. "The lesson is still the same. Kit is gone. I cannot have his laughter anymore. I cannot have his passion for life. Not unless I create it on my own."

He tilted his head, his brow narrowed in thought. "It is

funny," he said softly. "I would say that you taught me that. To keep *living* despite everything."

She heard the stress on the word "living" and knew that Brandon had indeed changed. That he would never seek his own end again. "Then Kit is doubly missed," she said.

He leaned forward and gently wrapped her fingers around the ring. "Keep his ring so that you will remember his lesson."

She nodded, more because of the warmth of his hand surrounding hers. Once again, she felt cocooned with Brandon, tucked away in a place that was safe for such discussions and self-examinations. She took a deep breath and released it, feeling the tension in her body ease with the movement.

"Thank you," she said. "For everything."

He arched a brow as he pulled back from her, leaning against the squabs. "Do not thank me yet, Scheherazade. Not until you know what I have done."

She frowned, and at her silent question, he waved to the window. Looking out, she saw that they were nowhere near the Tavern Playhouse. That they were, in fact, leaving London.

"What?" she said as she twisted to the window. "Where are we?"

"I'm taking you to Pottersfarm. It's a village near Greenwich where I have a house. Everything is all arranged. You needn't worry about the playhouse or anything. Just come to my home and rest for a time."

She didn't answer, her gaze picking up the green of trees and grass and all sorts of things that were incredibly rare in London. There were still buildings, houses, even inns, but the feel of space out here was marked. She sighed and closed her eyes, dropping her head back against the squabs. What would she give to live out here forever? Could she give up her life in London?

"Please, Scher. I'll take you back if you want, but don't you think you deserve a rest? Just for a few days?"

She smiled without opening her eyes. She took deep breaths of the air, enjoying the scent of flowers and sunshine, of less coal and no stale sweat. Of Brandon and his mint. It was perfect. The thought of staying for a little longer in that cocoon of peace with Brandon was beyond perfect.

"Thank you," she said again. "I would love to visit your home for a while."

She felt his hand slip over hers, warm and large. Comforting. And without even thinking, she flipped her hand over so she could hold his.

She nearly said it right then. She nearly spoke the words: Yes, I will be your mistress. She wanted to more than anything. Except then she thought of Seth's boys, of her dead sister, and all the actresses who became mistresses only to become pregnant despite precautions. She could not do it to her future child. And she could not trust in their restraint the next time he touched her. Eventually, there would be a child, and she would not have one out of wedlock.

She pulled her hand out of his, covering the motion by shifting so she could see better out the window. "Green and more green," she said. "It's so beautiful."

"Whatever you want, Scher," he said softly. "However long you want. This I swear to you."

She turned back to look at him, seeing that he had somehow guessed her thoughts. He was offering her carte blanche in the literal sense. He would give her everything she wanted for as long as she wanted. Everything, that is, except marriage.

"Not for long," she said. "Just a few days' holiday." Then she turned back to the window to hide her tears.

He must have understood. Indeed, how could he not? They had both been quite clear in their positions. So rather than argue, he shifted so that he could look out the window with her.

"That's where Bob Neely found his lost hog," he said as he pointed over her shoulder. "Unfortunately, it had already trampled all of Miss Stevenson's prize pumpkins. Quite the scandal."

She smiled. "I hope he has found a way to contain his pig better."

"No, not really. But as his attempt to make restitution resulted in Miss Stevenson becoming Mrs. Neely, everyone has decided the pig's escape was a benevolent act from God."

She twisted slightly, shooting him a look over her shoulder. "Shouldn't that be an act from Cupid, not God?"

"Hmmm, perhaps it should. Perhaps they should have renamed the pig to Cupid."

She smiled, relaxing to the side so that he could tell her more. "And what about this patch of land? Is there any great love match to be found here?"

"Sadly, no," he returned. "This is where I spent an hour watching the progress of a spider attaching a web to my arm."

"You did not!"

"I assure you I did. On the way from London sick from my wounds. It was at least an hour before I could manage to sit up. The bread you gave to Hank helped enormously."

Scher smiled. "So he didn't eat it then. I thought he wouldn't, but you can never tell with boys that age. Hunger is a powerful thing."

"He forced it on me. Said he wouldn't let me make him a liar to Lady Scher," he returned.

She smiled, the expression easing tension she hadn't even realized she was carrying in her face. "I hope you rewarded him adequately for his loyalty."

"He's eating me out of house and home! Mrs. Wiggins had to double the food budget because of him!"

Her smile widened at that. She wasn't quite up to laughter, but he made the gray fog lighten with every moment in his presence. They passed the rest of the distance in comfortable discourse. It wasn't that he was particularly witty in the London way, with sarcasm and veiled innuendo. Far from it. He had a sense of humor completely absent in London. He gloried in the bucolic joys of pastoral life, poking fun at it even as he seemed to admire the quieter rhythms. And as she had never seen this side of him, Scher found herself extremely happy to explore this calmer, happier Brandon.

By the time they arrived at his house, she was in the perfect mood to appreciate its beauty. It looked exactly like an English village manor ought to look. Two stories, green lawn, near to the village, but enough removed to be private. He told her he'd purchased it off a young lord who had decided life here was much too dull.

They disembarked into fresh air, blue sky, and the anxious expression of Brandon's housekeeper. She was a rotund woman with rosy cheeks who fussed with her apron as she spoke.

"My lord! My lord! I didn't realize you'd be bringing a guest. Oh, dear. The doctor is here, you know. And he brought his mother, lovely lady. Those foreign ways makes the misses more comfortable even if they are odd. And we're full up to the rafters, so I had to hire on Missy from down by the church. Oh, dear."

"Mrs. Wiggins, Mrs. Wiggins!" Brandon said with an easy smile. Even his posture had relaxed. His body somehow looked less predatory Londonite, more country baron. "You look delightful this afternoon. Do tell me that Cook has made those tarts that are so excellent. I'm sure Miss Martin will find them delicious."

"Oh. Well, as to that, I'm not really sure. I can inquire, of course, but . . ." She looked embarrassed and awkward as the coachman lifted down Scheherazade's bag. "So you are to be staying, then?"

"The doctor is here?" Brandon put in before Scher could answer. "And he has brought his mother?"

"Yes, my lord. Yes. So you see—"

"We have a lack of bedrooms, then. No matter. Is there any bed at all for Miss Martin?"

"Well, one could be made up in the nursery, I'm sure, as the doctor is sleeping in the room you usually have. His mother has settled in with Nidra right next to the missus. It's been quite good for her, what with their language being spoken at all hours, but you—"

"Excellent! Put Miss Martin in the nursery then. You won't mind, will you, Scher? It's quite clean—"

"Of course I won't mind—"

"And I shall bunk in the library then."

Mrs. Wiggins' eyes widened in horror. "The library, my lord?"

"Of course. There's an excellent settee in there, as I recall. Quite comfortable. Just get me a pillow and a blanket."

The housekeeper stared at him goggle-eyed.

"Really, Brandon," Scher said, touching his arm. "I don't need to—"

He rounded on her. His movement was slow enough to appear casual, but the intensity that burned through his gaze revealed . . . something. Emotion. Blistering heat. Need? Her breath caught in her throat, and she was stunned to feel an answering swell in her own heart.

"You will stay, Scher," he said with a falsely casual wave to the sky. "It's too late to go back now anyway." Then he sobered. "Please."

She nodded. "Of course. Now that I have seen this beautiful village, I cannot think to leave. At least not until I have met Mr. Neely's pig."

"Oh, and what a story that is!" said the housekeeper as she began leading the way inside. "It's been the talk of the parish for years."

They climbed the step to the front door, Mrs. Wiggins chatting the whole way. Scher glanced toward Brandon as she maneuvered the front walkway, only to have her gaze caught and held. He stood there, his body relaxed, but his expression still intense.

"Thank you," he mouthed.

She nodded and was about to say something, but her words were forestalled as Mrs. Wiggins turned abruptly.

"Oh, your lordship, you'll want to see the missus right away. She's at her best now, after her nap. And this morning was ever so lovely. She likes her bit of home."

Brandon's gaze shuttered as he turned his attention to his housekeeper. "Of course. I'll go there now." Then he hesitated, turning slightly to Scher. "Would you care to meet . . . my wife?"

The offer was sincere. That much, at least was clear. As was Brandon's anxiety with that slight hitch in his question. Scheherazade swallowed. Of course she wanted to meet Brandon's wife. But it wasn't something to do unprepared. She needed to feel stronger, needed to know how she felt about Brandon before . . .

"Of course," she heard herself say. Then she was climbing the stairs right beside him, her mind spinning with anxiety.

"Just mind not to make any sudden moves," the housekeeper admonished. "And mind, my lord, the doctor's made some changes to the parlor."

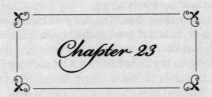

Chapter 23

"Change" was an understatement for what the doctor had done to Channa's parlor. Brandon stepped into the denuded room and felt his anger start to rise. The place was stripped of all furniture completely! His wife was sitting on the floor like a peasant! Nidra and an older woman, probably the doctor's mother, were sitting with her . . . folding laundry?

He restrained his fury and a bellow for the doctor, mostly because a shout would certainly startle Channa. But also because there wasn't quiet enough to speak. Unlike the usual morbid silence, Channa and her companions were chatting with animation, perhaps even girlish excitement.

He frowned and looked closer at his wife's face. Yes, indeed, she seemed happy. And she certainly wasn't reaching for her scissors to stab him.

"Quite the difference, my lord, isn't it?" It was a male voice.

Brandon turned again, this time to see the warm, olive face of Dr. Dandin. In his hands, he carried a bowl of something that reeked of curry. Brandon stepped aside, the scent mixing in his mind with smoke and ash. He had never wanted to smell that particular mixture again. His stomach churned in disgust, but everyone else in the room seemed to look up with pleasure.

The older woman, Mrs. Dandin presumably, came forward with an excited chatter. Nidra brightened as well, but Brandon's focus was on his wife. How would she react to her native dish? The last time they had tried such a thing was a year ago. Channa's fit lasted nearly a week, but today was different. The girl looked up just as expectantly as Nidra. Or at least she did until she caught sight of Brandon.

There was a long frozen moment between him and his wife. Around them was chatter and movement. Even Scheherazade faded somewhat from his attention, though he was very aware that she stood a few inches behind him, no doubt watching everything with her keen gaze. But what would Channa do?

She shifted to her knees, her gaze puzzled, almost as if she didn't recognize him. As if he hadn't been here just yesterday morning when she'd thrown her breakfast at him. Then her expression changed. He saw it coming immediately and tensed himself for the blow. She was on her feet in a second, launching herself at him with a scream of fury. He stepped forward to grab her, but Dr. Dandin was before him. He grabbed Channa's arms and held her firmly.

"Enough of this!" the man snapped. "You will spill the food!"

Channa continued to screech, her eyes wild as she stared over the doctor's shoulder at him. Then Mrs. Dandin smoothly stepped between Brandon and his wife, cutting off Channa's view.

"Such nonsense!" chided the woman in Channa's native dialect. "You will ruin the meal."

Channa, still restrained in Dr. Dandin's arms, stopped her scream on a toddlerlike hiccup.

"That's better," the older woman said. Then she glanced over her shoulder at Brandon. "Men do not belong here. This is a woman's place. Go! Go!"

Her words were stern, but he saw a silent plea in her expression. He nodded in assent and bowed out of the room. He knew better than anyone how Channa reacted to his presence.

"Then I must leave as well," said Dr. Dandin. "And you must sit and eat." He guided Channa to where Nidra had laid out a blanket on the floor like a picnic. "I hope you enjoy it," he said warmly before he too gave a slight bow and backed out of the room.

Brandon stayed out of sight, watching as the doctor shut the door quietly behind him. On the opposite side of the hall, Scheherazade stood silently, her steady gaze absorbing everything. Brandon sent her a desperate glance, silently pleading with her not to be afraid. Her response was a soft reassuring smile.

He stared at her a moment longer while a weight rolled off his shoulders. A weight he hadn't even realized had been there. The last two housekeepers and a score of maids had run screaming at the sight of Channa in one of her fits. And all Scher had done was step silently backward out of the way.

Meanwhile, Dr. Dandin turned to him, a grin on his face. "Do you see?" he asked with a smile. "Do you see how much better she is?"

Brandon gaped at the man. "She . . . She . . ." Words deserted him. His wife had descended into a screeching madwoman the minute Brandon came into view. That was hardly better.

"Ah," said Dr. Dandin, with an understanding nod. "You are focusing on the worst, but think back to how she appeared before."

"Before she caught sight of me?" Brandon drawled.

"Er, yes, before then. Did you see how she was happy?

How she interacted with my mother? They were doing chores all morning. It's mother, really. She has a way with the girls. I should have brought her to England long ago."

Brandon nodded slowly. "Yes, I suppose that is improvement. But . . . why is there no furniture?" He ran his hand over his face, struggling to order his thoughts. "I can't be in the room with her, I can't help her mind. At the very least I can see that she lives in comfort."

Dr. Dandin took his arm, leading him down the hallway toward the stairs. "We can talk more comfortably in the library," he said, as he cast a curious glance at Scheherazade.

She immediately took the hint, smiling sweetly. "I should just freshen up. If someone could point to my room?"

Mrs. Wiggins was coming up the stairs, likely to do just that, but Brandon abruptly touched Scher's arm. He would have yanked her to him if he could, but even he was not that uncivilized. Still, he couldn't deny the surge of need that coursed through him. He wanted her with him. He needed to know that she wasn't going to run away the moment he turned his back.

"Scher—" he began, wondering just what he could say. So many thoughts jumbled together in his mind. But he had brought her here for her to recuperate, not so he could burden her with his problems. She looked at him expectantly, but words failed him. What could he say to her? He glanced at Dr. Dandin and found help in polite introductions.

"Dr. Dandin, please allow me to introduce Miss Martin. She is . . . She was . . ." He swallowed. "She was lately engaged to my cousin. We were at his funeral this morning."

"My goodness, I had no idea! Please accept my condolences," the doctor returned.

"Thank you," both Scher and Brandon responded together. And then another awkward silence descended as his two guests tried to take their cue from their host. But Brandon was still at a loss.

"Uh," he stumbled into speech, "I, uh, met Dr. Dandin in India. He wanted to come to England to study, and I have followed his career with interest."

"He has done more than that," Dr. Dandin continued. "He has been an enormous help in opening doors in England."

"In return, he has been Channa's doctor and a much-needed friend."

The mutual admiration ended then, and once again they stood awkwardly in the hallway. Only now it was worse as Mrs. Wiggins topped the stairs to stand expectantly just to the side. Eventually, it was Scher who managed to end the difficulty.

"It is lovely to meet you doctor. I am sure you are a great aid to Lord Blackstone. No doubt the two of you wish to discuss matters in private."

"Scher—"

"It has already been a long day, my lord. Perhaps we could speak again this evening at dinner."

He wanted to speak more now. He wanted to explain about Channa, about how all this mess came to be. He thought she would listen this time, but he couldn't take the time to explain right here in the hallway. Most of all, he wanted to have her beside him when he discussed whatever it was that Dr. Dandin wanted. Those conversations were never easy, and he simply wished she could be there with him. He wanted her thoughts on the problems at hand. He wanted . . . well, he wanted her, and that, he thought as he glanced back at Channa's door, was never going to be.

He executed a deep bow, using the motion to force himself to look at something other than Scheherazade. "Mrs. Wiggins will show you the way. Please let her know if you need anything at all."

He spoke the words to her shoulder, then with a stiff spine and a sense of doom, he turned toward the library and whatever new problem the doctor wished to lay at his door.

The nursery was a small room set with a bed and a cradle. The doctor, apparently, resided in the attached bedroom designed for the nanny.

"It ain't much but the linens are clean," said Mrs. Wiggins.

"It's fine. It reminds me of my bed as a child. And I am not so tall as to have my feet stick out."

Mrs. Wiggins nodded with professional detachment, but her eyes held a bright curiosity. "Right sorry I am to hear about your fiancé, miss." She hesitated. "If I might be so bold . . . Which cousin was it? Who has . . . er . . . passed on, miss?"

"Master Kit Frazier," she answered, surprised that she could speak his name without her voice breaking.

"Oh, miss. I'm so sorry, miss."

Scheherazade allowed herself to drop slowly onto the bed. "Do you ever think, Mrs. Wiggins, that some things were just never meant to be? That nothing good ever comes from trying to reach for something that . . ." She stared down at her hands, her words faltering.

"Well, I don't know, miss," the housekeeper said, her tone warm and motherly. "Seems to me this house is filled with things that shouldn't be. Indian wives not right in their head. A lord whose brother is the real lord while his is a given title." To her credit, there wasn't any disdain in her voice. It was a simple recitation of facts. "Seems as though we all muck along best we can, and there's no accounting for what should and should not be."

Scheherazade felt her lips curve in a fond smile. "You sound like Pappy."

"Well," said Mrs. Wiggins, "your father was clearly a good man." Then she patted Scher's arm. "You rest now. Dinner will be served at six, but you can have a tray sent up if you like."

"No, I won't put you to the trouble. I will be down for dinner. Thank you."

The housekeeper nodded and left, and all the while, Scher was thinking that Pappy was also another thing in her life that ought not to be. Pappy wasn't her father but had been more of a father to her than whoever had sired her. Was there anything in her life that was right?

Scher came down late to dinner, her hair mussed and her eyes red from tears, but when Brandon looked questioningly at her, she managed to pull together a blank, false smile very reminiscent of her nights in the Green Room. She probably guessed he wasn't fooled, but his other guests would be. She was good at hiding her personal feelings.

Bloody hell, Brandon thought, he had made a complete hash of this. He should not have brought her here. But she needed a rest from the troupe and he had needed to converse with Dr. Dandin. It had seemed logical at the time. Or, perhaps, he had simply wanted to be with her.

"I am so sorry," she apologized again as they went in to dinner. They were a small party of four, consisting of Scher, Brandon, Dr. Dandin, and his mother. Channa, as usual, ate in her room.

"Think nothing of it," Dr. Dandin returned. "You should allow your body to take its rest when it can. Life can be too rushed sometimes and we forget about the basics of sleep and nourishment."

Brandon doubted Scher had slept much at all. There were still smudges under her eyes and a sallow cast to her skin. She had made some attempt to straighten her hair, but . . . bloody hell, he didn't think the nursery even had a mirror. He made a mental note to change that immediately. Mrs. Dandin was chatting with animation, obviously happy with the company. She probably thought Scher was one of those perpetually wan Englishwomen. But he had seen her sweetly competent in the Green Room, her very essence exuding strength. He had known it when she was facing down harridans in Hyde Park. And, of course, he could not forget how wonderful she was writhing in the throes of ecstasy. She was not a wilting English flower, and that made her present condition all the more worrisome.

Or perhaps he was pushing off his own worries onto her. After all, this afternoon's discussions with Dr. Dandin had given him a great deal to think about. What he wouldn't give now to have Scher's clearheaded thoughts on his future.

"I'm afraid we have nothing but honest country fare here," he said, taking refuge from his thoughts in polite banter.

"On the contrary," inserted Dr. Dandin as he turned to Scheherazade. "Lord Blackstone's cook has proved herself quite adept at Indian cuisine as well as English. I believe we are to experience the best of both tonight."

"How delightful!" Scher said with an echo of her usual animation. "I'm sure I shall be most interested."

"Well, don't expect Brandon to take any. He has foresworn curry as the devil's scourge!"

"Not true!" Brandon returned. "I am merely being a polite host, allowing my guests to take the best morsels. You must take some, Miss Martin. Take a great deal. Finish it, so that there is none left for me. Please, I beg you!"

His florid speech brought a smile to her lips, and he was disgustingly pleased to have accomplished such a thing. She dipped her head to everyone.

"I shall be most honored to take a taste, but I would never dream of eating it all!"

Brandon groaned in mock horror while everyone—Scher

included—laughed at his antics. Odd. He had rarely stirred himself to such levels of polite silliness, but he found that he could attempt such things here. Away from London, he felt less of the weight of his political responsibilities. Plus, he had the added incentive of seeing Scher smile. For that, he would dress as a court jester and do flips across the table.

The meal continued. Scher began a lively inquiry into India, showing her intelligence as she asked Mrs. Dandin for more details of her life in a country so far away. Though she did little more than prompt the doctor and his mother to elaborate on their culture, Brandon could see her skill in keeping the conversation flowing without resorting to banalities about weather and food. Were Scher of different birth, she would have made an excellent political wife.

The meal ended, and the evening began, but night comes hard in the country. Without gaslights to lighten the darkness, the manor felt very isolated. The land settled into sleep whether or not his own body was used to country hours.

Dr. Dandin and his mother made their excuses and headed to bed. Scheherazade rose as well, and he held his tongue, refusing to beg her to stay awake a little longer with him. She was beyond tired. He could see that. He would not—

"I find I am not yet ready to sleep, my lord," she said. "Do you perhaps have a book or something in your library that I could read? Perhaps something about India, as I would love to learn more."

"Of course," he answered smoothly. Politeness demanded such a response. "Please follow me."

Then, while his other guests climbed the stairs, he calmly led Scheherazade into his bedroom.

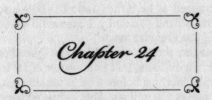

Chapter 24

"Sadly, I have only a few books on India, but I suppose it is more than you could easily find in other places."

Scheherazade nodded politely as she followed Brandon into his library. He lit the candelabras spaced about the room while she looked at the place that was clearly his. It was a small parlor outfitted with a couple bookcases, a desk pushed against the wall nearest the window, and a chair facing the fireplace. It was obviously his desk chair simply moved for companionable conversation with someone who would sit on the short settee, now covered with blankets and a pillow.

"This is ridiculous," she said, not just about the bed linens, but the entire understated room. This was all he had in his own home?

"What?"

He was looking at titles on the lowest shelf while she struggled for the right words. She could hardly criticize the size of his library, so she gestured to the bed linens instead.

"You can't possibly expect to sleep there. Your feet will stick out the end!"

He shrugged as he turned from the bookcase, a slim volume in his hand. "Actually, I expect I'll stretch out on the floor. I don't require much."

"But you are the master of this house. You should—"

"Scher, I have found that I am master of far less than I ever thought. Sleeping before a fire is the smallest of sacrifices if it means you will stay here awhile with me."

She flushed, embarrassed by his words. She knew he spoke of her visiting Pottersfarm, but her thoughts went straight to last night when "staying" meant being in his bed. He seemed to have followed her line of thought as well, and he began to stammer out an apology.

"I-I mean . . . Scher, I want you to rest, not . . . This visit was meant as a restorative for you. Not . . . I didn't think we would . . ."

She stepped forward, placing her hand on his arm to stop his babbling. "I know, Brandon," she said, laughter lacing her tone. "I know why you brought me. And I thank you."

He touched her face, a reverent stroke of her cheek. "I just wanted you to relax somewhere. Not think of anything or anyone for a while."

She smiled. "Can I think of you?"

His eyes darkened, and his breath stopped, but he didn't move any closer to her. In the end, he exhaled gruffly, his mint scent perfuming the air. "You must be dropping with fatigue."

She arched a brow. "Actually, I find I'm bursting with questions. There are some things I need to ask you."

He nodded, pushed the book into her hands, then stepped away with a firm stride. She felt bereft by his sudden absence, but she had no time to object as he began speaking.

"I suppose you want to know about Channa. Well, it is a sad tale, to be sure, filled with my own stupid arrogance."

"No, I—"

He turned to her, his expression bleak. "I want to tell you. I have a decision to make about her and I would value your opinion."

She closed her mouth, momentarily silenced by his words. How novel it was to have a man say that to her: that he valued her opinion. And how wonderful that it was Brandon.

"I'm sorry I wouldn't listen before," she said. "You tried to explain, but I was so angry."

He shook his head. "I should have told you from the very beginning." Then he turned away from her, his gaze sliding to the dark window. "I was trying to do business with her father. Channa was the condition of the joint venture."

Scher blinked. "You married her so that you could create a factory with her father?"

"It certainly seems that way, doesn't it? I wish you could have known her then. Channa was lighthearted, funny, and a real beauty. She was shy at first, as all good Indian girls are, but I could see a spark in her. A mischief in her eyes. I wasn't supposed to see her at all, you know, but she found ways to talk to me. We both did."

Scher bit her lip. She could hear the affection in his voice, true warmth. "You loved her."

He laughed, the sound bitter. "Oh, yes, I was in love, but not with her. Not really."

She set the book down and crossed closer to him. "I don't understand."

He sighed as he turned away from the dark window to lean against his desk. "I was such a rebel. I wanted to change the world."

She folded her arms across her chest. "I believe you still do, Brandon."

"Yes, I suppose so. But I was going to forge a new world

where English and Indian lived and worked together for great profit. It was my vision, and Tapas's daughter was another symbol of that unified vision."

She lowered herself onto the settee, accidentally displacing the pillow as she sat. "I can see that in you," she murmured, picturing him as a young man, brash and idealistic. "Very like Kit, in some ways."

He laughed, and this time the sound was bitter. "Oh, very much more idiotic than Kit would ever be, I'm afraid. I lived with Tapas, you see. Fully half the time I was in India, I spent in his home. Not long by their standards. Did you know that India has been around for thousands of years? They had a great civilization while we were still squatting around fires and hunting with arrows."

She shook her head. "I had no idea."

He toyed absently with papers stacked neatly on his desk. "I hadn't gone native, as everyone thinks. It would take much more than a couple years for that to happen. But I do respect their ways and their people. They're not English, you know, but that doesn't make them barbarians."

"I know," she said. She had heard him say things like that in the Green Room a time or twenty. She always believed that was why he avoided the after-the-show group. Someone inevitably asked him about his politics and he was forever "defending the heathens," as Mr. Phipps would say. Mr. Phipps was an idiot.

"So you married Channa," she prompted.

"In an idealistic fit. And because it was what her father demanded as a condition of the joint venture. And because she was pretty and mischievous, and I liked hearing her laugh." His gaze slid to the cold fire grate. "Many English marriages are built on less, and I thought I loved her."

She could well believe it. "But then her family died in the fire."

"Then her family was *murdered* and their home burned to the ground. She was nineteen. We didn't even have our wedding night because I was drugged with opium and tossed into a den."

He lifted his face enough that she could see how haggard he appeared. These were the memories that haunted him. She had already known the particulars, but having now seen his wife, she had a better perspective on how deeply they continued to affect his life.

She leaned forward on her elbows and touched his arm. The room was so small that she could do that from where she sat. "It is no crime to believe in a better world, to live your passion and your beliefs. You married her and have done everything you can by her. I find that incredibly honorable."

"Dr. Dandin wants me to renounce her."

She blinked, stunned. How could one of Channa's own countrymen suggest something so cruel?

Brandon pushed up and away from Scher, pacing about the room with agitated steps. "I had to leave India. They made that clear." He paused to glare at the fire grate. "After the fire, after I screamed that I would bring the murderers to justice, after I ranted and wailed like a madman, I was arrested and dragged to a jail. My captors, of course, were men from the East India Company."

She closed her eyes, not wanting to imagine Brandon screaming in the debris of a burned factory, grieving for his lost friends, outraged by the horror, only to be dragged away by his coworkers. How could people like that live? People who used the veneer of civilization to cover heinous crimes? "I'm so sorry," she murmured, but Brandon wasn't finished.

"I was taken before my superior, Charles Cornwallis." He practically spat the name. "I was given a choice: jail in India, probably for the rest of my life, or I could return to England a rich man with a title. The only condition, of course, was that I never return, never speak my ridiculous accusations again. Either way, of course, I would be branded a madman."

"All because you spoke the truth."

"Because I accused wealthy, titled men of murdering six Indian craftsmen, then burning their factory to the ground."

She twisted her hands in her lap. Even now, seeing his distress, knowing Brandon would never lie about something like this, Scher still had trouble believing it was true. Someone from England, a member of the English elite, could be that immoral? It was hard to believe, but she did. All it took was one look at his face, and she knew it was true.

"I am very careful in my politics," he said gravely. "I have to work for justice without ever mentioning Cornwallis's true crimes. I shouldn't even be saying his name to you." He sighed. "Perhaps I would have done better to stay in India."

"In jail? You could do nothing from there. Of course you had to leave." But what a horrible end to an idealistic heart.

"Actually, I spit in his face the first time." He released a rueful laugh. "That is one of my favorite memories of India. But two days in jail changed my mind." He rubbed a hand over his eyes and she could see how weary he was. "You are right. I could do nothing from jail. And Channa was ill. They made sure I knew how vulnerable she was too." He looked at her, silently begging her to understand. "I couldn't abandon her. She was nineteen, with no family left, and branded as a traitor for marrying an Englishman."

She stood up, moving to stand before him. She touched his face, bringing his gaze up to hers. "Of course you had to leave. You had to take their money and their title. What other means of support did you have?" She pressed a tender kiss to his lips. "You did nothing wrong."

"Really?" he said, his gaze searching hers. "Because it feels as though I have been damned every step of the way."

"It is no crime to be young and idealistic."

"But you see what two years in England has done to Channa. Her mind is broken, she cannot see me without having a fit, and now the doctor . . ."

She dropped her head to his, forehead to forehead. She smelled the mint of his breath and knew that his eyes watered from the frustration of it all. "What does the doctor think?"

He sighed. "That it would be best for her to return to her native country."

She stilled, her mind thinking furiously. She ought to be feeling the pain of the nineteen-year-old girl who lost everything in a fire. Instead, her thoughts were on herself and what her life would be like without Brandon in it. "You are planning to go back to India with her?"

His hands went around her hips, not pulling her to him, but keeping her close. "I can't. If I return to India, I will be killed. They made that quite clear as well." He sighed. "I thought I could take her to a different part of India, someplace far away from where she grew up, but Mrs. Dandin says that Cornwallis has expanded. The East India Company is everywhere. There is no place that I could go that would be safe for me."

"Or for Channa then, as your wife." Scher was beginning to understand. "So Dr. Dandin thinks you should renounce her, turn her aside as if everything you ever did in India never happened." Oh, what a terrible choice. The one thing he clung to was his honor. "What are you going to do?"

He didn't speak. He just sat there, leaning against his desk while she stood before him. Their foreheads still touched. He still held her hips in hands that clenched without hurting. She could feel the struggle within him with every breath. The tension in his body was palpable.

She wanted to say something that would ease his choice. But only he could decide what his honor was worth, what his bargain with Channa's father was worth. How best to respect their memory. All she could do was love him, she realized.

So she kissed him. She poured all of her heart into that kiss. She pressed her mouth to his, she stroked her tongue across his lips, and when his hands drew her tight between his thighs, she opened herself up to him.

He plundered her mouth, slamming himself into her with a passion born of pain. She arched into him, letting her head drop back as he did what he willed. Thrusting, stroking, even tiny nips of his teeth when he chose. She didn't resist. If anything, she matched his passion. She wanted to show him without words that she was his. No matter what he chose, no matter what he had done before, it didn't matter to her. It would never matter. Because that is what love meant. She loved him completely independent of the world's constraints, of the rules of society. Love was free of all those restrictions. And love was more important.

She stilled, her thoughts and body spinning to a halt. He didn't notice at first. He continued to dominate her body, crushing her against his groin, thrusting into her mouth. But in time, he realized her lack of response. His mouth slowed, his hands tightened then released, and he once again dropped his forehead against hers, pulling back enough so that they could speak. "Scher?"

"I love you," she said. "I think I have loved you for a very long time."

She felt the words hit him, his body clenching with the impact. He even stopped breathing. It took a few moments, a long suspension of everything, but then his body eased. He took a slow stuttering breath, and with his exhale, his hands softened, his shoulders lowered, and his eyes slipped closed.

"Scher," he breathed, but she stopped him from saying anything more. She pressed her hands to his mouth and said the one thing she never thought she would.

"I will be your mistress, Brandon. Whatever you choose, however you want. This love I feel for you is more important than anything else to me. And even if we have children—"

His hands spasmed on her hips when she said that, tightening to draw her close. She understood because the thought of having his babies, of raising his children made the love in her heart swell even further.

"If we have children," she continued, "I will love and care for them. I will make sure they lack for nothing."

She touched his cheek. He still didn't speak, though his eyes were open again. They watched her with a gaze so intense he stole her breath.

"Our children will have the money to be whatever they want," she finally said, her words shaping her thoughts as much as the other way around. "Kit was right in that, but he didn't see what you did. He didn't see that it is a large world." She smiled. "Our children can have a future, just not in the English peerage. Illegitimate or not makes no difference—"

"It makes a difference," he said, his voice thick.

She bit her lip. "Then we will not have children," she said, already mourning the loss. "But I will have you, and I will have your love."

"Would that be enough?" he asked.

"Yes," she said. "All this time I thought my fears were because I wasn't respectable." She shook her head at her own stupidity. "The unsettled grayness of my days, the despair, I blamed it all on being locked out of the respectable world. But that wasn't it at all."

He touched her face and spoke the same words he had said so long ago. "Tell me. Let me make it better."

"You already have!" she said with a smile. "It's love, Brandon. I was missing love. Mine for you. Yours for me. With you, I'm not so afraid. Life suddenly has hope instead of—"

"Despair. You take the despair away."

"Not me," she returned. "We. Us. Our love." Then she lifted her lips up for a kiss. He allowed their mouths to touch, they shared a few kisses, but he did not allow it to go further. In the end, he pulled back.

"It is not enough for me," he said. "I will find a way, Scher. I will find a way to help Channa and honor you."

"You don't need—" she began.

"I will," he said firmly. Then he smiled, his eyes and his touch growing gentler. "I do."

"I do," she echoed. It wasn't a marriage, it wasn't a church wedding, but it was good enough for her. It was his promise and hers in return.

This time, they kissed each other at the same time, moving together as one. There was no restraint, no reservation, just deep penetrating kisses and the sweet build of passion. Her gown came off quickly. He undid her buttons even as he plundered her mouth. And when she stepped back enough to shrug out of her dress, he took the time to rip off his cravat. His shirt came off next with both of them fumbling at his buttons. Then he held her face in his hands, both of them panting, as he looked at her. "This should be done in a bed—"

"I don't care."

"You shall have a church wedding with all your friends around—"

"I don't care."

"This should be done carefully with tenderness—"

She reached down through his waistband to grab him. She tried to be gentle, but she was trying to make a point. He gasped, his words cut off by her action.

"I want you now," she said. "Quickly." Then she squeezed him for emphasis. "Right. Now."

His eyes darkened, his nostrils flared, but his lips curved in a smile. "Very well then, Scher. Your wish is my command." And with that, he eased her hand off his organ before he quickly shucked all his clothes.

She stood back a pace, watching him undress. The candlelight turned his skin to gold, but she watched the promise in his eyes. She saw his passion and his hunger. What a difference from the man who had come to her room so many nights ago. This man could see a future. And she knew it would be filled with love.

She thought he would come to her when he was naked, his organ jutting proudly before him, but he didn't. Instead, he crossed to the settee, carefully laying out a blanket before the fire. The pillow came next, and then he bowed to her.

"Your bed, m'lady."

"No," she said as she stepped forward into his arms. "I want to lie on you. You will be my bed."

He grinned as he slipped his hands beneath her shift. Though she'd already discarded her gown, she still wore her shift and stockings. At least she had managed to kick off her shoes. "I believe that can be arranged," he said.

His fingers were warm where they stroked over her belly and ribs, but she still shivered at the caress. And as he raised his arms, taking her shift along with him, she arched herself into his hands. Oh, she would never tire of feeling his hands, large and hot as they stroked her breasts. Unwilling to let him abandon her chest, she managed to pull off the shift herself. And while she was tossing it aside, he bent his mouth to her nipples.

The feel of his lips on her breast, the way he sucked and stroked, made her knees go weak. She had to grab on to his shoulders for balance, but he knew of her difficulty before she did. He wrapped his hands around her, then supported her gently down to their makeshift bed. Then, when she was on her back, he began to stroke her body in earnest.

With both hands and his mouth, he traveled over her body. He stroked her breasts, her ribs, her hips. His mouth tugged at her nipples while she grasped the blanket and arched into his embrace. She tried once to bring his mouth to hers, to touch him as she wanted, but he firmly pushed her hand back to the blanket.

"Let me make this perfect for you," he said as he began kissing down her belly.

"It is!" she gasped. "It—" Her words were cut off as his hand slipped into her curls.

He spread her legs. His fingers stroked deep inside her, pushing inside, rolling upward and over while she writhed. He stroked his thumb across her once, twice, then pressed his tongue right there. She shifted restlessly, using her knee to settle him more deeply between her thighs. But she didn't want his mouth, she wanted him. She wanted him inside her.

"Brandon," she cried. "Oh, please, Brandon. I want you!"

She didn't know if he understood her. But before the tension became too great, before she was swamped in ecstasy, he abandoned her intimate place. He kissed down her thighs, one after the other, untying her stockings as he went. Then he rolled them down and pulled them off her with a flourish.

Then he stopped. He was kneeling between her legs while she lay wide open before him. "I will never tire of seeing you this way."

She had no words to respond. The heat in his eyes robbed her of everything—shame, embarrassment, even coherent thought. So her words spilled out without conscious intent.

"I love you," she said.

His eyes darkened, his nostrils flared, even his organ jerked, stretching for her. But he didn't move to where she wanted. Instead, after a long, heated look, he shifted his gaze to his desk. He didn't even have to stand up to open a drawer. The room was that small. He reached inside, rooted around a bit, then pulled out a French letter. He was carefully pushing it on his organ when he spoke.

"This will prevent pregnancy," he said. "It's called a—"

"A French letter," she said. "I know." She had been raised around whores, after all. And while they didn't often have them, they absolutely knew what they were. "Thank you," she said, sitting up enough to pull his face up for a kiss. "Thank you for having them."

"I will always have them," he said softly, as he rolled the thin bladder onto his organ. "Until we are both sure."

She grinned. "I'm sure now," she said as she began to lean back, bringing him with her. "I'm sure I want you now."

She didn't allow him to argue but possessed his mouth in a demanding kiss. She had wrapped her arms around his shoulders, and when she finally lay on her back, he was stretched on top of her. His elbows settled to the side, his weight pulling off her as he placed himself right where she wanted.

He was hot, she realized, even through the covering of the French letter. Hot and hard and slowly pushing himself inside of her. Thick, he stretched her. She arched her back, lifting her knees to both give her more room and allow him to push deeper.

He continued his insistent pressure and she groaned at the wonderful feeling. She liked the push, liked the feeling of being filled by him. She tightened her knees, silently trying to pull him closer.

"More," she murmured.

"Are you ready?" he rasped.

She opened her eyes at his words, pleased when she saw the stark tension in his face. He was holding himself still for her, keeping it slow for her.

"Don't hold back," she said. "Give me everything."

He nodded but he didn't move. Instead, he lowered his face to hers, kissing her with such incredible hunger. And while she was arching into his kiss, he thrust the rest of the way.

Oh! Nothing had ever felt more right. She tightened her legs. She wanted him to do that again. He began a slow withdrawal, and she whimpered at the loss.

Then he thrust into her again. *Yes!*

His withdrawal was faster this time, the return harder. His pace increased. She gasped with every thrust. She clutched him ever harder. Tighter.

He was looking down at her, and she up at him. She saw his face, tight and hungry. Her own breath was short with quick pants. The pleasure built. Her body tightened. Her soul leapt. Love! Such love!

Yes!

And while she was still soaring from her peak, he shuddered with his own release. He gasped, his cry half strangled, half awed. His eyes shuttered, but they didn't close. Neither did hers. And in this way, their souls flew together.

Chapter 25

The week flew by like a moment out of time. Except this
moment, this life, felt more real to Scheherazade than anything else. The shocking thing to her was that it was *easy*.
Once she surrendered to her absolute love for Brandon, all
the rest fell into place. The staff treated her with defer-
ence, even taking her direction when needed. Channa continued to improve, so long as Brandon stayed away. Talk
of returning to India made the girl especially happy and
Indian songs could often be heard from the master bedroom. As for Brandon, he spent his mornings in his library
on his political correspondence, and his afternoons and
most especially his nights with Scher. Even more amazing:
She had heard him laugh. Daily in fact, if not hourly.

In short, by the time she packed up to return to London,
her heart and mind were filled with her love for Brandon.
She had done the right thing, she was glad to be his mistress.
Their moments together had been at times tender, thrilling,
incredibly erotic, and an absolute joy. But now . . . now she

had to return to London alone. Brandon had to stay and finalize details regarding his wife. He'd said nothing about what those details would be except that he wasn't sure of all the legalities. He swore he would tell her as soon as he could. Then he had kissed her. They had made love one last time on the floor of his library, and then . . . now . . . she had to leave.

She slept the entire ride back to London. Nightly confidences and other activities took their toll, and she fell asleep almost as soon as the wheels started rolling. She didn't even dream, so when she next opened her eyes, she was at the Tavern Playhouse and the entire troupe was waiting to greet her. By the time she had disembarked, she felt the pattern of her regular life assert itself. Like a second skin, it attached itself to her body, and she became Lady Scher again. She settled too easily into a regular life of costumes and shows, gossip and the Green Room, but inside she felt a new shimmer of joy. Deep down, she knew she was loved, and that made all the difference. For a week.

By the second week, doubts began to creep in.

Four days after that, and she felt the first echoes of despair. Brandon had not come to see her. She had received letters, of course, terse notes filled with frustration. Communication with India was impossibly difficult, he wrote. His banker was being stubborn. He longed to be with her but would have to wait another few days. Then he signed it with the letter B.

She knew Brandon was not a man who expressed his feelings well. She further knew that what feelings he could express would certainly not pour out on paper. And yet, she had gone nearly two full weeks without the sight of him, and it was making her insane. Had the things they had shared been all a fantasy? Would it all come crashing down now that she was back in London? How had he become so integral to her life that she was on the edge of despair in so short a time?

Her letters to him, of course, were probably no better. She filled them with the details of her day, the gossip in the Green Room, and nothing of any substance at all. Yes, she penned more than he did, but the message was the same: My life is nothing without you. When can I see you again?

Three weeks after returning to London, she was practically drooping with the same gray cloud that used to surround Lady Scher. Long before Brandon or even Kit had come into her life, the gray dullness had surrounded her. It had been gone for a time, but now it held on to her more stubbornly than ever before.

She was on the way to the Green Room after another Tavern Playhouse performance. The stage was being set to rights, the noise from down the hallway was pleasantly loud. That meant the crowd was good and sales would be solid. Her mind was busy tallying up receipts in her head and her body was moving quickly, but that seemed like only a small fragment of her existence. Her chattering mind, her busy body, all moved through her days while the rest of her—the bulk of her spirit—waited in silence for Brandon.

So when a shadow caught her in this one place of quiet, when a large dark man snatched her around the waist and pushed her against the wall, she didn't fight in the least. Some part of her had caught the scent of mint a split second before she was touched, and that was all she needed. Her mind stilled, her body stopped, and her spirit soared to the heavens.

"Brandon," she whispered.

"Scher," he said at the exact same moment.

Then they were kissing, their bodies wrapped together beneath the cocoon of his cloak. Suddenly, wonderfully, she was alive again.

He stopped when they could no longer breathe. He pulled back when her breasts were on fire from his caress, her mouth swollen and hot from his lips. They panted in the darkness, their foreheads pressed together, the scent of mint filling the air between them.

"I couldn't stay away any longer," he breathed into the darkness.

"I have been mad waiting for you. Have you come back for a while? Can you stay?"

He sighed. "It is all so complicated."

Her heart sunk, and she clung to him. "It's all right," she lied.

"No, it is absolutely *not* all right," he said as he tucked her tight against him. "I have something to ask you, Scher. Something that cannot be discussed in the middle of a dark hallway."

"Come to my room tonight. Give me an hour in the Green Room and then—"

"I want to take you on a carriage ride. May I call on you tomorrow?" he asked. His voice was formal in its accents, as if he spoke to a real lady.

"Of course," she said, "but . . ."

"Tomorrow, then," he said. Then he kissed her again, long and thorough until she heard Seth's heavy tread coming down the hallway. She had to leave or be caught like a trollop against the backstage wall.

"Brandon . . ." she gasped, breaking away from his kiss.

"Tomorrow . . ." he whispered, and then he was gone.

Scher dressed with particular care. She wore the green dress he so admired and left off the paste that he did not admire. Then she paced in the Green Room, not even bothering to glare at the members of the troupe who gathered to see her off. Except no one had gathered. She was alone in the Green Room, which was all to the good, of course, but it was strange. Why wasn't anyone here? She tilted her head to listen more closely. She heard nothing, which wasn't all that odd given that it was the middle of the afternoon, but still. Shouldn't there be someone around?

Then there was no more time to wonder because she heard his footsteps. In her mind, she imagined mint and a large greatcoat, though it was early summer now and he likely wouldn't be wearing it. She folded her hands together and waited for the door to open. And when it did, her breath caught in her throat. He was dressed exceptionally fine this afternoon! Black coat, white linen shirt, and a green cravat that perfectly matched her gown. His eyes were warm, his smile especially beautiful, and she was in his arms before he had released the door.

"You look wonderful," she said, though in her mind she was thinking, *Do we really need to go driving? Could we not go upstairs to my bedroom right now?*

"You are perfect," he said as he pressed his mouth to hers. "Absolutely perfect," he repeated when he finally pulled back from her. Then he gazed at her, his eyes dark with hunger. She was just about to ask, just about to suggest that perhaps they need not enjoy the fine day outside when he abruptly spun her around.

"Go!" he said. "My carriage is outside and if I do not get you there right now, then we shall never make it at all."

"Would that be so bad?" she asked.

He paused, and his expression turned serious. "I have something important to ask you, and I will not be deterred."

Her heart squeezed in alarm, but she kept her expression neutral. "Of course, Brandon. Whatever you want."

He smiled at that, though his expression was rueful. Then before she could ask anything more, he opened the door and escorted her into the hallway and then into the main playhouse. She walked beside him, her mind whirling, but she didn't say anything. And in her silence, she had a moment to notice something else. The Tavern Playhouse was indeed empty. Absolutely empty.

"Where is everyone?" she murmured.

"Hmmm?" he asked, though she was sure he had heard her. How could he not with their steps echoing in the empty building? Then he opened the front doors and there was Hank grinning at her as he held the horses' heads. He had a new uniform on, his face was clean, and even his hair had been cut.

"My, look how handsome you are, Hank!" she said.

The boy bowed with excellent manners and intoned, "Thank 'ee, miss."

She nodded her approval and then had to turn her attention to climbing into Brandon's high-perch phaeton. "I shall never tire of this carriage," she said as she settled onto the thick cushion.

"Then I shall never sell it," said Brandon as he leaped up and gathered the ribbons. Hank followed a moment later. Soon they were moving down the streets, thankfully turning away from Hyde Park. In truth, Scher was pleased that he didn't intend to showcase her to the snobbish *ton*. She had no wish to spoil this day with them.

"How is Channa?" she asked when the silence became too much for her. "Is Dr. Dandin still with her?"

He took a moment to answer, his attention caught on maneuvering the horses. But then the difficulty passed and he slowed them down. They were now on a relatively secluded path about the park and he could direct most of his attention to her. "Channa left yesterday morning. She travels with Mrs. Dandin to India. The doctor left more than a week ago. He is going to open a hospital, Scher. Someplace where patients like Channa can heal."

Scher touched his hand. She knew what it had cost him to surrender his wife. "It must have been hard, Brandon, but I think it was the right choice for her."

He quirked an eyebrow at her. "It wasn't hard at all, Scher. It feels too convenient, but I think I have found a way to satisfy the dictates of honor as well as look out for Channa's welfare."

She waited, knowing he would explain when he was ready. It took him some time, but he finally spoke.

"I have surrendered all my money to her, Scher. To Channa as dowry, should she ever choose to marry, and a huge amount to Dr. Dandin as well for the creation of his hospital. If I could give up the title to her, I would, but that will not help her. So everything I made from the East India Company has been given over to Channa and to the creation of Dandin's hospital."

He said his words in a rush, but she caught every syllable. It took longer than that, though, to understand the implications. So they sat in silence for a time, while he directed the horses in a lazy slow drive beside the park. In time, she was able to speak.

"You foreswore her? She can marry again?"

He nodded, his lips tight. "The legalities are . . . complicated, but Dr. Dandin thought it best. She is still a virgin. No one need know of our marriage unless she chooses. She has all the money she needs to live a full life alone, but if she falls in love . . ."

"Dr. Dandin will watch over her," Scher said, knowing it was true. "He is a good man."

"Even if he doesn't, I have made some contacts through friends in India. I will always watch out for Channa. She is still my responsibility until such time as she can care for herself."

Scher squeezed his hand. "I find that a most *honorable* solution."

He quirked his lips at her, obviously aware of her choice of words. "Honorable or not, it is the best solution I can manage. It gives her the best chance at a good life and leaves me free to be with you."

He maneuvered the carriage to the side of the street, stopping the horses in an area of London that Scher rarely visited. The neighborhood was too elite for her, and so it was unfamiliar. He turned to her and held out his hand.

"Would you care to walk for a bit?"

"Of course," she said. She would go anywhere with him.

He passed the reins to Hank with a wink, then jumped down. Scher came next, wondering all the while at the boy's grin. "Can you manage them?" he asked Hank.

"Yes, m'lord. I know just what to do."

Brandon gave the boy a nod, and then he turned back to Scher. "Let's go this way." He led her along a path, moving easily through the greenery. His stride was matched to hers and his manner was easy, but there was still an underlying tension in his body, an anxiety that she felt without understanding why he was so nervous.

"What is it, Brandon?" she finally asked. "What is the matter?"

He tightened his hold on her hand, turning her slightly so she looked directly at him. "I am penniless, Scher. I have retained the manor in Pottersfarm, but I have no funds to keep it. My title barely sustains itself. I have managed that, at least, in the last two years, doing renovations and the like so that it no longer requires huge infusions of cash. But there is no income whatsoever." He shrugged, and she could tell he was trying to appear casual. "I have nothing."

She smiled, touching his face. "You have yourself, and that is more than enough for me."

"Is it?" he asked. "Are you sure?"

"Absolutely." She stretched up on her toes, pressing a kiss to his lips. She didn't deepen it because he didn't allow her to. So she tried to communicate in that sweet touch all the love she felt for him. It had nothing to do with money or titles or anything the world valued. He loved her, and that was all the treasure she needed.

She broke the kiss and settled back onto her heels, but to her shock, he also moved his body down. Not closer to her face, but down onto one knee right there before her. He still held her hand, and his expression was filled with yearning. Then he pulled a piece of paper out of his coat, along with a jeweler's box.

"I have a special license, Scher. If you will have a penniless aristocrat for your husband, then we can be married immediately." He opened the jeweler's box to a modest ring in a modest setting. "I kept back some money, the same amount I had before I left for India. I used it to buy you this. I will get you a better one eventually, Scher, but this was all I could afford." He swallowed and gazed into her eyes. "Scheherazade Martin, will you do me the greatest honor and be my wife?"

She looked at him, her throat too closed up to answer. Everything she had ever wanted was right here before her. A man who loved her! She didn't need money, she had plenty. And her time among the *ton* had told her that she had no interest in the elite. What she cared about was the love shining through his eyes. The love that lit up her heart and dispelled the gloom that had become an integral part of Lady Scher.

Without speaking, she pulled off her glove so he could set the ring upon her finger. He did so with shaking hands. And when it was done, she leaned down to kiss him.

"I love you," she whispered just before their mouths met.

He kissed her deeply, thoroughly. And when they broke apart, he pushed up to his feet and pointed up the path. "I have a surprise for you, Scher, if you are amenable."

She fell into step with him without thought. She didn't care where they were going or what they were doing. She was going to be his wife, a respectable woman and a beloved wife. No surprise he gave her now could compete with the joy of that. Nothing . . . until she saw where he was headed. They were walking onto the steps of St. James's Cathedral.

"Brandon?"

"Everyone is here. We can be married this moment, if you like. No interfering families, no *ton* to try and pry us apart."

"They couldn't do it anyway," she said.

"No, they couldn't. But why put ourselves through it?"

She grinned as the doors to the church opened and she spied the people twisting in their seats to see her. The entire troupe was inside! That is where her friends had gone. They were inside waiting for her and Brandon! And on the opposite side of the aisle sat a few gentlemen and ladies. Politicals, she realized, including William Wilberforce the champion of the black slaves, all sitting there to see them marry. Apparently, Brandon had friends who would still support him no matter who his wife was.

"You were quite confident of me, weren't you?" she said. "You planned this all in advance."

"I hoped," he answered. "I prayed. And, yes, I believed."

"I love you," she said.

"And I love you."

She took his hand, and together they walked into the church.

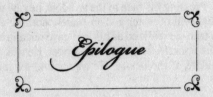

Epilogue

Kit groaned as the world tilted on its axis. It tilted, it rolled, it sloshed. Sloshed?

He opened his eyes, waiting impatiently as shadows resolved into form. But what he eventually saw made no sense. Wood room. Round porthole. The obvious sound of water against the side.

He was on a boat? But why? The last thing he remembered was being carried from the playhouse to Michael's home. Then all was misery and wretchedness until now. How did he get on a boat?

He closed his eyes again, trying to remember. Images floated through his mind, disconnected and jarring. Then he remembered Michael standing right beside him. Light was streaming in from the porthole, so it must have happened here. Right here in this very room. What had the man said?

"It's for the best, Kit. A man can make a fortune in the colonies. You'll see. It's for the best."

Kit's eyes popped open, horror forcing him to stagger to his feet. His muscles groaned as they adjusted to his weight. Everything ached! How long had he been asleep?

He stumbled forward, half falling, half walking to the porthole. Pressing his face to the window, he saw water. He saw a great deal of water and absolutely nothing else.

It was true, he realized as his legs gave out and he slowly sank to the floor. He wasn't just on a boat. He was on a boat in the middle of the *ocean*. He was bound for the bloody colonies!

Turn the page for a special preview of
Jade Lee's next historical romance

Wicked Seduction

Coming March 2011
from Berkley Sensation!

Prologue

One English boy shackled to the mast. That's what Kit Frazier saw as he crept over the side of the slave ship. One boy of about seventeen years, feet tied with rope, arms shackled with iron. There was blood dripping to the deck too but Kit couldn't see from what wound.

Bloody hell, this was a trap.

He wasn't sure what tipped him off. Everything was silent. The man on watch stood like a statue on the foredeck, not even bothering to whistle. Kit cocked his ear toward the hold. No sobs. No low moans. So, no slaves trapped below either. Just the one English adolescent, his dirty-blond hair a mat that obscured his face.

Kit crept around the edge, slipping through shadows. He'd spent years on this boat as a slave, and coming back now made his hands slick with sweat. If he had any sense, he'd turn and run now before it was too late. What did he care that another English aristocrat had been abducted for ransom? But once, long ago, he'd been chained to the mast,

waiting for a ransom that never came. He couldn't leave
this boy to the same fate.

A flash of yellow teeth caught his attention. Kit froze,
peering into the blackness, waiting until he heard a telltale
pop of knuckles. That had to be Abdur, the one who liked
to whip the children. Kit smiled. Suddenly he didn't care
if it was a trap so long as he could strike against the night-
mare of Venboer's slave ship.

Kit crouched, wiped the sweat from his hands, and then
struck. After two years as a free man, he was faster than
Abdur. And stronger too. The bastard collapsed to the
deck. Kit even remembered to cushion his fall so that all
was done in silence. Then he looked around. One down,
but how many more?

Three that he could see, spaced behind barrels set much
too obviously along the rail. Perfect spacing from which to
attack. Not so good for defense. Kit slipped behind each
one, his panic easing now that he was in action. One by one
they fell. Easily done, but it took too much time.

Kit looked around again. The boy had raised his head to
listen. Sharp ears on that one, but was he smart? Would he
know to keep quiet until Kit could effect a rescue? Taking
a huge risk, Kit slid Abdur's knife across the deck, wincing
at the sound. Not so loud, but not so quiet either. And sadly,
no help against the shackles. But at least the boy would be
able to defend himself while Kit went in search of the key.
Or a heavy axe.

The boy didn't appear to move as the blade settled
against his leg. But a blink later, the knife was gone and he
was drooping more where he sat, presumably so he could
cut the rope at his ankles. So, the kid was smart too.

Kit began to creep toward the forecastle. The slave key
was kept . . .

Three figures stepped out of the shadows, two large men
flanking their very large captain. Kit spun around. Two

more men stepped behind him, one of them the watchman who had jumped down to join the fray. Five to one with the boy still chained to the mast.

Hell.

Then a miracle happened. The boy stood up, his iron shackles dropping to the deck with a clang. Kit raised his eyebrows in surprise. Apparently, he was rescuing a lock-pick. Which narrowed the odds to five against two. Better, though he doubted the boy really knew how to fight. Still, things were definitely looking up. Especially since he could see the boy's wounds now. Swollen face from a beating, jagged cut along his arm, but nothing that would keep him from swimming to safety.

"I knew you would come," Venboer gloated, and Kit slid his attention back to the bastard who had destroyed so many lives, Kit's included. "He looks like you, yes?"

Kit shifted into the cocky drawl that he knew irritated Venboer. "We English are a pretty lot."

The bastard released a growl, low in his throat. It took a moment for Kit to realize he was trying to chuckle. "He will do well in the dens, I think. Pretty enough for the women, but strong enough to be used by men."

To the side, the boy stiffened in horror, his jaw clenched tight. Kit too had to repress his visceral response. He'd seen what happened to the pretty ones in the dens. Some things were worse than death, and that was one of them. Meanwhile, Kit tried to appear as if he weren't choosing between death and worse than death. "No one paid the ransom then?"

Venboer shrugged. "Not enough."

"How much? Maybe I'll buy him." Kit drawled as he turned to inspect the boy. It was a ruse. He didn't have near enough to buy a slave, but it gave him an excuse to catch the prisoner's eyes. With a tiny flick of his eyes, he indicated the far rail. That was their best escape, assuming the boy could swim. He took a step forward. "He looks a little sickly—"

Venboer's men attacked. The bastard never had been one for idle chat. Kit had been ready for it, but had been hoping to get in a better position first. No time now as the two back men suddenly lunged. They were trained sailors, well versed in sea fighting, and armed with cutlasses. Kit, on the other hand, had only his daggers, which were light enough for swimming and little use against a large, heavy sword. But at least the boy could escape.

Kit leaped aside, then began the game of feint and dash while simultaneously listening for Venboer's other men behind him. He narrowly missed being gutted, but was being slowly, steadily pushed back into Venboer and his other two men.

Hell. He was running out of time. His two attackers had slowed down, stepping sideways in order to flank him better. It was now or never. Kit abruptly spun around, giving his back to his attackers while he threw.

Venboer's first mate fell to the ground, a knife sticking from his throat. Kit didn't allow himself the time to even smile. Later he would relish the satisfaction that the man who had beaten him nightly for months was finally dead. Right now, while the others were gaping at the first mate, Kit spun back and threw again. The one closest to the boy dropped.

The boy? Bloody hell! The idiot was supposed to be over the side now and swimming for his life. But no, in an admirable show of bravery, the kid was lifting the dead man's cutlass—in the wrong kind of grip—and closing to Kit's side. Damned English honor. Now they were both going to die.

Except they didn't. The fighting closed in tight, with even Venboer lending a hand. Against cutlasses, Kit wouldn't usually have stood a chance, but the boy had a special genius for interfering at just the right time. First it was a rope, kicked beneath one man's feet. That gave Kit time to use his last throwing knife and thin their opponents to two.

Then the boy tossed Kit the cutlass. No small feat given the weight and heft of the blade, but Kit was able to snatch it out of the air in time. Better and better. But two against one was still hard fighting, and Venboer was smart. Kit couldn't hold them off for long.

"Go!" he barked at the boy. "Swim!"

There was a moment's hesitation, then the boy abruptly spun on his heel and ran. A moment later, Kit heard a tell-tale splash and felt an inner release. If he did nothing else in his misbegotten life, at least he had saved one boy. He grinned at Venboer.

"Your prize has escaped."

The bastard actually grinned. "The boy is nothing. You are the prize."

"That's what I meant," Kit countered with a maniacal laugh. "I'm leaving." It was a bluff. Kit threw himself into a rush of speed and ferocity that would never win him freedom against these two. They were too good and he was too tired, and all three of them knew it. But it was Kit's only hope. With luck, it would force Venboer to kill him. He'd rather die than be enslaved to this bastard again.

Luck was on his side. Venboer hated the sound of joy, especially a slave's. So while the bastard flinched away from Kit's bizarre laughter, Kit was able to press close and slice him across the chest. But he paid dearly for that victory. The other sailor struck before Kit could move aside. A crippling blow to his leg that had him crumpling to one knee. He felt the slick wash of blood and knew the gash was deep. He was done for, but maybe he had one more swing left in him. He took it gleefully.

"For Jeremy!" he bellowed, then stabbed upward. Throwing all his weight behind his thrust, he pierced Venboer like a fish on a stick. The bastard's mouth gaped open, his eyes shot wide, and then he dropped in the slow fall that men take when their heart has been pierced.

Victory! And now . . . death. In order to make the thrust, Kit had exposed all of himself to the other man's swing. His neck, his arm, hell, his whole right side was open for gutting. And yet in that moment, a sense of satisfaction entered his soul. He'd saved a boy and ended Venboer's reign of terror. All in all, a good way to die.

Except the blow never came.

Confused, Kit pulled his guard back up, scrambling for footing while trying to figure out why he wasn't dead. His enemy's cutlass was raised for the strike, but his eyes were wide and his back was arching in clear agony. What had happened?

The boy! The damned stupid, honorable, wonderful boy had not swum away! He'd merely pretended to jump over-board, then had grabbed a cutlass from somewhere. He'd used it to cut open the bastard's spine.

They would live! They would both live!

Kit tried to grin. He tried to laugh and dance a jig. Instead, he dropped to all fours, his breath shallow with pain. Looking down, he saw his leg was slick from blood. Not as bad as it could be. He'd live if it could be stitched up and he didn't die of fever. But he was sitting on the deck of Venboer's slave ship with no surgeon in sight. He couldn't swim now, not trailing blood the whole way. Couldn't run far either. And he damn sure couldn't man the slave ship with just himself and the boy.

He quieted his breath a moment, willing his pound-ing heart to ease. He eased himself to the side and then stripped off his shirt to bind his leg. And as he worked, he listened for a human sound. Nothing. No pounding feet. No screams of outrage. Just himself and the boy on the quietly rocking boat. Was it possible? Had Venboer been so confident that he'd put no more than nine men on the ship? Was Kit now in possession of a fully sea-worthy galley ship?

Kit suppressed a grin. A dozen things had to line up perfectly for this to work. But he'd just cheated certain death and killed Venboer, the worst of the Barbary pirates. On tonight of all nights, he was feeling lucky. He looked at the boy who was still standing frozen, his gaze locked on the body at their feet.

"Look at me, boy. What's your name?"

The young boy complied slowly, his words barely audible. "Alexander Jacques Morgan, sir."

"Well, Alex, can you row? Can you row a boat straight and for a mile?"

The boy blinked and then nodded. He was coming back to himself, clarity finally entering his eyes as Kit gave him something new to focus on. "I'm a damned fine rower, sir."

"Good man, Alex. Now listen. I can't leave the boat. There's things to be done here."

"But you're hurt." The boy's eyes dropped to where the shirt was already turning red.

"I've had worse," he said in return, which was true enough, but he'd never had to stitch himself up while preparing a ship for ocean voyage. "Now see those two lights over there? You're going to row straight over there. Up the beach two yards is a shack that serves the best rum in Africa. There's a man behind the bar who knows English. I named him Puck since he looks just like you'd expect, 'cept he's black. Give him this, and tell him it's time." He yanked a chord off his neck and passed it to the boy, who blinked down at the ugly brooch.

"What is it?"

"A peacock, I think, but that doesn't matter. Tell Puck we sail tonight."

"Tonight?" the boy asked, hope sparking in his eyes.

"For . . ." He couldn't even say the word, so deep ran the desire.

"Yes," Kit answered, his own voice cracking on the words. "For England." After seven years, Kit was finally going home.

Enter the rich world of
historical romance
with Berkley Books.

Lynn Kurland

Patricia Potter

Betina Krahn

Jodi Thomas

Anne Gracie

Love is timeless.

penguin.com

The "masterful"* *New York Times* bestselling author

MADELINE HUNTER

presents the first book in
a magnificent historical romance quartet

Ravishing in Red

Audrianna Kelmsleigh is unattached, independent—and
armed. Her adversary is Lord Sebastian Summerhays. What
they have in common is Audrianna's father, who died in a
scandalous conspiracy—a deserved death, in Sebastian's eyes.
Audrianna vows to clear her father's name, never expecting
to fall in love with the man devoted to destroying it . . .

*Booklist

penguin.com